The Last Bloom

by

Roberta C.M. DeCaprio

Between The Rifle and The Spear,
Book 6

The Last Bloom

COPYRIGHT © 2018 by Roberta C.M. DeCaprio

Cover Art by *RJ Morris*

The Wild Rose Press, Inc.
PO Box 708
Adams Basin, NY 14410-0708
Visit us at www.thewildrosepress.com

Publishing History
First Cactus Rose Edition, 2018
Print ISBN 978-1-5092-1907-0
Digital ISBN 978-1-5092-1908-7

Between The Rifle and The Spear, Book 6
Published in the United States of America

After one glance she thought

life had been kind to Brodie. Truth be told, life had been downright generous. The lean, baby-faced young man she bid farewell to had returned a well-built, muscular gentleman with a strong, handsome face. But the russet curls and large green eyes were the same, as was the genuine, kind smile that spread across his semi-freckled face when he spied her entering the door.

In an instant he came to her, his strong arms circling her waist in a familiar embrace. She immediately, standing on tiptoe, wrapped her arms around his neck and inhaled the clean scent of spice that was his aftershave. "Thank God you're finally here," she whispered, meaning her words more than even she realized.

"Did you have any doubt I'd come?" He pulled back to search her face.

Her cheeks warmed beneath his scrutiny. She stepped from his embrace, confused. What had changed between them? This was Brodie, the neighbor and friend who was more like an older brother—looking out for her and buying her ice cream with the first pay he earned mucking the local stables. He picked her up when she fell, wiped her tears, and carried her to his father when she'd skinned her knee. He kept bullies from teasing her as she walked home from school. Why did she now feel so strange in his presence?

She cleared her throat nervously. "No, I had no doubts at all."

Dedications

To the memory of my dog, Kitty Girl,
and my mother-in-law, Helen Watson Lemke.
Both passed away during the writing of this book.
~*~
And to my maternal great-grandmother,
Carmela Calandro Formichelli,
who was also a midwife.
The heroine of this book is fashioned after Carmela,
who carried a gun, the same depicted in this novel, due
to a similar "Gipsy" incident, which is also mentioned.
~*~
And I'd like to thank my cousin,
Marylou Formichelli Jaeger,
for all her help in supplying the correct information
concerning the make and model of the gun
my great-grandmother actually carried.
~*~

Also, a heartfelt thanks to my editor, Allison Byers,
who continues to make me shine as a writer.
Having her in my corner has been a major blessing.

There comes a time, in spite of protocol's voice, whereby a woman must listen to the calling of her own heart...and follow it!

Prologue

Eagle's Landing, Arizona, January 1996

The weather was cooperating with the Sunday event, as it turned out to be an exceptionally pleasant Arizona winter day. In fact, it was the nicest Cassia Rose had seen in a while during this season. She smiled, thinking how the beautiful afternoon, of this 14th day of January, fit right in with the town's plans to celebrate its one-hundredth year…and her birthday.

Cassia snuggled comfortably in the back seat of a shiny, black limo the mayor, one of her many great-nephews, had sent to pick her up. She straightened the collar of her new, blue tweed coat and gave her twenty-five-year-old great granddaughter's hand an affectionate pat. "Can you believe the fuss they're making over me?"

Amanda smiled, her sapphire blue eyes twinkling with excitement. "I think it's wonderful. After all, Granny, you were the first child to be born in this town."

"Actually, my nephew, Ethan Soaring Eagle, was the first. He was born in November of the previous year…exactly two months before me." She shrugged. "But as the story was always told to me, the legality of the town's standing wasn't officially registered until a few weeks before I arrived." She frowned. "I always thought it was terribly unfair to Ethan, especially since my half-brother, Gabriel Golden Eagle, was the town's founder."

"And a chief, since your mother was first married to an Apache before the Reverend Holmes," Amanda added, raising her dimpled chin proudly.

Cassia chuckled. "You know the story as well as I do, child." She cast a sideways glance at the beautiful, pale-haired, young woman sitting beside her. "You're named after her...my beautiful, precious mother. And you pose a striking resemblance as well, right down to the sapphire blue of your eyes."

Amanda gazed out the window. "It always brings a flutter to my heart, when I think of her once walking about the same grounds I have all of my life. Though they appeared much different than they do today."

Cassia nodded. "And only fifty-seven acres made up the township's grounds at that time."

"I've also always admired your mother's tenacity," Amanda added.

She arched a brow. "Mother's willfulness did not always please my father."

"Still and all," Amanda began, keeping her eyes on the passing scenes. "I admire her strength to listen to her heart's calling and follow it during a time when women weren't allowed the freedom to make their own decisions."

She followed her great-granddaughter's gaze, watching the streets fly by, as the limo made its way to the town's arena—flashes of the sun's ray reflecting now and then off a store window, or the shiny chrome of a high-rise. So much had changed since she was a girl. And yet at times it seemed the same.

"Sometimes I can still picture my mother taking her strolls. Or my father unlocking the chapel doors each morning in case someone needed its sanctuary for prayer." She sighed. "I can picture them all: the expressions upon their faces, the sound of their laughs, and the pitch of their voices. The way Mr. Washburn raised a brow, the way Mrs. Granger scolded her children, or the music at the ice cream socials." She tapped her right temple with a forefinger. "It is all stored here inside my head, the scenes playing out like a moving picture show behind my eyes."

Amanda smiled, her full lips spreading over even white teeth. "You've had so many adventures, Granny."

She sighed again. "Ah, yes—there were quite a number of them, as it was a time when many milestones were made—innovations and inventions...the quest to make life easier." She gave her great-granddaughter's hand an affectionate pat. "Nothing like the technology we have today, mind you. But then—then we thought we'd reached our peak—never realizing all the things yet to come for us to learn." She chuckled lightly, shaking her head at her youthful tenacity. "I thought I knew so much back then, so sure I had it all under control. After all, I had studied midwifery in England. I remember clearly the day I returned." She paused and added, "Sometimes it seems like it was just yesterday."

Chapter One

Arizona, April 1919

Cassia Rose Holmes literally felt every weary bone and aching muscle in her body. Such an exhausting condition was the result of wayfaring throughout the night, a circumstance she'd hoped to avoid but wasn't spared. Traveling alone, something her family frowned upon, was tedious enough…traveling all night made it even worse. But she couldn't wait any longer for an available escort. She missed her homeland. She'd been gone eight long years, two years more than planned due to the outbreak of the First World War—or The Great War, as it was often called—the summer of 1914, three years after she arrived in England.

Cassia had been visiting a half-sister, Sunny Cavendish, and her family living in Brighton, England. It was bittersweet—sad to leave the many nieces, nephews, parties, and spectacular events taking place at Bentwood's Bentley Manor—yet glad to return home to Eagle's Landing where her parents resided.

She had spent most of her stay in London with her father's sister, Marrietta Cavendish. Cavensworth, the family's estate, was her home away from home while she attended The Royal Collage of Nursing for three years, developing her education into midwifery services and nursing.

However, the last five years were spent working in camps and clinics, caring for the British soldiers returning from the war and other war victims. Due to starvation and an epidemic of typhus, thousands immigrated to England from other war-torn countries. The sights she'd seen no one should have to be subjected too, all the pain and suffering, the blood, disease, and human desperation. The men returning from the war couldn't find jobs and begged on the streets for whatever handouts came their way. They congregated in the alley ways between the London buildings, picked fights with passersby, and even at times went so far as to accost women—compromising virtues. No woman walking alone, day or night on London's streets, was safe.

Those who secured employment couldn't keep a job for very long because they suffered from something called *shell shock* which had them reliving the horrors of war. In a strange sense, she also was a victim. After a long day of caring for the sick and maimed, seeing all the death, watching minds decay, she was somewhat shell shocked too. She was not without her own nightmares, waking with a start, her heart racing and her nightwear soaked with perspiration. But her time in those clinics prepared her for just about everything in the medical field there was to come. So the thought of tending to womenfolk's issues and childbirth was a welcome change.

Auntie Marietta, now widowed, cried when Cassia left for Brighton. It broke her heart to leave the elderly woman after they'd spent such a long time enjoying each other's company. But her time in London ended, as well as the last holiday she would have at Brighton's shores, feeling the beach sand sift between her toes and the ocean waters swish against her ankles, before she'd be made to buckle down at her medical training and join Dr. O'Clarity's practice at Eagle's Landing.

As long as Cassia could remember, she wanted to help others—especially women. As soon as she turned thirteen, she assisted the town's Apache Shaman, Owl Woman, and Dr. Sean O'Clarity birth the many babies born at Eagle's Landing and surrounding counties. She learned a lot from the pair, as well as from her mother's dear friend, Rowena Cooper, an herbalist who had a garden stocked with nature's cures. Rowena's *Calendula* or Pot Marigold plant saved Cassia's father's life after a gunshot wound.

With Owl Woman's passing and Dr. O'Clarity getting on in years, her services were needed. She would also work with Rowena's daughter, Clara Morris, who had taken over most of the herb garden's daily care from her mother. And she couldn't be more excited over the opportunity to put her midwifery education to good use. The only regret she had was she would not be working with Tucker, Doctor O'Clarity's youngest son.

As children, they'd been close friends, even though Tucker was almost two years older. At first she was like a little sister, and he'd look out for her. But as she grew, they'd fish in the creek, pick berries, plus save and care for injured animals. They laughed at the same things, confided in each other, and shared secrets. They also shared the same hope—to ease folks' pain and suffering.

She was fourteen when Tucker left to attend medical school in Boston, joining his brother Brodie who had already been there for two years. The night before his departure, they pledged their hearts to one another, sealing the agreement with a kiss...their first and one Cassia would never forget. Thoughts of working side by side as husband and wife to serve their town with quality medical care was something they had promised each other they'd accomplish...until Tucker decided medical college wasn't right for him, and he joined the railroad.

Tucker wrote her, releasing her from their secret vows, chalking them up to childish dreams with no real regard for a future. And just like that, he was free to take the path he'd newly mapped out for himself.

She sighed; thoughts of living minus Tucker, always brought a pain to her heart. And the only thing that helped push that pain aside was her goal to become the best in her field, help women during childbirth, and share all the safe, modern day medicine she'd learned.

The train's conductor called out, "Five minutes to Willow Creek."

Cassia reached for her hat lying on the seat beside her. This would be her stop, anticipation welling up within her at seeing her family. She combed her fingers through her hair. The short, sassy golden curls bounced against her cheeks. It was all the fashion now—hair bobbed to chin length and bangs lying straight across the forehead. Of course, Cassie's hair curled around her face. The thick, short locks seemed to stray this way and that, but nevertheless, she was fashionable. How would her father react when he saw her waist-length curls gone? Frowning, she placed her hat atop her head and hoped he'd be so happy to have her home that he wouldn't scold overly much at her new appearance.

Reverend Joshua Holmes was a strict parent to a degree, but loving and kind as well. He never raised a hand to her, nor did her mother. When Cassia misbehaved, her punishment was doled out differently—in the form of chores or privileges taken away, instead of the spankings many of her peers endured.

Mary McCrea's parents weren't too bad, although Mary and her siblings got what was coming to them when they misbehaved. Mary was a bit older than Cassia and Nora Granger a bit younger. The three of them got into scrapes and antics that would try any parent's patience. Nora, however, was punished the worst of the three.

"Poor Nora Granger," she whispered, thinking of her best and dearest friend. Nora was the oldest of the seven children of Maggie and Eli Granger. Daily, Nora kept her siblings in line for a few hours after school, until Maggie closed her general store. And if she failed at the task, Nora promptly got her backside tanned when Maggie arrived home.

Now Nora Granger was Nora Dodd. A year ago she was married to Cameron Dodd who worked at his father's modest firm as a law clerk, hoping to become a lawyer and take over the family business. The letters Cassia received from Nora painted a heartwarming story of her love for Cameron. She regretted missing Nora's important and special day. But sad as she was to miss her friend's nuptials, Cassia would share another important and special day with Nora, due at any time to give birth. Her child would be a first on two levels...for Nora as a parent and for Cassia as the town's licensed midwife.

In some ways she envied Nora, the blessing of discovering true love and being able to go through life with a deeply caring man. To have a home and a family with that special someone, and to grow old together, like her parents, was something Cassia had hoped for herself. She believed since she was a young girl, that she'd have the same with Tucker O'Clarity.

"I couldn't have been more wrong," she whispered.

Her mother's words echoed in her thoughts. *"You're still so young, my darling—beautiful, intelligent, and caring. Do you truly believe Tucker O'Clarity will be the only man you'll ever love?"*

A resounding *yes* echoed in response. Tucker knew her hopes and dreams, shared her likes and dislikes, was her best friend. How wonderful is it to be in love with your best friend?

"Debarking now in Willow Creek," the conductor proclaimed.

Cassia sighed, straightened her shoulders, adjusted the brim of her hat, and stood.

Chapter Two

Willow Creek was a bustling town, the main street becoming longer and wider within a few decades. There were sidewalks and paved roads. High buildings replaced the smaller ones, turning a once quiet, western town into a busy little city. Nothing, except the old church and parsonage, remained of bygone days. Those two old structures are what her mother called an old stand-by, the safe haven where anyone could go for help in a storm. And if anyone knew this first hand, it was Amanda Holmes.

Amanda Gregory Eagle Holmes was first married to an Apache Warrior named Proud Eagle, during a time when the white man and red-skinned man were enemies. Amanda bore three children from this union— Gabriel Golden Eagle, Raven Eagle, and Sunny Eagle.

When Proud Eagle died, Amanda wed the Reverend Joshua Holmes, Cassia's father. Both were past their prime, her mother fifty and her father sixty-two, when she was born which was why Cassia's birth was such a miracle—or a *down-right-shock*, as Sylvia, Reverend Ben Newcomb's wife and Amanda's close friend, always stated. The Apache people living at Eagle's Landing entitled her *The Last Bloom*. And truly, for Amanda and Joshua, that's just what she was.

By the time she was born, Cassia's half-siblings were old enough to be her parents. Thus now the reason all of her nieces and nephews were around her age. Those that were older than she, refused to call her *auntie*, as they felt more like cousins. However, even though the family dynamics was not like that of other families, there was lots of love and cooperation among the members as everyone looked out for each other.

Her brother Gabriel and sister-in-law Riley lived next door and became like second parents. Many times she was left in their care when her parents went on a holiday. She respected their word, obeyed their rules, and accepted the punishments they doled out to her when she was naughty. They nurtured her when she was ill, supported her goals, and cherished her humor. Their three children, Ethan Soaring Eagle, Silas Warning Eagle, and Anita Awakening Eagle were like siblings and best friends rolled into one. She loved them all dearly and couldn't wait to see them again.

As she stepped down from the platform, she spotted one of her nephews. Silas was sent to fetch her from her travels and welcomed her with a warm smile spreading across his young, handsome face. At twenty, Silas was a formidable male specimen, muscular and over six feet tall, possessing his mother's large green eyes. And like his father a splash of gold hair swept across one side of the very black, thick curls that just reached the rim of his shirt's collar. That very streak was what won him his name, after his great-great-grandfather, Lord Silas Collins. It was a well-known fact Lord Collins owned the same unusual shock of the sun throughout his hair, as well as a crescent shaped birthmark on his abdomen.

He closed the distance between them with a few long strides. She dropped the baggage she carried before Silas embraced her, lifting her off her feet and swinging her around.

"Ah, you're home at last," his newly grown-male voice cracked, the pleasant aroma of leather and spice emanating from his skin. "Dearest Auntie Cassia," he teased, "all grown up and now a proper professional." He gasped as he glimpsed the short curls peeking out from beneath her hat. "And you've cut your hair."

She giggled. "It's all the fashion." She wrapped her arms around his neck and planted a kiss upon his cheek. "And look at you." She changed the subject and pulled back to look into his eyes. "My little nephew, all grown up."

He placed her upon her feet and stared down into her eyes, before reaching to retrieve her baggage. "This is all you have after all this time…only two bags?"

She nodded. "It's always best to travel light, if one can."

He frowned. "Well, I guess I should take note of that advice, although I'm sure my dear sister, Anita, won't be so cooperative."

She looped a hand through his arm. "And where are the two of you going?"

He sighed. "We are bound for England, along with Mama, in ten days. Now that the war is over and it's safer to travel overseas, Anita and I will be embarking on our futures. Mama, of course, will stay on until Papa joins her at the end of the summer…possibly sooner as he can never manage to stay apart from Mama too long."

She searched his face. "So it is time, then, for you to take your rightful place as heir?"

"That it is," he answered softly. "Though it is

customary for the oldest son to fulfill such a task, Ethan must remain here. Should anything happen to Papa, Ethan will be named the next chief of the Western Apache tribe…or, what's left of them."

"You always knew this day was coming," she said. "Your father promised Lucinda Collins that one of his sons would take over Collins Stead so the family bloodline would continue."

"I know," he said. "And it's not like I'm not familiar with the place. I've traveled to England every year since I've been born—not counting the war years. Oliver and Leah Mills, the grounds overseer and close friends of my parents, will be there to guide me. Plus, Glenshire Sussex is a mere three quarters of an hour from London, by horse." He arched a mischievous brow. "And I've been doing a bit of reading about the numerous adventures to be had in large cities."

She chuckled lightly. "Not to mention the very pretty Danica Mills who is close to your age and living on the grounds with her parents."

Silas blushed. "Yeah, that's true as well."

She frowned. "Then what troubles you?"

He shrugged. "The fact I'll never again be able to call Eagle's Landing my home. Once I step foot into that mansion, I'm there for life."

"It's not like you can never return to Eagle's Landing for a visit," she offered.

"But I will never be able to permanently stay," he said. "I'll be expected to marry an English woman, my children will be British citizens, not Americans, and when I pass away, I'll be buried in the Collins family plot."

"And you will be the lord of a manor, rich enough

to travel anywhere in the world you desire, influential and respected by others, and served daily by a staff of servants," she countered.

A slow smile spread his lips. "I will, won't I?"

She giggled. "Not such a bad trade off after all."

He joined her mirth. "No, not so bad at that."

"And why is Anita joining you?"

"She'll be staying in Brighton for the summer with Auntie Sunny and Uncle Rafe, where she will be able to fine-tune her skills as an artist," Silas explained. "It's what she always dreamed of doing, and now that she's sixteen, it's time she begins her career. So she's very pleased…extremely excited to leave."

"Ah, if anyone can introduce her to such a career, it's my sister, Sunny, an amazing artist herself, who has many connections in that field," she said. "By the time Anita returns, she'll have a résumé grand enough to enter a good college here in the states."

"That's what Mama thought as well."

She squeezed Silas's arm affectionately. "Then I'd say we'll have to make the best of these next ten days, since it might be some time before I see you again."

He nodded, escorting her from the station terminal, out into the beautiful Arizona spring day.

As Cassia made her way to the horse and carriage, she raised her face to the afternoon sun blazing in the cloudless sky. "One thing I missed terribly while in England is the warmth of the sun. All it ever seemed to do in London is rain, a thick mist of fog blankets the earth whether it is early morning or late at night."

After Silas helped her step up into the carriage and stash her baggage in the back of the wagon, he ran around to his seat. With a tug on the reins, he set the vehicle in motion. About a mile down Main Street's thoroughfare, they were abruptly halted by a horseless carriage emerging from Summit Street to drive ahead of them.

Silas scowled. "That's the bank manager's son, Willis."

She frowned. "Flora Washburn's grandson?"

He nodded. "He thinks he's something grand because his father runs the bank and his mother runs Remington's Department Store."

Cassia gasped. "Flora's Boutique is now a department store?"

He nodded again. "A lot has happened in eight years."

"I can see that." She glanced around as they passed through the town.

"Since Flora's daughter-in-law has completely taken over the business, she's had the building renovated, made it larger and two stories high. They sell everything from women's clothes to furniture."

"No doubt Flora's husband, Vernon is the creator of the furniture," she added. "I remember how he built things in his barn, even helped him sand and paint a few chairs when I was younger."

"Yup, Vernon has gotten pretty famous for his handmade furnishings. And folks from all over, especially Phoenix, who want the country look in their homes, flock to Remington's for the perfect table or chair."

"How many around here have a horseless carriage?"

Silas shrugged. "Besides the Remingtons, I'd say about twenty to thirty families. Though I've seen the streets full of automobiles, which is what they're called, when I accompanied Papa on a trip to Phoenix last summer."

"What do you make of them?" She settled herself for the forty-five minute ride to Eagle's Landing.

"They fascinate me."

"I hear they can be quite costly," she said.

"They were at one time, but Henry Ford with his Model T has changed all that." He glanced her way. "I read a magazine article on Ford's automobiles and learned quite a lot."

"What did your efforts discover?"

"They are the traveling mode of the future," he said. "And it was two Hungarian immigrants that helped design the vehicle. When I read their names, Joseph A. Glamb and Eugene Farkas, I began wondering about them."

She frowned. "What do you mean?"

"Well, maybe at one time they were just two poor farm boys, living in a modest wood-framed home, running around barefoot and spending Saturday afternoons fishing at the nearest waterhole. They dared to be different, challenged themselves, and against all odds they came to America to pursue their dream of success, to seek their fortune," he said, his voice growing in awe for men he never knew. Never would meet.

"Yes, daring to be different," she whispered. It was what she wanted, to be different. To be book-learned in the medical field, and not just a country woman birthing babies. The challenge to be knowledgeable and skilled, the ability to really help the patients she treats. It was what she always dreamed of doing while she tagged along with Owl Woman and Doc O'Clarity.

"Then they meet Ford and his team of men who all wanted to think of ways to make life easier," Silas said, bringing her thoughts back to their conversation. "And they come up with a design whereby no one would ever have to walk or ride a horse far distances or in bad weather again."

"Strange how life works. They came to America for a better way of life, and you're leaving America to seek your success and fortune," she said.

Silas turned briefly to look her way, excitement filling his green eyes. "I think I'm going to buy an automobile when I get to England." He squared his shoulders. "After all, the lord of a manor must have a way, other than a horse, to get around."

She returned his exuberance with a smile. "Perhaps leaving Eagle's Landing might not be so awful after all."

He chuckled lightly. "No, perhaps it won't be too bad at that. And as you mentioned," he added, "there's always Danica Mills."

Chapter Three

Upon entering Eagle's Landing, Tribal Square is what a traveler first saw. This was not always the case. Until Cassia was ten years old, this part of the town was secluded and set aside only for the few Apaches who chose to continue living traditionally, their wickiups in a small cluster by the creek.

Wickiups were made of a framework of poles and limbs tied together over which a thatch of bear grass, brush, and yucca leaves were placed. The wickiup was then topped with a canvas like material that was stretched over the structure on the windward side. An opening at the top allowed smoke to escape from the fire pit, situated in the center of the abode. But as the elders died, and families grew, the primitive dwellings were abandoned for modern-day, wood-framed houses. Now the square was a tourist spot, complete with a visitor's center that housed a small museum, an eatery serving sandwiches, hotdogs, ice cream, coffee, tea, and soda pop, and a gift store selling Apache and other handmade items. Revenue from tours and other festivities helped to improve and sustain the town, as well as educate the populace on the Apache way of life. The Pow Wows held also helped to keep the Apache tradition alive for the younger generations born into the tribe.

Another great change since 1906 was the town's

expansion. Around 1905 her brother, Gabriel, purchased the land across the bridge, known as Beaver's Bluff. The one hundred eighty acres of land was once used during the Gold Rush days as a stop off to and from California. Nothing much made up the town even then but a saloon, a small boarding house, and a place to stable a horse.

Shabby and falling into disrepair, Beaver's Bluff later became open to vagrants and other undesirables. After Cassia was born, her mother was kidnapped by a white agent named Denton Hall and held captive in a shack at Beaver's Bluff. It was then Gabriel worked very hard for many years to own the land and clean it up. That area is now known as South Eagle's Landing, or SEL.

When she was a youngster, she watched the men erect the covered bridge joining the two parcels of land. The efforts to complete a hotel, a small medical clinic, and even an agricultural college have all these years been in the works. The extended town offered jobs and more land for homesteaders to build on. What started out as fifty-seven acres of land owned by Cassia's grandfather, Ethan Gregory, were now a quaint yet thriving town, home to many, and a historical site as well.

As the wagon made its way farther into the town, they passed the cemetery. She'd come many times to these sacred grounds with her mother, to pay their respect and lay flowers upon her grandparents' graves, as well as her mother's first husband's resting place. As she grew older, she often wondered why her father wasn't bothered by the fact his wife still held dear in her heart the memory of another man.

Once Cassia questioned her brother Gabriel on the matter, and he had told her, "Your father and my father were good friends. Upon my father's death bed, his last wish was for your father to take care of our mother. They had an understanding with each other…a code of honor, as they both shared the bond of loving our mother. Your father loved her first and has her last. My father loved her when their time was right. Since there is a season for all things, there is no need for jealousy or hurt feelings."

And so, in the Holmes's household it became perfectly natural to include Peter…which was his Christian name…Proud Eagle's memory into their lives. Both her parents shared stories about the Apache chief, conjuring up a picture of a very brave, wise, and kind man. Her siblings talked about their father with fondness and absolute reverence, so much so, that Cassia almost felt like she was related to the man as well.

"You're overly quiet," Silas commented.

She sighed. "I'm just taking in the sights of home." She inhaled deeply the scents of spring, memories of the days she romped and played in the woods and by the creek, catching fireflies or listening for an owl's hoot at night. Summer evenings spent sitting on the porch eating homemade ice cream or popcorn with Nora, while they shared their deepest secrets. They were the times when parents did all the worrying, comforted her, and were the wisest humans she knew. And when her head hit the pillow, she fell into a deep, sound sleep, fearing nothing and dreaming all her hopes came true, and how much the future held.

As Silas brought the horse to a halt in front of the

modest, two-bedroom bungalow on the corner of Amelia Lane and Ethan Drive, Cassia's heart raced with anticipation. Home...she was finally home, where tonight she'd sleep in her bed surrounded by all her familiar things. She'd wake to her mother's cinnamon toast filling the house with delicious aromas and a hot cup of ginger tea. Her father, dressed in his clergy clothes, would have just finished reading the daily newspaper and ready to walk to the church, preparing for the morning service. He'd plant a fatherly kiss upon her cheek and give her a quick hug before he departed. How she'd missed this routine.

"Are you ready to go in?" Silas asked.

She smiled. "I couldn't be more ready."

When Silas opened the front door, an array of voices shouted "Surprise."

She scanned the living room, glancing at all the familiar faces. Her mother came forward first, cupping Cassia's chin between her small hands and kissing each cheek.

"How glad I am to see you," Amanda whispered.

"And I you, Mama." Her eyes welled with unshed tears. From the letters she received from home, her parents worried endlessly about her welfare, being overseas during such dangerous and troubled times.

Then her father made his way to her. Frowning, he tugged on a strand of her hair peeking out from beneath the brim of her hat. "Where have you left your hair?"

She pulled off her hat and shook out her curls. "It's all the style, Papa." With a hopeful smile and looking deep into the light blue eyes that matched her own, she added, "The good thing about hair is that it always grows back."

He chuckled lightly. "Aye, that it does." He enveloped her within his strong arms and kissed the top of her head. "I'm just glad to have my baby girl back home where she belongs."

"I am twenty-three, Papa," she whispered.

"You will always be my baby girl." He pulled her close enough to feel the beating of his heart.

She relaxed against his chest, his crisp, white shirt smelling like starch and sunshine. She wouldn't correct him again, for it would do no good. Papa would never see her as anything more than his little girl. He had carried her whenever he could until she neared the age of four.

She remembered her mother saying, "Joshua Holmes, mark my words when I tell you that child's never going to learn the God-given ability she has in using her legs if you persist on carrying her around like an infant."

But he would smile at his wife and nod, while he continued to keep her close…never wanting or letting her far out of his sight. He was the one who read her a story before bed, came to soothe her in the middle of the night after a nightmare, was the hero who squashed the spiders and fixed her toys.

With his large hands spread across her back, Cassia felt safe, loved, and content. It was how her parents always made her feel. It was how Papa took care of his girls. She and Mama were the reason he woke each morning…the joy of his heart and the happiness in his life. Without them, her father would crumble and die. Without him, she and Mama would do the same. And as he was the age of eighty-five and her mother seventy-three, Cassia worried more and more at how much longer she'd have either of them. Though both were in excellent health, strong and vibrant for their age, the nagging realization they were getting on in years always crossed her mind. The others came to greet her now—her brother, Gabriel; his wife, Riley; their oldest son, Ethan; and their daughter, Anita. Then she found herself hugging her best friend, Nora, her stomach large with child bulging between them.

Pulling back, Nora turned toward her husband. "You remember Cameron, don't you?"

"Of course." She regarded him briefly. Cameron had grown into a very tall and handsome man of medium build and broad shoulders, not the scrawny boy she remembered from her teen years.

"Nora and I are both pleased you will be helping her through the birth of our child." He reached for Nora's hand.

"I'm so glad you're home," Nora added.

"Me too." Her heart warmed by the affection between her dearest friend and the man she'd chosen for a lifetime mate. And in the next instant, she was pained at the thought of not having a love of her own.

But her thoughts were cast aside as Rowena Cooper,; her daughter Clara; and Clara's husband Owen, were next to welcome her home, as well as Dr. Sean O'Clarity and his wife, Sadie. The small gathering lasted a few hours with everyone eating, drinking, laughing, as well as sharing fond memories. As Cassia glanced around the room, settling her gaze upon the smiles and features of each person, her heart swelled with love. These people made up her life and had something to do with who she was today, especially her parents. She'd been so blessed, so fortunate to be born into a loving, caring family who fostered her intelligence and independence, even though she was a woman.

As Doctor O'Clarity was leaving, he gave Cassia a brief hug. "Take a few days to settle yerself in, Lass, to get reacquainted with yer home and family before ye report to work." He smiled warmly, his emerald green eyes reminding her so much of Tucker's. "I can't tell ye how happy I am to have ye back home. I'm in need o' a helper, especially now that I've been takin' meself over to the new clinic three times a week to attend the folks there." He sighed heavily, suddenly appearing worn. "Sadie's on me all the time to slow down, take a bit o' time for fun, but there's always someone needin' me services."

She smiled reassuringly at the elder man. "I will do all I can to lighten your load, Doc. It's what I've dreamed all my life of doing."

He gave her hand an affectionate pat. "I know 'tis, Lass. And a fine helper ye'll be at that."

Clara took her aside before departing. "I've got a fresh bunch of herbs a waitin' for ya," she said. "Come by for 'em soon, won't ya? We'll have lunch and talk more."

Cassia nodded. "I'll be by tomorrow, so I can fill my bag and have it ready for house calls."

Clara giggled. "Can ya believe yer now a full-fledged midwife, Cassia? With credentials and all."

She shook her head, giggling as well, the thrill of the truth giving her such joy. "Sometimes I can't imagine it, but then other times I remember all the hard work, the book learning and studying it all took to get here, and I feel so…so…"

"Proud," Clara supplied.

"Yes, I guess you could say that," she admitted.

"Well, ya should be proud; none of it was easy to do," Clara countered. "Especially being female and all. Anyway, I'll be lookin' forward to yer visit."

After everyone was gone, she began to help her mother clean up.

"No, child," her mother said softly, taking the dishes she'd collected from her grasp. "It's been a long day for you, and I can't imagine you being anything but totally exhausted."

She sighed, relinquishing the stack of dirty plates. "I am rather spent."

"Go," her mother urged. "Take a hot bath and get into bed. I can handle all this myself."

She frowned. "I don't want you to do all…"

"Oh for heaven's sake, Cassia, I'm not on my last leg yet," her mother interrupted. "Now go."

This time she obeyed, drawing herself a hot bath and sinking beneath the relaxing waters to soak away the tension of the long day. Closing her eyes, she smiled. She couldn't think of a time when she was so happy. Coming home was so needed. The only thing that would have made it even more perfect, was if Tucker O'Clarity were here, waiting for her.

Chapter Four

Doctor Brodie O'Clarity flopped with total exhaustion onto the single-sized, iron-railed bed. Still half-dressed, he sighed. His long, busy shift at Boston General had left him too weary to even remove his trousers and socks. All he wanted was the solitude to stretch his aching back, prop up his sore feet, pass some gas as loudly as he wished in the privacy of his rented abode, and fall asleep. But the air was hot and stale in the tiny attic apartment, which would eventually cause him to sweat and chafe if he didn't rise to open a window. He sighed again as he threw his long legs off the bed and sat on the edge, glancing around the space he'd come to call home for the last three years.

The furnishings were sparse, old, and cheap, but clean, which was more than he could say for most of the boarding houses of modest and economical means. And he'd seen the insides of some horrendous row houses on the many house calls he made. The Widow Danfield kept a strict place—no smoking, drinking, food, or women allowed past the first floor, and if each apartment wasn't kept clean upon her weekly inspection, the renter was evicted. The layout was compact but efficient and met all his needs.

On one end of the studio dwelling sat a bed, along with a three-drawer dresser, which also served as a nightstand. Outer clothes were hung upon the many hooks nailed to a wall. On the opposite end, there was a table and two chairs, which served as a writing table, a small three-shelved wooden cupboard for toiletries and other belongings, and a wood-burning stove for heating the room. Although the large Victorian style home had electricity on the first and second floors, the attic apartments did not. Gasoline lanterns were used for lighting. In another corner, there was an arm chair with an ottoman and a bookcase.

He shared the bathroom, which was down a flight of stairs to the second floor, with the fellow across the hall—a young lawyer from Atlanta by the name of Paul Rhinehart—and an old ship captain from Nantucket. Captain Jack Crawford, or Cappy Jack as the sailor was called, lived opposite the bathroom, confiscating it first each morning, and leaving it smelling like death and decay. Whatever the old bugger was eating, certainly wasn't agreeing with him or the pipes. Widow Danfield, on many occasions, was forced to call a plumber to unstop the clogged toilet.

Brodie yawned and pulled off his socks, tossing them aside as he wiggled his toes. Standing, he removed his pants and hung them neatly on a hook before making his way to open the window nearest to the bed. A slight, cool breeze flowed into the room, chilling his bared chest. He inhaled sharply, closing his eyes while enjoying the night air. Back home at Eagle's Landing, fresh, clean air was easier to come by. Nights were cool, even in the dead of summer, making it comfortable to sleep. And there was lots of space, grass, trees, and flowers.

Slowly he opened his eyes to glance out at the crowded scene: rooftops in a row, cramped quarters and people on top of one another. He could hear a baby crying and a couple fighting from the house next door. At times like this he longed for home, the quiet privacy of country life, his mother's cooking, and his father's company.

Doctor Sean O'Clarity was a man Brodie admired and the reason he became a doctor. However, practicing medicine in a small town was not as lucrative a career. Besides, his life was shaping up nicely here in Boston, now that he met Dorothea Malone and asked for her hand in marriage.

Beautiful, rich, intelligent, and stubborn Dorothea, the chief of staff's daughter, had turned his head and made his heart race the first time he set eyes upon her auburn curls and hauntingly large brown eyes as she lunched one afternoon with her father. Doctor Hemsley Malone seemed interested in Brodie's career, many times admiring his dedication to the patients. So, inviting him to join them was not only a feather in his cap professionally, but personally, as he was able to charm Dorothea as well. Of course, it was also obvious that Dorothea was her daddy's girl, spoiled and coddled. Never had she felt the sting of a paddle upon her backside, been spoken to harshly, or been denied a single request. Cherished and indulged, she never did a day's chores or shared anything with a sibling. Pampered, she got her own way, whatever that might be, even a husband in a high position at the hospital. After his proposal and engagement, doors had suddenly opened for him.

Doctor Hemsley Malone would further Brodie's career faster than anything he could accomplish on his own. Watching Doctor Malone's rich lifestyle put stars in Brodie's eyes. Being paid a good wage for medical services rendered was so much better than receiving a bag of flour or a basket of eggs, which his father had accepted as pay for being a country physician.

After all the years of hard work, Brodie wasn't ashamed to admit he wanted the prestige Hemsley Malone had. Doctor Malone spent his life giving all the best things in the world to his precious little girl, and that fact was in Brodie's favor. There's no doubt the elder Malone would want for his daughter an accomplished spouse who could keep Dorothea in the manner to which she'd become accustomed. What was so wrong with him being that man?

Brodie yawned and scratched his testicles. While making his way back to the bed, he loudly released the gas he suffered, due to the hurried pastrami sandwich he consumed too late in the day, before climbing into bed. Then he pulled the sheet over his legs and fell asleep.

****

Spending Sundays with the Malone family was an experience to behold. Their mansion, three blocks from Widow Danfield's boarding house, was a white, three-story, Victorian dwelling set quite a distance from the road and privately enclosed by an eight-foot wrought iron fence. Brodie rode his second-hand bicycle the distance, happy for the sunny morning, and arrived in time to accompany Dorothea to Sunday service at the Grand Street Presbyterian Church.

A Catholic, Brodie was use to worshipping with another denomination's congregation. Since his family had migrated to America and lived at Eagle's Landing, they spent Sundays at the Baptist church in town which was much easier than traveling two hours to the nearest Catholic church, especially during winter. Reverend Joshua Holmes and his wife, Amanda, had welcomed the O'Clarity family with open arms and caring hearts.

Brodie halted at the large gate, hopped off his bike, and pulled the bell's rope to summon the grounds keeper. Within a few moments, Hank, short and stocky, waddled over to unlock the gate.

"Good morning, Hank." He walked his bicycle through the entrance.

"A-yup, to you as well, Doctor O'Clarity," Hank countered. Gazing at the sky, Hank shielded his eyes from the sun. "Looks like we're gonna have a scorcher on our hands today." He pointed to Brodie's jacket. "You'll be wishing to shed that soon enough."

Brodie frowned. "And it's not likely my wish would be granted, my friend." Already he felt the sweat trickling down his back and soaking his last clean, white shirt.

Dorothea would throw a tantrum if he accompanied her looking anything less than dapper. How she, in such heat, could wear all the frills of her frock—complete with hat and gloves—was amazing.

Hank nodded sympathetically. "I hear ya, Doc."

Brodie chuckled lightly. "I suppose you do." All the household's staff heard Dorothea's tantrums, making her spoiled defiance a well-known fact.

"A-yup," Hank muttered. "It would've done a heap of good, back in the day, for that young lady to have had her backside warmed now and then." The grounds keeper frowned. "Ain't no cause at all for some of the lip that sassy girl gives her parents, after all she's given. If she were my daughter, she'd have been over my knee the first time she threw one of her fits." Then he looked around suspiciously. "But let's just keep that between us, hey what?"

Brodie nodded. He didn't trust Hank by a long shot so any sort of verbal agreement to anything the elderly man said wouldn't be wise, even agreeing to share his confidence. Hank loved to gossip and so did his wife, Blanche. If Brodie added a comment to Hank's venting, his words would find their way straight to Blanche's ears and in turn to Mrs. Malone's ears at some interval. As well as to her husband's attention, which Brodie certainly didn't want or need to happen. Dr. Malone favored Brodie by sharing medical counsel and bringing him in on all the most interesting cases. Angering such a mentor would not be a smart, professional move. Neither would the chance of provoking Dorothea's dander in an uproar and being the brunt of one of her tirades.

Brodie sighed heavily, his jacket stifling him just as much as his awareness to keep quiet. "I'd better get going, as Dorothea hates to be kept waiting."

Hank winked. "A-yup, I hear you." One of his weather-beaten gardener's hands reached for the hedge clippers hanging from his utility belt. His large, green thumb with a dirt-laced nail and cracked skin at the cuticle pulled the implement free from a loop. "A good day to you, Doc," he called over his shoulder, walking away to sculpt a nearby hedgerow.

"And to you as well, Hank." He made his way to the mansion's front, double doors.

Blanche opened the door, wearing a crisp, white blouse beneath a light gray pinafore, a white apron with two deep pockets tied around her plump waist. Her silver-streaked hair was pulled back tightly into a bun that rested at the nape of her neck, causing the flesh at her temples to slant the corners of her greenish eyes.

"A-yup, finally here you are," she mumbled, beckoning him inside.

The large foyer, with flowered wallpaper done in cream and accented with gold leafing, against the shiny mirror-like-luster of the marble floor, was as extravagant as the rest of the mansion.

Brodie could hear his mother say, *"'Tis a mighty grand entrance way, to be sure."*

Quickly he pulled out his pocket watch. "I am only about ten minutes late," he said in his own defense, replacing the timepiece in his vest pocket.

"A-yup, but just the same," she countered. "Miss Dorothea's a stickler for punctuality."

Immediately a knot formed in his stomach. If Dorothea decided to take him to task for his tardiness, no matter how slight, it was destined to be an unpleasant day.

"But you are in luck, Doc," Blanche whispered. "Miss Malone's been otherwise distracted with her step cousin, Drake Nolan, also a doctor," she added. "He arrived from New York late last night." Blanche shut the door behind him. "Seems he's Mrs. Malone's sister's stepson and will be touring the hospital tomorrow with Dr. Malone." She shrugged. "Appears he's thinking of staying, getting into practice with Dr. Malone."

Now his stomach sank to his knees. There was enough competition already to work with and beside the great Doctor Hemsley Malone; he certainly didn't need an added obstacle. And a family member at that, which would take priority over any hopes he had of obtaining a valid position after Doctor Malone retired.

"Where is Miss Dorothea, Blanche?" He forced himself to appear confident and unconcerned, in spite of the turmoil rioting within.

"In the garden with Doctor Nolan," Blanche explained. "But it might be best if you didn't interrupt them, a request of Mrs. Malone's."

He frowned. "I don't understand."

Blanche sighed heavily. "Don't go saying I told you, but I think the missus is hoping Doctor Nolan will take a fancy to Miss Dorothea." She arched a brow. "Family is family, after all, and when they both were youngsters, they did take an unusual liking to each other. Mrs. Malone, I'm surmising, hopes something between them will spark again. Plus, she wants to please her sister by giving the stepson a chance at a good career and a high-born wife."

He felt his face grow hot. Clearing his throat, he forced himself to remain calm. "Well, that can hardly be the case now, can it? Since Dorothea and I are engaged."

Blanche screwed up her large, pepper-shaped nose. "Well now, there lies a problem. The missus feels if Dorothea isn't wearing a ring, then she's still available."

He could feel the perspiration wetting the underarms of his shirt. "I've explained to Dorothea the reason why I haven't yet…" he began, and then deliberately clipped his words. He wouldn't discuss the situation any further with someone who had no business conversing on the matter in the first place. Besides, no matter how carefully he retorted, whatever he said would be contorted, then spun throughout the household. With Drake Nolan's arrival, he was working at a disadvantage. Certainly, he didn't need to add to the problem by fueling gossip.

"Where is Mrs. Malone?" He hoped she wasn't hold up in her chambers, as she was most days at this hour, sleeping off the liquor she consumed the night before.

Charlotte Malone, or Lottie as she was called, partook nightly in alcohol…a nip here, a dram there, soon became her comfort from the loneliness of an absent husband and a sanctuary from a spoiled, overbearing daughter. He often wondered why Doctor Malone didn't seek professional help for his wife, being in the high medical position that he was. He had to know someone who could bring a remedy to Charlotte's daily stupors and incapacitations. Then again, his wife's absence left him free to dabble in all sorts of pleasures away from home, which his close association as of late with Doctor Malone had brought to his attention, as well as Hemsley's habit of overly catering to Dorothea by granting her every whim. How Charlotte stood a chance to have any sort of voice in her own home— ever, especially when Dorothea was a child—was a mystery to him. No doubt, thus the reason she chose to numb herself from the frustrations and confrontations surrounding her with spiked tea or coffee during dinner and many glasses of port wine that followed.

Blanche smoothed her apron, looking slightly peeved she'd no longer be privileged to continue the conversation. "She's having tea in the dining room."

Charlotte Malone being up early and having breakfast in the dining room came as a shock. Most evenings, dining at the mansion ended with Hemsley and Blanche escorting Mrs. Malone to bed. He'd offered to help, but Dorothea always distracted him in some way to remove focus from the embarrassing situation. And it was rumored Mrs. Malone would not be heard from again until late afternoon the following day.

He inclined his head politely. "Thank you, Blanche." He forced a smile in her direction before making his way to the dining room.

Surprisingly Charlotte Malone looked particularly pulled together; eyes clear and bright watched his entrance. Smiling like the cat that got the cream, she greeted him with a lilting tone to her otherwise drone of a voice. "Well, the good Doctor O'Clarity has arrived."

So sorry to complicate your plans, he wanted to say, but instead he nodded politely. "Good morning, Mrs. Malone."

Her smile froze upon her face, looking stale and unnatural. "I suppose you're looking for my daughter."

"I was told she's in the garden with a visiting family member," he said.

She arched a brow. "Yes, but you see, he's not really a blood relative," she retorted, emphasizing *blood relative.* She waved a hand casually in the air. "But I'm sure Blanche has sufficiently explained the situation," she added sarcastically.

"She has." He moved to take a seat opposite her at the dining room table. "But suppose you explain the reason you didn't want me, your daughter's fiancé, to interrupt them?"

Mrs. Malone reached for the teapot resting beside her plate, then motioned for him to hand her the cup in front of him. He complied, and she poured him the tea. After handing him the cup, she indicated the cream and sugar decanters upon the table. "Please, help yourself."

"No, thank you. I drink it black.".

She sat back in her seat. "You're a nice enough young man, Doctor O'Clarity. My husband is very fond of you and raves about your work, but you are not right for my daughter."

"Because I have not yet placed a ring upon her finger?" he snapped. Before the elder woman could answer, he went on. "I explained to Dorothea my desire was for her to wear my great grandmother's ring which I plan on getting the next time I travel to Eagle's Landing to visit my folks."

Mrs. Malone locked her gaze on his. "I was thinking more because you are sincere, polite, and ready to please my daughter at every turn."

He frowned. "And don't those qualities make for a loving and successful marriage?"

"For Dorothea, yes. But not for you." Mrs. Malone sighed heavily. "My daughter, though I love her dearly, will make your life miserable. She will walk all over you in no time, if she hasn't already. You will never satisfy her, no matter how hard you try. I've spent the better part of twenty years giving all I could to that child, only to learn it's never been enough…or exactly what she hoped. Trust me on this. Dorothea won't appreciate or be content with anything you do, nor will she wear your great grandmother's ring."

"Dorothea and I love each other, things will be different for us," he said. "She will accept my great grandmother's ring because I've told her how much her wearing it means to me…to my family."

Mrs. Malone chuckled lightly. "Oh, you think so?" She leaned forward in her seat. "The two of us went shopping a few days ago to Unser's Jewelers. Do you know what my daughter tried on for the better part of an hour?" She didn't wait for his answer. "Diamond rings. The stones of ample size…rings you could never afford to purchase. And when I pointed that fact out to her, she informed me that if you truly loved her, you'd find a way."

Brodie's face burned with rage. "And you believe Drake Nolan can find a way?"

"Yes, he has better means," she said softly. "He's known Dorothea longer and better than you do. Since they were children, he had a knack for how to handle her, with just enough control to keep her in line, yet still pampered and treasured."

Brodie's heart raced. "Why then, if he's such a perfect match for Dorothea, has he not claimed her hand before now?"

Mrs. Malone folded her hands in her lap. "He did, before he left for Germany to complete his medical studies."

He arched a brow. "Obviously Dorothea refused his proposal because she doesn't love him."

"Dorothea refused his proposal because she wanted him to finish his studies here," she said. "When Drake held strong to what he wanted to do, Dorothea decided to teach him a lesson. And you were just…"

"Convenient for her to carry out her plan," he finished.

Mrs. Malone nodded. "I'm so sorry, Doctor O'Clarity." She sighed again. "Now that Drake's returned, I'm sure Dorothea will decide to marry him."

Despite the broken heart he now felt, he squared his shoulders and stood. "I need to talk to Dorothea."

"Talk to me about what," came a voice from behind.

Brodie turned to see Dorothea entering through the doorway, her hand familiarly looped around the arm of a tall, thin man standing way too close beside her.

Chapter Five

Cassia Rose woke, inhaling the fragrant spring air ruffling her bedroom curtains. She smiled to herself. She'd missed the warmth of an Arizona morning. England, with all its charms, lacked the frequency of the sun's heat. Even on the nicest of days, she sensed a bit of a chill in the air.

She inhaled again, this time filling her nostrils with the delicious aroma of pancakes, sausage, bacon, and coffee. Her mouth watered as she remembered how pampered and satisfied she felt after one of her mother's home-cooked meals.

"The woman is a genius," she mumbled, throwing aside the quilt and draping her legs over one side of the bed. To be able to make something from nothing, and have it taste amazing, seemed to be Amanda Holmes's specialty.

Cassia yawned and stretched before reaching for the robe across the foot of her bed. "Poor man who marries me will probably starve to death." Even though her mother taught her to cook, her focus was practicing medicine. Donning the robe, she glided her feet into her slippers and made her way to the kitchen.

The scene greeting her was heartwarmingly familiar. Mama was busy at the stove, bustling around like a busy bee, with frying pans cooking on every burner. Papa was seated at the table, hunched over his open Bible with several sheets of paper and a pencil in hand while composing his sermon for Sunday's service. It mattered not it was only Wednesday. Papa's routine was to contemplate a new sermon on Monday, write a rough draft of his thoughts on Tuesday, do research on the subject on Wednesday, combine the outline of thoughts and the element of research on Thursday, edit on Friday, and make a finished copy on Saturday.

Looking up from his work, he smiled at Cassia. "Did my baby girl have a good night's sleep?"

She nodded, coming over to plant a small kiss atop his head, which still housed a crop of thick hair. Though, most of it now had turned gray. "It was good to sleep in my own bed." She stole a piece of bacon set aside on the counter. "Is there anything I can help with, Mama?"

Amanda, working right along at flipping pancakes, glanced in her direction. "You can help us eat it all."

She giggled. "That won't be a problem, especially with the bacon." Her mother always made the bacon crisp, the way Cassia liked, and lots of it, too, as it was her favorite breakfast meat.

"What are your plans for today?" her father inquired.

Before she could answer, her mother indicated a satchel hanging from a peg by the back door. "Clara Morris dropped that off earlier for you."

She frowned, reaching for the satchel and pulling out a large-brimmed straw hat, a red checkered shirt, and a pair of denim overalls fit for a teen boy, but surprisingly her size as well.

Her mother chuckled lightly. "Aha, you've been gifted with gardening clothes. Must be Clara needs help

40

with tending the herbs." She brought the plates of food to the table and set them down. "I'd say Clara's just planned your first day back home."

"Well, we did talk of readying my medical bag with healing properties," she mused aloud. "I'd say it was only fitting to get that task done before I'm called into service by Dr. O'Clarity."

Her father, eyeing the overalls, arched a brow. "I remember a time when men's trousers were only worn by men, and if a woman donned them… Well, it would be quite scandalous."

She placed all the items back into the satchel, hanging it again on the peg, and took a seat beside her father at the table. "Mama wore trousers, didn't she?"

"Aye, only once," her father emphasized. "While she induced me to help save Proud Eagle from the clutches of Lieutenant Ryan Duffy."

It was a story Cassia knew well. Her mother's plan to rescue her first husband called for Amanda to dress like a man while she entered the military fort where he was being held before a hanging sentence was carried out.

"And I've always said, wearing trousers to work or ride in is much easier, very comfortable, and more efficient than a skirt," her mother added. "I'm pleased to see my idea has finally caught on and become permissible."

"I second that notion," she said, diving into the bacon.

"Hmmm," her father grunted.

Both women giggled at his retort.

****

Cassia, carrying the leather, monogrammed

medicine bag Aunt Marietta gifted her with, made her way to Clara Morris's home. Walking the two short blocks to her destination, garbed in her new clothes, she inhaled the warm breeze playing with the curls framing her face. Cassia was content and hopeful. Finally she was beginning her medical career. It took forever to get to this point, but hard work and determination had paid off. And today, though it only concerned her with preparations, was her first day on the job.

She found Clara in her yard, dressed in clothes similar to her own, snipping plants. The Morris's garden was nature's apothecary, stocked with several types of healing herbs, their properties shared and passed down through Rowena Cooper's family and used by the entire Western world for over a hundred years. As well as generations of many Indian tribes, thanks to the Western Apache Shaman, Owl Woman.

As she and Clara worked into midafternoon, the Arizona sun grew hotter. Clara handed her a red, paisley-printed bandana for wiping her brow. The material's pattern was similar to what the railroad workers wore tied around their necks. And in an instant, Tucker O'Clarity filled her thoughts.

Where was he now? What was he doing? Was he well? Did he have someone to love? A family? Did he ever think of her as she so often thought of him?

Cassia sighed heavily, her anguish over Tucker coupled with the heat. "I forgot how intense Arizona's sun can become, especially when one is out working beneath it."

Clara, resting back on her haunches from her work, glanced over at Cassia. "I believe we've got enough to make several jars of salve, bottles of tincture, and pouches of tea." Her eyes rose to the afternoon sky, and with her own bandana, she wiped her neck. "And the sun's only goin' get fiercer from this point on." She stood, brushing dirt from the worn knees of her overalls. "I'd say it's about time to splash our faces with cold water and enjoy a cool glass of lemonade."

Cassia stood, brushing her clothes. "I'd say that's a capital idea."

Clara laughed. "Ya sound like one of those English gals."

She joined in on her friend's mirth. "I imagine after eight years some of their phrases were bound to rub off on me." She smiled and bent to retrieve the basket she'd been filling with herbs. "But at heart, I'm still just a prairie girl. And this prairie girl can't wait to drink a glass of lemonade."

Clara's home was efficient with all the modern conveniences of a stove, ice box, and indoor plumbing. The décor, however, was modest. The furniture was well worn and mostly hand-me-downs, yet it all came together with a down-home, cozy look.

The walls, scatter rugs, and upholstery consisted of light colors and soft tones. Her kitchen, like all country homes, was the center of Clara's household where everyone gathered the most to eat, drink, and tell stories. The kitchen table served many purposes: turning into a desk when paperwork and ledgers needed tending, a seamstress's surface where patterns and material was spread for sewing, as well as Clara's apothecary counter where she bottled her herbs for medicinal purposes.

Clara's husband was a dairy farmer. The milk, butter, eggs, and cheese Eagle's Landing residents purchased at the town's general store were the product of his efforts. He also added home delivery to those town districts too far from the store. Her children, ten-year-old Morgan and eight-year-old Blythe, helped before and after school, and during the summer. Clara did her share, as well, making the farming business a family affair.

Clara placed a cool glass of lemonade before her friend and made up two finger bowls filled with hot soapy water. "Can't be havin' a medical person, such as yerself, carin' for folks with dirt beneath the nails, especially since they're such nice hands to boot." Clara held out her hands, scrutinizing the condition they were in. "Mine have seen their days for sure," she added with a frown, before placing a bowl in front of Cassia and a small scrub brush. She set a bowl and brush for herself, and for a time the two women tended their nails and sipped the lemonade in silence.

Clara's hands were small, but strong and muscular. The tips and pads of her fingers were laced with cuts and scars from the laborious chores they helped her perform. Her nails were short but evenly cut and filed, not ragged or yellowed, yet still very much a farmer's wife's hands: sun-kissed, wind-blown, and freckled.

Cassia finally broke the silence. "Applying lotion will help to mend the cuts," she offered.

Clara chuckled. "The number of times I wash my hands in a day…well, let's just say I'd be usin' a powerful heap of lotion." She sighed. "Nope, these hands don't have time to be pampered, never have, come to think on it. If I wasn't helpin' Ma with the chores when I was a youngun', I was doin' my share as a wife, and a very young wife at that, since I married

Owen the day after I turned eighteen. Between plantin' in my garden, milkin' the cows, collectin' the eggs and feedin' the chickens, washin' the clothes, cleanin' everythin' from wood floors to baby bottoms, and makin' the meals, these hands have been in and out of hot water more than a provokin' child."

She studied Clara's face. "Do you ever regret getting married and being a farmer's wife?"

Clare screwed up her freckled nose. "I wouldn't go as far as to say I regret my choice, because I love my husband and my children with everythin' inside of me. But I think it would've been nice to be me, for a while…travel a bit, like you've done…see places other than Willow Creek and Eagle's Landin'." She giggled like a school girl. "Wear fancy clothes, put on fancy creams like those I see advertised at Remington's Department Store, to make a woman feel pretty, like them there city gals in the ads with their hair all done up in curls. It would have been nice to be able to meet new folks, see how they live, and such the like." She wiped her hands on her apron, stood, and gathered the bowls. "But that wasn't the way of it for me. I went from my parents' home, doin' what they told me, to my husband's home."

She frowned. "Isn't Owen good to you?"

"Owen's a good man, and as a good man he treats me fair and righteous, loves and protects me. He's never raised a hand to me, and for that I'm grateful. I know plenty of women puttin' up with husbands who beat them. Constance Wilson, who lives at the edge of town, has a sister livin' in Alaska. She's married to a logger and gets her bared bottom switched by her man like she was one of the children."

Cassia gasped. "Why does she stay?"

"Where's she gonna go, with five children, no schoolin', and no money?" Clara countered. She shook her head. "Besides, the Bible's rule is that women must obey their husbands. It's a vow we take on our weddin' day. That's why I count my blessin's every night I bed down that I've a reasonable spouse instead of one that's ruthless, imposin' upon his wife such violence." Clara arched a brow. "But still and all, as good and kind as Owen is, I'm held accountable for fixin' the meals, sewin' the clothes, keepin' the house, teachin' the children right from wrong so they'll grow to be fine adults, and the like, for him to be doin' what needs to be done to keep this farm goin'.'"

"And if you didn't do all those things, strayed from protocol, do you think Owen would beat you?"

Clara cocked her head to the side, contemplating the question before answering, and that slight pause gave Cassia chills down her spine.

"I don't rightly believe he'd beat me," Clara finally said. Her brows furrowed. "But he'd be mighty mad." She shrugged. "I probably couldn't blame him much. Without my help, Owen would have an overwhelmin' work load, one that would put any single person into a grave much sooner than need be. And as long as I'm healthy, can do my share, I don't mind." She glanced around the room. "This is my home, a home I want to keep for my family. It's just sometimes I would like to do somethin' for just me."

"What would that something be, Clara?" she said softly.

Clara smiled. "I'd like to travel and see new places. And maybe buy a store-bought dress now and then, instead of always wearin' the home-made kind. Or go out to one of those fancy restaurants for dinner. Have someone serve me a meal for a change and do the cleanup."

Long after Cassia left Clara's house, she thought of their conversation. Lying in bed that night, she began to wonder. She had always hoped to fall in love, marry, have her own home and a family. But in doing so, would she have to give up her wants and desires for a medical career?

"No, not me," she whispered to herself with conviction. "There comes a time, despite protocol's voice, whereby a woman must listen to the calling of her heart...and follow it. I intend to do just that," she vowed through a yawn. After rolling onto her side and fluffing her pillow, she reassured herself once more before sleep claimed her senses. "I will find a way to have it all."

Chapter Six

The next day was the first day Cassia was officially on duty. Because she had also taken nurses training, as well as midwifery, her medical duties in town and at the SEL clinic would be extensive. She would be taking care of more than pregnant women throughout the day, so her uniform and medical bag would be different from that of only a midwife's.

Dressing in a short-sleeved, gray dress neatly belted at the waist and falling to mid-ankle length, she felt her heart race with anticipation. This was the day she had waited for, for so very long. Over the gray dress she wore a crisp, white apron with two deep pockets placed on each side, white hose kept up by garters, and white front-laced shoes with ample arch support for all the hours she'd be upon her feet.

Her hair was too short to put up in a bun, so she smoothed and pinned back the curls framing her face, keeping the hair out of her eyes or from being a distraction. She secured a small, white nurse's cap on the crown of her head. A hip-length, light-weight navy blue cape would suffice to keep her warm, if the spring temperature should call for it. But come the winter months, a long-sleeved dress would be worn beneath her apron, along with a mid-knee length, hooded cape of a warmer material and white gloves for outdoor use.

Doctor O'Clarity would be by at seven a.m. to pick

her up. The doctor confirmed the time last night when he called her using the telephone which was a wonderful invention. It made communication between homes available without making a trip to the person's residence. City phone systems were more advanced then rural areas, so any household able to afford a phone had one. However, Eagle's Landing was not yet as large a township. Therefore, only certain homes had phone service.

Cassia's house had a phone, since her father was the town's clergyman. Doctor O'Clarity had both a phone at his office and in his home. The Eagle's Landing General Store had a phone as well. This phone was the favorite of Maggie Granger, the store's keeper. Her time on the device, mostly gossiping for her entertainment, interfered with the entire town's use of the phone since lines were connected, thus called party lines.

The delicious aromas from the kitchen had her hurrying to add a few finishing touches to her appearance. When she entered the dining area, her father looked up from the morning paper and smiled.

"Now, there's my baby girl, ready for her first day on the job," he boasted with pride gleaming in his light blue eyes.

"For Lord's sake, Josh, when are you going to stop calling her a baby?" her mother scolded, turning from the cupboard and casting an adoring smile.

"Never," her father replied.

Cassia sighed, taking a seat at the table. "Truth be told, I feel as vulnerable as a child. I'm just as scared as when I left for my first day of school."

Her mother placed a cup of tea in front of her.

"And so, I will advise you the same way I did on that morning so many years ago. Pay attention to what you're doing, and always do your best."

"And remember, it's not about folks thanking you for their care, but instead you thanking God for the skills He's given you to be of help to them," her father offered. Leaning forward, he gave her hand an affectionate pat. "Always make time to talk to God throughout the day, Cassia. Having His ear will give you the strength to make difficult decisions, or accept those results you cannot change."

She nodded, knowing the difficulties her father spoke of. In the medical field, there was a lot of satisfaction in making someone well, in being instrumental in the recovery. But there were also those times when a doctor couldn't cure a patient. The suffering continued despite all training and efforts, and the patient died. If a doctor didn't have the strength to move past those times, he couldn't continue to help the countless others who would soon need him next.

"Staying sharp with a heavy heart is not always that easy." She sipped her tea.

"Then change your viewpoint," her father advised. "Bring forth your ease, draw upon your comfort, by looking at the situation from a different angle. Calling attention to something other than your own hurts, fears, or distress, will give you the strength and clarity to cope with the situation at hand, and perform adequately."

"Protect me, O Lord, with Your refrain of liberation," she muttered.

"Aye, Cassia," her father whispered. "And He will at that."

A knock at the back door ended their conversation.

The doctor, ever reliable and punctual, declined the cup of coffee Amanda offered with a polite reply and the fact of not wanting to make Cassia late on her first day. Then he escorted her to his old, worn, partially covered, horse-drawn wagon.

As she settled her backside upon the wood-planked seat, she sighed. "There are much quicker and more comfortable ways to travel now, Doc."

He chuckled lightly. "Aye, I'm well aware o' the alternatives, as me children and dear wife have been singin' such praises. But nothin' is more reliable than this old mare hitched to this trusty wagon."

"And I'd have to say, mighty cold to ride in during the winter months." She turned to look at him.

"I get where 'tis I need to go, so I'm not complainin'. Besides," he added, "I'm still hardy enough to cope with a bit o' cold weather."

She looked deep into his emerald eyes. Instead of the usual twinkle she remembered, they appeared tired, red-rimmed. His gentle face was now haggard and worn. No doubt he sat up half the night with a sick person—stopping home long enough to change into clean clothes and grab a bite to eat...the eating part, she was sure, optional. It was how this man took care of his patients—thorough, with dedication and complete devotion. She had been on the other end of that professional concern when she was six years old. For days her body burned with fever, and throughout her illness Doctor O'Clarity was present, taking turns with her parents to swab her burning flesh with cold water, even going so far as to emerge her into a cold bath. This, she hoped, was the kind of medical caregiver she would turn out to be. Under Sean O'Clarity's guidance, there would be no other way, as he would accept nothing less.

I just pray I'm up for the task.

"Not to fear now, Lass. Ye're goin' to be doin' a fine job."

She arched a brow. "And now you can read minds?"

He chuckled lightly. "Well, 'tis not so much yer mind I'm able to read, but the scared look upon yer face."

She sighed. "Am I that obvious?"

"Aye, Lass, but all will be fine. I don't plan on leavin' yer side until I know yer confident. Besides, 'tis always a bit easier seein' sick folks at the SEL clinic, then 'tis trapsin' all over the countryside. 'Tis exactly the reason I chose the location for yer first day." He turned her way and smiled. "And by tonight, when I return ye to yer folks, ye'll be too tired to ever remember how fearful ye were."

She frowned. "But with both of us at the clinic, who will be on call at Eagle's Landing?"

"Sadly there will be no one, for today. So, we must pray the good Lord sees fit to direct all ailin' humans to our clinic door. But when yer confident to make calls by yerself, we will split the work. Then both areas will be covered. 'Tis what I always hoped would happen when Brodie and…" He swallowed the end of his sentence.

Cassia finished it for him. "When Brodie and Tucker became doctors." It was her hope too—the Tucker part, anyway.

"Aye, Lass, 'tis the truth o' it." He shrugged. "But Brodie didn't want a country doctor's life, and Tucker didn't want a doctor's life at all."

She cast her eyes to the folded hands in her lap. "Do you ever hear from either of them?"

"Aye, from time to time," he said. "Brodie is meetin' well the demands o' practicin' medicine at a big hospital in Boston. Last he wrote us, he had himself a lady love." He shrugged again. "Tucker hasn't written in almost a year. Too busy, I suppose, with his duties and travelin' all over God's creation for the railroad."

She cleared her throat and gave the doctor's hand a quick pat. "Well, you've got me, and together the two of us will do just fine."

He smiled. "I'm not worried in the least, Lass."

The two of them were silent for the remainder of the ride. The carriage wheels thumping over the covered bridge connecting Eagle's Landing and South Eagle's Landing lulled her, allowing her thoughts to wander. How was Tucker, and where could he be now? Was he happy with the choices he'd made for his life? Did he have a lady love too, like Brodie? Would he one day return to Eagle's Landing, married?

It was Doctor O'Clarity's declaration of, "Well, Lass, here we be," that pulled her back to the present, as well as all the people lined up outside of the clinic's doors. Mostly women and children—lots of children—sick, crying and fussing as they waited for the clinic doors to open. And suddenly dread overcame her. An overwhelming lump forming in the pit of her stomach and a dull pain at the base of her neck reminded her of the days during the war, overseas. Never did the sick or injured let up, the constant flow, the immediate tasks, and doing her best at all times. It was stressful and exhausting.

She sighed heavily. "Oh, my."

"Don't let them take ye back, Lass." Dr. O'Clarity pulled the horse to a stop. "All will be fine. We can only administer our attention to them, one at a time, and do the best with our God given skills." He made a gesture with his hand to the waiting crowd. "They understand that and are thankful to be able to come to a place that'll give them the help they seek and need."

She nodded, climbing down from the wagon and reaching for her bag which would be filled further with various clinic supplies for use during the home visits. As she followed Dr. O'Clarity through the doors, a strong, clean aroma of ammonia and bleach filled her senses. The clinic, consisting of basically one large room, was divided up by a series of screens and curtains arranged to form individual dressing and examining rooms. In each cubicle there was a linen covered examining table, a large stand holding a sufficient number of clean gowns, a wash basin, soap, towels and washcloths, gauze for bandages, rubber gloves, and cotton balls. Two chairs were provided, one for the patient's clothes to be placed on and the other for the parent to sit upon while the child was examined. A second table held instruments and products used in addressing ailments, a garbage pail for discarded supplies, and a laundry bag for soiled linen, gowns, and towels. In another section there were two bathrooms, one for the men and another for the women, a patient waiting area furnished with twenty to thirty straight-backed wooden chairs, and a receptionist's desk. At the end of the large room was a walled off area, which was the doctor's private quarters. This room was furnished with a desk, file cabinets, bookcases filled with large leather-bound medical volumes, cabinets stocked with drugs, and a sink.

Cassia's first patient of the day was the baker's son, nine-year-old Arnie Harland.

"He's gone and ate himself sick on a batch of molasses cookies," Mrs. Harland explained, while drying Arnie's tears with a handkerchief. "He knows better," the mother grumbled. "Those cookies were for sellin' in the store—not for little boys to be hoggin'. And when he's done ailin', he's gonna get a switchin' he'll never forget," she added. This announcement only made Arnie cry all the harder and louder.

Cassia helped the blubbering boy onto the examining table. "Let's get him undressed and in a gown so Dr. O'Clarity can examine him."

Mrs. Harland nodded and pulled off Arnie's shoes and socks, while she removed his jacket and shirt. Then the boy's mother undressed him from his trousers and underwear which Arnie definitely didn't like.

Covering his genitals with a hand, he sobbed, "I don't want her lookin' at me."

"It's her job to take care of sick folks, so she ain't payin' no mind to whatcha got or haven't got," Mrs. Harland snapped. "Besides, ya should've thought about that before ya ate all them cookies."

Cassia reached for a gown. "Here, Arnie, let's get this on you."

The boy nodded and put his arms through the gown's sleeves.

Cassia tied it securely at the nape of the neck and reached for a thermometer. "Roll over now, so I can see if you're running a temperature."

"I can take it in my mouth," Arnie informed her,

sitting ridged on the table.

She stifled a smile and replaced the rectal thermometer with the oral kind. Cassia looked into his ears and throat, listened to his heart, and took his pulse.

When Dr. O'Clarity arrived, he listened to Cassia's patient update as he hurried along with the examination, asking Arnie where it hurt. He felt along the child's stomach and checked him for a hernia. "Well, me lad," Dr. O'Clarity concluded. "Seems to me those cookies ye ate have left ye as full as anybody has a right to be. So, we need to clean the buggers out o' ye." He turned to Cassia. "A soapy enema will do the trick."

"Yes, Doctor," she said.

Upon leaving the cubicle to fetch an enema bag and bed pan, she heard Arnie shout, "Oh nooooo!"

As the day progressed, she assisted in setting a broken ankle, a broken wrist, attended to diaper rash, coughs, allergies, headaches, upset stomachs, examined a few pregnant women, cleaned and bandaged a few burns, stitched up a few cuts, and gave another enema.

On the ride home, she struggled to keep her eyes open and understood why Dr. O'Clarity looked so worn out. When he halted the horse at her house, she wearily climbed down from the wagon.

"Eat a good dinner and get yerself to bed, Cassia," he advised. "Tomorrow is the home visits."

All she managed was a nod.

Do I even have the strength to chew dinner?

She felt it doubtful as she slowly trudged her way to the front door.

Chapter Seven

In the days that followed, Cassia became busier and more exhausted than she ever could have imagined. She felt torn with so many wanting a piece of her time and attention. Besides the patients she helped care for, and helping her father clean the church for Thursday evening and Sunday services, her mother needed help putting together and cooking for a small going away gathering. Cassia's sister-in-law, Riley; nephew, Silas; and niece, Anita would be traveling to England in a matter of days, and sending them off with a family dinner to remember was something very important to Amanda Holmes.

It was important to Cassia as well, since this would be the last time for a long while she'd see her nephew, and the final time he'd be a permanent resident at Eagle's Landing.

The day of the event fell on a beautiful Sunday afternoon, following the church service. The guests arrived after changing from their Sunday best to comfortable clothes. The family sat around the dining table to feast on duck in orange sauce, asparagus, boiled potatoes, cranberry bread, and lemonade.

As coffee was served, Silas stood, slowly glanced around at all his loved ones sitting at the table, and smiled. "I've been an extremely fortunate person, to have so many wonderful kin folk to love and who love me in return." He swallowed hard, blinking back the tears welling in his eyes. "That's probably why leaving Eagle's Landing will not be easy." He took a deep breath. "I've always known this time and my obligation to continue our blood line at Collins Stead would come one day, just didn't think it would be so soon." He squared his shoulders and lifted his chin. "And I am both proud and excited to fulfill my duty, even if I am sad to leave. I only ask that you don't forget me, will come often to England, and I will visit as well. I don't want to—can't lose sight of my family."

Cassia, tears cascading down her cheeks, stood and rushed to her nephew. As she embraced him, she whispered, "You will never be far from my heart."

Everyone took a turn hugging and kissing Silas, reassuring him of his place in the family and promising to visit at every chance available. It wasn't long after that the gathering dispensed, all those invited departing for their homes and readying for a new day to dawn.

As she said one last farewell at the door, she kissed her nephew. Standing on tiptoe to reach his cheek, a profound sadness enveloped her. She enjoyed the eight years she lived in England, but there was always the fact she'd return home to live out her life among those closest to her. How would she have felt if she had to live in England permanently?

"You are quite a man, Silas," she said. "And we're all so proud of you."

He kissed her forehead. "I wish there had been more time for us to spend together."

"I do too," she whispered.

He laughed. "Then again with you so busy caring for sick folks, I probably wouldn't get to see you much anyway."

"I should have made more time," she said.

"No, you should be doing just what it is you planned to do," he countered. "And I'll be doing what was planned for me to do."

"Take heart, Silas. Knowing you as I do, I don't doubt for a second you won't make it all your own with the unique and responsible way you do everything." She smiled. "It will be all right, my dear nephew." She patted his chest. "Trust your heart in all matters, as it is usually the first instincts we should listen to."

As she watched him walk down the front path to his house next door, she whispered a little prayer for his safety, happiness, and prosperity in his new life as master of Collins Stead.

She slept fitfully, her dreams a jumble of what transpired throughout the day. That was always the way for her. What she lived by day, she replayed by night. And by morning she was drained, wishing she could just pull the quilt over her head and stay in bed.

But that wasn't an option, especially today, the day she was scheduled to pay a professional visit to Nora, who was nearing her due date. She smiled as she swung her legs off the bed. Who would have thought little, skinny, shy, Nora—her childhood friend and confidante—would one day be the wife of an attorney in the making and soon to be a mother?

She frowned. "And who would have thought I'd be the one to deliver her baby."

After a quick meal of porridge and fruit, she reached for her bag and made her way out the door, only to find a bike waiting for her beside the front steps. In England she had used a bike to get around. All the nurses did, going to and fro through the streets much quicker and faster than those using other modes of travel. But this particular bike she knew well, as she had ridden on the handlebars many a time in route to childhood adventures.

The note, attached by a pink ribbon, read:

Not as fancy as a Model T Ford, but better than walking.

Love,

Silas

She smiled through the tears welling in her eyes, glancing over at the house next door. It was quiet, except for one shutting and locking the front door. Upon spotting her, Ethan waved, then made his way to where she stood, a knapsack thrust over his right shoulder and dressed in traditional Apache garb.

He smiled, his large green eyes glancing over at the bike. "He finally willed ole Nellie to you, huh?"

She laughed. "That's the truth, and I appreciate the gesture as I have quite an area in town to cover." Then frowning, she indicated his mode of dress. "And where are you off too dressed traditionally?"

"Well, my dear auntie," he teased. "I'm on my way to fulfill my vision quest." He sighed. "I've put it off for way too long." Shrugging he added, "I thought if I didn't fulfill this rite of passage, I'd be free from the responsibilities of being the tribe's next chief, should anything happen to my father. But in view of the fact Silas is moving forward to his duties, shucking my own is no longer an option." He glanced at his house. "This seemed like the ideal opportunity, with Papa bringing Mama, Anita, and Silas to catch the train, to slip away without a fuss."

"How long will you be gone?"

"About five days, whereby I will channel the spirits of my ancestors, come back wise, and ready to do what the chief's son must do when the time comes."

"Rites of passage," she mused aloud. "We're finally there—old enough to pick up where those before us left off and carry the torch until the next generation arrives."

"Both exciting and frightening," he admitted. Glancing up at the morning sun, he added, "And it is time for me to be on my way."

"Godspeed," she said.

"And to you as well," he countered, before making his way down the path.

Sighing, she placed her bag in the front basket and released the kickstand. She wadded her skirt between her knees before climbing onto the bike's seat. When she passed Ethan, he waved. She smiled and returned the farewell gesture before she rounded the corner, heading the bike toward Nora's house.

This morning's call on Nora would be the very first time she visited her friend's home. On the outside it was nicely landscaped with bushes and flowers, shuttered windows, and a porch complete with a swing. Nora and Cameron's home stood out among the others on the street, Nora's homey touches easy to spot. As well as the fact finances to keep the property well-kept wasn't a problem.

Cameron's parents, though they couldn't be classified as extremely wealthy, were comfortable financially. Edmond Dodd, a successful attorney with a thriving clientele in Eagle's Landing, also tried and won cases in Willow Creek and even as far as Phoenix.

Muriel Dodd, a school teacher who also did private tutoring, weaved and created beautiful blankets and sweaters that sold quite steadily at The Eagle's Landing General Store and Remington's Department Store in Willow Creek.

Cameron Dodd, being the only child of such successful parents, became the recipient of an ample start to his law career, as well as owning a home of good means. Nora's parents, Maggie and Eli Granger, weren't struggling folks either, even with a crew of children to support. Maggie was the general store's shopkeeper, and Eli ran a successful sheep ranch.

When she knocked on the door, to her surprise Maggie answered, appearing somewhat harried, her graying, auburn hair in disarray around her plump, fair skin textured face.

"'Tis by the grace o' God yer scheduled to come by today," she said breathlessly.

She frowned. "Is Nora all right?"

"Nay." Maggie beckoned for Cassia to follow her down a long hallway to the last room on the left. "Her pains started about an hour ago, just as I arrived with homemade biscuits for the two o' ye to enjoy with tea. And she's been in labor ever since."

"Has Cameron been called?" She tightened the grip on the handle of her bag.

"Nay, he can't be reached. He's gone with his father to Willow Creek on a case," Maggie said. "But I've been able to get a hold o' Muriel." She opened the bedroom door. "She should be arrivin' at any moment."

The bedroom was bright and airy, yellow flowered wallpaper accenting the pale yellow curtains, which were pulled back on the two windows situated on a far wall. Cassia smiled encouragingly at her friend and set her bag at the foot of the bed. "It's time, then," she said.

Nora responded with a taut nod, her freckled cheeks flushed and the wisps of auburn curls framing a face glistening with perspiration. "And my husband's not in town," she sobbed. "I knew this was going to happen."

Maggie went to her, sitting beside her daughter on the bed. "There, there, now love; ye've got yer ole mama here to help ye along. I've had seven o' me own and helped many in town have theirs, so I know a thing or two about birthin' babies," she said with bravado. Then she motioned to Cassia. "And yer dear friend is a trained midwife, so all will be well."

"But I wanted Cameron to be here," Nora whined. "He wanted to be here."

"Most times men are a nuisance in these matters, love," Maggie said. "Best he's not here and can give us women room to help ye to get the job done."

Cassia moved to close the curtains. "I want to cool you down, Nora, make you feel refreshed. So, I'm going to bathe you." She turned to Maggie. "Can you fetch me a basin of warm water, a wash cloth, soap, and a few towels?"

Maggie stood. "I sure can." She forced a smile. "And after this we'll have tea and those biscuits I brought."

Cassia gave Maggie's arm a reassuring pat, coupled with an encouraging nod. There wasn't a doubt in her mind, even though Maggie was involved many times with the birthing process, that things would be different for her today since the expecting mother was her own daughter.

While Maggie left to retrieve the items requested, Cassia opened her bag and pulled out the items she would need. After securing a cap upon her head to keep her short curls in place and donning a surgical gown, she assisted Nora in removing her nightgown. Then she placed a protective rubber sheet beneath Nora's lower extremities.

When Maggie returned with the requested bathing items, Cassia first scrubbed her hands before pulling on the rubber surgical gloves that had become a part of every medical kit. Cassia examined Nora's breasts, took her temperature, listened to her heart and the baby's heartbeat, and checked between her thighs to see how many centimeters she was dilated.

"You're too far along to be issued the standard enema," she commented.

Nora pulled a funny face. "Lucky me. I always hated those things." She motioned to Maggie. "Mama thought they were the cure-all for whatever ailed you, especially after we ate a bunch of candy from our Easter baskets."

"There's nothin' wrong with a good cleanin' out to set the body straight," Maggie said.

Nora frowned. "Come to think of it, I don't believe the enema bag was ever taken down from that hook over the toilet, that's how much use it got."

"'Tis still hangin' on that hook," Maggie confessed.

Cassia giggled. "I've had my share of the dreadful things too, as well as castor oil."

Nora joined in on her mirth. "Oh, please, don't even get me started on castor oil. It was a Sunday night ritual in the Granger household."

Maggie laughed. "If I remember right, I had ye all line up before bed to get a spoonful."

"You remember right for sure, Mama," Nora said.

The doorbell chimed, and Maggie left to see to the caller while Cassia bathed Nora. Murial Dodd's perky voice could be heard as she spoke to Maggie.

Nora sighed. "Now, isn't this just what I need, my mother-in-law watching me have a baby?"

She frowned. "Don't you like Muriel?"

"Of course I like her," Nora said. "I'm just not fond of her watching me, lying buck naked and spread eagle on my bed, pushing out a baby."

"That's understandable," she sympathized, not wanting to ever be a part of such a scene herself. "And what's important is you feeling as relaxed and as comfortable as you possibly can throughout all this, so I will politely ask Muriel to leave."

"No, Cassia, please don't," Nora pled. "It would hurt her feelings, and in turn upset my husband."

"You are my primary concern here, Nora…and this baby," she added.

"I know, I know." Nora grimaced with the pain of another contraction.

"I need you top notch and focused throughout the delivery, and if Muriel's presence is going to be a negative distraction or upset you in any way, then…"

Nora interrupted her. "It will be fine… I'll be fine, just don't send her away."

Cassia nodded, their conversation ending just in time for Muriel and Maggie to enter the room. As time progressed, the extra hands proved extremely helpful, each one of them taking turns to rub Nora's back after each pain, help her to the bathroom when needed, and keep her flesh cooled.

An hour had passed, and Nora's contractions were coming every eight minutes. "I'm going to check your cervix again, Nora, to see how the baby is lying," she explained. "To get a proper read, I'll need you, after the next contraction passes, to bend your knees, draw them up, place your heels together, and then let your thighs fall as far open as you can."

Nora complied, and she could thoroughly examine the vulva, as well as feel the cervix.

She sighed, relieved, and gave Nora an encouraging smile. "The baby is lying in a proper position for delivery."

"Saints preserve us," Maggie mumbled.

"How far along is she," Muriel inquired.

"Almost three quarters dilated," she said.

But as she moved her fingers around one more time, she felt something odd. With a bit more probing, she realized it wasn't the vaginal wall but a soft mass attached from above. It pulsed with the baby's heartbeat as it hung beside the baby's head. Terror seized her to the very core. Slowly she removed her hand, which began to tremble.

Her inner turmoil must have played upon the features of her face, because Nora gripped her arm. "What's wrong, Cassia?"

She swallowed hard. "The cord has prolapsed and is wrapped around the baby's neck.

Tears welled in Nora's eyes. "My baby will strangle."

"Saints preserve us," Maggie gasped.

Muriel's voice shook. "What can be done?"

Cassia closed her eyes while she called upon her

studies and what she'd been taught in such a case. When she opened them, they locked with Nora's. Tears spilled down her friend's flushed face.

"Tell me, Cassia," Nora whispered.

She inhaled sharply. "Usually a cesarean section is performed."

"That's an operation whereby the baby is delivered through an incision in the mother's abdomen, I believe," Muriel clarified in her teacher's voice. It wavered now with emotion but still held the calm, authoritative tone it did when conducting class.

"Yes, and even if I could perform such a procedure, which I'm not," she added quickly, "it cannot be done here. We'd need to get Nora to the hospital in Willow Creek."

"There's no time to get her to a hospital that far away," Maggie said, her face pale with fear for her daughter's well-being.

Cassia's rapid heartbeat echoed in her ears. Maggie was right; there wasn't enough time to get Nora to Willow Creek. And the clinic, where Dr. O'Clarity was on duty all day, wouldn't be equipped either for such a procedure. Besides, as Nora's labor progressed the cord would be crushed and the baby would die.

Muriel's fearful but controlled voice broke through her thoughts. "Is there another alternative that comes to mind, Cassia?"

Again she called upon what she'd been taught. "Yes, there might be. If the amniotic sac hasn't been broken, sometimes it is possible to raise the mother's pelvic area so the baby's head can be pushed back a bit. In this way the cord can be moved out of harm's way."

"Has the sac broken?" Muriel said.

"No, not yet," she said.

"Then do whatever you must to save my baby, Cassia," Nora choked out.

She looked around the bedroom and spotted a foot stool with a fairly wide dimension in a nearby corner. "Maggie, I believe we can raise Nora's bottom with that footstool."

Maggie immediately went for the stool, draped a clean towel over the seat, and brought it to the bedside. Together with Muriel, the two women managed to prop Nora's buttocks on top of the stool. Then taking a place on each side of Nora, they lifted her legs, securing one over each of their shoulders, before holding her rear steady upon the stool.

Nora grunted with discomfort; as her head and upper half of her body was considerably lower than her bottom half. She grimaced in pain as she reached up to grab the spokes of the brass headboard.

"I know this has to be a terribly uncomfortable position for your back, Nora," she sympathized. "But it's the only way to take pressure off the cord, allowing the baby to pull back into the uterus."

"No mind, Cassia," Nora gasped. "Just do whatever needs to be done to save my baby."

"And I've only a few moments to push the cord away at best, because with the next contraction the baby will be pushed forward again."

"Then best you get to it," Nora said.

Inserting her fingers again, she felt the dilated cervix and the pulsating cord. Then she felt for the baby's head, being very careful not to put pressure on the fontanelle, which would bring instant death to the baby.

God be with all of us, here…please, guide my hands.

She glanced at Maggie and Muriel. "Now, hold her bottom as still as possible, ladies."

"She's not movin' if I can help it," Maggie boasted.

"I've got a good grip as well," Muriel countered.

Gently Cassia pushed the baby's head. Slowly it moved, shifting about two to three inches. Then she felt for the cord…nothing…the cord was gone. She stretched her fingers farther, but all she could feel was the baby's head.

"I've done it," she said relieved. "The cord has been moved, but I fear it will fall back if you're taken off the stool."

"Ye mean she's got to deliver the babe like this?" Maggie said.

"Yes, I'm afraid so." She pulled back her fingers. "So hold her firmly in place."

At that point Nora's face, red and wet with perspiration, contorted with the pain of a contraction. Her grip on the bed spokes left her knuckles white. Then her water broke, and from that point on, her labor continued, progressing normally. Slowly and steadily the baby's head crowned.

"Just a bit more now, Nora," she encouraged her friend, as she cupped the baby's head in her hands.

Nora hollered in pain as each of the baby's shoulders appeared. One last push and the baby slipped from Nora's body. Cassia placed the baby on the bed and cut the cord.

"You've got a son, my friend." She held the baby upside down by the heels to clean the mucus from the throat. After she gave the infant a quick and gentle pat on the back, he cried.

While Maggie and Muriel helped Nora off the stool, she wrapped the baby in a clean towel.

"He's a handsome one, Nora, with all his fingers and toes." She placed the baby into his mother's outstretched arms.

"Hello, Cameron Dodd Junior. I'm your mama," Nora whispered.

After Maggie and Muriel cried with joy, hugged, and cooed at the baby a bit, they helped to clean Nora and the room. Cassia removed her rubber gloves and wrapped them in the rubber sheet that was once beneath Nora. All such items and instruments would be sterilized once she returned home. Then Maggie brought in a tray of tea and biscuits. Never had Cassia tasted anything so satisfying, as she watched her friend nurse her new son.

"You did it, Nora," she said, tears welling in her eyes.

"I couldn't have without you." Nora gazed lovingly down at the infant. "You're one fine midwife, Cassia Rose Holmes. You saved little Cameron, here." She sighed. "And for that I'll always be truly grateful."

"Here, here," Muriel chimed in, raising her tea cup.

"Aye, 'tis the truth for sure," Maggie added.

Spending so much time with Nora made for a longer day, as Cassia was late to the other five households she was scheduled to call upon. By the time she finally rode her bike home, the sun had set and her back ached. A small bowl of lamb stew for dinner was all the strength she could muster to eat. And after making sure all her medical instruments were properly cleansed, she fell into bed.

Two, quick and sharp rings of the telephone brought her awake. She glanced at the clock, it was almost midnight, as she awkwardly climbed out of bed, and hurried to answer the phone before two more rings woke her parents.

Sadie O'Clarity's out-of-breath voice sounded from the other end. "Cassia, I'm with Sean here at the Willow Creek Hospital."

She shook her head to clear it. "Why, what's happened?"

"We were enjoyin' dinner with Vernon and Flora Washburn when Sean took ill. Thankfully, Flora's grandson, Willis Remington was also a guest. He was able to take us in his automobile to Willow Creek," Sadie explained.

Cassia's mouth went dry. She nervously cleared her throat. "Have the doctors yet discovered what ails him?"

"Aye, Cassia, they have at that." Sadie inhaled sharply. "Sean's had a heart attack."

Chapter Eight

Brodie sat in the parlor of the boarding house, sipping on a glass of wine while fellow resident, Cappy Jack, nursed a glass of whiskey in a chair opposite him. It had been a long, tiring day. In fact, it was the first night out of four this week he wasn't spending at the hospital, now that one of his patients had passed away, and another was finally stable. He pushed a wayward lock of russet hair from his forehead and sighed. He was also weary to the bone of Dorothea's actions as of late and was voicing his concerns to Cappy as they relaxed together with an after dinner drink.

"Seems to me," Cappy began, "it's time you faced the facts, Mate. This gal has decided to be with another. The writing is as plain as the nose on your face."

He nodded. It had been three weeks since Drake Nolan arrived in town, and he had made no bones about occupying Dorothea's time. Nor did she have any difficulties accepting his invitations. She seemed to relish and savor the times she spent in the other man's company.

When he tried to confront her with this fact on an evening he'd happened to catch her home, she'd brushed him off or accused him of overreacting. At one point she had the gall to act appalled over his jealousy. But he stood his ground on the matter. An engaged woman doesn't take up with another man and leave her intended to spend his time alone. Doctor Malone was also standoffish, catering to Doctor Nolan's wishes, and bringing him on board first to accompany him on interesting cases. A position Brodie once held. Now he was pushed aside, like a pair of old shoes.

"Does it take a brick to fall on you, Mate?" Cappy continued, taking a sip of his whiskey and wiping his mouth with the back of his hand. "If you want my advice…"

He chuckled sardonically. "Looks like I'm going to hear it whether or not I want to."

"Darn tootin' you are," Cappy snapped, placing the glass aside on a nearby table. "I stand by those I care for and respect. And I respect the hell out of you, Mate."

He tipped his head politely. "I feel the same about you, Captain."

"I'd say it's about time you give up on this fickle female," Cappy quipped. "Set her free."

"It strongly appears she's already done that to me," he mumbled.

Cappy removed a pipe from his jacket pocket, readying it with tobacco. "Good riddance to her, I say, because the last thing you need is a woman whose head can be turned so quickly by another." He took a puff on the pipe; the tobacco's spicy aroma filled the room.

As the smoke encircled Cappy's white-haired head, Brodie couldn't help but compare the scene to the words of "'Twas the Night Before Christmas" he learned as a child.

The stump of a pipe he held tight in his teeth,
while the smoke encircled his head like a wreath.

Cappy chuckled lightly. "I had me a couple of that

sort of woman, myself. Truth be told, I wasn't such a trustworthy soul either. But you're a different breed than me—loyal, devoted, settled, a homebody—the sort of a man who deserves a woman who sets her sights and heart on just one fella." He squinted one of his light blue eyes before he continued to calculate the situation. "You need the kind of gal who wants a family, a home, a long life with the man she chooses. One who shares the burden the trials of life has a knack for throwing at a person." He took another draw on the pipe. "Yessiree, a true partner is what you need, not a spoiled brat who demands her own way."

He sighed and nodded again. Cappy Jack was right. Dorothea wasn't really what he wanted. "I probably should admit I was taken by her beauty more so than her attributes."

"And the prestige her papa could give you didn't hurt none, I suppose," Cappy countered.

"Yes, shamefully that was a winning factor as well."

"Then bless your lucky stars, Mate, that this Nolan fella made an entrance when he did." The elder man puffed again on the pipe and broke into a coughing fit.

"That thing's going to kill you." Brodie gestured to the pipe.

Cappy shrugged and placed the pipe into an ash tray. "If not this, it'll be something else as we've all gotta go somehow." He reached for the glass to take one last swig of whiskey. "Have you thought of what you plan to do next?"

Before he could answer, Widow Danfield waddled into the room. "I'm sorry to interrupt you gentlemen, but a telegram just arrived for Dr. O'Clarity."

She handed the envelope to Brodie and made her way slowly to the parlor windows, taking her sweet time to open one wide and air out the smoke-filled room. No doubt, to find out what the telegram was all about.

He read the message in silence, his brows creasing with worry at what the news relayed.

"What is it, Mate?" Cappy sat forward in his seat.

He inhaled sharply, pausing for a moment before he spoke, allowing the words to digest before he could speak them. "Well, I'd say it's just been decided for me as to what my next plans will be."

Cappy frowned. "How so?"

"The telegram is from my mother." He cleared his throat from the emotion suddenly forming to choke him.

Mrs. Danfield stepped closer, hungry for gossip. "I pray all is well."

He stood and squared his shoulders. "It appears, about three days ago, my father suffered a heart attack."

Mrs. Danfield gasped and covered her mouth with a hand.

Cappy shook his head sadly. "So sorry, Mate."

He stuffed the telegram inside his vest pocket. "I need to return home immediately."

The next day, after a trip to the locomotive station to purchase a ticket for a train bound for Arizona early the next morning, he sent his mother a return telegram. Then he went to the hospital to hand over his resignation. When he couldn't find Doctor Malone, he made his way to the business office. He learned from a thin, peevish-looking woman that Doctor Hemsley Malone and his family, along with Doctor Drake Nolan, were spending the week at the Malone summer home in Cape Cod.

"I'd be happy to forward anything you have for him." She peered over the round, black-rimmed glasses too large for her face and sitting half way down her long, narrow nose.

He handed over the letter of thanks and appreciation he'd written for Doctor Malone but decided to hang on to the farewell letter he'd comprised for Dorothea. Perhaps he wouldn't send it at all. In view of the fact she took Drake Nolan on a trip to her family's summer home, when she indeed still considered herself engaged to him, spoke volumes.

"So, it's over then," he whispered to himself, as he rode his bike back to the boarding house.

As he gathered his belongings, he couldn't help the memories flooding his thoughts. For five years he dwelled in this attic room. They were hard years, but for the most part interesting and exciting. He enjoyed the friendships he'd made, his work, and learned a lot from his colleagues—especially Doctor Malone. He should have quit while he was ahead, concentrated on his profession and left love, romance, and Dorothea out of the picture.

But none of that mattered now. His father was ill, and his family needed him. Dread took over his thoughts, and a heavy worry enveloped his heart. Just how ill was his father? His mother hadn't said. Many he'd seen after suffering a heart attack did quite well in resuming their lives, with only minor restrictions. Then there were some who didn't, and others still who died. What was his father's prognosis? And what would he face while recovering? Besides, his father wasn't a man to be coddled nor would he sit still while others cared for him. It was true, doctors made the worst patients.

He sighed heavily. "Either way, I will be there to help him through it."

"Have you taken to talking to yourself now?" said a voice from behind.

He turned to find Paul Rhinehart, the young lawyer and fellow tenant, peering around the half-opened door.

"I knocked, but obviously you were too preoccupied to hear." He made his way into the room and secured the door behind him.

Brodie continued to stuff his suitcase with the few sweaters he owned. They came in handy on a cold, Boston night. "Sorry, Paul, I've a lot on my mind."

"Understandable." Paul moved aside a pile of socks stacked upon the bed, before he sat. There was a long pause before Paul spoke again. "I'm really going to miss you, my friend."

He sighed. "I feel the same toward you, Paul." He forced a smile. "But there's nothing that says you can't come to Eagle's Landing for a visit. Hell, even to live, should you decide."

Paul chuckled sardonically before commenting. "And if your Irish mama is anything like my Southern mama, I'd probably be well fed," he joked, his accent thick and soft.

He chimed in on his friend's mirth. "Not to mention being introduced to just about every eligible girl she could find."

"Well, now, how can I refuse an offer like that?" Paul countered. Then his face grew serious. "What about Dorothea?"

He shrugged. "Dorothea, her parents, and Doctor

Drake Nolan are vacationing at the family's summer residence in Cape Cod. So, I'd say that chapter of my life is over."

Paul frowned. "Does she know about your father and the fact you're leaving town?"

He sighed heavily. "No, she has no idea."

"Hmmm," Paul responded. "It appears you're correct in thinking things between you are over. But the lawyer in me can't help but advise you to send the woman some sort of word, whether by mail or telegram, of your departure. Something in writing has a way of covering your ass should legal problems arise."

He arched a brow. "What legal problems could stem from this situation?"

"Breach of promise," Paul said. "You asked the woman to marry you, now you're fleeing town."

He inhaled sharply. "And she's gone off with another man."

Paul held up a finger. "Accompanied by her parents, for one, and didn't you say Drake Nolan was Mrs. Malone's step-nephew?"

His brows furrowed. "Yes, but clearly he's after much more than being on a holiday with his family."

"Aha! Speculation," Paul snapped. "Nothing can be proven."

His frown deepened. "What should I do, then? I am scheduled to leave early tomorrow morning, and Dorothea is not even in town."

Paul scratched his chin. "Are you privileged to know the address of the Cape Cod residence?"

"I could get it easy enough." He remembered how much Hank and Blanche loved to gossip.

Paul smiled. "Splendid...do that, then, and send

78

Dorothea a telegram. The slip of paper you'll receive upon sending word is proof you made an honest attempt to notify her of your departure. And…" He held up his finger again. "To be completely secure in the matter, I advise you to draw up a letter of farewell to Dorothea. When you've finished, give it to me. I will sign it as witness and send it by messenger to her home, making a copy for my files first, of course," he added.

Brodie nodded, making his way to the vest hanging upon a hook, and took from the pocket an envelope. "I've already written such a letter to Dorothea."

Paul stood and took the envelope. "Splendid." He shook Brodie's hand. "Consider your ass legally covered."

Chapter Nine

"Brodie's comin' home," Sadie announced with a great measure of relief, as she placed a cup before Cassia and her mother. "Sean didn't want me to be botherin' him, but after three days o' seein' me husband so ill, I knew 'twould be a while before he'd be back upon his feet." She shrugged. "Nothin' else made sense but to be contactin' Brodie, askin' him to come home." Turning to retrieve the whistling tea kettle from the stove, she added, "So, he'll be arrivin' on tomorrow's train."

Cassia was also greatly relieved to hear this news. Even though Willow Creek's hospital had been diligent and thoughtful to supply a doctor at the clinic, she was on her own with town house calls. In the last three days, she'd delivered three babies and given prenatal care to four expecting mothers.

"Don't go to any fuss on our account now, Sadie." Amanda looked at the floral tea cup Sadie had begun to fill. "We came by to see if there was anything we could do for you, not the other way around."

"Hush now. What good am I if I can't be offerin' me dear friends a cup o' tea?" Sadie teased.

Cassia studied Sadie's face. Her fair, freckled, Irish complexion was slightly marred by the dark circles beneath her eyes; no doubt from a sleepless night over concern for her husband's well-being. And her auburn hair, now paled with streaks of gray, was pulled back with a ribbon instead of neatly piled atop her head in the usual bun. Still, the lilt in her voice remained, obviously to put her company at ease. Cassia admired the woman immensely and how she kept up a brave front in the midst of fearing for her husband's life.

Cassia's medical profession taught her life was precious and could be snuffed out at any age. But Doctor O'Clarity, Sadie, and Cassia's parents were in their golden years, and how much time any of them had left was something that worried her often.

Cassia watched Sadie buzz around the kitchen, making her home hospitable. Never did she hear a mean word or hurtful remark uttered from Sadie's lips. She would feed anyone coming to her house, even if it were her last morsel of food.

"Besides…" Sadie placed a plate of chocolate chip brownies on the table. "Me lovely daughter, Shailyn, as well as continuin' at her clerical duties in Sean's office, is cookin' up a storm. Saints preserve us. I sure can't be eatin' all o' this food meself. And me other daughter, Betsy, has given me shelter at her home in Willow Creek while Sean's in the hospital. That's where I've been stayin' for the last four days and will continue until Sean's released." She sighed heavily. "I just came home for a day or two to get the place ready for Brodie's arrival. I want to make sure he's got enough food in the ice chest to warm while he's stayin' here."

"If there's anything else Brodie needs, you can count on us to help," Amanda reassured her friend.

Brodie was coming home. Betsy and her husband offered lodging for her mother while Sean is hospitalized, and Shailyn is baking and cooking. What about Tucker?

As if Sadie read Cassia's mind, she responded, "I tried to send word to Tucker's last known address, but since I haven't heard anythin' as o' yet, he must have moved on to another location."

Or else he remains as self-centered as always, not caring about the promises he makes or the people he hurts.

Amanda reached out and gave Sadie's hand a reassuring pat. "I'm sure once he gets the news of his father's illness he'll be home directly."

"Aye, I'm sure o' it as well." Sadie forced a smile. "In the meantime I've got me a close bunch o' folks ready to pitch in, and me other three offspring lookin' out for me and the house while I'm in Willow Creek with Sean."

Children taking care of their parents—Cassia saw this more and more in her line of work. Daily a son or daughter would bring a parent into the clinic, be their spokesperson, caregiver. It would be her brother, Gabriel and she who would take care of her parents when the need arose. As it was, she helped her father ready the church for services, to relieve her mother.

"Have the doctors an idea when Sean can come home?" Amanda inquired.

"Not at this time, but I'm sure I'll know more when I return with Brodie, who'll know which questions to ask." Sadie smiled again, this time with full gratification. "And I thank ye, Lass, for all the help yer givin' with the clinic and townsfolk while we wait for Brodie to take over for his papa."

"No thanks needed, Sadie," she said. "I'd do anything to help Doc O'Clarity. And I'm sure Brodie and I will do just fine together."

"Aye, I know ye will." Sadie wiped a tear from her eye with the back of a hand. "And 'tis good folk like ye, ready and willin' to do all ye can, that make the hard times easier to get through."

****

The morning after Brodie O'Clarity arrived in Eagle's Landing, he was ready to take over his father's duties. When Cassia entered the office, Brodie was packing his father's well-worn doctor's case and suited up for town visits. Doctor Sean O'Clarity's medical headquarters was moderate in size and adjacent to the family's home. The front part of the building was the waiting room, stocked with wooden chairs and a receptionist's desk where a phone and typewriter sat. This is where Shailyn O'Clarity McCrea, Sean's daughter, took appointment calls and completed the daily schedule. Down a long hall, a back room served as Sean's private office. Off from that room was a supply room, and across the hall was an examining room. All rooms were painted in light colors, clean, with polished hardwood floors. Office hours were later in the afternoon, as morning hours were dedicated to home visits. Two days a week the office was closed so Sean could work at the clinic. Since Sean's heart attack, the office had been closed every day. Shailyn took calls from her home and dropped off a schedule each morning for those house calls Cassia was qualified to make. Everyone else was directed to the clinic. Until now, that is. With Brodie home to take over for Sean, she was sure her days would resume as before.

It had been almost ten years since she'd last set eyes on him. He left to attend college in Boston when she was thirteen and at fifteen she left to attend to her studies in England. The first three years Brodie was studying away he didn't come home. His schedule was too intense. So, the O'Claritys' went to see him. Consequently, by the time Brodie could come back to Eagle's Landing for visits, she had already left for England.

After one glance she thought life had been kind to Brodie. Truth be told, life had been downright generous. The lean, baby-faced young man she bid farewell to had returned a well-built, muscular gentleman with a strong, handsome face. But the russet curls and large green eyes were the same, as was the genuine, kind smile that spread across his semi-freckled face when he spied her entering the door.

In an instant he came to her, his strong arms circling her waist in a familiar embrace. She immediately, standing on tiptoe, wrapped her arms around his neck and inhaled the clean scent of spice that was his aftershave. "Thank God you're finally here," she whispered, meaning her words more than even she realized.

"Did you have any doubt I'd come?" He pulled back to search her face.

Her cheeks warmed beneath his scrutiny. She stepped from his embrace, confused. What had changed between them? This was Brodie, the neighbor and friend who was more like an older brother—looking out for her and buying her ice cream with the first pay he earned mucking the local stables. He picked her up when she fell, wiped her tears, and carried her to his father when she'd skinned her knee. He kept bullies from teasing her as she walked home from school. Why did she now feel so strange in his presence?

She cleared her throat nervously. "No, I had no doubts at all."

He arched a brow as he took in the length of her hair. "And what happened to all those long, golden curls?"

She brushed back a wayward strand from her forehead. "Shorter hair is all the style now."

"So it seems." He crossed his arms. "Well, at least it suits you. Really brings out those large baby blues of yours. Did you know your eyes always reminded me of my favorite marble?"

His small compliment made her heart race and left her tongue-tied; therefore, she chose to make no reply to his confession. At this point she felt it was much safer to stay silent, for fear her voice would crack. But his approval, for some strange reason, left her self-conscious. Again she wondered why.

The awkward silence filling the room brought an immediate change to Brodie. "Yes, well, I'd say we'd better get going on these house calls. I've picked up a schedule from Shailyn earlier. So, I trust you'll fill me in on each patient, Nurse Holmes," was his stern response as he turned to retrieve his bag.

She wiped her sweaty palms on her nurse's apron, worried she'd offended him. Not wanting to do any further damage, she also responded in a professional manner. "Yes, of course, Doctor O'Clarity."

He turned to face her. "Have you a bag?"

"Yes, waiting for me in my bicycle's basket," she replied.

"Well, that way of travel would be most inconvenient for the two of us, so we'll be using a horse and wagon. I've one ready and waiting out back." He walked in the opposite direction.

"I'll meet you there." She hurried out the front entrance to secure her bike and get her bag. As the door closed behind her, she couldn't help but feel this day was going to be a long one—very long indeed.

Chapter Ten

As Brodie went out the back way of the medical office, he hoped Cassia would take some time before joining him. He needed a moment to clear his head and regain his composure.

Frowning now, he mentally chastised himself.

How stupid of me to have expected her to be the same young woman I left.

Suddenly, he must face the fact that Cassia was three years older than Dorothea. When he'd embraced her waist, which was much slimmer and shapelier, he was caught off guard. Then, when her full, firm breasts pressed against his chest and the delicious scent of lavender invaded his senses, a whole lot of other thoughts flooded his mind—thoughts he never pictured having toward Cassia. Her nurse's pinafore, which draped over curvy hips, had a hemline reaching only to an inch below her knees, leaving in full few the remainder of two, perfectly shaped legs and dainty ankles.

She'd always been like a little sister. She grew up with his baby brother, the two playing and napping together on a quilt spread upon their parlor floor. He watched his older sister bathe Cassia when she was brought over to be looked after. She ran around their kitchen in diapers, laid down on his bed to take a nap while sucking on her bottle. He stood guard so she wouldn't roll over and fall off. He carried her on his shoulders, wiped her tears, and bought her ice cream. This was the Cassia he knew and remembered—not this beautiful woman with golden hair framing an angelic face—a goddess in a nurse's uniform.

Saints preserve us, she's completely undone me.

The anticipation of working side by side with someone he knew well, felt relaxed and comfortable with, just clouded. Now, this day would be awkward and tense. Exquisitely profound womanhood radiated from her like the heat from a large bonfire. How would he sit beside her in the wagon, or work near her with thoughts of caressing her soft skin? Were her thighs as perfect as her ankles? How would those ample, firm breasts feel cupped in his hands? And those full, pouty lips had to be soft, taste as sweet as she smelled.

Agitated by his thoughts, he raked a hand through his hair.

I must get a grip on what's important. The patients, helping those that are sick...other than that, nothing else matters.

"I'm ready when you are, Doctor O'Clarity." A voice from behind pulled him from his lewd longings.

He turned to gaze into the light blue eyes of this gorgeous woman. And instantly he was disgusted with his mindset, embarrassed over the feelings she invoked within him. This was someone he once protected, cared about, and respected. Nothing needed to change.

He smiled and softened his tone. "I'm still just Brodie, Cassia."

Her return smile melted his heart. "And I'm still glad for that." When he took her hand to help her into the carriage, she squeezed it affectionately. "Welcome home, Brodie."

He paused, glancing down at how perfectly her tiny hand fit in his. And in that fleeting moment he knew he belonged...in a way he never did in Boston or with Dorothea.

He'd learned, growing up with a doctor father, it was important to know the patient fully. Treating the person, both medically and emotionally, gave a clearer, well-rounded look at the malady troubling the patient. It also fostered trust. So, before visiting each name on the patient list, he asked Cassia to give him a brief insight into to what to expect of the person, the household dynamics, as well as the illness being treated. He could do this to some degree in Boston. However, the quick-paced, high-level turnover of sickbeds made it a time-consuming process, frowned upon by his superiors and many of the other hospital staff. So, his duties were done on an automatic speed—efficient, yes—personal, no.

Now, this wasn't the case. Though he had to keep to a schedule, time was there for his using. And making house calls more personal than professional, but still accomplishing the task at hand, seemed a better idea. His father had built the clientele of the town, and these folks built a trust in Sean O'Clarity. If Brodie was to successfully fill his father's medical shoes, for whatever length of time needed, he had to come across in the same friendly, yet qualified manor.

Cassia held the list while he drove the wagon. "Our first patient this morning is Mr. Ned Beachum. He's suffering from rectal bleeding, can't sit for long periods of time without a lot of pain and itching." She lowered the list of names and began to give him a brief insight on the patient. "First, Mr. Beachum drives a milk wagon for Owen Morris. He and his wife, Clara, run a small dairy farm located a few blocks away from your house. Daily he covers a large route and spends long hours sitting on a hard, wooden seat."

"Sounds like Ned's got a case of hemorrhoids," he diagnosed.

"That would be my idea on the matter," she agreed. "And I've seen some very painful cases in pregnant women."

"Has Ned got a wife?" he inquired.

She lifted the list to read further about the patient. "Yes, and four children, so I imagine taking time off from work is setting the family back financially."

"Then the problem needs to be addressed correctly, efficiently, and hopefully without having to schedule a surgical procedure. I haven't a problem with you sitting and chatting with the wife while I take care of Ned."

"Well, I do..." she snapped.

A quick glance in her direction found her frowning.

His own brows furrowed. "Have I said something to offend you, Cassia?"

She met his gaze. "Would you expect the nurses at the hospital in Boston to sit out of a patient's room and chat with the wife while you did an examination?"

He brought his eyes back to the road. "I just thought, because you're a midwife, that this case might be...would be rather..."

She interrupted. "Awkward for me to handle?"

He cleared his throat. "Well, yes."

"Do you feel awkward when you are needed to handle cases involving female patients?" she shot at him.

His frown deepened. "Of course not, I'm a doctor. I've taken an oath to care for the sick—period. No matter their sex or anything else."

"Exactly," she snapped. "And I have taken the same oath."

He tried again to explain. "I just thought since you basically administered to women's needs, you'd feel uncomfortable with this case."

"Brodie, I studied nursing as well as midwifery, and it was a blessing I did because while I was in England a war broke out. All available medical people were called upon to perform all duties that arose. Because of my dual training, I was able to answer that call." She inhaled sharply. "To be perfectly blunt, I've seen more men minus their trousers—examined more genitalia and buttocks then I care to remember—in all stages of disease and lack of cleanliness, from a horrible case of poison ivy to bullet wounds. First and foremost in my mind was not my girlish virtue but to help that soldier the best way I could...hopefully, to save his life and definitely to relieve his pain."

"I'm sorry, Cassia," he apologized. "I meant no disrespect."

The rest of the way to the Beachum homestead they remained silent. He spoke the truth; he didn't mean any disrespect, but then, what did he mean? Certainly he'd expect any nurse he worked side by side with in Boston to help him administer to all patients. Why did he think differently when it concerned Cassia?

Because I'm still thinking of her as the innocent little girl I used to protect. For God's sake, she's a professional woman now with an educated brain to go along with that woman's body...a body I can't take my eyes off of. Tormented, he briefly squeezed his eyes shut. *She is a fellow colleague. Thinking of her as anything other than that is wrong. So, get a grip, Brodie O'Clarity before you make a fool of yourself.*

"We need to turn left here, Brodie." She pulled him once more from his thoughts.

The Beachum house, a small, clapboard framed, single story dwelling, was situated a mile down a very desolate and winding road. A woman in her forties answered the door. Her light brown hair was pulled back into a bun at the nape of her neck and dark circles colored the flesh beneath large, brown eyes. She wore a a well-worn green skirt and a faded, flowered shirt, stained with what looked like baby vomit. Her feet were bared and dirty. And the toddler she balanced upon her right hip was naked.

While he introduced himself and Cassia, he took in the poor, unkept condition of the kitchen.

The woman, somewhat embarrassed, also glanced around the chaos of the unorganized room, as she in turn introduced herself as Olivia Beachum. "Sorry for the mess," she apologized. "Been tryin' to bathe little Anna here before my other three youngin's get home from school, and I keep gettin' disturbed." She sighed. "Ned's really feelin' poorly and needin' a lot of my attention this mornin'."

Anna was indeed in need of being washed, as the strong odor of urine and vomit rose to meet him when they stepped farther into the home. "Is the baby ill?"

Olivia frowned. "Just teethin', I 'spect. Feelin' fussy an' all from sore gums."

"Still, after we have a look at your husband, I'd like to examine Anna," he said.

Olivia hoisted Anna farther up on her hip. "We ain't got enough for ya to be lookin' in on Ned and the baby. And right now, my husband is worse off. Can't sit to do his job or on the pot to do his business without a lot of pain. If he don't get back to workin' soon, ain't none of us gonna be able to eat."

It was Cassia who spoke, nearing Olivia and gently placing a caressing hand upon little Anna's head. "You need not concern yourself with payment, Mrs. Beachum. Whatever we need to do for both Anna and your husband, will be done." She turned her large, blue eyes to look at him. "Isn't that right, Dr. O'Clarity?"

And here was the plight of a country doctor. How many times had his father been at a patient's bedside throughout the night, only to come home with a dozen eggs, sometimes empty-handed? But he never went hungry nor was deprived of the essentials a boy needed to grow up strong and educated. He and his siblings had everything they needed—food, clothing, a good home to live in, and lots of love.

"That's right, Mrs. Beachum," he said. "There's no call for concern."

Upon his reply, Cassia's features softened, a look of admiration shining in her marble-swirled orbs. And that one, brief but adoring look, caused his heart to skip a beat. In an instant he found himself addicted to her admiring glance. How perfect it would be to have this enchanting woman looking upon him in such a manner for the rest of time, in every instance. For all the times he looked into Dorothea's eyes, never did he think to want such devotion from her.

"I thank ya both, kindly," Mrs. Beachum said. Then she indicated with the wave of a hand to a doorway at the far end of the kitchen, its frame covered with a curtain. "My Ned's yonder, layin' on the bed."

The room was dark, except for the dim glow of a small, oil lantern sitting on an old chest of drawers. Bad lighting was a doctor's worst enemy. Cassia must have read his mind, because immediately she reached for the lantern and brought it to a rest on a small bedside table.

The light shed a better look at Ned Beachum—a man of medium build, black hair peppered with gray, mussed up and longish. He appeared to be in or about his late forties and wore a blue striped night shirt that fell above a set of bony knees. Curled up on his side, facing them, the man slowly opened his eyes and then shielded them from the light.

"Good day to you, Mr. Beachum," he began. "I'm Doctor Brodie O'Clarity, and I've come to look at what ails you." He gestured to Cassia. "This is Nurse Holmes."

Cassia gave the man a warm smile. "Please, call me Cassia." She placed her bag on a nearby chair.

Mr. Beachum frowned. "Ain't the sight of my bleedin' ass gonna scare ya any, Miss Cassia?"

"It won't bother me, if looking doesn't bother you," she said.

"I just want this pain and itchin' to stop," he mumbled.

"And that's what we're here for, Mr. Beachum," she said softly.

"If you could roll onto your stomach and get up on your knees, Mr. Beachum, I can examine the affected area," he said.

Cassia pulled from her bag a rubber sheet and placed it beneath Mr. Beachum as he turned onto his stomach. "We'll have you feeling better in no time," she promised. After the man crawled upon his knees and jutted out his buttocks, Cassia lifted the night shirt, rolling it to stay around the patient's waist. "And back to work doing your deliveries."

"Yup, gotta get myself back on the job. Got mouths to feed and bills to pay," the patient commiserated.

"I understand completely," Cassia continued. She kept Ned Beachum talking about his job, Olivia, and his children throughout the examination, even during the painful internal check necessary to see if surgery was needed. Her distraction not only helped the patient, but him as well. Her diversion put them all at ease and as comfortable as Ned could possibly feel, despite his painful, bared, hairy, and bloody backside in full view for all to see. Brodie was also pleased with the fact Cassia's conversation with the patient took nothing away from the efficient way she assisted him.

"I feel no internal problems, Mr. Beachum," he said finally.

The man groaned as Brodie removed a gloved finger from the area he probed. "What's that mean, Doc?"

"It means there's no reason to anticipate surgery. But you need to get the outer problem healed, so there won't be further complications," he said.

"I have something that will help," Cassia offered. Referring to her bag, she pulled from it a small bottle and a packet of cotton sheets. "Jojoba oil is known to help in such matters." She soaked a piece of cotton with a bit of the oil and applied it to Mr. Beachum's affected area. "I'll leave this bottle and several cotton balls, here for your use. Applying it three to four times a day will give you much needed relief, as will putting more fiber in your diet to help you move your bowels easier."

"We'll return in a couple of days to see how you're doing," he promised.

"I ain't got a couple of days, Doc. I gotta be able to sit on that wagon by tomorrow and make my rounds," Ned whined.

Just as Mr. Beachum moved to his side again, his wife walked into the room. She still held Anna, but now the child was clean and wearing a diaper and a shirt. "How's it goin' in here?"

He explained his findings and the remedy left at their disposal. "But if he doesn't use the oil, eat more fiber, and stay off the area for a few days, I can't guarantee the situation will improve." He pulled from his bag a bottle of medicine and set it on the bedside table. "And I'll leave something a bit stronger for the pain."

"I ain't got much of a choice, Doc. I've got to get back to work tomorrow," Ned grumbled.

"Mrs. Beachum, I noticed when I came through the kitchen you own a foot-peddle sewing machine. Do you do a lot of sewing?" Cassia asked.

He frowned. What on earth did Mrs. Beachum's sewing talents have to do with the matter at hand?

"Yup, it's the only way to keep our backs covered since store bought cloths cost too much."

Cassia then turned to Mr. Beachcum. The frown upon his face indicated his confusion on the question of his wife's sewing ability as well. "Do you have a small tire, perhaps one that came off a child's tricycle or a baby's carriage?"

"Yup, I believe we do...a tube of a child's wagon

wheel is in the shed out back," Ned said, his frown deepening.

Cassia's light blue eyes twinkled. "Well, I was just thinking, if Mrs. Beachum could cover that tire with some cloth, you can sit upon it, leaving your troubled area to fit in the hole and off the wooden wagon seat. That might help you to continue healing without missing any more days of work."

Mrs. Beachum smiled. "I know exactly what yer after and what yer wantin'." She handed Anna to Cassia and took off after the wheel.

Cassia hugged the child affectionately. "And now let's see what ails you, little Miss Anna."

Anna Beachum was just suffering from teething gums. Again Cassia pulled a tincture from her bag to remedy the problem. And the Beachums gave them each a jar of homemade bread and butter pickles as payment for their services.

Back in the wagon, Cassia licked her lips. "I love bread and butter pickles, don't you?"

He chuckled lightly. "I can't think of anything better."

Chapter Eleven

As the week progressed, Cassia accompanied him on all the house calls, maladies ranged from toxemia to a broken foot. At the clinic she was beside him as well, preparing each patient for examination, reading the next step of the procedure without him telling her what he needed or what he wanted her to do. They worked together like a well-oiled machine.

On one rainy day, they found themselves behind on their calls, wagon wheels sinking into the muddy road, and summoned to the Wexley home. Thankfully, it was the last stop on their schedule. Colin Wexley, a ten-year-old boy suffering from a mental disorder since birth, raged with fever. In his delirium, his mental issues became out of control. He not only thrashed around in the bed, tearing it apart, but took to racing around and destroying the bedroom. The mother, Edna Wexley, was a widow. She was heavy-set and appeared to be somewhere into her fifties. Certainly she was neither young enough nor fit enough to stop Colin, also heavily built and tall for his age. Consequently, the poor woman was beside herself and at a complete loss as to what to do, other than cover her face with her hands and cower in a corner.

Examination of any sort was impossible. Colin continued to shake his head and moan as he pulled repeatedly on his left ear. Brodie suspected an ear infection. No doubt, with the boy's inability to relay his discomfort, the infection had climbed to extremes before help had been called.

"Nothing can be concluded without an examination, but there's a strong possibility Colin has an ear infection. With his mental disorder hampering care, the best place for him to be is in a hospital," he conferred with Cassia. "But I'll never get him to settle down long enough to get him into a medical transport."

"What about sedating him first," she suggested.

His frown deepened. "We've got the same problem there too, getting him to stay still long enough for me to administer a hypodermic of morphine."

Before they could come up with a strategy to the problem, Colin ran out of the bedroom. In a flash Cassia was right behind him. By the time he came to his senses to follow them, Colin had run out the back door. Cassia remained in hot pursuit.

"Get the sedative," she yelled to him, leaping over a large branch.

Quickly he ran back to the bedroom, where he'd left his bag, and prepared the injection. He made it back to the yard just in time to witness Cassia cutting Colin off at a mud puddle. She jumped, actually leaped off the ground, and pounced upon the boy. Mud flew everywhere.

"Now," she yelled.

He waded into the puddle, pulled Colin's wet, muddy pajama bottoms down to his kicking feet, and stuck him with the needle. Cassia continued to hold the child, keeping his head from flopping into the puddle, while the sedative worked. Then he carried Colin back to the house.

Edna Wesley covered the kitchen table with a towel, and that is where he laid Colin. He watched as the two women stripped the boy of the rest of his nightwear and washed him clean. He was a mess himself, mud soaked shoes and trousers soiled to the knees. But Cassia was worse for wear. Mud covered her crisp, neat pinafore from her neck to hem, as well as her legs and white shoes. Her stockings were torn and hanging in shreds around her ankles. And the cap, which once sat prim and proper atop a head full of golden curls, hung down the side of her face. If the situation weren't so dire, it could almost be comical. Despite all her disarray, Cassia worked on at her duties. Not once did she complain or worry about her appearance. Her only concern was for the patient.

He'd never catch Dorothea in such a state. Truth be told, Dorothea would never so much as soil her hands. Cassia was dirty from head to toe. And he found her positively radiant, even with the mud caking around her nose and down the side of her face. Never did he admire or respect a woman more.

"He's ready now to take to the hospital, Brodie," she said.

He nodded, taking the child's temperature rectally before helping Mrs. Wexley to re-dress the boy and get him into bed. And Cassia did her best at the kitchen sink to scrub her hands again, as well as cleaning her face, and repositioning her cap upon a tangled mass of muddy curls.

"I'm sending for a medical transport when I get to the office, Mrs. Wexley," he said. "Colin's temperature is nearing 104. He is far too ill to remain home. He needs round the clock care and attention only Willow

Creek General can give." He sighed. "He should remain asleep until the transport arrives."

Edna Wexley nodded, looking very relieved over his decision and the fact her child would stay sleeping until help arrived. "Thank you, Doctor O'Clarity." She turned to Cassia. "And you too, Nurse Holmes." She bit her bottom lip as she surveyed Cassia's filthy, disheveled condition. "I'm so sorry for all your trouble. I'll be more than happy to clean and starch your garments."

Cassia gave the woman an affectionate pat on the arm. "That won't be necessary, Mrs. Wexley."

The older woman gasped. "But how on earth will you continue your day looking like that?"

Cassia giggled. After all they'd gone through on this call, she could still bring forth a measure of mirth. "Thankfully, you're the last call on our list."

When they were back in the wagon, he had to ask. "Saints preserve us, where did you learn to run and tackle like that?"

Again she giggled—a sound he found most enjoyable and refreshingly uplifting. "Nora and I would help her father shear the sheep. On occasion there'd be one or two who decided to make a run for it." She squared her shoulders proudly. "Doubt this or not, Brodie O'Clarity, I always got my sheep."

He smiled, completely enchanted and thoroughly amused. "Believe me; I have no doubts at all."

A small town doctor was always on call, but if there weren't emergencies, weekends were days of rest—days he didn't see Cassia. Better yet to say, days he didn't need to see Cassia. If it were at all appropriate, he'd try his best to make up some excuse to be in her presence, as he truly enjoyed her company. She was smart, funny, and interesting. And the thought of spending a day without her dampened his spirits.

His mother still stayed at Betsy's home in Willow Creek but left meals for him to eat and the entire house at his disposal. So, he lacked for nothing. However, the quiet only pleased him for a morning, before boredom and a bit of loneliness crept in.

"This house was never meant to be so still," he mumbled, while fixing himself another cup of tea. His mindset stemmed from the fact the O'Clarity household, with four very verbal children, was constantly brimming with many voices of opinion, vivacious action, both medical and domestic drama, and the constant clatter of dishes being washed after the many meals prepared.

He looked at the empty chairs at the kitchen table. The vacant seats were almost an affront to their existence. If they owned faces, their mouths would be turned down in sadness. As grown children left their childhood homes for lives of their own, parents felt empty and lonely, evermore so if spouses had passed. Thankfully his parents still had each other, but now with his father suffering a heart attack, his mother had to be worrying about the length of time they still had together. It was clearly a factor on his mind. And when that time came, she would sit at this kitchen table by herself, as he was doing now, and remember the times when her family dwelled beneath one roof.

No doubt either Betsy or Shailyn would want Sadie to come and live with them, as each one has said as much since their father's illness. But his mother's will to remain independent and the ruler of her own roost, as she's already voiced, will keep her from accepting their offer for a long time.

He closed his eyes and dove deep within to his own heart's desires. He wanted what his parents had, the deep and loyal, devoted and passionate love for one another, and a house full of children. He briefly thought he'd have a chance at such a life when he met Dorothea. But as things transpired, she'd never be his *better half*, working alongside of him, as his mother complemented his father, and vice versa.

"Cassia would be that type of mate," he whispered. She'd be the sort of wife who would stand beside her husband, take responsibility for what needed to be done with the children, the home, and even with her medical career. This last week, working with her as he did, it didn't take him long to realize if any woman could accomplish it all, it would be Cassia.

He opened his eyes and once more scanned the quiet room. The kitchen was the hub of the house, the family's central meeting ground. Not only were meals served and shared, but at times it was where babies were bathed, skinned knees were dressed, punishments were handed down, late night studying was done, and bills were paid. He wanted a kitchen just like this, in a house of his own, with a wife and children. Never had he wanted these things as much as he did this very minute.

He drank the rest of the tea, grown cold with all his musings. Taking the cup to the sink, he washed it and placed it on the drain board to dry. Then he made his way to the telephone and removed the earpiece. Clicking the earpiece's holder a few times brought him an operator's attention, thus connecting him to his sister, Shailyn's phone.

"McCrea residence," his sister's smooth, soft voice announced.

"Hi, Shail—it's me. Thought I'd go for a walk," he said.

She giggled. "Is that big old quiet house getting to you?"

He sighed. "Yup."

"Well, if anyone should call in for medical help, I'll send Patrick Jr. out looking for you," she offered. "If there's one thing P.J.'s good for, it's hunting down life. I can attest to that with all the injured critters he's brought home over the years. He and that dang bike can scout out places I never knew existed. The investigator instincts he's inherited from the McCreas...taking after his grandpa Mickey, Uncle Michael, and his own father at various times when he's not doing the blacksmith work."

He chuckled, picturing P.J. his awkward, but gentle, eleven-year-old nephew going to heroic lengths to save a sick or wounded animal.

"But his desire to heal the wounded reminds me of you and Tucker," she continued.

"I'd say, that side of him is from our blood," he supposed. "And as long as you mentioned Tucker, has anyone heard from him?"

"Not so far. Mama sent word to his last known address when Pa first took ill," she explained. "I reckon when he returns from whatever he's doing, wherever he's doing it, he'll see it. And then I hope he's got the good sense to make his way home."

He frowned. Tucker had proven to be unreliable. Selfish too, looking only out for himself. "I hope so too.

But you know how he is—how he can be."

Shailyn sighed. "Yes, I know, but fretting over what Tucker will or won't do isn't going to change things."

"You're right about that," he admitted.

"Come over later for dinner. I'm making corn beef and cabbage—Mama's recipe—just the way you like it. We'll talk more then. I don't want to get into too much over the phone. You never know what other ears are listening."

He arched a brow. "And isn't that the truth."

"Now, go take your walk," she concluded.

The day was exceptionally warm for early spring, a bit of a breeze helped to evenly distribute the heat from a scorching sun. His parents' home was located on a tree-lined street, the main street where the business district of town sat. It was two minutes by foot to his father's medical office, as that building was next door. And beside that, the General Store. Needless to say, they'd lived in a prime location, privileged to the goings on about time, yet a comfortable distance for the sake of privacy.

Once he was down the front steps and onto the road, he veered left. He made his way about two blocks down Bentley Drive before making another left onto Cornelia Road. At the end of this short causeway on a corner lot sat a brick, two-story home with a side-view yard, enclosed with a white picket fence. As he made his way past the house and rounded the corner, he heard familiar laughter.

Cassia, dressed in men's denim overalls and a red checkered shirt, leaned against the fence, chatting with Clara Morris, the dairy farmer's wife. Her golden curls peeked out from beneath a wide-brimmed straw hat, and her high cheekbones were flushed a deep shade of pink.

"I reckon we've got enough plant matter now to start with the boiling," Clara commented.

Cassia, wiping the back of her hand across her forehead, nodded. Shielding her eyes from the sun, she glanced skyward. "It's getting too hot to do any more work out here anyway." As she turned to gaze back at Clara, she spotted him. A large, welcoming smile spread across her beautiful face. "Why, Brodie, what brings you to this part of town?"

He shrugged, nearing the fence. "Just thought I'd take a walk." He returned her smile. "I could ask the same of you."

"On Saturdays I help Clara with her herbal tinctures," she explained. "In that way I'm able to stock my medical bag with fresh balms and syrups for the week."

"Aha! So this is where you get your inventory. And all this time I thought those bottles just magically appeared," he teased playfully.

She giggled—the sweet, lilting expression of mirth he had so quickly grown to enjoy. "Would suit me just as well if that were true," she kidded back. "Then I wouldn't have to help plant, hoe, pick, and boil down the contents that go into each bottle."

He glanced over the fence, down to the freshly turned earth, spotting her tiny feet clad in fishermen's sandals. Peeking out from the cut-out tips of her shoes were light pink, polished toenails, evenly filed. As his eyes roamed upward, he caught sight of her dainty ankles, as well as the rest of her shapely legs since her trousers were rolled above her knees.

His face grew hot with the thought of viewing her thighs, and he averted his gaze to Clara. "How are Owen and the dairy business going, Clara?"

"Better now that Ned Beachum's back to work. Before that, my Owen was fillin' in for him and havin' to do all the deliveries besides the rest of what he's gotta do. Was a hard week, but thanks to you and Cassia fixin' up Ned like ya did, he's back to work."

"I'm glad to hear all is well. I know Ned was concerned to miss too much time," he said, fighting to keep his eyes from wandering back to Cassia's legs.

"Yup, he's a good man. Very reliable. When his wife told me he was ailin', I talked her into callin' ya to help." Clara sighed. "They ain't got too much of anythin' to speak of. We pay Ned what we can, but with four youngsters to feed…"

"Perhaps we can help them in some way," Cassia interrupted.

Clara shook her head. "They're mighty proud—the two of 'em. Owen and I tried a few times to send over cheese and clothes my youngins outgrew. I think they took offense."

"What would make you come to that conclusion?" he said.

Clara shrugged. "Just the way Ned looked away when I handed him everythin' one day when he returned from a run. His face reddened—embarrassed, he was at first—and then he appeared annoyed." She shook her head again. "Ya can't help folks if they don't want ya to."

"But that's just foolishness on his part. Clearly Ned knows they could use a measure of help," Cassia said.

He glanced in her direction. The frown creasing her brow was of deep concern. "Not at the expense of his pride, Cassia," he said, understanding fully Ned's mindset.

"He's right, Cassia," Clara said. "A man's pride is…"

"Stupid," Cassia interrupted. "Especially when it gets in the way of him accepting aid to help his family."

He softened his tone, endeared by the fierce way she felt moved to help the Beachums. Her kindness and caring moved him. "It's how it is, Cassia. Some things, no matter how stupid or miniscule they seem, are not worth relinquishing your pride for."

Her eyes widened. "Even if others are hurt in the process?"

"Mrs. Beachum's just as proud," Clara said.

Cassia sighed. "Then I feel sorry for those poor children. With two proud, stubborn parents, they're caught in the middle and denied the things they need."

"As sad as that is, it has to be. Can't be offendin' folks," Clara said.

"Then perhaps there's another way," Cassia said, her face brightening with her thought.

He could almost see the wheels of her mind working to concoct an alternate plan of action. "And what other way might there be?"

"Well, hiring someone to do a job isn't charity, right?" she said.

"Right," he agreed.

Clara frowned. "Other than Ned workin' for Owen, what else can he do?"

"Not him…her. Perhaps Mrs. Beachum can work at something," Cassia countered.

Clara arched a brow. "What's the poor woman gonna do with the youngins while she's gone?"

"She doesn't have to go anywhere," Cassia said, a smile spreading across her face. "Mrs. Beachum can sew. When we were at the house to care for Ned, I spotted an old treadle sewing machine in the kitchen. And when I asked her about her sewing ability, she admitted to making their clothes. Now," she went on without taking a breath, "I have tons of things needing to be mended. With my busy days and my mother liking the task less and less lately, the work is piling up. I'm sure, when I tell Mama my plan; she'll be more than pleased to hire Mrs. Beachum."

Clara smiled. "I think ya just might be on to somethin' there, Cassia."

"I do too," he said, admiring the beautiful woman standing before him—her brains, her heart, and, aha yes, her body.

"Well, now that we've got that settled, we best get to makin' a batch of tinctures and balms," Clara pointed out.

"Would you like to join us, Brodie?" Cassia said. "We can always use an extra set of hands."

"I accepted an invite to Shailyn's house for dinner," he said.

"Well, then, perhaps another time." Cassia sounded disappointed as she bent to retrieve the shovel she'd been using.

His eyes were drawn to her well-rounded hips, attached to a most inviting bottom. The denim overalls hugged her form in all the right places. Nervously he cleared his throat, shifting his gaze to the pocket watch he freed for a quick glance. "And yet, it appears I do have some time before I'm due."

She turned to face him, looking deep into his eyes. "I'm glad you don't have to leave yet."

He matched her gaze. "So am I."

Chapter Twelve

Cassia controlled the urge to become positively giddy.

What was it about Brodie that turned her insides into mush? His mere presence had her acting like a school girl on her first date. She felt awkward, clumsy, and worried about her appearance. Was it the way he scrutinized her every move with those lush, emerald green eyes, or the way he smelled of musk and spice that left her weak in the knees? Was it the deepness of his voice, the muscles in his arms, or how tall he stood, that made her heart race? Maybe it was everything blended so perfectly into one caring, intelligent package—the combination giving her sweaty palms and a dry throat. What baffled her as well was the fact she'd known Brodie all her life and never, ever did she have these self-conscious moments. He was like a big, protective brother.

She'd climbed on his shoulders as a toddler for piggy-back rides and sat upon his lap to be read a story. He'd wiped her tears, a snotty nose, a chocolate ringed mouth, and muddy hands. He'd seen her naked and diapered when his sisters watched over her on many occasions. If there was anyone in the world she could be herself with, it was Brodie. And yet, right now as he helped her and Clara chop herbs to make tinctures, oils, and medicinal balms, she was completely out of place working beside him.

"A penny for your thoughts," he said playfully. His unexpected comment, pulling her from her musings, nearly made her jump out of her skin.

"Yup, was just about to ask ya the same thing. Not to mention yer a bit jumpy to boot," Clara added.

Then please don't mention it.

Instead she shrugged, trying to act nonchalant. "Just wanting to make sure we accomplish all that needs to be done."

Clara's two children, Blythe and Morgan, joined the task at hand. Cassia secretly admired how well Brodie interacted with them, making them laugh and getting them to enjoy doing the work their mother set before them.

One day he will make a good father…and a good husband. How fortunate his lady love is to have him.

And suddenly, to her complete surprise, Cassia envied the nameless, faceless woman in Boston. Truthfully, she felt a bit jealous the woman had been able to win Brodie's heart. Frowning over her selfish and inappropriate thoughts, she stood. Leaving the table to check on the pot boiling on the stove, she tried to wipe her misplaced musings from her mind. She had no right whatsoever to be jealous. If anything, she should be happy for her dear friend. How wonderful to find that forever person—true love and companionship. Isn't that what she hoped would happen for her? So, how could she begrudge Brodie such happiness?

His hand upon her shoulder pulled her back to the present situation. "Is everything all right with you, Cassia?"

The rich, warm tone of his voice went straight to

her core. She nodded. "Just a bit tired," she lied, turning from the pot to face him. He was so near, so very close. It would take nothing to reach out and trace the strong line of his jaw or the inviting curve of his full lips. She was sure they'd feel soft and warm against hers. She closed her eyes briefly to gain control. "It's been a long week."

"I agree," he said, not attempting to move.

For a moment they just stood looking into each others' eyes. And she could have sworn there was something more in his gaze. Did he have the same thoughts about her? And if he did, what would she do? After all, he was spoken for. Any decent woman, and she was a decent woman, wouldn't allow herself to be involved with a man promised to another. But it would be so easy to…so wonderful to…

It was then that Clara cleared her throat, and instantly the enchantment forming between them was broken.

He stepped back.

She sighed, both relieved and disappointed.

He took out his pocket watch and checked the time. "I really must be going." He turned to smile at Clara. "It's been interesting."

She glanced over at Cassia and arched a brow. "It sure has."

Quickly she averted her glance, busying herself in packing the bottles and jars of finished products into her bag. "After I help to clean up, I should be going as well."

"Ya go on, before it gets dark. My youngin's can help clean," Clara said.

Both Morgan and Blythe groaned simultaneously.

"Never mind, now," Clara scolded. "Ya know what's gonna happen if I have to ask ya again."

Both sighed heavily, and together mumbled, "Yes, Mama."

"I've got to pass your house on the way to Shailyn's, so why don't I walk with you? Then I can help carry the bag," he offered.

"Oh no, Brodie, that's not necessary…" she began.

He interrupted. "Nonsense, I won't have you lugging that heavy bag home on your own," he countered.

"But I have…" she began again.

This time Clara interrupted her. "Now, that's a right nice offer. And whatever else ya need, I'll send Morgan to yer home with later."

She frowned, realizing Clara was preventing her from mentioning she rode over on her bike, as she was accustomed of doing, and able to place her bag in the basket.

"Best ya both be gettin' on yer way, now," Clara urged.

On the walk home, the wind picked up. She raised her eyes to the sky. "It looks like we're in for a bit of rain."

He chuckled lightly. "Do you remember the fun we had playing in the rain?"

She joined in on his mirth. "Oh, I do… I came home caked in mud. Mama wouldn't even allow me to walk through the house in such a dirty mess. I was stripped by the back door and partially scrubbed down in the kitchen before I was permitted to walk through to the bathroom."

He laughed harder. "My mother wet us down out in

the yard, then made Tucker and I change in the woodshed."

"What about the time we all ate the blueberry pie your mother baked for the church social and ended up having a bad case of the diarrhea all night," she reminisced.

He arched a brow. "I remember quitting after the third piece. You and Tucker finished off that pie. The two of you were smothered in blueberries."

She laughed again. "Another night I was washed in the kitchen."

"How did our parents put up with such antics? At least your mother had only one naughty child to handle. Mine had four." He shook his head. "I often wonder now, between the children and the medical practice my mother helped my father build, when the poor woman ever did a single thing for herself?"

"Well, like my own mother, your mother loved the church socials," she reminded him.

"And then we went and ate her pie," he countered.

They both broke out laughing.

"I can't wait to have a family of my own," he blurted out.

The thought of him sharing such affections with another woman suddenly dampened her spirits. The laughter froze on her face, as she tried desperately to hide her feelings. "Well, I'm sure, once your father's back on his feet, you'll be able to return to Boston and the life you've made there with…with…"

"Dorothea Malone," he interrupted.

Now, with the woman's name known, Cassia felt even more envious of the situation. "Yes, with Dorothea."

He sighed heavily. "Truth be told, Cassia, Dorothea has chosen to be with another."

She stopped walking. "I don't understand."

Nervously he cleared his throat. "There's not much to understand. Dorothea found a man more suited for her, and so we've parted."

"And how is all that setting with you?" She hated Dorothea Malone with a vengeance. How could she discard such a kind, handsome man as Brodie for another?

"I won't deny how much her actions hurt at first, but as I look at the relationship, I don't believe Dorothea and I were ever right for each other," he said. "We come from different backgrounds and have different ideas on what love and marriage is all about."

"And what do you believe love and marriage is all about?" she countered, surprised at herself for asking such a bold question.

"Sharing while caring," he began. "Loyalty, friendship along with the love and passion. Sometimes sacrificing for one another, definitely cooperating, and most certainly trusting and being trusted in return."

She smiled to herself. All the things he wanted, she wanted too. Once again they picked up their pace, walking the rest of the way in silence. When they'd reached her house, he turned to her and looked deeply into her eyes.

"And what does love and marriage mean to you, Cassia?" he asked softly.

"Everything you mentioned, except for two things more," she confessed.

"And what might they be?"

"Faith and hope," she said. "Without faith we lose

sight of humanity. Without hope we lose the courage needed to journey on through our challenges."

His smile was one of immense approval. "Yes, faith and hope," he repeated with a whisper. "I'm not surprised to hear such wonderful virtues spoken from a reverend's daughter."

She shrugged. "It has been a staple in our household, and never has the duo done us wrong."

He handed her the bag he'd been carrying. "It's been nice spending time with you, outside of our workdays that is," he quickly added.

"I feel the same," she agreed.

He glanced at the heavens. "Hopefully Morgan will get here with your bike before it rains."

She gasped, feeling her cheeks warm. "You knew?"

He nodded with a devilish grin. "I saw the bike parked on Clara's porch when I came around to the front door."

She frowned. "Then why did you offer to…"

"Because I wanted to walk you home," he interrupted.

She arched a brow. "It seems we've both left out something on our love and marriage ideal list."

He frowned now. "What's that?"

"Honesty," she said.

Chapter Thirteen

She thought of Brodie all through the Saturday night service, while she made ready the chapel for the next day, and during dinner. Even while she sat at her dressing table brushing her hair before bed, her mind wandered to him again. He'd known about her bike yet still asked to walk her home. He wanted to have the opportunity to spend time with her outside of work. Didn't a man, interested in a woman, go out of his way to be in her presence? She felt at a loss, only having a school-girl crush on Tucker as any sort of an example.

All these years she fashioned herself in love and jilted. But in all truth, she'd built dreams on vacant hopes. What she and Tucker had was a childhood fancy. No wonder it didn't hold up. And all this time she'd blown up their time together as a love affair. And when she lost his attention, she stupidly vowed to keep her heart safe from ever being broken again.

"How foolish I've been," she whispered. Certainly there was no long-lasting, real relationship between her and Tucker. Lord sakes, they were just children. What did either of them know about commitment? Blaming Tucker all these years for abandoning his promise to her suddenly seemed unfair now—to both of them. As a grown woman, able to see clearly the way love with the right man really can be, she realized her mistake. She regretted all the time she wasted being resentful, or thinking her time to love and be loved had passed.

"You were right, Mama," she mumbled.

"About what?" came her mother's reply.

She turned to see her mother standing in the bedroom door's frame. Amanda Holmes, now in her seventies, was still a formidable woman. Even dressed in a faded pink robe, with her long golden braid streaked with silver and hanging down one shoulder, she looked beautiful. Her sun-kissed complexion was flawless. The signs of aging looked appealing on her. No wonder she turned men's heads, captured their hearts. Her father adored her. The Apache risked his life for her. Oh, that she could ever be that sort of woman to a man.

"I was heading to the kitchen for a drink of water and saw your light on." Amanda made her way into the room. "Now, what was I right about?"

"That Tucker O'Clarity wouldn't be the only boy to win my heart."

Amanda took the brush from Cassia and began brushing the short curls, which had grown a bit since she'd returned from England. As she wound a lock around her finger, Amanda reflected. "That's because the key word here is *boy*. You were infatuated by a kiss from your very first love…a childhood sweetheart."

She gasped. "How did you know Tucker kissed me?"

Her mother smiled. "Because when you came home, you were elated. There was a flush upon your cheeks and a twinkle in your eyes. Only a girl's first kiss can render such a glow."

She cast her eyes to her lap. "And now I am so tormented."

Amanda chuckled lightly. "I see no reason why you should be." Her mother went on before Cassia had a chance to explain. "You and Tucker were mere children when your hearts took notice of one another. What did either of you know about life, or death for that matter? Now, with the work you do, you've been on both ends of the spectrum. You've seen things most young women your age don't even read about. And you've grown—matured. As I knew you would. And so, it is quite natural you'd no longer draw satisfaction or loyalty from a childhood crush, or its memory."

She raised her gaze to catch her mother's in the mirror. "Is it even right to love two men in one lifetime?"

Amanda stopped playing with her daughter's curls to gently stroke her cheek. "Oh, my darling child, how can you ask that of all people—me, when I've done exactly that?"

She reached for her mother's hand and held it, remembering the warmth of them as they lovingly cared for her as a child. "And how could you, Mother?"

Amanda sighed. "If anyone had asked me that question when I was young, I wouldn't have been able to give an answer, as I believed true love only happened once. But since then I've learned the heart is resilient…large enough to truly love someone again." She smiled. "And I'm so blessed I discovered how wonderful second chances are, as now I have you—my last bloom."

"Papa always says there are reasons and seasons for all things," she said.

"He speaks the truth, Cassia," Amanda said. "And if you're as smart and as resourceful as I believe you are, you'll take that advice and embrace the changes presenting themselves."

"It's Brodie O'Clarity," she confessed. "He's filling my thoughts, touching my heart in ways I never imagined were possible." She frowned. "But I don't understand how this can be happening? Brodie's been a good and dear friend...almost like a big brother to me all of these years. Why now are my feelings for him turning into something more?"

Amanda's smile returned. "I can't tell you the *why* of it, my darling daughter. Matters of the heart can be mysterious. But I can tell you it is positively enriching to fall in love with your best friend." Softly she kissed the top of Cassia's head and stroked her hair. "Will you decide to let it grow again?"

"Yes, I believe so," she said.

Amanda nodded and handed her back the hairbrush before making her way to the door.

"Mother."

Amanda turned to face her daughter, the true beauty of her face softened by a mother's love. "Yes, Cassia?"

"Please keep this between us," she whispered.

Amanda nodded, her sapphire blue eyes twinkling. "Never fear, your secret's safe with me."

Alone again, Cassia studied her reflection in the mirror. Her eyes weren't the dark blue of her mother's, but the light blue of her father's. "And they remind Brodie of his favorite marble," she whispered with a smile.

The next day in church, sitting up front with her mother, she took special notice of the love her parents shared. Joshua Holmes, into his middle eighties, stood straight as he preached at the pulpit. His shoulders were still broad, though not as muscular, and a crop of white hair replaced his dark curls. His eyes caught Amanda's several times during the Gospel. Truth be told, he never really let her out of his sight when they were together. And he always held her hand, or placed his palm at the small of her back when walking beside her.

Cassia glanced over at her mother. Amanda's face radiated with love and pride for her husband. Her focus was only for him. The words he spoke and the kindness he bestowed upon his congregation made him more endearing. And briefly she felt a pain of sorrow, for the time when her parents' endearment, to one another and all others, would no longer be shared. With each passing year, they grew older. What would happen to one without the other? She bit the inside of her lip, not wanting to dwell further on such a thought.

Before returning her gaze up front, she glanced around the church—spotting Brodie sitting a few pews away in the opposite aisle. He was dressed in a dark jacket and matching trousers, white shirt, and no tie. His semi-casual look screamed Boston on a late spring day. She admired how handsomely his clothes fit him, his tall and muscular form sending ripples of excitement through her body. When his eyes locked with hers, heat radiated from the top of her head to the tips of her toes. Embarrassed for being caught gaping, she quickly turned her gaze back to her father and pretended to be engrossed in his sermon for the day.

After the service Brodie approached her, his easy smile and twinkling green eyes robbing her of any resolve. "I've taken the liberty to pack a lunch basket...nothing extravagant, just a few pieces of cold chicken I found in the ice box, cheese, rolls, a few homemade cookies I took from my sister's house last night, and a jug of water. I thought we could go to the creek, the place near the rocks where we'd fish, and talk."

"I'd like that," she said. Then, glancing at her church attire, she added. "I'll go home and change and meet you back here in about ten minutes."

He nodded.

Her heart raced, her mind swirled as she hurried to remove her Sunday frock and slip on a casual spring dress, sandals, and a straw hat. She reached for a few items, like cloth napkins, cups, butter, utensils, a container of potato salad left over from last night's dinner, a couple of apples, and a blanket for them to sit on, and threw everything into a picnic basket her mother kept by the fireplace. She met Brodie by his wagon in front of the church. "I added just a few things to our picnic lunch." She handed him the basket and climbed into the wagon.

The day was warm but with a gentle breeze. The sun shone bright, and memories of the time she spent with the O'Clarity boys, fishing and eating plums by the creek, filled her thoughts with a yearning for such carefree days.

"A penny for your thoughts," he said.

She sighed. "I was just thinking of how we ate plums by the creek while we fished."

He chuckled lightly. "Tucker and I fished; you kept throwing them back."

She smiled. "I did, didn't I?"

"Yup, irritated the hell out of me, but you felt sorry for the poor fish," he reminisced. "And I couldn't help but comply with your wishes, especially after you'd put on such a pathetic pout, your eyes filling with tears that spilled delicately down your cheeks with one, slow blink."

How her sympathy for the fish affected him, melted her heart. "I'm sorry if I was a pain, but I couldn't stand to watch the fish as they gulped for breath with sides heaving and gills flapping. And I saw no reason to rob anything of its time here on earth just for sport. After all, we had food at home and didn't need to eat what we caught to survive."

"I suppose your kind heart, the empathy you had for others is what brought you to the medical career," he said.

"I've been told I'm much like my sister, Sunny. She was always coming to the rescue of injured critters and nursing them back to health."

"Then the kindness runs in your family," he observed.

"And what of you…your reasons for becoming a doctor?"

"The same feelings—the desire to help others. I saw my father doing his best to cure, heal, and save lives. I wanted to do the same. But the times you can't help, no matter how hard you try, stays with you." He sighed heavily. "Ahh, to be back there again, our childhood trauma only being for the life of a fish."

She nodded. "And to have that carefree feeling about us, letting our parents worry for our needs and wants." She arched a brow. "It's a dang good thing we can't see what's ahead for us, or else we'd be too frightened to get out of bed each morning."

"So true," he agreed. "Such a foresight could drive

a person crazy."

"I believe that's exactly why the good Lord kept such information a secret from us," she philosophized. "The same goes for when it's our time to pass from this world."

"Don't you think it would be convenient sometimes to know when we're scheduled to die?" He quickly added, "I mean, so we can be prepared, settle things for our loved ones."

She cocked her head sideways, contemplating her answer. "I think men more so than women have such a mindset, as most of them are the breadwinners for their households. Without the man around to financially care for a family, the wife and children would suffer greatly and quickly be thrown into poverty and despair."

"But you'll never have to worry about such things, Cassia, as you've gotten an education, have a profession whereby you can supply for yourself whatever you might need."

"Yes, I suppose you're right about that, but…"

"But what?" he interrupted.

"I still want to be a part of a family," she admitted. "Living life alone, without someone to love and share things with, as well as having children, isn't what I hope to do…despite my ability to support myself financially."

"Me either," he agreed softly.

His words set her mind thinking. The handsome, strong, intelligent man sitting beside her shared the same ideals and desires, as well as her love for family and in helping others. He was beginning to touch her heart.

"Are you bothered by the fact women are moving

ahead, learning ways to be independent from a man." She turned to look him straight in the eyes while he answered her question.

He glanced her way and held her gaze. "I might be unusual in admitting this, but I think it only fair women have an equal opportunity to live their lives as secure and as free as any man. I've seen the devastation from a broken home too many times, whether the situation has come by the husband's death or abandonment. I wouldn't want that sort of sorrow for my sisters or the daughters I might one day father."

"Then you wouldn't stop your wife from continuing or pursuing her dreams?"

He chuckled lightly. "Well, I can't say I'd be pleased with her choice of pursuing something of an indecent or illegal nature. But for her to have a legitimate and wholesome career, yes, I believe I'd support her fully, even be proud of her."

She smiled. "You're a good man, Brodie O'Clarity."

He chuckled again, her compliment bringing a slight blush to his cheeks. "And you are a good woman, Cassia Rose Holmes."

Her cheeks warmed. Shyly she cast her glance aside, remaining silent the rest of the way to the creek.

After helping her down from the wagon, Brodie handed her the basket she brought and reached for a blanket and his basket. "I've brought one as well." She helped him spread both out beneath the tree and then set their tiny feast upon them.

As they ate, they reminisced about their childhood.

"I'd sneak out of the house on late summer nights and skinny dip," Brodie shared. "One night a few boys from Willow Creek decided to do the same and thought it would be pretty funny to steal all of my clothes."

She giggled. "Oh, no! What did you do?"

He shrugged. "What else could I do but walk home naked? Thankfully the little thieves left my shoes, as they were hidden behind a rock. And it was late, so no one was about…and very dark that night as well with no moon." He sat back against the tree's trunk. "I made it as far as the bend by the Hendrick's farm before a wagon came into sight and stopped right in front of me."

She gasped. "Oh my stars, how humiliating."

He chuckled. "Well, it could have been, but the driver was your father."

Her eyes widened. "Why in the world would my father be out so late?"

"I learned later, hearing my parents talk, Reverend Holmes had been summoned by my father to the deathbed of a dying neighbor, asked to give a last blessing. Obviously, he was on his way home when he discovered me."

"And what happened then?"

"Well, he motioned for me to get into his wagon, and after I did, he handed me a blanket to cover myself. I braced myself, thinking I'd be getting a real scolding…a lecture on the sinfulness of a thirteen-year-old young man walking around town late at night, naked. But he never asked one question as to why he caught me in such a situation. In fact, he never uttered a single word. He just kept his eyes on the road and drove me home."

She arched a brow. "Imagine, he never mentioned your strange encounter, but I'm not surprised. My father is an honorable man, doesn't gossip, hates anything that can cause trouble, and never takes credit for what he does for others."

"Much like my own father, I'd say," he countered.

"So true," she agreed.

He sighed. "Do you think you could handle our patient schedule on your own tomorrow?"

"Yes, no problem…but why?" she said.

"I've only been to the hospital once to see my father, and that was when I first arrived home. Since taking over his duties, the opportunity to travel to Willow Creek hasn't been available."

"Oh, Brodie, I'm so sorry. How inconsiderate of me not to have offered to take over for you before this." Shame for her thoughtlessness pierced her conscience.

"No. No, none of this is your fault." He reached out to give her arm a reassuring pat.

His hand lingered, his fingers gently encircling her arm. The warmth of his touch penetrated to her very core. As her gaze locked deep with his, she experienced a tingle of excitement. This moment sitting here with Brodie, his strong yet gentle hand heating her entire body, was the best time she'd ever known to date. And she wished—no, she prayed he'd lean over to kiss her lips.

But instead he cleared his throat, removed his hand, and offered her more cheese, breaking the beautiful moment they shared. Embarrassed by the strange feelings weaving throughout her existence, she declined the cheese and stood.

"I think I'll wade a bit in the water." She slipped off her sandals and ran ankle deep into the creek, reveling in the way its coolness calmed her hot flesh.

To her relief, he remained sitting on the blanket. She moved upstream a bit, away from his immediate view, and inhaled sharply.

"What an idiot I'm being," she whispered to herself. To think for one moment Brodie would consider her in any way other than a good friend, a colleague was the most idiotic thing that had ever crossed her mind.

Just as she neared the shore and was beginning to wonder how she'd return with dignity, he approached her. "If you walk to the blanket, your feet will get all sandy."

And with that, he picked her up and carried her back to the tree. Silently he dried her feet with the edge of the blanket he brought, making sure to get between her toes. His gentle administration again left her insides the consistency of jelly.

"Your pink toes," he said, in reference to the polish she wore. "Is this something new for women to do?"

Nervously she giggled, pulling her dried foot from his grasp and slipping on a sandal.

"Actually, no… I learned from a history professor while in England that the mummified pharaohs decorated their nails using henna, and African women have also been known to dye their fingertips. Of course, we don't use henna now but instead nitrocellulose the United States acquired from Germany during the war, which allowed them to produce nail polish in this shade of pink." She dried her other foot herself. "I met a young woman from New York City by the name of Celeste Foster," she went on further. "She was one of my classmates, and she wore the polish on her fingernails which was soon frowned upon by our instructors." She shrugged. "No doubt due to patient concern involving sanitary purposes."

He nodded. "I would agree."

"So, Celeste began to paint her toes. I liked the idea, and when we parted, her gift to me was the bottle of pink nail polish." She put on the other sandal.

"And cutting off all those long curls." He glanced at her hair.

She self-consciously combed her fingers through her shortened locks. "Yes, that as well."

A slow smile spread his lips. "Cassia Rose Holmes, you certainly are unique—indeed."

Chapter Fourteen

Brodie woke early to beat the heat while making his way to Willow Creek's General Hospital. His heart was hopeful, as his father was recovering nicely. A call to his mother last night updated his father's progress. In a few days, he might be able to return home.

The birds were in good form this morning as well. A Mourning Dove, sitting on the fence, greeted him as he hitched the horse to the wagon. Tree Swallows sang, their chirping tune echoing throughout the early hour. Even a Ruby-throated Hummingbird entertained him a bit. As he made his way farther out of Eagle's Landing, he was graced with performances from the Cactus Wrens and the Black-capped Chickadees.

He smiled, soaking in the beautiful spring day he was blessed to see and thinking of Cassia. He could still feel the soft flesh of her tiny foot in his hand, pink toenails peeking out from beneath the blanket he used to wipe her feet. Everything about Cassia intrigued him: her giggle, the way her marble-blue eyes locked with his, how she listened intently to whatever he said, her pale, bobbing curls framing an angelic face, the dimple in her chin, the cute wrinkle of a dainty nose when she smiled, her full pouting lips, as well as her independence, intelligence, and kindness. The way she walked, her shapely legs, rounded hips, tiny waist, ample breasts, even the softness of her voice—all of it held him spellbound. In only three short weeks, he'd grown from once being like her big brother to wanting a chance at being her man.

The thought of her wrapped in his embrace, her warm flesh against his, made him shift uneasily on the hard, wooden seat of the old wagon. If he were made to stand and walk right now, it would be difficult. He was suddenly thankful no one was around at this early hour to view his condition, and that he had a very long way to go to reach Willow Creek. Hopefully it would be more than enough time to calm the goings on beneath his breeches.

The town had grown considerably within the last five years. Taller buildings, longer and wider streets, as well as automobiles, put a different perspective to the entire area. Brodie felt ancient, traveling in a horse and wagon. Though many still navigated the old way, the automobile was quickly gaining recognition in Willow Creek…as it had done in Phoenix and Boston. It wouldn't be long until small, sleepy hamlets, like Eagle's Landing, would soon join the modern-day mode of travel.

"The world is changing," he whispered to himself. He was changing too. Working these last few weeks as a small town doctor wasn't as boring or unrewarding as he'd thought. The fancy restaurants, pubs, and theaters weren't readily available to enjoy. But Eagle's Landing held a warmth Boston lacked. "And the warmest attraction just happens to be named Cassia."

He had thought long and hard on his decision, and he was about to present it soon to his father. No doubt, Sean O'Clarity wouldn't be able to ever take on the full load of patients he had been seeing before his heart attack, even with Cassia's help. He frowned. Knowing his father as well as he did, sitting at home would drive him crazy. But if the three of them pooled their skills, his father would only have to work a day or two in the office, once he got back on his feet. And he and Cassia could pick up the slack with the clinic and the house calls. He smiled, anxious to reach the hospital and tell his father his plan.

Willow Creek General Hospital in no way could be compared to Boston's Medical Center. With only two floors other than the basement, which housed the operating rooms and morgue, it could still handle the influx of sick folks living in the small city and surrounding hamlets. As he entered the main foyer, a whiff of ammonia met his senses. His heels clicked noisily on the shiny linoleum floor as he made his way to the reception desk. A young woman with jet-black hair pulled back into a bun at her nape, smiled up at him.

"Can I help you, sir?" She pushed the wire-rimmed glasses she wore higher up on the bridge of her nose with the tip of a finger.

"I'm Doctor Brodie O'Clarity, here to see my father, Doctor Sean O'Clarity."

She nodded and then frowned as she scanned the roster of names listed on a sheet of paper. Once she found his father's name, she smiled and raised her eyes to meet Brodie's.

"He's been moved to a regular room, here on the first floor." Her smile broadened. "Which you know, of course, happens when a patient is doing better."

He smiled now. "And that is a very good thing, indeed."

"Yes, it is." She continued to stare at him.

He cleared his throat. "And the number of the room, please."

"Oh, mercy me, I am so sorry." She blushed as she looked again at her paper. "Room 6A."

He inclined his head politely. "Thank you, miss, and you have a nice day."

"You as well, Doctor."

He found his father sitting in a reclining chair by the window. The sun's light cast a ray of warmth across his face. His complexion was not as pale as when he first saw him within a few days after his heart attack, but a worn look remained in his eyes. Brodie swallowed hard, the emotion rising to choke him. His father was always a hardy man, a gentle giant, able to do all things, from saving lives to fixing the roof. Now he appeared so small and frail.

He forced a smile as he entered the room. "And so you're out of bed?"

His father turned from the window. "Brodie, me lad, 'tis so good to see ye."

He made his way to his father and bent to kiss him quickly atop the head. "It's so wonderful to see you sitting up."

"Aye, and 'twould be even better if I was allowed me pants," he mumbled. "Sittin' here in this airy gown and robe, bare-assed, is not to me likin' for sure."

He chuckled lightly. "Doctors make the worst patients."

"Aye, well, I've had enough o' it all," he grumbled on. "Time for me to be on the other end o' this thing, doin' what I do best—helpin' others get well."

"And you will, as you're coming along nicely," he

encouraged. "But you know rushing a recovery will only end up with a relapse, and none of us want that."

"Aye, especially yer mother...she can't take seein' me like this." He looked down at the way he was dressed.

He frowned. "Where is Mama?"

"I told Betsy to keep her home today," he said. "The poor woman's been by me side from the start, sleepin' in a hard chair with her head restin' on the bed. Every time I opened me eyes, I saw her."

He smirked. "And you truly believe Betsy's going to be able to stop Mama from making her way to you?"

His father rubbed his chin, the way he always did when he was frustrated or annoyed. "Nay, but I had to try. I can't be seein' her sick because o' lookin' after me." Sighing, the elder man continued, "I couldn't bear life without that woman, as stubborn as she can be at times, she's me everythin'."

He searched his father's eyes; they were the same emerald green as his. "When did you know Mama was the right woman for you?"

His father smiled. "The moment I set me eyes upon her, waterin' her father's horse out in front o' the barn. She caught me fancy with her long, curly hair blowin' in the wind." He laid his head back against the reclining chair as he continued the memory. "I was just startin' out as a doctor when I'd been summoned to see what ailed yer grandmother and had to pass by the barn to get to the house. There yer mother stood, takin' care o' the horse, her full lips mumblin' calmin' words to the animal. I wondered to meself...why would a daughter be tendin' to a horse, instead o' her mother, who was lyin' ailin' inside the house? So, the bold lad that I was…"

"And still are," he interrupted.

"Aye, I suppose… Anyway, I stopped to ask her."

He chuckled. "And what was Mama's answer?"

"She looked me straight in the eyes, squared her shoulders and said, 'Can't feed me sick Mama without workin' the farm, and this here horse helps with the farm work. If 'tis any o' yer business.' And right there and then I knew I'd be makin' this woman me wife. Six months later I did."

Brodie moved to the window, looking out at the busy street. "I envy you and Mama. To have such a love for one another all this time—strong together and for each other—working side by side to make a good life for your children by leaving all you knew and loved and coming to America." He turned to look down at his father. "I want what you two have."

"Well, me handsome lad, 'twill help to find yerself a woman first," his father teased. Then added, cocking his head sideways, "Unless ye already have."

He gave a taut nod, his face warming.

"Ahhh, 'tis like that, is it?" his father marveled. "And would I be accurate in assumin' yer eyes have been caught by a Miss Cassia Rose Holmes?"

"My eyes and my heart."

His father arched a brow. "Well then, there's only one way about it, son."

"How's that, Papa?"

His father sighed. "Ye must tell her how ye feel."

He inhaled sharply. "Then what?"

His father arched a brow. "I suspect yer plannin' on stayin' then?"

"Yes, I came to tell you exactly that."

His father smiled. "Then ye marry her, son—make her yers forever more."

Just then a familiar voice from behind interrupted their conversation with, "I'm home."

Both turned to see his younger brother, Tucker, standing in the doorframe.

His father whispered a warning, "And I'd say ye better be damn quick about it."

Chapter Fifteen

Cassia's legs, heavy with fatigue, dragged her bone-weary body up the front steps to her home. She'd ridden the bicycle all over town, as it was an extremely busy day with three mothers giving birth, a case of severe ulcer pain for one woman, a fungus problem in an elderly man's toenails, and coming to the aid of a young girl having an asthma attack. At a few patients' homes, she trudged on foot through backwoods, the road too bumpy for bicycle wheels, while toting her nurse's bag. Her back, legs, and feet were tired and sore. She missed lunch, hadn't even taken the time to have a drink of water or use a bathroom. At any rate she couldn't wait for Brodie to return. Another case load like today's would be too difficult to handle alone. If such a schedule was exhausting for her, at twenty-three, it must have been grueling for Doc Clarity, a man in his early sixties. He took on days like this on a regular basis, and that wasn't even factoring in the times he worked at the clinic.

"No wonder the poor man had a heart attack," she mumbled.

When she entered the house, her parents were in the parlor. From the doorway she saw her father reading a book and her mother engrossed in her embroidery. Too tired to talk, she made her way to the bathroom, used the toilet with great relief, stripped off all her dirty, sweaty clothes, and washed at the sink. She covered her nakedness with a robe she always left hanging on a hook by the door, before making her way to her bedroom. After quickly brushing her short curls, she climbed upon the bed and fell asleep.

A gentle touch upon her brow woke her. She opened her eyes to find her mother sitting at the edge of the bed.

She blinked her eyes into better focus. "What time is it?"

"Nearing seven," Amanda supplied, the warm look of a loving, adoring mother twinkling in her sapphire eyes. "Oh, how I miss those long golden locks." She pushed aside the wisps of hair covering her forehead.

Cassia sighed. "Hair grows, Mama."

"I suppose," she whispered, caressing Cassia's cheek. "Did you have a rough day?"

She nodded and yawned, turning onto her side.

"Well, your father and I have already eaten, but I saved a dish for you." Amanda gave Cassia a light pat upon her behind, the way she did when she roused her on Sunday mornings for church as a small child. "Come now, before it grows too cold, unless you think you haven't enough energy to chew?"

"I'll manage." She felt the gnawing pangs of hunger rumbling within her stomach.

Her mother gave her one more loving pat before she stood and made her way to the door. "Oh, by the way…" She paused to look over her shoulder. "Tucker O'Clarity's home."

Her mother's last words shot through her like an adrenalin infusion. In one fluid motion, she was on her feet. "Do you know this for sure?"

Her mother turned to face her squarely and arched a brow. "You know I don't take well to gossip and would never spread a falsehood."

She swallowed hard. "I'm sorry, Mama. I only meant…"

Amanda folded her arms beneath her bosom. "Truth be told, he was here this afternoon, looking for his mother. I told him she was staying in Willow Creek with his sister Betsy so she'd be closer to his father while he was in the hospital. I also told him Brodie was back from Boston and was taking over for his father, but he'd gone today to Willow Creek to visit Sean. Then he explained how he hitched a ride with a traveling salesman who happened to be passing Eagle's Landing, so he had no way to see his father. That's when your father offered him the use of our horse and wagon."

Her heart raced. "Did he ask about me?"

"He did at that," her mother said.

"What did you tell him?"

Her mother frowned. "Why, the truth, Cassia—that you returned from England about a month ago and had been working side by side with Sean until he became ill. Now you are seeing patients with Brodie, but today you were covering calls alone so he would be free to visit Sean."

Suddenly every nerve in her body felt like it was beating. "How did he look?"

"Well, I reckon you'll have a chance to see for yourself, when he brings back the horse and wagon," Amanda said.

She gasped. "I can't have him seeing me like this?"

Her mother smirked. "No, you can't."

140

She hurried to her wardrobe. "Oh mercy, what should I wear? And my hair's such a fright."

Amanda chuckled lightly. "I'll leave you to your task at hand while I go upon my own mission."

Frowning, she glanced at her mother. "And what mission is that?"

Amanda sighed. "That being the effort of trying to keep your food warm."

Food. She'd completely forgotten how hungry she was. Could she even eat one morsel right now? Her stomach rumbled with an answer.

"Yes, please, if you don't mind, Mama. I'll be done here quickly."

Amanda shook her head. "You will have to decide, Cassia."

"All I need to decide right now is which blouse to wear." She reached into the wardrobe for both a light blue and a pale green one and held them up for a better look.

"The blue. It will go nicely with your navy blue skirt," her mother advised, before leaving the room.

Her mother was right, about the blouse and the men, as she once faced the same dilemma. And it couldn't be said of Amanda Holmes that she didn't follow her heart against all protocol. Becoming the wife of an Apache and going to live with him in his village wasn't something a white woman in 1864 did. And yet her mother made the choice she desired, despite all those who frowned upon her decision.

Making her way to the bed, she sat on the edge and closed her eyes to calm the storm of doubts rising inside of her. "I don't have to do anything I don't want to because I am a smart, resourceful young woman and can take care of myself." The positive affirmation strengthened her resolve. Opening her eyes, she squared her shoulders and stood, continuing to dress for the evening.

She loved her mother's cooking, but tonight she tasted nothing she ate, automatically spooning the lamb stew into her mouth to quiet the rumblings of a hungry stomach. After washing her dinner plate and tea mug, she chose a book containing verses by Keats from the shelf and tried to become absorbed in the words. Never did she have a problem enjoying the author's work, but tonight her attention drifted constantly to the mantel clock. The anticipation of seeing Tucker again after so many years rose like the morning sun—bright and warm. Her parents said nothing, keeping their eyes and minds on their past times or making small talk between them. She swallowed the mixed emotions threatening to choke her, as her parents' oblivious actions made Cassia want to scream, yet their refusal to notice her behavior was appreciated.

Around eight a knock sounded at the door, Cassia hesitated to stand for an instant seemingly riveted to the chair.

"I'll go." Her father held up a hand for her to stay seated and placed the book he was reading aside. As he stood, she watched him stifle a grin. "It's probably that young chap, Tucker O'Clarity, returning our horse and wagon."

"No doubt," her mother nonchalantly commented.

Cassia clasped her hands in her lap. "I don't even know what to say to him after all of this time."

"Hello, might be good for starters," her mother quipped.

She frowned. "I'm glad you and Papa find this amusing."

"I'd say more interesting than amusing." Looking up from her embroidery, Amanda searched her daughter's face. "Cassia, neither Brodie nor Tucker has asked you for or promised you anything. So, the way I see it, all three of you are free to do whatever you want and more than able to give the situation time."

"Yes, time," she whispered. "I need time."

"And you should take as much of it as you need," her mother advised. "Because whatever you do decide will affect your life for the duration."

Her frown deepened. "But what if there isn't a lot of time. Brodie might return to Boston and Tucker to wherever his job takes him."

Her mother leaned forward. "Cassia, the man who is right for you will find a way to never be without you." She smiled fondly. "Proud Eagle crossed barriers that almost cost him his life to be with me. And your father never gave up hope for us, which I am so thankful for," she added. "If a man loves you, he will go to any extreme to be with you. And if you really love him, you won't mind doing the same."

She cast her eyes to her hands. "You gave up your home to be with Proud Eagle."

"No, I gave up a house—and one burning to the ground at the time—not my home," Amanda corrected.

It was moving and heartbreaking to listen to her mother speak of Proud Eagle. A tender expression crossed her visage, the memories both wonderful and painful. To love someone, bear their children, and then lose them had to leave a deep scar etched into the heart.

Amanda's voice softened. "Home would only be

where the love of my life lived."

"But what if the love of my life wants me to give up being a nurse and a midwife?" she worried. "Lots of husbands don't want their wives to work."

"True, but times are changing. Your occupation can successfully continue in any part of the world, as there's always a need for medical help. So, wherever your husband's career takes him, it can take you as well."

She bit her bottom lip. "All you say is true, Mama, but there's no guarantee I'll marry an O'Clarity man. Neither has made any proclamations. No promises have been spoken."

Amanda frowned. "Have I not raised a wise and independent daughter who cuts her hair, wears toe polish, and occasionally wears men's trousers?"

She gave a taut nod.

"You will know not to choose a mate that does not foster and support the woman you are and want to continue to be," her mother countered.

"And what if I never find that mate?"

"Then you will go on fulfilling your life with the work you've chosen to do," Amanda said. "Life does not end because marriage and children aren't a part of it. Helping others can be just as rewarding, but in a different way. And that's completely fine. It would be a very dull world, indeed, if we all did the same things."

She smiled. "Dull, indeed."

Their conversation was cut short as her father entered the room. "Well, Tucker was kind enough to help me get Henry unhitched from the wagon and tucked away in the barn for the night."

Tucker followed her father close behind, looking

more muscular and taller than when she'd seen him last. But what could she expect? At their last meeting, he was a teen-age boy. Now he was a man, and a very handsome one at that with large green eyes staring at her from beneath thick auburn brows. His hair, a deeper auburn, hung in waves to his collar. His skin was bronzed by the sun.

"Hi, Cassia." He eyed her with a similar awe.

Her father cleared his throat. "Come, my love." He extended a hand to his wife. "The hour is late."

Amanda nodded, accepting her husband's help to stand. "Nice to see you again, Tucker," she said, as the two of them departed the room.

And there she was, left by herself, facing the man she believed would be her husband and share with her the medical profession. She stood on shaky legs. Beside her heartbeat, the only other sound she heard was the ticking of the mantel clock.

It was Tucker who finally broke the silence. "You've cut your hair."

Self-consciously she ran her fingers quickly through her short curls. "It is all the fashion."

A slow, easy smile spread across his face. "I like it; it fits you now."

Her face heated. "You're different too."

He chuckled lightly. "Yes, in a scrappy sort of way."

"No. I didn't mean…"

"I've missed you, Cassia," he interrupted, nearing her.

Her stomach clenched. "And yet you never attempted to contact me."

He stood before her, looking down from his tall

stance, smelling like leather and bay rum. "That doesn't mean you weren't always in my thoughts."

They were close, oh so close. All she had to do was lift her face a tiny bit and raise on her tiptoes, and her mouth would easily meet his lips. Did she dare?

And then something strange happened. Unexpectedly she pictured the first day she saw Brodie, remembered his embrace and the confused feelings it sparked within her. Looking into his eyes was different than peering into Tucker's, though they were the same shade of green. Brodie's orbs held sincere warmth, a deep righteousness and respect. He was seeing her—and only her—and she felt admired and thrilled. Whereby Tucker's gaze appeared like he'd practiced such a glance and probably used it often to melt the hearts of women. The thought offended her, and suddenly she felt cheap and used. The only thing special about her presence was she was the woman with him now and would suffice.

She stepped around the chair she'd been sitting in, putting a distance between them. "It grows late, Tucker, and I've an early shift in the morning."

He arched a brow. "You wish for me to leave…so soon?"

"Yes, please. I'll see you out." She made her way to the front door.

He followed her in silence but stopped at the heavy oak portal. "I'll be in Eagle's Landing for a while. Long enough to see my father resting comfortably at home."

"I'm sure that will please him greatly." She opened the door.

He placed a hand on her arm. "I'd like to call on you, Cassia."

She pulled her arm from his grip. "My days are so busy, I really don't know when…"

"If nothing else, are we not still friends?"

She sighed. She didn't hate Tucker, just disliked how he ran out on his promise. Then again, they were just children, too young to have made such promises. "Yes, we are still friends."

He smiled. "Then you will agree to see me?"

"Yes, I agree," she said, resigned. "Now, go home."

He chuckled and gave her a peck on the cheek before she shut the door behind him.

With mixed emotions, she remained for a few moments standing in the foyer and gazing at the door, as she rubbed the spot where he'd kissed her.

Chapter Sixteen

Brodie's heart fell to his toes when he turned to see his brother standing in the door of his father's hospital room. And the uneasy feeling increased as the day wore on. People were drawn to Tucker's personality, and because of this, he was used to being the center of attention. He was funny, quick witted, and interesting. No doubt the reason Cassia always enjoyed his company. Even at the hospital, while visiting their father, the room came alive when he stepped inside. He had a few nurses laughing, as well as his father. In no time all ears were listening to Tucker's adventure of how he finally made it into town.

The fact Brodie arrived immediately when his mother summoned him, and Tucker was weeks late, seemed not to matter. And thinking back it was always the case. Tucker could get out of every selfish, self-centered thing he did. He wasn't held up to responsibility, wasn't expected to tow the mark. As the youngest he was doted on, given several chances to redeem himself, which he rarely did.

Driving separate wagons back to Eagle's Landing gave Brodie time alone to evaluate the situation—that being Cassia's first inclination was to favor Tucker. He was the older one, and the person Tucker and Cassia always looked up to. He got them out of trouble and scolded them when they misbehaved. Because of his

148

elder stance and wisdom, he was excluded from their friendship in many ways. Their little schemes, their childhood jokes, secrets, and other things they enjoyed together built a relationship between them, a strong bond. Now, did he even stand a chance with Cassia? Could he successfully come between all she and his brother previously built throughout the years?

He made his way to the kitchen for a drink of water. From the small window above the sink, he spotted Tucker walking up the backdoor's path. With both hands thrust deep into his jacket pockets, Tucker sauntered closer to the house, shoulders squared and looking very pleased. Brodie's heart sank. Tucker had gone to the Holmes's residence to return the horse and wagon he borrowed. Obviously, he would have had a chance to speak with Cassia. In what way did their encounter contribute to Tucker's good mood?

"Christ, you're grinning like the cat that got the cream, little brother," he whispered. Brodie's flesh heated, jealousy spreading like wildfire through his entire being. Taking a deep breath, he filled a glass with water and drank, allowing the liquid to quench his thirst and cool the smoldering heat within. Just as Tucker opened the back door, Brodie briefly closed his eyes and took another deep breath. The last thing he wanted was a confrontation with his brother. Both were here to help with his father. Being at odds with one another wasn't the way to accomplish that.

Finishing his drink, he cleared his throat and placed the used glass in the sink, then forced a civil tone. "Are you hungry?"

"Ravenous." Tucker moved to the ice box. "What's good to eat?"

"Mother's left a few dishes," he responded. "I've put quite a dent into the beef stew which is in the large brown pot. But I'd say there's enough for a couple more bowls."

"Swell, then, I'll warm it up for the two of us." Tucker brought the pot to the stove.

Brodie set the table and sliced a loaf of homemade bread a neighbor lady brought over the night before.

The two worked in silence until seated, and Tucker spoke between mouthfuls of stew. "I see Cassia eventually forgiving me."

He frowned. "Her father's a reverend; she was taught to forgive."

"That's not what I mean, and you know it," Tucker muttered.

"Oh, then you're referring to the way you shattered the hopes she had for the two of you?"

Tucker nodded. "We agreed they were childhood hopes, nothing that should hold anyone accountable forever."

He sighed heavily. "How gracious of Cassia to let you off the hook."

Tucker sat back in his seat. "Aw, come on, Brodie. Don't tell me you would have honored such a commitment uttered at such a young age?"

He locked eyes with his brother. "I would have— yes. And you know why, Tucker? Because I am a man of my word. Something you are not," he added beneath his breath.

Tucker chuckled lightly. "Then you are a chump. No one pays any mind to a kid's musings."

He arched a brow. "Cassia did."

Tucker leaned forward. "And now, she, too, has

realized how stupid the whole thing is…was."

"Are you so sure about that?"

Tucker smirked. "Well, she agreed to see me as a friend." He shrugged. "Who knows what can develop again from there."

He swallowed hard the anger rising to choke him. "And what then, Tucker? What happens then, after you and Cassia have rekindled the flame?"

"Well, hopefully, we'll be together again," Tucker spat.

"Together where?" He didn't wait for his brother to answer. "Are you planning to stay in Eagle's Landing, make a life with Cassia here?"

"Well, no… I don't know." Tucker shrugged again. "What's the big difference where we live, anyway, as long as we're together?"

"The difference is that Cassia has very much made a place for herself in this town, doing what she went to school to learn. What she has always wanted to do with her life."

"She can minister to the sick and deliver babies anywhere, Brodie," Tucker snapped.

"What about her family and friends she holds near and dear?"

Tucker frowned. "She didn't have a problem leaving them to study in England."

"But Cassia's father is in his eighties. She might be reluctant to leave him again."

"Other women have followed their men, like Mom did Dad. For cryin' out loud, Brodie, Mom left her country, all her family and friends, to come to America with Dad."

"Times were different then, Tucker," he said.

"Mom didn't have a career outside of the home. Cassia does."

"No one's asking her to give up her career," Tucker said. "Just to do her nursing someplace other than Eagle's Landing." Glaring across the table, Tucker pushed away his bowl of stew and set his spoon aside. "What's it matter to you anyway?"

He looked down at his bowl of half-eaten stew. By now he'd completely lost his appetite. How could he tell his brother he saw Cassia in a different light—as a woman he was attracted to, instead of the little girl he once looked out for? How could he explain the feelings of desire and the emotions that overtook him while he was in her presence? He hadn't even told Cassia how he felt.

Slowly he raised his eyes. "It matters to me because I don't want to see Cassia hurt again by you or anyone else."

"In case you haven't noticed, Brodie, Cassia's a big girl now."

Oh, little brother, I've definitely noticed.

"And she doesn't need you to look after her anymore," Tucker concluded.

Brodie stood and picked up his bowl, spoon, and water glass. "I will always have Cassia's best interest in mind, no matter how old any of us get. I won't stand for her to be abused by another's control or saddened by anyone's selfishness. And you'd do best to keep that in mind." He took his dishware to the sink, rinsed them in silence, and left the room.

Chapter Seventeen

The next few days following Brodie's talk with his brother were awkward. By day he went with Cassia on house calls and worked side by side with her at the free clinic. They even took a few office visits together, as she was good with children and put the women patients at ease just by being in the room. By night Tucker took her to dinner, for a walk one night by the creek where they all once played, or had dinner at the Holmes's residence. Brodie was always invited, but declined, which made working with Cassia the next day even harder. The distance growing between them worried him, wore on his heart, and kept him awake at night in his bed. He realized he had to do something soon to bring her back and closer to him. But with Tucker in the picture, he feared the confession of his feelings for her would look like sibling rivalry.

The silence that hung between him and Tucker grew thicker, as his silent resentment and jealousy continued to get the best of him. He was grateful when the day for his father to return home arrived. To have others in the house to converse with, keep his attention elsewhere, was a welcomed thought. He hoped Tucker would, once he saw his father home again and doing well, leave Eagle's Landing.

He and Tucker shared a wagon to Willow Creek, bringing it to a halt in front of the hospital. In silence they walked together to their father's room, where they found their mother in charge. She was rummaging around the place, packing his father's belongings, making certain not to forget a thing. A familiar expression was upon her face—the one she wore when she was fully into organizing and completing a task properly. He remembered it from the days she planned holiday meals, ladies' luncheons, or church socials. Nothing got past her. She was thorough, efficient, and fiercely protective of her duties. His father's recovery would be her first and foremost project, and she'd be very protective of him as well while she accomplished her mission.

Brodie had a pang of envy for what his parents felt for each other. His father cared for and protected his mother, and vice versa. They looked out for one another, finished each other's sentences, and understood the silent requests. And they really enjoyed each other's company. Not only were they in love, but they liked each other, were best friends. This was what he yearned for in his life with Cassia. In many ways she reminded him a lot of his mother—their strength, intelligence, loyalty, and love for their families mirrored one another. And if he didn't speak up soon, let Cassia know how he felt toward her, he just might lose the chance to ever make her his or to ever experience the happiness his parents shared.

"Tucker's got yer papa's bags, and ye can be pushin' him in this chair on wheels to the wagon, while I visit the nurses' desk. I'll be wantin' to make sure I've got all the paperwork and medicine right we'll be needin'," she said, bringing Brodie from his thoughts.

"I can do that, Mama," he offered.

154

She paused with a frown. "I suppose ye'd know better than me if all was in order with the medicine, but don't be long." She pointed a finger at him. "I want to get Papa home and to bed then fix him somethin' to eat and get some meat back on his bones."

"Now, Lass, I've been in bed long enough. I won't have ye coddlin' me like a wee babe," his father objected.

"Ye'll be doin' whatever it takes, Sean O'Clarity, to get yerself well again, and I'll be hearin' nay another word on the matter," his mother countered, with hands on hips and a stern face.

With a heavy sigh, his father nodded.

Brodie stifled a smile and made his way to the nurses' desk. They all knew by now challenging Sadie O'Clarity would get them nowhere.

Once home, he had an opportunity to speak privately to his father while Tucker put the horse and wagon to bed and his mother made them all lunch. While putting away his father's toiletries, he caught a glimpse of him donning his nightshirt. His brief nudity proved his mother's worries. Sean O'Clarity was gaunt and frail. As a son, the thought caught in his throat and nagged at his heart. As a doctor he knew his mother wasn't the only one who would be helping to put the meat back upon his father's bones. He'd be right there as well to make sure his father got both his mother's homemade love and his professional care.

Making his way to the bed, he assisted his father in sitting on the edge. "Would you like me to line the bed with a few towels before you get in?"

"Ye mean in case I piss meself?" his father snapped. "I'm not so feeble-minded I can't be taken meself in to do me business properly." He arched a brow. "Hope it'll be a long while before I'll be needin' me wife or sons to help me onto a pot in bed or changin' me bedclothes like a babe in nappies."

He sighed. "I didn't mean to imply you are feeble minded, but you of all people know how it is when a person is weak and been through what you have. Sometimes in such instances a person can lose control of bodily functions and…"

His father frowned. "I'm still in control o' every bodily function the good Lord gave me, Lad," his father interrupted gruffly. "And I know ye were just tryin' to be helpful. So, I'm thankin' ye for yer concern and advice and then askin' ye not to be harpin' on me about such things again." His father stood before climbing into the bed.

"Point taken." Brodie covered his father's bare, thin legs with the quilt. "I'll keep my silence about me, then."

His father nodded. "Sometimes silence is best, and other times not so good."

He frowned. "What now are you implying?"

His father's gaze locked with his. "Did ye ever tell Cassia how yer feelin' for her?"

"No," he whispered. "Not yet."

"Saints preserve us, lad, what the hell are ye waitin' for?"

"It hasn't been the right time," he said.

"Wait long enough and some other lad's goin' come and say the words first," his father warned. "And there's nay another, other than ye, that's goin' to make a right life for that sweet lass."

He arranged a few pillows behind his father's head.

"How are you so sure of that, Papa?"

"I know her, and I know ye," the elder man said with conviction. "And the two o' ye are what the other needs." Resting back against the pillows, he went on. "One time, after the first encounter I had with yer mama in front o' her parent's barn, I caught her havin' a lemonade at an outdoor café with a few friends. If me memory serves me right, she was laughin' and enjoyin' the company o' a lad by the name o' Timothy Darby."

Brodie sat at the edge of the bed. "I've never heard this story."

His father arched a brow. "Aye, well, there never was a need before for me to be tellin' it."

"Well, don't keep me in suspense," he complained.

His father relaxed deeper into the downy soft pillows. "I never liked Timothy—thought him to be a selfish sort—worryin' only about what baubles and such he could buy to make himself better than others. And he flaunted his family's wealth, used it to impress folks. Yer mother was taken with him for a wee bit o' time." He shrugged. "I suppose flowers and candy, lace ribbons, and other such delicate things can turn a lass's head."

"And you were a struggling young doctor, overworked, underpaid, and exhausted," he added.

"Aye, that was the way o' it for sure," his father agreed. "But one night I was called again to yer mother's home. This time yer grandpapa took ill. He'd gotten an infection from a small wound made by a rusty nail. All night I stayed to care for the old man, as his body raged with fever. Yer grandmamma and mother took turns helpin' me swab him down with cool cloths. Ye learn a lot about someone—their likes, dislikes, values, and faith while sittin' quietly beside a sick bed in the wee hours o' the night. Yer mama and I did just that. By mornin' the old man's fever broke, and he was better. And from that time on, yer mother looked at me in a whole different way." He smiled. "Knowin' at first glance she was the lass for me, I didn't hesitate to move further into her good graces. I even had it out with Timothy, findin' him to be just as big o' a fake as he was a coward. 'Tis a recourse that had to be taken, as the other man lost and the better man won the lady."

He sighed. "And what recourse do you take if the other man is your brother?"

His father leaned forward. "Do ye truly believe Tucker's sincere in his intentions toward the lass…that he wants or is after the same outcome as ye are?"

"No," he said. "I believe she'll only fill his fancy for a time, before he moves on."

"Aye, 'tis me own take on the matter as well. So, then, the only recourse to take would be to tell the lass how yer feelin' about her," he said. "And ye need to do it soon."

Brodie frowned. "Why is it you're taking my side over Tucker's?"

"I'm not takin' anyone's side, lad. I just don't happen to believe Tucker's up to the call. And ye are," his father added. "Tucker hasn't found himself yet. A man needs to know where he's goin' in life before he can take another person along with him. And ye've been headed in the right direction for some time now, as is Cassia. 'Tis only right, since ye've got strong feelin's for the lass already, that ye save both o' ye the sorrow o' bein' apart and act on yer heart's desire."

Before Brodie could comment, his mother entered

the room carrying a lunch tray. "Enough now with the visitin'." She placed the tray on the bedside table and pulled a nearby chair closer to the bed. "Yer meal's on the kitchen table, Brodie," she said, not looking up from her task of separating her food from his father's.

"Thanks, Mama," he said. Then to his father, "Enjoy your lunch, and then get some rest."

His father chuckled lightly. "Doctor's orders?"

He smiled. "Exactly."

Tucker was making headway on a roast beef sandwich when Brodie sat down to consume his meal.

Between mouthfuls his brother mumbled, "Do you think Pa's ever gonna be back to his old self again?"

"With the proper care, I see no reason he shouldn't make a complete recovery," he said before biting into his sandwich.

"Complete enough to get back to his practice?"

He swallowed hard. "He won't ever have to take on such an immense load again, Tucker, because Cassia and I will be doing most of the work."

"Did Cassia agree to that?" Tucker wiped his mouth on a cloth napkin.

Brodie placed his sandwich on the plate and reached for his napkin. "I assume that's the reason she returned to Eagle's Landing in the first place...to help Papa with his practice."

Tucker arched a brow. "Well, maybe now you shouldn't assume anything for Cassia."

He frowned. "And would that be because you waltzed back into town?"

Tucker's brows furrowed. "I didn't waltz anywhere. I answered a family call." He leaned forward in his seat. "But now that I am here, I see no reason why I can't…"

"Complicate Cassia's life," he interrupted.

Tucker's voice rose. "How about maybe enhancing it?"

"More like destroying it," Brodie snapped loudly.

"Well, that's only your version," Tucker bellowed.

"Saints preserve us," his mother gasped from the doorway. "What in God's name has gotten into the pair o' ye sittin' here shoutin' at each other and bickerin' like little children, when yer Papa's tryin' to get some rest."

Shame hit him square between the eyes. "I'm sorry, Mama."

"Same for me, Ma," Tucker said.

She moved closer to the table and pointed a scolding finger at them. "I'll not be havin' either o' ye upsettin' yer father. His recovery is o' the most importance, do ye two hear me?"

They answered, "Yes" simultaneously.

"Ye might be too big now to be taken over me knee for a paddlin'," she pointed out firmly. "But I can kick ye out o' me home."

The thought of his mother administering such a punishment heated his face. Those times hurt his pride—the humiliation great, even though he was a small boy.

"And I'll not hesitate one moment to be doin' just that if I hear any more o' this sort o' nonsense." With hands on hips, she concluded, "Do I make meself clear?"

"Yes," they responded in unison again.

A knock at the back door ended the scolding. When answered, John Tyler Boyd, the brother of one of his patients, stood on the stoop. The young man, a tall, thin-framed fellow about sixteen, with a mop of pale, yellow hair and a pimpled complexion, politely removed his sweat-stained hat before stating his business. "Sorry, ma'am, to be botherin' ya, seein' as though ya just got home from the hospital with Doc Sean and all."

"Nay a problem, Mr. Boyd," Sadie reassured the man, gesturing him inside. "What has you comin' our way this afternoon?"

John Tyler's gaze fixed on Brodie. "I'm meanin' to fetch Doc Brodie, here. Nurse Holmes sent me."

Brodie stood, knowing Cassia would have never sent for him unless she was in dire need of his help. "What's wrong, John Tyler?"

"It's my sister, Alma Lee. She's havin' a heap of trouble birthin' her babe." John Tyler wiped the sweat forming on his brow with the back of a hand. "Nurse Holmes is with her—my ma too—both have been with Alma Lee since early this mornin'. There's been a lot of screamin' and cryin' from the bedroom, but still no baby's come. Nurse Holmes's pretty troubled and thought ya all would be back from Willow Creek by now, so she asked me to fetch ya." John Tyler frowned. "Said to tell ya she's sorry to be botherin' ya all, especially today, but…"

"No. No, it's not a bother," he interjected. "Nurse Holmes's was right in calling for me."

Sadie brought a hand to her heart. "Saints preserve us. If I'm rememberin' right, Alma Lee's not due to birth that babe for another two months or so."

"Yup, you'd be thinkin' right on that account, ma'am," John Tyler agreed. "But she's havin' the

161

pains, been in pain all night. So early this mornin' Ma told me to fetch Nurse Holmes since she heard Doc Brodie weren't gonna be around today."

"Just give me a moment to get my bag." He raced to the table by the door where he kept his medical gear.

"I'll hitch the horse to the wagon," Tucker offered. And then turning to John Tyler he said, "Did you walk here?"

"No sir," the younger man said. "I rode Nurse Holmes's bicycle so's I'd get here faster which is much quicker than tryin' to saddle the horse or takin' the time to hitch him to the wagon."

"Come with me to the barn, and bring the bike with you. I'll put it in the back of the wagon, and you can catch a ride back to your place with Brodie," Tucker suggested.

John Tyler inclined his head politely. "Much obliged."

As soon as they left the room, his mother neared him, "Brodie, ye must try with everythin' possible to save Alma Lee Sloane's babe."

He sighed heavily. "I try to save everyone in my care, Mama."

"Nay, 'tis not what I meant," she said, biting her lower lip. "Alma Lee's been through a lot in the past two years with her father dyin' o' the cancer and then losing her husband, Vincent Sloane, in a loggin' accident not even a year later. This babe is all Alma Lee has left o' Vincent. 'Twas only a few months after he was killed the poor girl found out she was carryin'. If this babe is lost too…"

"All will be well." He placed a reassuring hand on his mother's arm. "I will do everything possible to save them both, Mama." He kissed her briefly on the forehead and headed for the back door.

But before he closed the door behind him, he heard his mother say, "God be with ye, son. God be with ye all."

Chapter Eighteen

When Brodie halted the wagon in front of the Boyd's modest, two-story and wood-framed home, Trudy Boyd and her youngest daughter, Ruth Ann, waited on the front porch. With her semi-graying hair pulled back into a sloppy braid that hung down her back, Trudy, a thin wisp of a woman, paced nervously, wringing her hands in front of her. Ruth Ann, no more than twelve, sat on a wicker chair watching her mother as closely as a cat would watch a mouse. Her long, pale curls fell in disarray around a thin, somber face. As Brodie made his way up the stairs to meet her, the elder woman's eyes filled with tears.

"Thank God ya finally got here." She led him to the door. "It ain't like Nurse Holmes ain't done her best to help Alma Lee," she went on. "Just somethin' ain't right."

Placing a hand on Trudy's trembling arm, he spoke calmly. "I'm going to do my best to help your daughter and her baby."

She nodded, then turned to John Tyler and Ruth Ann. "You two youngin's stay put, and I'll come fetch ya after the baby's born." Once inside she ushered him up the stairs. "The room to the left is mine, but Alma Lee's room's the first door to the right. My poor girl came back after bein' up north with her husband and seein' him pass from a loggin' accident. Now she's sleepin' once again in her old room."

He halted Trudy at the bedroom door. "I want you to go downstairs and make yourself a cup of tea. Sit with John Tyler and Ruth Ann, and wait for me to call you."

"Oh, no, Doc. I need to be with my girl," Trudy protested.

"It's best for Alma Lee not to see you so upset," he said softly. "Let me and Nurse Holmes take care of her."

Reluctantly Trudy nodded. "I reckon I could use a cup of tea," she whispered, then added, "Probably wouldn't hurt none to make the youngins a bite of lunch as well."

He forced a smile. "That sounds like a good idea."

The room he entered was small and hot, despite the two windows opened wide for air. He had to crouch down, after passing through the door so his head wouldn't hit the slant of the ceiling. The room was sparsely furnished with just a small bed to one corner, a night table beside the bed, a three-drawer dresser in another corner, and a baby's cradle beside a rocking chair. A small set of shelves was stocked with baby items—diapers, blankets, booties, and the like, as well as a white teddy bear with a gold ribbon tied around its neck. As he neared the bed, he passed a heap of soiled linens lying on the floor, and the stench of sweat and urine filled his nostrils.

Alma Lee, garbed in nothing but a nightgown rolled up to beneath her breasts, was lying on her side. Her knees were curled to her swollen belly, and she faced the wall. Cassia, kneeling beside the bed, spoke softly to the patient while rubbing her back. Again, as he'd done so many times before, he revered Cassia for the deep and thorough care she gave her patients. Admiration and respect for the beautiful and intelligent woman assisting him daily surfaced stronger and stronger as time went on. And her kindness didn't end with each call but carried over into the patient's lives— spilling over into Cassia's private time. He'd heard of the trips twice a week to Ned and Olivia Beachum's home, carrying with her clothing in need of mending and alterations so Olivia could make an income beyond what Ned brought to the table. Cassia's efforts brought Olivia customers as far away as Willow Creek, and their standard of living within the few weeks had greatly improved.

When Cassia spotted him, she stood. "Dr. Brodie's here, Alma Lee."

Alma Lee cried out to Cassia, turning slightly to reach for her hand. "Please, don't leave me."

"I'll only be a moment," Cassia reassured her, bending to cover Alma Lee's bared bottom with the nightgown. "I just want to fill Dr. Brodie in on your condition." She motioned for him to step outside of the room.

"How far apart are her contractions?"

Cassia's blonde curls were in disarray across her forehead, and with a trembling hand she pushed them aside, biting her bottom lip. "I've never seen anything like this, like what Alma's going through."

He frowned. "What do you mean?"

Cassia sighed exasperated. "After all the pain…the pushing…still nothing is happening."

His frowned deepened. "What did you discover with an internal?"

"Nothing—there's nothing there—no fetus," she whispered.

He searched her face. "What are you saying?"

"I'm saying, Alma Lee Sloane has no baby inside of her," Cassia said. "That's why I sent for you."

"Sounds like a case of pseudocyesis." He placed his bag on the floor and combed his fingers through his hair.

She arched a brow. "False pregnancy?"

"Yes, also known as phantom or hysterical pregnancy," he said. "A patient with pseudocyesis has the appearance, signs, and symptoms related to pregnancy—interruption of the menstrual cycle, swollen belly, enlarged and tender breasts, and changes in the nipples, possible milk production, and nausea. Even signs of preeclampsia or constipation can occur," he explained. "Are you familiar with the syndrome?"

"I've heard of such cases but never cared for a patient experiencing the problem."

"I'm not surprised. Phantom pregnancy is extremely rare."

Frowning, she glanced at Alma's bedroom door. "What could cause such symptoms, and why would this happen to Alma Lee?"

"In some cases causes for the condition can be a tumor, the inability to conceive, multiple miscarriages, or the loss of a child."

"But Alma Lee hasn't experienced any of those things," she pointed out.

"And still another cause is a manifestation of psychosis—the simple wish to be pregnant. A dissociative disorder, whereby the mental state becomes irrational, yet the rest of the patient's thinking remain intact."

"I don't understand. Why would Alma Lee think she was pregnant when she wasn't?"

"She recently lost her husband, didn't she?"

"Yes, in a logging accident up north, a little over seven months ago. And it was just after Vincent's death Alma Lee found out she was pregnant."

"Alma Lee wished she was pregnant," he corrected.

She frowned again. "Why would she wish to be pregnant when she wasn't?"

"It was the only way to keep a tangible hold onto her husband." He sighed heavily. "I saw such a case only one other time while in Boston, the wife of a Washington diplomat. The pressure to give her husband an heir brought upon phantom pregnancy. She went into labor while in Boston but…"

"She wasn't really in labor," she interrupted, "because there was no baby."

"Exactly," he whispered.

"Oh, Brodie," she gasped. "This baby means everything to Alma Lee. The poor girl's lost so much already. What will she do if there's no child for her to hold…for her to go on for?"

Reaching for his bag, he moved toward the bedroom door. "Let's hope I'm wrong."

Alma Lee had rolled fully onto her back, her long, pale-yellow tresses fanning out over the pillow. Her nightgown, cocooning her enlarged abdomen, twisted around her thighs. Brodie couldn't help but think how young she looked. What was she, maybe eighteen the most? Cassia was right; Alma Lee Sloane was just a girl. Too young to have all this pain and sorrow running through her body, desperate—through this baby—to keep the love she felt for her man alive. Suddenly, at twenty-nine, he felt so old. Literally he was witnessing a child having a baby. Pity for the young woman swelled his heart as he once again approached the bed.

"I need to examine you, Alma Lee," he said softly, as not to frighten her any more than she already appeared. "Would you allow me to look?"

Alma Lee bit her bottom lip and nodded, tears pooling in the large, blue eyes that seemed to plead for his help. Pulling her nightgown to her waist, she braced the bottom of her feet against the mattress and spread her legs.

Cassia, the compassionate, caring, and loving human she was, knelt again, this time at the head of the bed, and caressed Alma's face. "Take a deep breath, Alma Lee, and relax your body."

Brodie's examination proved his false pregnancy theory correct, conveying the diagnoses to Cassia with a quick nod. She blinked back the tears forming in her eyes and took a deep breath.

"Should I fetch Trudy?" she whispered.

He nodded again. "But tell her to come upstairs alone." It was best for Alma Lee to have her mother present when he broke the tragic news.

It was almost twilight before he and Cassia left the Boyd residence. Alma Lee went into uncontrollable hysterics upon learning there would be no baby...that there was never a baby. Her uncontainable grief later consumed the entire family, and he and Cassia tried desperately to console them all. In the end, after Alma Lee realized her symptoms of pregnancy were just manifestations of her mind, she became totally undone by messing herself and the bed with vomit and urine.

Brodie took John Tyler downstairs with him, embarrassed for Alma Lee that her sixteen-year-old brother should witness the horrible ordeal of her anguish. Cassia, Trudy, and Ruth Ann bathed Alma Lee and cleaned up the room. Then he gave her something to make her sleep until morning.

"Trudy, your daughter has experienced extreme physical and mental trauma," he explained. "It's a great possibility she'll need more than a medical doctor, but also to speak with a psychologist."

"You mean one of those head doctors?" Trudy wiped her red-swollen eyes with a handkerchief.

"Yes, I fear her mental state will be sorely compromised in the days to come," he said. "She'll need someone to talk to, to help her adjust."

Trudy wrung her handkerchief in trembling hands. "Well, I reckon that's what she's got a mother for. I don't plan on leavin' her side 'til she gets past this whole nightmare."

"The truth of the matter is, Alma Lee may not fully come out of this—not without professional care. And every moment she's left untreated, she could become a danger to herself," he explained.

Trudy raised a defiant chin. "Ain't no way a child of mine's gonna be put into one of them there nut houses," she snapped. "I've heard what happens in those places—how they tie people up, operate on their heads, leave them naked and dirty." She folded her arms in front of her. "No. Not my girl. We Boyds take care of our own."

Both John Tyler and Ruth Ann nodded in agreement to their mother's statement. It was then

Trudy made her way to the front door and opened it wide. "I thank ya kindly for the help ya gave Alma Lee, Doc Brodie, but now I reckon its best ya both leave us to our sorrows so's we can get through this as a family."

He inclined his head politely. "Very well, but I'd like to stop by in a few days, just to see how all of you are doing."

"Ain't no reason to be concerned for my sake, or the youngins," Trudy boasted.

"Then for Alma Lee's sake," he countered.

"Seems like my girl's taken a shine to Nurse Holmes." Trudy pointed to Cassia. "I'll allow her to come back, but just her."

"Very well." Turning to Cassia, he motioned for her to precede him out the door, as they took their leave.

Cassia sat silently on the way back home, her back ridged, hands clasped in her lap, and eyes straight ahead. Her professional conduct and emotional restraint in such an instance had his admiration for her rising to a new level. Not once did she falter in her duties as a medical caregiver, keeping her wits about her even in the throes of witnessing a complete and utter human breakdown. But now her silence concerned him.

"Are you all right, Cassia?"

Keeping her eyes ahead she whispered, "What happened to the Washington diplomat's wife?"

He swallowed hard. "I don't know," he lied, casting a quick eye in her direction.

She met his glance. "Did she hurt herself, like you warned Trudy Alma Lee might do?"

"Cassia, please... I don't think..."

"Tell me what happened to her, Brodie."

"I believe... I heard she hung herself," he finally admitted.

Cassia gasped. "And if Alma Lee doesn't get the help you suggested, do you think she'll do the same?"

He slowed the wagon and pulled off onto a dirt road. Upon coming to a complete stop, he turned to fully face her. "The circumstances weren't the same, Cassia. That other woman had a history of miscarriages and stillborn pregnancies. She was under great pressure because her husband wanted an heir, and she couldn't seem to give him one. And when he left her for another woman...a woman who later bore him a son..."

"The first wife couldn't handle it," she concluded for him.

"But Alma Lee's situation is different," he added quickly. "She has a family that loves her and is standing by her. Plus she's young and has the chance to marry again one day and have a family."

"And yet you still thought to mention psychiatric help," she countered.

"I'm a doctor, Cassia. My job is to make every patient aware of the medical help available. If they decide not to heed my advice and suggestions, that's their choice. But I'm bound by oath to do no harm, and that means doing everything I can to heal and cure those in my care. And to shed hope by delivering accurate information on further treatment, if in fact there should be any available."

"Oh, Brodie, a terrible—horrible thing happened today," she whispered, tears slipping down her face. "To love and wed a man, have him die, and then to be so grieved that you conjure up being pregnant just so…so…" Her sentence ended in a heart-wrenching sob.

He slid closer and pulled her to him, cradling her body against his. The feel of her so close warmed every fiber of his being. "Cassia. My sweet, Cassia," he muttered against her temple.

She nestled her face beneath his chin and wrapped her arms around his neck. "Why do bad things happen to good people, Brodie?"

He caressed her soft hair. "I wish I had an answer for that, Cassia. But you know, as a reverend's daughter, there's a reason for all things."

"Maybe so, but that doesn't mean we should like it," she sobbed.

"No, we never have to like it."

"Alma Lee loved Vincent so much. Can you even imagine such a love?" She pulled back to look into his eyes.

"Yes." He wiped a tear from her cheek with his thumb. "I can imagine such a love." He gently traced the outline of her full lips. "I can imagine it clearly."

"Oh, Brodie," she whispered.

Before she could say more, he covered her mouth with his. Her lips were warm, soft, and sweet. By her design the kiss deepened, as she cupped the back of his head with her palm and pressed him closer. His heart raced, his body heated in the throes of passion, and he became totally lost within her embrace. And it was at that very instant he knew he'd never want to stop kissing this woman or ever be too far away from her. He never wanted a day to begin or end without her beside him.

"Cassia," he whispered against her lips, "I've

wanted to kiss you from the moment I saw you in my father's office."

She pulled back to search his face. "I've wanted the same."

He raised a brow. "You have?"

"Yes," she breathlessly admitted. "I can't begin to tell you the nights I lay awake in my bed, trying to figure out a way to let you know my heart."

"I know perfectly well about those nights, as I've been plagued with them too. So much I wanted to tell you how you make me feel…how I feel about you…every bit of you. From your eyes the color of my favorite marble to your perfectly painted pink toes."

She giggled. "And so what's taken you so long?"

"When Tucker came back I thought…"

"Tucker and I are friends." She emphasized the word *friend*. Then caressing his cheek with a finger, she added, "And that's all we'll every just be." She cocked her head sideways, her light blue eyes twinkling now with seduction instead of tears. "And what of you and me, Brodie, what will we be?"

He smiled. "If I have my way—forever bound, my love—forever bound."

****

Upon entering her home, she found her parents in the parlor, sitting in their usual chairs. Her father read the newspaper, and her mother worked on her latest piece of embroidery.

"Are you hungry, honey?" Her mother never looked up from her work.

"I don't think I could stomach anything at this point, Mama." She sat on the sofa.

Immediately her mother raised her gaze. "Aren't

you feeling well?"

Her father lowered his newspaper and waited for her reply.

"No, not really," she admitted, and then through more sobs she explained what happened to Alma Lee. "I asked Brodie why bad things happen to good people, and he pointed out something Papa preached—there's a reason for all things."

Her father arched a brow. "Well, I'm sure glad someone was listening in Sunday school." He shook his head and smiled. "I always liked that lad." He leaned forward and reached out to lay a consoling hand upon her arm. "Obviously you still question Brodie's recall."

"I believe my answer to him was there's nothing that says we have to like the reason," she said.

Her father squeezed her arm affectionately, his large, smooth hand now dotted with age spots. "Aye, that's the truth of it. But if you're a strong believer in the Lord, you know that He is always present and at work in your heart and on your behalf, even if you can't see that at the time. And in faith, one day, you'll understand God's reasoning, as you realize His love has a hand in everything."

"It was all so horrible, Papa," she whispered. "I just wish it were in my power to help that family…more than in a medical way."

"You do have the power," her father said.

She frowned. "What power is that?"

"Knowing the Lord as you do has given you strength and motivation, and you rest in the power of His many extensions of grace, passing them onto others," her father explained.

"And what are extensions of grace, Papa?"

"There are all kinds of unselfish acts we can do for one another," he said. "Like the hope you've given the Beachums when you got Olivia's sewing business started."

"But what then can I possibly do for Alma Lee and her family?"

"You'll know what grace to extend when the time comes, baby girl."

Cassia left the bedroom door ajar, as she combed out her hair. Every bone in her body screamed with fatigue, but her spirit was renewed—thanks to the ever wise and loving father she'd been blessed with. His words circled in her thoughts as she readied herself to climb into bed.

"Could you use a bedtime story?" her mother joked, peeking into the room.

"Have you got a good one to tell me?" she teased in return.

Her mother opened the door wider and came to sit on the edge of the bed. "If I remember right, you were always partial to the one where the elves helped the shoemaker."

Cassia smiled, sitting beside her and sighed wistfully. "If only that's what it would take to appease me now."

Her mother wrapped an arm around her shoulders, pulling her close. "Then what would it take to appease you now?"

She giggled nervously. "Well, Brodie had a really good idea. The best ever, actually."

Her mother rested her forehead against Cassia's. "Do tell."

Cassia's cheeks warmed. "He…well he…he kissed

me."

Her mother pulled back, arching a brow. "And what did you do?"

She cleared her throat and sighed again. "I kissed him back."

Chapter Nineteen

Alma Lee's medical circumstance fell on a Tuesday, and Cassia was scheduled for a follow-up by Friday. But on Thursday she ran into John Tyler at the general store purchasing lye soap. When she inquired about Alma Lee, John Tyler assured her everything was fine, and she needn't rush to visit their homestead. Since spring was the time flowers bloomed and babies were born, her caseload of birthing mothers had her working from sunup to sundown. So, after John Tyler's affirmation that Alma Lee was doing well, Cassia thought pushing the follow-up visit to Monday of the following week wouldn't hurt anything until she met Murial Dodd at a church function on Friday night. From the very reliable mouth of Eagle's Landing's school teacher, she learned John Tyler and Ruth Ann hadn't attended class all week.

Obviously, John Tyler had lied about what was really going on at the Boyd household. Therefore, waiting until Monday for a visit was no longer an option. And so was the reason, though it was her only day off in over a week, Cassia rose early on Saturday morning. After downing a cup of coffee, she gathered her medical gear and headed over to check on Alma Lee.

When she rode her bicycle into the Boyd's back yard, she spotted Ruth Ann standing on the porch, her thin arms reaching out to the clothes line to hang towels, or what appeared to be towels, except they were all cut into a V-shape with lace-like ties hanging off from each side.

"Mornin' Nurse Holmes," Ruth Ann greeted her, never missing a beat as she hung one triangle towel after another. Though the young girl was nearing thirteen, her tiny, thin frame gave her the appearance of being much younger. And her short stature left her struggling to reach the clothesline. "Looks like we might be in for some rain. I'm hopin' it comes after I've taken in the wash, though."

After securing her bicycle against the side of the house and grabbing her medical bag, she climbed the porch stairs. "What are these you're hanging," she probed, reaching out to touch one.

Ruth Ann halted her work. "They're special undies. I made them for Alma Lee to wear."

She frowned. "Why would Alma Lee need special undies?"

Ruth Ann bit her bottom lip and hung her head.

"Ruth Ann, look at me," she coaxed.

The young girl slowly raised her gaze, deep blue eyes pooling with tears.

Cassia reached out and pushed aside a long, golden strand of Ruth Ann's hair from her forehead. "Tell me what's going on, Ruth Ann, so I can help."

"I had to cut down the towels like this and sew them as I did so's they'd fit Alma Lee's bottom 'cause she don't know how to use the outhouse anymore and does her business in her pants," Ruth Ann whispered.

Her frown deepened. "When did Alma Lee's incontinence begin?"

Ruth Ann's blond brows furrowed. "Her what?"

Cassia rephrased the question. "When did Alma Lee begin messing herself?"

"Right that next morning after learnin' she weren't gonna have a baby. She never came down to breakfast, so Ma went upstairs to check on her and found Alma Lee had wet herself and the bed. It took two of us—me and Ma—to wash and change her and to clean the mattress which was nearly ruined. And when Alma Lee kept making a mess, Ma figured she couldn't sleep in her bed no more. So we piled a bunch of quilts on the floor for her to sleep on since it's easier to keep washin' them instead of the mattress."

A lumped formed in her throat. "So you're using the towels as diapers?"

Ruth Ann nodded, the tears spilling down her cheeks. "Best I could come up with since ya can't buy real diapers for grown people."

She swallowed the nausea rising to choke her. "What else is going on, Ruth Ann?"

The younger girl hesitated to answer.

"I'm here to help your sister—to help all of you," she added, taking Ruth Ann's hand in hers. "But I can't do that if I don't know what's going on."

"Alma Lee's actin' like a baby now, Nurse Holmes." Ruth Ann sobbed. "She don't know how to do nothin' for herself. Me and Ma feed her, change her, dress her, and bathe her."

Cassia blinked back her tears. "Oh, sweet Lord, no."

"She don't talk no more either, just sits and stares. And when she lies down to go to bed, she cries and cries until Ma goes into her room to sing her a song."

"You hush your mouth, Ruth Ann," John Tyler snapped, as he swung open the back door and walked onto the porch. "What did Ma say about ya tellin' our business to others?"

"I ain't gossipin', John Tyler, honest I weren't," Ruth Ann quickly added in her own defense. "Just lettin' Nurse Holmes in on what's goin' on so's she can help."

"It's true, John Tyler," she said. "I mean no harm, really. I just want to help, that's all. I want things to get back to normal for all of you. I want to see Alma Lee well again and make it possible for you and Ruth Ann to be able to attend school."

John Tyler crossed his arms across his chest and blocked the entrance into the house. "It ain't no one's business if we don't go to school, or what's goin' on here with Alma Lee. We Boyds can take care of our own."

"That's not true, John Tyler. If you two stay absent from school for too long, the authorities will come by to see why," she explained. "And with your sister now as sick as she is, the last thing your mother needs or wants is any attention called to this household."

"Alma Lee's just sad now, is all, 'cause she ain't havin' no baby. But she'll come out of it, and until she does, we're gonna be here to help Ma. And there better not be no one settin' foot on our land 'cause that's trespassin'."

"I promise, none of that needs to happen if you'll let me help," she vowed.

"We can trust Nurse Holmes, John Tyler. I know we can. I feel it in my bones," Ruth Ann said, then quickly added. "After all, Alma Lee herself took a shine to her."

"Hush, Ruth Ann," her brother snarled. "Ya need to leave things up to me, now that Pa's gone. I'm the man of the house." To Cassia he said, "It'd be best if ya left us alone now, Nurse Holmes."

"Please, let her have a chance to help our sister," Ruth Ann pleaded.

He squinted at Ruth Ann. "All Alma Lee needs is her family, and if ya can't understand that, then I'll have to take ya into the woodshed and give ya another whoopin' like I had to do two nights ago when ya left Ma's sewing scissors in Alma Lee's room, and she cut off all her hair."

Cassia gasped.

Ruth Ann's face reddened. "Ya had no right to shame me like that, John Tyler, 'cause ya ain't my ma or my pa. Besides," she added, "Pa stopped takin' the paddle to me when I was nine 'cause it weren't no longer fittin'."

"Didn't ya hear what I said, little sister? I'm the man of the house now," he shouted. "And it's up to me to keep ya in line so's ya don't go astray. And if that means taken ya over my knee so's ya behave yerself, that's what I'll do."

Tears of humiliation and frustration wet Ruth Ann's cheeks. "But it weren't fittin', John Tyler. Ma even said what ya did to me was wrong…said it weren't decent 'cause yer my brother. I'm growin' into a young woman."

John Tyler chuckled sarcastically. "Ya ain't no young woman. Yer just a skinny little girl who still sucks her thumb at night and is afraid to sleep in the dark. Shucks, ya aint even grown boobs yet."

"That ain't so!" Ruth Ann shouted, her pale complexion reddening. "And if ya ever try to spank me again, Ma said she'll give ya a whoopin' ya won't forget."

"Well, she'll have to catch me first," John Tyler retorted sharply.

"Stop it—both of you." Cassia placed her bag at her feet. Her outburst gained their silence and immediate attention as both siblings turned their gaze to her. With hands on hips, she continued to reprimand them. "Do you two really believe you're helping your mother get through this time with Alma Lee by fighting like a pair of vicious dogs?"

"No, ma'am," they answered in unison.

"John Tyler, a man…a real man, one who is smart, kind, and good, as I know your father would expect you to be in his absence, doesn't run his household with violence."

"I know lots of people who have a Pa who does just that—rules the household with a stern look and a switch to the backside." Then he added, "Ain't no one disrespecting their word, that's for certain."

"That's not respect their families have for them, but fear. Would you rather be feared or loved?"

John Tyler hesitated. "Loved, I reckon."

"Then from this day on, you are to keep your hands off Ruth Ann, or any female, for that matter. It doesn't take much of a man to beat on a woman. A man like that, in my eyes, is nothing but a coward. And skipping school will not make you a wise man, or a man who can work a decent job for decent wages. Without a good pay, you'll never be able to support this family very well, or any other family you might have."

John Tyler hung his head. "I'm sorry, Ruth Ann, for beatin' on ya the way I did. It was purely indecent of me to take such liberties." He leveled his gaze to meet his sister's. "Can ya find it in ya heart to forgive me?"

Ruth Ann ran to throw her arms around her brother's neck. "Yes, oh, yes. I forgive ya, John Tyler. Make sure it never happens again."

Her heart warmed at the love the two siblings held for each other. Their misguided behavior was a direct result of a home in horrible discontent and sorrow. "Now," she said, retrieving her bag, "will you step aside, John Tyler, and let me enter the house?"

He nodded, pushing his sister gently from him, and opened the screen door.

"Come, Nurse Holmes." Ruth Ann reached for Cassia's hand. "I'll take ya to see Alma Lee."

John Tyler made his way to the kitchen, shoulders slumped. "Hold on a moment, Ruth Ann." She followed the young man.

He sat at the table and cradled his head in his hands. Cassia glanced around the small kitchen—poorly furnished with old-fashioned appliances, as the Boyd home still had no electricity or indoor plumbing. Yet everything was in its right place and scrubbed clean. Touches of family life surrounded her at every turn…newly washed and starched curtains hung on the windows, a freshly baked pie sat cooling on the counter, dirty boots were respectfully left at the back door, not to mar a clean floor, laundry was neatly folded in a wicker basket, waiting to be put away, and the sound of a clock, faithfully striking the hour. This was home to these people—and its serenity, its

184

structural dynamics, had been sorely compromised and turned upside down and inside out by death and sorrow.

Placing her free hand on the young man's shoulder, she softly encouraged him. "All will be well."

"I feel so useless since I can't actually go into Alma Lee's room and tend to her, like Ruth Ann can, 'cause it wouldn't be fittin'. And it just seems nothin' I do for Ma or Ruth Ann works out well either," he muttered into the palms of his hands. "For all the good I'm doin', I might as well not even be here."

"I know it's all so frustrating, but I'm sure just having you in the house to protect everyone is extremely appreciated. And I will do my very best to help all of you find a way to aid Alma Lee," she promised, silently praying she'd be able to keep what she vowed.

"Much obliged, ma'am," he muttered.

Returning to Ruth Ann, who waited now for her at the foot of the stairs, she forced a smile. "Lead on, my friend."

"Ma's feeding Alma Lee now," Ruth Ann offered. "We've been smashin' and mushin' up the food so's she don't choke."

Holding tightly to the banister, as the steps were steep and narrow and her medical bag cumbersome, she followed Ruth Ann. "What has she been eating?"

"Mashed potatoes with butter. Ma makes them nice and creamy. As well as smashed up bananas, squash, peas, and carrots. For breakfast she's fed oatmeal, a soft-boiled egg, applesauce, and pear puddin'. If ya put a cup between Alma Lee's hands, she'll raise it to her mouth and drink on her own. 'Course we've got to stay right with her so's she don't drop it when empty," Ruth

Ann added.

"And what sort of liquids has she been drinking?" she said.

"We've been givin' her lots of orange juice, chicken broth, and water and at night an herbal tea to help her sleep."

When Ruth Ann opened Alma Lee's bedroom door, Cassia glanced around the tiny room. The cradle and shelves lined with baby items had been removed, and the rocking chair pushed to the side. It was then she spotted Trudy on her knees beside a pile of blankets and quilts. She was spoon-feeding Alma Lee what appeared to be applesauce. The younger woman's long, beautiful, golden curls were chopped off, hanging in uneven strands to the middle of her neck. She was uncovered and staring straight ahead. Propped up with several pillows behind her head, she sat atop a few layers of towels. She had an apron tied around her neck like a bib, and beneath that she wore a shortened version of a nightgown coming only to the middle of her abdomen. One of the towel diapers covered her bottom, and socks were on her feet.

"I cut down a few nightgowns, 'cause she kept wettin' the long ones," Ruth Ann explained. "And I even sewed lace along the hem so's she would look pretty."

Ruth Ann's last words caught Cassia's heart. To think this young girl, in the midst of such trauma, still wanted her sister to look pretty. "You did a fine job, Ruth Ann."

Trudy stood when Cassia entered the room, placing the bowl and spoon on the table beside the bed. "Much obliged you came, Nurse Holmes."

"I'd like to examine Alma Lee now, if I could." She knelt with her bag beside the pile of quilts. Alma Lee didn't make a sound or blink an eye while the three of them removed her clothes. Cassia listened to her heart and checked her breasts, which had now returned to a normal state. Her stomach, once swollen with the appearance of pregnancy, was flat. She enlisted Trudy and Ruth Ann to hold Alma Lee's thighs apart for the internal examine and was pleased to see there was no infection or abnormal swelling within. "I'd like to see if she's running any sort of a fever, but I fear she's incapable of holding the thermometer beneath her tongue."

"I reckon yer right, Nurse Holmes," Trudy agreed. "And should she bite down on it, she'd get glass in her mouth. We sure don't need her doin' that."

"No, we sure don't." Cassia sighed. "It looks like I'll need you two to help me roll her onto her side, so I can take her temperature the alternative way."

It was at that point Alma Lee began to sob. Trudy reached over and caressed her oldest daughter's face. "Ain't no cause for them tears, my sweet girl. Only folks here are one's tryin' to help ya get well again."

"I can't blame her," Ruth Ann chimed in. "I'd cry too if everyone was lookin' at me, lying naked as a jay bird, and gettin' a *thee-mom-mee-ter* shoved up my…"

"Hush now, child," Trudy interrupted. "Ain't no cause for ya to be speakin' disrespectfully."

"No fever," she reported after reading the thermometer. "Has there been further vomiting or diarrhea?"

"No, Alma Lee's stomach seems to be settled now," Trudy said.

Cassia smiled and happily pronounced. "I believe physically Alma Lee's on the mend."

"Too bad her head ain't matchin' her body." Ruth Ann looked down at her older sister with pitiful eyes. "Where do ya think her thoughts are at, anyway...with her husband, maybe? Or could she be thinkin' she's off somewhere takin' care of her baby?"

Cassia sighed. "It's hard to tell, as the brain is such a complicated part of the body, and many times it takes longer to heal when we've experienced so much hurt. I've cared for soldiers wounded in battle, and lots of them have a hard time forgetting all the horrors of war they experienced. They call what they have, *shell 'shock.*"

"Do ya think Alma Lee has this *shell shock*?" Trudy inquired.

"Well, a form of it—yes," she admitted. "Her brain is having a hard time processing the grief of all she's lost. It's just easier to retreat into a safe and private cocoon, block out the outside world, where she's made to face and deal with reality and the sorrow, and instead dwell in a much happier world."

For a few moments stillness enveloped the room while her words sank in.

Clearing her throat, Cassia broke the silence. "But I do know, I always feel better mentally when I'm washed and smell clean." She directed her next words to Ruth Ann. "So, if you don't mind fetching a basin of warm water, a bar of soap, clean towels, and a few washcloths, I'd like to bathe Alma Lee."

"I'll get right on that for ya, Nurse Holmes." Ruth Ann stood and made her way out of the room.

Trudy, placing a hand on Cassia's arm, whispered,

"Do ya think my girl will ever come back to us?"

She placed her hand over Trudy's. "I do, Trudy. I believe there's always hope she'll come through all of this, but it will take time. And I plan on being here to help her through the recovery." She reached for her bag and pulled out a rubber sheet. "It will be easier on all of our knees and backs if Alma Lee is bathed upon the bed. This rubber sheet will protect the mattress." Then an idea came to her. "In fact, I've three of them in my satchel, and I will leave them all for your use. If you line the bed each night with one, Alma Lee will sleep more comfortably. And it's a proven fact, when rested we think and act clearly."

"I thank ya so very much, Nurse Holmes." Trudy helped her get the rubber sheet in place on the bed.

When Ruth Ann returned to the room, the three of them helped Alma Lee over to the bed and washed her. Cassia could feel the tension in her patient's body fade as lotion was massaged on her back and buttocks, down her legs to the thighs, calves, and ankles. She then spotted a birthmark in the shape of the number eight just above Alma Lee's left ankle bone. "My siblings all have birthmarks. They inherited theirs from their Apache father."

Trudy chuckled lightly. "Same goes for my youngin's. They got their birthmarks from my ma's side of the family. I've one on my lower back, John Tyler has one on his forearm, and Ruth Ann has one on her belly."

As Trudy and Ruth Ann were securing Alma Lee's towel undies, Cassia had another idea. "Ruth Ann, do you think it would be possible for you to make several pairs of panties from one of the rubber sheets I'm leaving here?"

"I could try," Ruth Ann said. Then frowning she added, "But they'd be awful uncomfortable to wear."

"I was thinking they could be pulled up over the towel coverings, to keep leakage from soaking whatever Alma Lee wears or wherever she sits. In this way she won't have to always stay up here in this tiny room, dressed only in a shortened nightie, but instead clothed as usual and able to come downstairs with the rest of the family. If she's going to regain her senses, she needs to have her mind stimulated, seeing and hearing all of you talking and interacting with each other will encourage her to communicate again."

Both Trudy and Ruth Ann smiled, their faces filled with new hope. "I can get on that after dinner." Ruth Ann reached for one of the rubber sheets and hugged it to her chest. "I sewed all the towel undies in two days, probably won't take me much longer to make the rubber panties."

"I'd like to fix Alma Lee's hair," she offered next, nearing the rocking chair and pulling it to the center of the room. Taking the other rubber sheet, she folded it thrice and placed it upon the rocker's seat. Then she helped Alma Lee over to the chair and sat her down. As she placed a towel around Alma Lee's shoulders, Trudy went to fetch her sewing shears. And in no time Alma Lee looked as fashionable as the girls in a magazine. Her golden curls were shaped into a short bob that framed her face.

"Why, she could be yer kin, Nurse Holmes," Ruth Ann commented. "The both of ya have the same color eyes and hair. And now ya both are wearin' the same style."

Cassia giggled. "Yes, we could almost be sisters."

"If ya cut my hair too, we'd all be like sisters," Ruth Ann pointed out.

Trudy arched a brow. "If ya take my scissors to yer hair, I'll be takin' the wooden spoon to yer bottom...reddenin' it so's ya won't be able to sit properly for a week." Moving closer to her younger daughter, Trudy added, "Do ya hear me, child?"

Ruth Ann scowled. "I hear ya, Mama."

Cassia couldn't help but pity Ruth Ann. She tried so hard and yet continued to come up against so many obstacles along the way. "Ruth Ann, while I was in England I admired and became dear friends with my Aunt Marrietta's cook, Inez. She is a wonderful woman from Algeria who made the most delicious meat pies. For thousands of years, Inez's people wore their hair plaited into a most unusual looking weave, whereby three strands are gathered and intermingled with other side sections of hair as the braid continues. Before I decided to cut my own hair, Inez taught me how to become accomplished in doing this fancy braid. Would you like, after I'm finished tending to your sister, for me to fix your hair in such a fashion?"

The younger girl's face brightened. "I'd be much obliged, Nurse Holmes."

It was then that Alma Lee, her arms crossed over her breasts, began rocking in the chair.

"She looks like she's rockin' a baby," Ruth Ann commented.

"I bet that's just what she's thinkin' she's doin'." Trudy sighed. "My poor girl, both of her arms and heart are empty."

"Maybe they don't have to be—at least for a

while—until Alma Lee regains her senses," she said.

Ruth Ann frowned. "But none of us here has a baby to give her."

"Where's that teddy bear I saw the last time I was in this room?"

Trudy bent and pulled a small wooden storage chest from beneath the bed. "I packed all the baby things Alma Lee collected in here and took the cradle to the barn. I figured it might help her to get past her grief faster with everythin' out of sight. My husband, Howard made the cradle after he found out I was carryin' Alma Lee. Then we used it for John Tyler and Ruth Ann when they were born. It seemed only right for my grandbaby to sleep in it as well." She wiped a tear from her eye and opened the chest's lid. "Here's the teddy bear. I wrapped it in this yellow blanket Alma Lee knitted."

"Perfect." She took the white stuffed bear and placed it into Alma Lee's arms.

To everyone's pleasant surprise, Alma Lee broke from her starring-state and looked down at the blanket wrapped bear. Then she smiled.

"Well, I'll be," Trudy said, her own lips spreading into a smile.

"She looks right happy and content rockin' that bear," Ruth Ann marveled.

"And I believe that happiness and contentment can play a part in Alma Lee's healing," she admitted.

As she turned to sit on the edge of the bed, Cassia's foot hit a pan. It must have been pushed out from beneath the bed when Trudy pulled out the wooden chest. When she reached down to push it aside, she recognized it as a chamber pot. Folks in homes without indoor toilets keep a chamber pot beneath the bed for those middle-of-the-night emergencies. Sometimes it's just too cold or dark to trudge all the way to the outhouse to do your business. Looking at the pot gave her an idea. "Trudy, when your children were small, did you have a certain plan or schedule that you used for potty-training?"

Trudy sat beside her on the edge of the bed, the two of them watching Alma Lee rock the teddy bear in her arms. Finally Trudy said, "I reckon I did, since I knew their habits well enough." She scratched her head as she recalled those days. "Alma Lee always did her messy business in the afternoon, so I put her on the pot right after lunch and kept her there a spell by givin' her picture books to look at." She chuckled lightly. "In no time she was leaving me a surprise in the pot. John Tyler was harder to keep still, and Ruth Ann was my easiest. I had her out of diapers at only two years old. I guess seein' the others makin' their way to the outhouse helped her in learnin'."

Cassia reached for the pot and analyzed its size and shape.

"That pot ain't getting' any use now," Ruth Ann said sadly, joining them on the bed.

"Trudy, do you think you can retrain Alma Lee to use the chamber pot by using your old system?"

Trudy frowned. "Ain't no way Alma Lee, in her present state of mind, is gonna be able to squat properly over that pot."

"What if she could sit again on a potty-chair?" she said.

"And where we gonna get a potty-chair for a grown-up?" Ruth Ann chimed in.

"Do you have an old wooden chair somewhere that you're not using?" Cassia inquired.

Trudy's frown deepened. "I reckon there's one or two in the barn."

Cassia stood with the pot in hand and made her way out onto the landing. "John Tyler," she called out. When he appeared at the foot of the staircase, she held up the chamber pot. "Your mother said there's an old wooden chair in the barn."

He gazed at the pot in her hand and frowned. "I reckon there's a few, some with arms and some without. But why would…?"

"Can you find one with arms," she interrupted, "and cut a hole in the seat, exactly as big around as the opening of this pot?"

He made his way half-way up the stairs. "I reckon that wouldn't be hard to do, but why?"

"I've found a way for you to help Alma Lee," she said smiling. "You're going to make her a private toilet for her bedroom."

Chapter Twenty

John Tyler cut a perfect hole in the seat of an old wooden arm chair, then sanded and smoothed the edges so splinters of any sort wouldn't be a problem.

"You did a perfect job," she praised him, "and this will be essential in helping Alma Lee regain her dignity and her life back."

The young man beamed as the three of them sat down to a lunch of homemade stew and bread. They talked a bit about Howard Boyd, the good and kind man that he was and the years he worked as a logger.

"In fact, it was how Alma Lee met her husband," Trudy said. "One Christmas, Howard brought Vincent home, 'cause he had no family, and my husband could never stand a person bein' alone on Christmas. They hit it off right from the start. Of course," she added, "Vincent was ten years older than my girl and had already been widowed five years at that time. Seems his wife died in childbirth."

"Poor guy," John Tyler chimed in. "Just wasn't his fate to ever have a child to carry on his name."

"Ain't it the truth," Trudy agreed.

"And so they married, and Alma Lee went to live up north to be with her husband?" Cassia inquired.

"Yup, that's how it went, 'til Howard got sick with the cancer," Trudy said. "Alma Lee came home for a spell to help care for her Pa. Stayed a bit after he passed, but then Vincent came for her…missed his wife, I reckon. It was time for her to be with her husband anyway, since all she did was sulk for him. So the two of them left, returned up north, but not more than a year later, Vincent died in a loggin' accident. That's when Alma Lee came home to Eagle's Landing for good. It was about a month later that she found out she was expectin' a baby or believed she was havin' a baby," Trudy corrected. "And now she don't know nothin' herself."

"She will again, Trudy," Cassia encouraged. "It will just take time before Alma Lee's fully healed."

After they had finished eating, Trudy prepared a bowl of mashed potatoes and carrots covered with gravy for Alma Lee. Before making her way upstairs she said, "I'm gonna sit Alma Lee on the pot after I feed her, so I'll be in her room a spell. In case ya leave before I'm through, I want to take this time to thank ya kindly for all ya done for my girl. By the grace of God ya stepped in to answer my prayers."

The extension of grace, like Papa said.

Ruth Ann grabbed her by the hand. "Come, braid my hair." She led her to the back of the home where two rooms were housed.

"That room there," Ruth Ann began, pointing to her left, "is where my brother sleeps. Ma keeps the door shut most times 'cause John Tyler's messy." She curled her nose. "And his room stinks too."

Cassia bit back a smile, as there was no doubt in her mind, having a room directly across from Ruth Ann, was the reason John Tyler knew she sucked her thumb and feared sleeping in the dark.

"And this room is mine," the younger girl

concluded, leading Cassia to the right of the small hallway.

Upon entering the small chamber, Cassia found it to be cozy, furnished with a small wrought iron bed covered with a pink and white checked quilt, a night table, a small bureau, and a dressing table with a mirror atop. After gathering a comb and rubber bands from a wooden box kept on the bureau, Ruth Ann pulled out a chair from the dressing table and sat.

"This here dressin' table was my ma's, and before her it was my grandmama's. But since it was too hard to get up those narrow stairs to Ma's room, it became mine," Ruth Ann boasted.

Cassia admired the mahogany wood vanity, framed by gold, ornate trim, and glass-ball drawer handles. "It is a lovely piece of furniture."

Ruth Ann sat quietly, engrossed as she watched Cassia plait her hair. At each step of the way, she explained just where, when, and how much hair to add so Ruth Ann could accomplish styling the braid herself.

"I want to do what ya do," Ruth Ann finally said.

"Well, if you pay attention to the way I form the weave, you will," she said.

"No, I mean, the way ya help folks, 'specially women," Ruth Ann said, her eyes meeting Cassia's through the mirror. "I watched the way ya washed Alma Lee, tended to her needs, so gentle and kind. I want to do that for others too."

"Well, it would mean you have to stay attending your classes at school, study hard, and get good grades so you can go on to further your education in the medical field."

Ruth Ann turned to face her. "Soon school will be

over for the summer, and I was wonderin' if I could be yer assistant."

The younger girl's request totally took her by surprise. For a moment Cassia hesitated to agree, but she thought back to when she wasn't much older than Ruth Ann and how Doctor Sean let her go with him on house calls when a child broke an arm or a baby was sick. His tutoring and guidance aided her when she finally made it to college. If Ruth Ann was serious about answering the call to work in the medical field, it was only fair and right for her to lend a constructive hand, as she had been given.

"Ruth Ann, I'd love for you to be my assistant."

Ruth Ann's face brightened. "Are ya speakin' the truth, Nurse Holmes?"

"I am at that, and I know just the place where you can begin, after school is out, that is," she added quickly.

"Please, tell me where I could start," Ruth Ann pleaded.

"At the clinic," she said. "I work there at least twice a week, and having another pair of hands to help with dressing wounds, taking temperatures, or recording patient information would be greatly appreciated."

The younger girl stood, wrapping her arms around Cassia's neck. "Oh, thank ya, thank ya, Nurse Holmes. And never fear, 'cause I plan on makin' ya right proud of me."

Gently she returned Ruth Ann's embrace. "I have no fears whatsoever that you'll do just fine."

On the way home, Cassia did a bit of mental planning. She figured she could make it to the Boyd homestead each day by six in the morning to feed and bathe Alma Lee, so Trudy could spend the morning making sure John Tyler and Ruth Ann get off to school properly. She would still have plenty of time to make it back home before Brodie picked her up at eight-thirty for either house calls or clinic duties.

And the days she was on her own, she'd make sure nothing was scheduled, outside of having to go on emergency calls, before nine-thirty. No doubt, with such a pending schedule, she'd be exhausted and too tired to spend time with friends or family, but it was the only way to help the Boyds and Alma Lee get back to normal.

Preoccupied with her thoughts, she didn't notice the wagon following her bicycle, until she heard a male voice call out, "Care for a ride, lady?"

Coming to a stop, she turned to find Tucker, his freckled face grinning from ear to ear, seated in a wagon about three feet behind her.

"Sorry if I startled you," he said with a chuckle. "I was returning from an errand and decided to take a short cut home, when I saw you peddling away." He brought the wagon to a halt beside her. "No sense riding all the way home on that," he said, indicating the bicycle, "when I'm going right past your house." He climbed down from the wagon and reached for the bicycle. "I'll just put this in the back of the wagon while you hop up on the seat."

As he handed her the medical bag, she found herself growing annoyed with his assumption she would automatically do whatever he said. If it weren't for the fact the day, so far, had been a bit tiring and a glance at the sky showed the possibility of a shower, she would have protested. Biting her tongue, she nodded, placed the bag on the floor at the front of the wagon, and climbed into the seat. In no time he was beside her, navigating the way to her house.

"Were you coming from the Boyds' house?"

"Yes, on a follow-up call," she said, smoothening her skirt over her knees.

"I heard Alma Lee miscarried," he went on.

"Yes," she lied, quickly realizing that was the word going around about Alma Lee's situation, and all the better for it. It wasn't anyone's business what really happened. Outside of Brodie and her parents, who wouldn't gossip if their lives counted on it, Alma Lee's false pregnancy would stay a secret between her family and her medical team. And if it weren't for the fact Brodie had to know about Alma Lee's mental state, she would have liked to keep that a secret as well.

Tucker shook his head. "Such a shame. That family has endured such sorrow."

"Yes, they have." She glanced ahead at the road.

He slowed the wagon and reached over to place his hand upon her arm. "Is there something wrong, Cassia?"

She met his gaze and forced a smile. "All is fine," she lied. Then sighing heavily, she added. "Just worn out, I'd say. It's been a busy week."

"And here you are, working on a Saturday," he concluded sympathetically.

"Yes…well, responsibilities must be met in my line of work. I knew that when I began."

"What if you didn't have to do this line of work?" He started the wagon moving faster again.

She frowned. "I do what I do because I like it."

"What if there was something else? Another way for you to work in the medical field?"

Her frown deepened. "You mean regular shifts, as one would work in a hospital?"

"Yes, exactly. A set number of hours, whereby you could set your free time…life with a family, as a priority."

"The only hospital around here is in Willow Creek which is too far away for daily travel." She arched a brow. "And I certainly don't want to live there."

He pulled the wagon off the road and turned to face her. "Would you like to live in San Antonio, Texas?"

Again she frowned. "Why on earth would I…?"

"Because that's where I'm headed in a few days," he interrupted. "And I'd like you to come with me."

She gasped. "What are you saying, Tucker?"

He neared her, taking her face into his large hands. His flesh felt rough against hers, calloused from his work. Yet they held her gently. "I made a big mistake leaving you behind. Now, with this second chance, I want to make things right again between us."

"Tucker, I just can't…"

This time the interruption of her words was smothered by his kiss. His warm, full lips sought her mouth with hunger. The lips she tasted in her dreams—wished for—yearned for the last five years, now caressed her lips with unbridled passion. This moment had woven over and over in her mind dozens of times. She waited for her heart to race, to dance, to leap with joy, but it didn't. She thought her arms would embrace him, pull him close, but they didn't. In fact, while Tucker kissed her, all she could think of was Brodie and how his mouth on hers stirred every fiber of her being.

Pulling back, she covered her mouth with her hand.

Tucker, stunned, searched her face. "What is it, Cassia?"

"We agreed to be friends, but…" she began.

He interjected with a raised brow. "But neither of us disagreed it couldn't be more."

"I know now, after…after…" She swallowed hard. "I know now," she began again. "We can only be friends. I'm sorry," she added. "I don't anymore… I can't… I'm not able to feel more toward you."

His face fell with disappointment, his large green eyes filled with confusion—then hurt. "Why…what has changed your mind?"

"Brodie," she whispered.

Chapter Twenty-One

Brodie watched his father, sitting ramrod straight in his seat, trying desperately to control the emotions running chaotically through him. His mother, biting her bottom lip, held back tears of frustration and embarrassment threatening her resolve. He sat at the kitchen table with them, a mixture of disappointment and disgust rising to choke him, as he tried to calmly process the situation. Sadly enough, he wasn't shocked or even surprised with what he was hearing from the man sitting across from him.

Clayton Matthews, gray-haired, short and stocky, sat beside his young daughter. Nervously he twirled the handlebar mustache covering his upper lip. Except for Jessica Matthews' soft weeping, the stillness enveloping the room was deafening. The young woman's large amber eyes were red-rimmed, as was the dainty nose she continually dabbed with a handkerchief. Chocolate wisps of hair fell from her chignon, framing a pleasant face. And beneath her plain, modestly cut green dress, her stomach swelled with child…Tucker's child. The Matthews had traveled all the way from San Francisco, California, to find Tucker and hold him accountable for his actions.

"Could I be pourin' ye another cup of tea, Jessica," his mother offered. Jessica declined with a shake of her head. "Perhaps then, ye would like to lie down a wee bit."

"I'm fine, thank you, Mrs. O'Clarity," the young woman's soft voice claimed.

"I only sent me son on a few errands," his father explained—again. "He should be back soon."

Mr. Matthews nodded, squaring his shoulders with determination. "We'll wait."

He couldn't blame the elderly man for his tenacity. If Jessica were his daughter, he'd go after the man who defiled her as well. With that thought in mind, he stood, going to the window. From this perspective he could see when Tucker rode onto the property. No doubt he'd head right for the barn, where he'd unhitch the horse from the wagon and settle him for the night.

Turning to face their guests, he forced a smile. "If you'll excuse me, I've some work to do in the barn."

Mr. Matthews politely inclined his head. "Please don't let us keep you from anything you need to do."

Making his way to the back door, he reached for his cap hanging on a peg and headed toward the outbuilding. Once inside, he sat upon a bale of hay to think. Jessica Matthews was a child herself...not more than seventeen or eighteen, like Alma Lee Sloane. "Children having children," he whispered. But that was the way of it. As soon as a girl hit puberty, she was conditioned to marry and birth babies. Except for the fact Jessica Matthews didn't have the sanctity of a marriage license. His brother's inconsideration and indiscretion had sullied her reputation.

He stood, removing his cap and running a hand through his hair. Placing the cap on the hay bale, he paced. "What in God's name is wrong with you, Tucker?"

Both had been brought up in the same household, by the same parents. How was Tucker so irresponsible and selfish when he was the complete opposite? The sound of an approaching wagon froze him in his tracks, and he debated his next move. Should he warn his brother of what waited him in the kitchen, or let him walk unprepared into the lion's den?

As soon as the wagon pulled into the barn, Tucker flew off the seat. "Damn you to hell, Brodie." Tucker reached Brodie in two long strides and punched him in the jaw.

Caught off guard, Brodie stumbled back, crashing into several buckets lined against one side of the stall. He stopped himself only seconds before he hit the dirt floor. "What in God's name's gotten into you?" He rubbed the side of his face.

"All this talk about not hurting Cassia, caring about her, looking out for her, was all because you wanted her for yourself," Tucker argued, shaking stinging knuckles from throwing such a blow. "When I tried to kiss her just now, she…"

Brodie's face heated; he saw red. "You tried to kiss her?" In one fluid motion, he was upon his brother, taking him by the collar and jamming him up against the wall. "You listen to me, you selfish ingrate, you have no right whatsoever to touch Cassia Holmes."

Tucker gripped Brodie's wrists to push him aside. "I have just as much right as you do."

"Wrong, little brother." He tightened his hold. "I didn't get Jessica Matthews pregnant. I would say that fact alone disqualifies you from making a commitment to Cassia, or any other woman for that matter."

Tucker's expression turned from angry to anxious.

"How do you know about Jessica?"

"She and her father have paid our parents a little visit." He released Tucker's collar and stepped away. "Their conversing over tea right now. Well, truthfully, all Jessica's managing to do is cry."

Tucker's voice shook "They're here—now—all the way from California?"

He nodded, rubbing again his sore jaw. "They've been waiting for you all afternoon."

"Holy crap," Tucker spat. "Damn, damn, damn." He turned to pace the barn. "I don't even want to imagine what Ma and Pa are thinking."

"Short of wanting to strip you naked, chain you to a wall, and beat the tar out of you, you mean?" He crossed his arms over his chest.

"Damn, damn, damn," Tucker ranted again, picking up the pace. "What am I going to do, Brodie?"

"You're going to face the situation like a man and make an honest woman out of that girl."

Tucker stopped dead in his tracks. "That's your solution…to marry a woman I don't love?"

He arched a brow, suddenly picturing himself giving Tucker a well needed thrashing and fully enjoying it. "And what's your plan? To run away?"

Tucker nervously combed his fingers through his hair. "Well, it beats marrying someone I don't love."

"Listen to me, Tucker," he grounded out through clenched teeth. "That poor girl sitting in the kitchen right now is due in about two months to have a baby…your baby. How could you walk away from that—abandon them?"

"You don't understand, Brodie," Tucker whined. "I didn't mean for all this to happen."

Brodie's fist's clenched. "What the hell did you think was going to happen if you bedded her?"

"I don't know... I reckon I didn't think..." he stammered. "I just thought it would be like the other times."

His nails dug into the palms of his hands. "You are a stinking louse. How could you be so rude, so disrespectful to other people's feelings?"

Tucker squared his shoulders. "I didn't do anything against anyone's will."

"Did you ever stop to think consent was due to the fact your conquests actually fell in love with you?"

"I promised them nothing," Tucker quipped.

Brodie arched a brow. "And you believe that stops a woman's heart from wanting...hoping for more?" He shook his head in disgust. "You're an ass, Tucker—a full-blown, thoughtless ass." He grabbed his brother by the arm. "And that sort of behavior ceases right now...with this girl and your baby."

Tucker protested and tried to pull his arm free. "Brodie, let go of me. I don't want..."

"This is no longer about what you want." He tightened his grip. "It stopped being about your needs and wants when you compromised Jessica's life—soiled her virtue and reputation. Now, for the first time in your life, you're going to do what's right. You're going to marry that girl, raise your child, and stop humiliating our parents, because none of these people deserve what you've inflicted upon them."

"All right, all right." Tucker freed himself from Brodie's grasp and raised his hands in a surrendering gesture. "But I walk into the house on my own like a man ready to stand up to his duty. Not dragged in by my older brother, like a bad child."

"Well, Tucker, isn't that what you are?" he snapped. "I mean, not more than ten minutes ago you were ready to flee to the hills."

Tucker cleared his throat nervously. "Well, I'm not now, am I?"

He chuckled sardonically. "And that's only because I won't allow it."

Straightening his collar, Tucker pouted. "You're really going to make me do this?"

"You did this to yourself." He reached for his cap and placed it upon his head. "Now, get your ass moving, little brother." He pointed to the doorway. "Yonder your bride awaits you, and it's not wise to keep a very pregnant woman and her irate father waiting."

Chapter Twenty-Two

Cassia had heard of shotgun weddings but only thought of them happening someplace far off, like in the mountains between feuding clans. She could picture the father of a disrespected young girl, holding a shotgun on her lover while vows were exchanged, forcing him to make an honest woman of her. Never did she think she'd be witness to such a situation in her parlor. But within the hour, she'd be standing up, along with Brodie, as a witness to Tucker O'Clarity and Jessica Matthews' nuptials, and her father would be the officiating clergy.

As she donned a light blue dress, her thoughts turned to earlier when Tucker asked her to leave with him, travel to Texas, before he kissed her. Now, his request and the kiss infuriated her. How could he, in good conscience, make such an intimate move toward her or ask her to go with him when he'd gotten another woman pregnant? How could he believe she'd agree to be just one more woman for him to use? And used she'd certainly be, for the request wasn't a proposal of marriage.

Sitting at the dressing table to fix her hair, she searched her reflection in the large, round mirror. Truth be told, had Tucker offered her the same invitation eight years ago, she'd have complied. At fifteen that's how enamored, how naïve and enchanted she was by him. She would have joined him anywhere, despite her age or her parents' protest…at any cost…even given up her goals, just to be by his side. And no doubt, she'd now be the one in Jessica Matthews' shoes. That thought caused chills to spiral down her spine.

"Oh, Jessica, you poor girl," she whispered.

Cassia's pity for Jessica Matthews grew stronger the very moment she set eyes upon the young, meek, woman who appeared to be in her seventh month of pregnancy. Jessica's soft, delicately sculptured face reflected a mixture of fright, shame, and misery. How humiliating to make a man marry you and for all to know you'd given your virtue to someone who took it disrespectfully and only for his own fleeting gratification. There was no sanctity, honor, beauty, or love in the marriage ceremony soon to take place or in the vows that would be recited.

When Jessica and Tucker looked back upon this day, it wouldn't be fondly with sighs of happy nostalgia. In truth, it was a sentence, something that would be a consequence lived out…caused by a night of passion. The horror of it already mirrored in Tucker's eyes. And if Jessica did hold love deep within her heart for him, as Cassia suspected, then she would forever be hoping and praying Tucker would one day feel the same about her.

Lord, move Tucker's heart to one day love this woman and his child, she silently prayed. It was a brief but cold glare Jessica cast her, leaving Cassia uncomfortable as she took her place beside her. It also left her to wonder if Jessica's instant resentment toward her was a product of Tucker divulging the history they had together. Dwelling on that prospect was soon put aside as her father began the ceremony.

The mediocre-sized living room was filled to its capacity as the O'Clarity family, Doctor Sean and Sadie, Tucker and Brodie; and their two sisters, Shailyn and Betsy who made the trek from Willow Creek within the hour while riding in her husband's police vehicle; and the rest of their family surrounded the newlywed couple. Of course, Mr. Matthews gave his daughter's hand in marriage and the traditional vows were said.

Amanda Holmes, always prepared, made ready a small bouquet of wild flowers and roses, cut from her garden and bound with white ribbon for Jessica to hold. Mr. Matthews supplied the rings, once worn by his grandparents, his large, weather-beaten hands shaking as he handed them over. After the ceremony everyone gathered in the dinette area to toast the newlyweds with wine. Cassia helped her mother and Sadie O'Clarity serve the fruit salad, custard pie, and tea thrown together quickly for the small reception. Shailyn brought a cake, and Betsy brought cucumber and roasted pepper finger sandwiches.

Periodically Cassia caught Tucker glancing with shame and regret in her direction. Twice he attempted to take her aside to talk, but she kept on the move by spending more time in the kitchen and cleaning up after the guests. Every time Tucker tried to get her attention, Jessica's eyes bore into her. The last thing she wanted was to make this day any harder for Tucker's new wife. She summed up, from her medical experience; Jessica had to be tired from traveling and emotionally drained. Cassia did not need to add jealousy to the younger woman's list.

Brodie stood beside her now, his hands full of wine glasses. "Thought you could use some help." He placed the goblets on the counter.

"Or were you also needing an excuse to put a bit of distance between yourself and everyone else?"

He inhaled sharply. "Am I that obvious?"

"Only because I'm feeling the same," she admitted. "Jessica's dagger-like glances are starting to give me flesh wounds."

He leaned against the counter, folding his muscular arms across his chest. "Not to mention being able to slice the tension. It is so thick it's smothering."

Before she could respond Amanda entered the room. "Mr. Matthews has an announcement to make, so leave the rest of the dishes for later and join us in the parlor."

Now she was the one to take a deep breath. "I've a feeling the tension in the air is just about to get thicker." She made her way to stand in the far corner of the parlor. Brodie followed and stood beside her.

Clayton Matthews, round and stocky, stood and looked around the room. His features were more relaxed; no doubt a great weight had been lifted from his conscience now that his daughter had been made an honorable woman. His gaze rested longer on Tucker. Under the older man's scrutiny, Tucker squirmed a bit in his seat.

"First, I'd like to thank the O'Clarity and Holmes family for opening their hearts, homes, and on such quick notice, supplying all this food to make this wedding day for my daughter and her husband a hospitable occasion," Mr. Matthews began.

Brodie whispered in her ear. "We weren't given

much of a choice."

Stifling a smile, Cassia whispered, "Hush."

"I only wish my dear wife, Gloria, were still around to also share this day." With that said, Mr. Matthews paused to clear the emotion from his throat. "I know Gloria would want me to extend something to the newlyweds as well," he continued. "And so, it is with great pleasure that I bestow upon my new son-in-law partnership in the small cattle ranch I own in San Francisco."

"Saints preserve us," Brodie whispered.

Tucker raised a defiant chin. "I already have a position with the railroad."

Mr. Matthews forced a smile. "And I'm sure you're excellent at your job. However, such a position has a way of taking a man away from his family too much and for too long." He glanced lovingly over at his daughter. "And there's no reason to leave my daughter's side if there's a way to make a good living close by." He leveled his gaze once more on Tucker. "As modest as it is compared to other establishments, my ranch is quite lucrative and has made a comfortable existence for me and my family all these years. I know it will do the same for you and my daughter."

"But I like working for the railroad," Tucker protested.

Mr. Matthews' smile froze upon his face. "And now you will learn to like something new, as well as having a chance to be near your wife and soon to be born child."

Tucker swallowed hard, his face turning red, yet he said not a word.

"Poor Tucker. He looks like he's ready to

explode," she whispered.

"I think he's getting what he deserves," Brodie responded quietly.

"Does your unsympathetic conclusion have anything to do with that bruise forming on your jaw?"

"Yup...and a whole lot more," he quipped.

Did Tucker tell him about the kiss? If so, that would justify Brodie's attitude toward his brother. And how did he feel toward her? Nervously, she bit her bottom lip and turned to look his way. "I think, after everyone leaves, we need to talk."

He caught her gaze and nodded. "I think you're right."

"Now, I believe it grows late, and we should be on our way," Mr. Matthews stated.

"I would be offerin' me home for the night, as it would be better for Jessica, in her condition, not to be so long on the road after an already exhaustin' day," Sean said.

Mr. Matthews inclined his head politely. "And although I am much obliged, Doctor O'Clarity, I will have to decline. I have rented two hotel rooms in Willow Creek that will be quite comfortable. Also, with the vehicle I've borrowed, it should only take about thirty minutes to reach our destination. In that way, come the morning we will grab a bit of breakfast and be able to board the first train heading for Phoenix where my sister lives. She owns a large estate there and has been generous enough to let us stay with her until after the baby is born, and it is safe enough for mother and child to travel to San Francisco."

Tucker sighed heavily, his resolve resigned, and stood. "Then I'd better go and gather my things."

"I will drive you to your parents' home," Mr. Matthews offered, making his way to Jessica and helping her to stand. "And we can be on our way to Willow Creek from there."

"Holy Mother of God," Brodie muttered.

She arched a brow. "Yup."

Chapter Twenty-Three

Brodie found Cassia in her mother's garden. She stood against the trunk of an old oak tree, hands behind her back, face raised to the glow of a twilight sky. As he neared where she stood, his senses filled with the heavenly floral aroma of the wild flowers, roses, hibiscus, oleander, and red yuccas he passed. The heady arrangement fit the scene before him—the one of a precious and beautiful woman enjoying a moment of a quiet, spring dusk.

He narrowed the space between them, and she leveled her blue eyes to meet his gaze. Gently she reached up to caress the bruise on his jaw. "Did you and Tucker fight because of me?"

He nodded. "He thought I poisoned you against him and came after me. Then when I learned he kissed you, I went after him."

She sighed. "Please believe me when I say his advances were totally unexpected and definitely not returned."

"I believe you." He turned his face to nuzzle in the palm of her hand. "But no man touches my woman."

She arched a brow. "I'm your woman?"

He nodded again. "But only if you want to be."

"I do, very much so," she whispered.

It was at this point he pulled her close and embraced her. She fit perfectly along the length of his body. Wrapping her arms around his neck, she closed what little gap there was between them. And as her firm, full breasts pressed against his chest, he could feel her racing heart keeping time with his. His body heated with desire as he lowered his mouth to cover hers.

Her immediate and passionate reaction drove him wild, and his senses spun. His pulse skittered alarmingly as he deepened the kiss. The air surrounding them became electrified. Slowly he dropped his hands from where they rested on the small of her back to the round of her backside. When she sighed, his male member swelled.

"You are most bold, Dr. O'Clarity," she whispered against his mouth.

"Forgive me for taking such liberties, as I didn't mean to offend you." He moved his hands to rest again at her waist. Reluctantly he stepped back, allowing a bit of space between them, least she feel him also growing moist.

She buried her face against his throat. "You don't offend me, Brodie. Besides, working in the medical field, I am quite educated as to how the male body works," she teased. Then sighing again, she added on a more serious note, "Anyway, I know you would never do anything to hurt me."

"Or to ever tarnish your trust," he said. "I hold immense respect and admiration for you, Cassia. That's exactly why I've spoken to your father before I came out here to speak to you."

She looked up at him with a frown. "My father? What does he have to do with anything?"

"I asked for his blessing," he said.

With lips still warm and moist from their union,

she kissed his chin…as tender and light as the spring breeze now rustling the tree tops. "And what did you need his blessing for?" Like the welding temperature that joins metal, his body heated with a fiery desire. Before answering her, he took her mouth hungrily.

She quivered and met his kiss with savage harmony.

"Saints preserve us, woman, you melt me," he whispered against her mouth, yearning now to taste her fully, every part of her beautiful body. Yet, he would not defile her, shame her as his brother had done to Jessica. Cassia deserved more; she deserved better. And with his body aching for the love of this woman, and his heart completely captured, he decided his next move. He brought his lips to kiss each of the lids that covered her marble-blue eyes and the tip of her perfectly shaped nose. "I asked your father's blessing to wed you."

"And did he give it?"

"Yes," he said, inhaling sharply. "Now, I will ask you." Getting down on one knee he took her hand. "Cassia Rose Holmes, I love you with every breath in my body. Will you marry me?"

"I love you too, Brodie," she breathlessly whispered. "And yes. I will marry you." Then she added, "When?"

He stood, pulling her closer. "Soon, my love…very, very soon."

He drove the horse and wagon to his house alone that night. Shailyn and her family had taken his parents' home after Tucker, his wife, and overbearing father-in-law left for Willow Creek. His mother worried that her husband had taxed himself overly much with all that had transpired throughout the day and was anxious for him to be home resting, preferably in bed. He worried as well, knowing his father would have never complained or let on to anyone if he felt ill or was tired. It was proven that doctors made horrible patients. But it was also a fact his father was still recuperating from a massive heart attack and needed to be cautious. With Sadie by Sean's side, Brodie wasn't too concerned for his father's complete recovery. His mother was like a watch dog and would make sure protocol, and then some, was followed.

He appreciated the solo drive as it gave him time to rehash the passionate encounter he'd had with Cassia. Just holding her body close to his, feeling her heartbeat and pulse of life, brought thrilling sensations throughout his entire being. The anticipation for a life time of such glory filled him with an excitement he could barely contain. The solitude of the ride home helped to calm him, as his body once more swelled with the thought of her. Inhaling sharply, he shifted his thoughts to the conversation ahead, readying himself to face his parents with the news they'd soon be attending another son's nuptials but this time for all the right reasons…love.

He lifted his gaze to the sky, allowing the night breeze to cool his face. Who would have thought through the tragedy of his father's illness and the hurt of Dorothea Malone's rejection, he would find himself in such a joyous place? His heart was content, his mind hopeful, and his spirit soared as he thought of the days, months, and years ahead with Cassia as his wife. She was a woman a man could be proud of, completing his very existence in an imaginable way.

To his surprise he found both his parents up, sitting at the kitchen table sipping tea. He made his way closer to the table. "I see sleep escapes you both."

"That's the truth of it," his father agreed.

He took a seat beside his mother, affectionately pulling her into a brief hug. "I would say it's been quite a day."

"Aye, that it has," his mother reflected. She frowned as she glanced at the bruise upon his jaw. Brodie waited for her response, but to his surprise she made no comment. Instead, she sighed and confided her thoughts on another matter. "Though me heart is at peace for the fact Tucker finally did right by Jessica, I have a feelin' all will still not be well for them." She shook her head. "A marriage startin' out without love from both ends is a poor beginnin' to be sure."

"Aye," his father agreed. "Me own gut says the same."

"I'd say, 'tis Mr. Matthews mostly troublin' me," Sadie confessed further. "Tucker and Jessica need to work out their lives in their own way like we did." His mother reached over to cover his father's hand.

He noticed the loving squeeze his father returned, their eyes meeting from across the table, and he smiled. This is the sort of love and devotion he always wanted one day when he married, and with Cassia as his wife, he was sure of just such a relationship.

He cleared his throat to gain their attention. "I have some news of my own."

Both his parents turned his way, slight frowns upon their brows.

He chuckled lightly. "Well, I assure you this news is good."

His father's face relaxed. "Well then, Lad, don't be keepin' us in suspense."

"Aye," his mother chimed in. "Good news would be a welcomed friend right about now."

He took a deep breath. "Tonight, after everyone left the Holmes's residence, I met with Reverend Holmes, to ask for his blessing, and then I met Cassia in the garden." Before he spoke further, he searched his parents' faces. Their gazes were intense as they listened to his words. "It was there I proposed marriage to her." Large smiles spread across their faces and his mother's eyes welled with happy tears. "And to my greatest joy," he added, his own eyes growing moist, "she agreed to be my wife."

"Saints preserve us, 'tis about time," his father blurted out, reaching to give his oldest son's hand a congratulatory shake.

"I'm so happy for ye, lad." His mother wiped her eyes with the handkerchief she kept tucked away in her sleeve before turning to give him a hug and kiss upon the cheek. "And I have somethin' special I've waited a long time to give ye." She stood and left the room for a few moments to retrieve the *something special*. When she returned she held a small, gold box in her hand. Gently she placed it down upon the table, in front of him. "Here, love…'tis me dear beloved grandmother's engagement ring. It was the only few belongin's I took with me from Ireland, along with the tea cups and me mother-in-law's veil. 'Twas to be given to the first son who planned to wed."

He reached for the gold box and paused, holding it for a moment before opening the lid. He'd heard of the engagement ring, and the stipulations, even though it was coveted by both of his sisters. It was also the ring he had planned on giving to Dorothea. He frowned. "But I wasn't the first son to wed."

"Ye are the first o' our sons to plan a marriage...not be forced," his father pointed out, gesturing to the bruise upon his jaw. "I'm sure the scrap ye had with yer brother was the result o' him takin' marriage vows this evenin'."

He only nodded.

"And knowin' me grandmother as I did," Sadie added. "I'm sure 'tis the way she meant the ring to be passed on." She gave him a pat on the shoulder "Open the box, Lad."

Slowly he raised the lid. There, lying in the white tissue paper, were two rings. One was his great grandmother's engagement ring. The rose gold setting held a small, round diamond between two small pearls. He picked the ring up and fingered the leaf etchings engraved along the shank.

"That second ring 'twas what I took when we left Ireland," his father explained. "I believe 'tis a very old piece of jewelry, Lad. 'Twas first me own grandfather's weddin' ring and probably goes back a wee bit farther than even that."

He picked up the second ring which was also a rose gold band but etched with a bit of fancy scroll work.

"And so, that ring me grandfather wore, will now be yours," Sean concluded.

"Me grandmother's weddin' band went to me sister, for her son's wife. So, you'll have to get yer bride a store-bought band," Sadie added. Then she sighed. "Do ye think Cassia will like it...the engagement ring, I mean?"

He smiled. "Yes, she'll absolutely cherish it," he said without a shred of doubt. Dorothea would never have valued it, as the stones were too modest. She wouldn't have appreciated the sentiment either. But Cassia, he already knew, would treasure the ring. "Strange how I know her so well. I can vouch for what she would like and how she will react."

"Well, 'tis the way o' it. How true love with the right lass is supposed to be," his father reflected.

His smile deepened. "Yes, true love with the right woman," he repeated, his heart swelled with happiness.

His mother hugged him. "I'm happy for ye, son. I've known Cassia since she was a wee babe, and the good family she comes from. I know she will make ye a loyal, lovin' wife, supportive o' yer work and be a good, carin' mother to yer children."

"And ye keep in mind her desires and goals as well," his father warned. "She's worked hard and long to be where she is. A woman workin' in the medical field goes through a lot to qualify. She's made it this far because she's good at what she does. So, if ye love her true in return, ye'll respect her right to continue her work."

He nodded again. "I have no intention of asking Cassia to put aside her career. In fact, I'm looking forward to her working with me here in Eagle's Landing. I want her to be my partner professionally and personally." He took a moment to try on the man's ring. It fit perfectly.

"Now, let's hope the engagement ring fits Cassia as well," his mother commented. "Otherwise ye will need to take it to Willow Creek for the jeweler to size it properly."

"Yes, that's what I'll need to do." He replaced both rings in the box and closed the lid. The excitement of slipping it on her finger coursed through his body. And from that moment on, he prayed it would never leave her finger…that they'd always be together until death do them part.

Chapter Twenty-Four

Brodie waited all week to present the ring to Cassia. Busy tending to the medical needs of the community left little personal time for either of them. Besides, he didn't want to spring such an important moment on her. Better instead to create a romantic backdrop before slipping the ring on her finger.

The next Sunday dawned with blue skies. An occasional warm breeze swept through the late spring day, and it seemed like the perfect day to present her with the ring. After church let out, Brodie invited Cassia to a picnic by the creek, their favorite place. While she went home to change from her Sunday clothes, he rushed to his house to pack a picnic basket. He wrapped a bottle of wine and two glass goblets in a table cloth to keep them from breaking, plus a butter knife to cut slices from the small brick of cheddar cheese he added along with wheat crackers. With two homemade brownies, his mother had baked the night before, his picnic menu was complete.

"Are you sure I can't contribute anything more than the napkins and blanket?" she inquired when he picked her up.

"No, this is all on me." He escorted her to the wagon, admiring the way her yellow sundress fit her perfect form.

Once at the creek, Cassia arranged the blanket

while he spread the table cloth. Then the two of them removed the goodies from the basket and began to eat. After pouring them each a goblet of wine, he held up his for a toast.

"To us," he began. "Here's to our love and our lives together." He smiled. "As well as the lives we'll make together."

She giggled. "Yes, we mustn't forget all of those lives yet to come."

The sound of her mirth, so pleasing to his ear, made his smile deepen. "Nor should this be forgotten." He placed his goblet aside and pulled the gold box from his shirt pocket. "I know I've already asked you this, on bended knee, but I wish to make it more…" he paused for the right word. "Binding." He opened the lid of the gold box and took out the ring. "Cassia Rose Holmes, I love you with all of my heart, and with that said, will you wear this ring, as a symbol of my love, devotion, and commitment to our future together?"

Her eyes widened when she saw the ring, and then they filled with tears. "Yes, Brodie O'Clarity, I shall be honored to wear your ring," she choked out, putting aside her goblet to stretch forward her hand. After he slipped it upon her finger, she gasped. "It's a perfect fit."

"That's because it was meant to be upon your finger," he said, before pulling her close. Their lips fused in a long, passionate kiss. Her warm, sweet mouth and the heady aroma of her lavender-scented skin brought sparks of desire throughout his being. He'd always crave her, just as strong and as much as he did this very instant.

She broke away, holding up her hand to admire the

ring. "This is absolutely beautiful, Brodie...the stones, the etchings—so amazing."

His heart swelled. "It belonged to my maternal great grandmother, and no doubt, many ancestor brides before her," he explained. "And this," he began, lifting the man's wedding band from the box, "was my father's grandfather's ring, and the one I will wear."

She took the man's band from him, and after examining it, her face lit with wonder. "Can you imagine the history we'll be wearing around our fingers? The love stories of each generation have been captured within these rings...each of them unique, with their own trials, tribulations, and victories. And now," she added, "we will add our own love story to the rest." She sighed, handing him back his ring. "Oh, Brodie, with so many beautiful spirits accompanying us through our life-long journey together, I know we will be happy forever."

Her words made his eyes brim with unshed tears, as he searched her beautiful face. Not only was every ounce of his bride-to-be's outer shell perfectly precious, but her kind and loving heart as well.

"I knew you'd feel the sentiment of this ring," he whispered. "That's another reason only you were meant to wear it again."

"My father believes there are no coincidences," she softly reflected.

"And I agree with him wholeheartedly," he countered.

"I do too." She traced the contour of his jaw with a finger. "We were destined to be right here, at this exact time, to do exactly what we are doing."

He leaned closer. "And to seal it all with this exact

kiss." Again he captured her lips with his.

After their picnic ended, he took Cassia home. Together they shared their news, Cassia showing her parents the engagement ring. Reverend Holmes shook Brodie's hand, tears of joy filling his eyes. Amanda Holmes hugged him, her tears of happiness cascading down her cheeks. He knew these people since he was a small boy, and now they'd be family. He couldn't be more pleased as they were kind and generous, always welcoming people into their home and hearts. They shared whatever they had, tried to see the best in everyone, and brought their daughter up to envy no one, never judge anyone, and appreciate what she had. He couldn't ask for better in-laws or a more loving and loyal mate.

"Is there a woman's wedding band to match the engagement ring," Amanda inquired, breaking through his thoughts.

"Yes, but my mother's sister was given that ring for her son's nuptials," he explained. He gazed over at Cassia. "We'll have to take a trip into Willow Creek and pick another out at the jewelers."

"Unless…" Amanda began.

"Do tell, Mama."

"I was thinking, if you'd like to continue to keep the bands traditional, I have one I've been saving for you," Amanda offered.

Cassia's face brightened like a child spotting gifts left by Santa beneath the Christmas tree. "The one you've always worn at the end of the gold chain around your neck?"

Amanda giggled. Cassia had inherited the same joyous and light laugh which he adored so well. "Yes, that very ring." Amanda reached beneath the collar of her blouse to pull the chain free. "It was my father's grandmother's, I believe. My mother wore it when my parents wed, and then I…" she clipped her sentence.

"And then your mother wore it when she wed Proud Eagle," Reverend Holmes finished. "Gabriel wears the man's band, as that is what my dear friend would have wanted," he added with a reassuring smile.

For a long moment, the room went quiet. Brodie knew all about Amanda's first marriage to the Apache warrior. His remains rest in Cassia's family's plot. He also knew Reverend Holmes held no malice toward the man or the union he once shared with Amanda, as Proud Eagle had also become his good friend. Brodie wasn't so sure he could be as congenial. He wasn't, by nature, a jealous person. But the thought of Cassia once loving and being loved by another man might cause him a strong bit of trouble.

Amanda broke the silence. "And I want you, should you agree, to wear the woman's band."

Cassia frowned. "Why wasn't it given to either Raven or Sunny, as they are older and were married first?"

Amanda sighed. "Well, I was still wearing it when Raven wed in Ireland and Sunny in England." Her eyes saddened. "I can't even begin to tell you how much my heart ached for missing their special day." She sighed again, heavily this time. "At the time it was impossible for me to attend either ceremony, and there wasn't anything I could do about the situation. But now, circumstances are different. I no longer wear the ring, and I can be at my youngest daughter's wedding."

Brodie turned to Cassia. "I'd say it is another ring

meant for only you to wear again."

Cassia leaned over to hug her mother. "I'd be honored to wear it, Mama." She tried the gold band on briefly, to make sure it fit, and it did, like it was made for her.

Cassia marveled at the way the rings sat upon her finger. "Although one ring is of yellow gold and the other of rose gold, the two look well together. In a striking way, they complement each other…like the union of two families, the bride's side and groom's joining together to make one large, new clan."

He pulled her close. "Somehow I knew such a symbolic notion wouldn't be wasted on you."

"And so, the next step would be to set a date," Reverend Holmes suggested.

Cassia looked up at him with a wistful expression. "I know you wanted to be married soon, but if we could wait until the fall, around October, then Gabriel will have fetched Riley and Anita from England. Sunny and Rafe will have already closed up Bentley Manor for the winter, so they'd be able to attend along with Raven and Braiton from Ireland." She smiled. "Perhaps even Silas could return, completing my family's attendance."

Here, it was nearing June, and his desire to make her his filled him continuously. But from the hopeful look in her eyes, his agreement to wait until her siblings could be present was extremely important to her.

"Besides," Amanda added. "Getting a gown made and making all the other preparations… Well, to do it properly, we'll need such a span of time."

"I concede." He leaned down to plant a soft kiss on Cassia's forehead. "October, it will be, but early October. In fact, the earlier the better."

Chapter Twenty-Five

Each day seemed like a whirlwind taking over every breathing moment of Cassia's life. School let out for the summer, and her promise to tutor Ruth Ann in the first waves of a medical career began. The two of them spent every Tuesday and Thursday at the clinic. Ruth Ann took to the training immediately, and Cassia couldn't help but believe the younger girl was made for helping others. She rose to the occasion when her sister needed great care. Ruth Ann did well with the elderly, the children, and the infants. Basically, everyone liked her and felt at ease with her either assisting Cassia or aiding a patient in an area she could handle on her own.

Every morning before work, Cassia kept her word at helping Alma Lee. Real progress over the weeks had been made, as Alma Lee no longer stared into the abyss, spoke when she was spoken to, could feed herself, and was able to use the outhouse by day. At night, because she was given medication to help her relax, she slept through nature's call. So, it was still necessary for her to wear the towel wrappings covered with Ruth Ann's creation of rubber pants. Each morning, when Cassia went into Alma Lee's room, it took some coaxing to get her fully alert enough for her to be changed, bathed, and dressed for the day. As Cassia made conversation with her, Alma Lee smiled and responded. Every day was better than the day prior, and she had real hope Alma Lee would pull through her breakdown and be back to normal.

One morning, when she entered Alma Lee's room, she found her sitting in the rocking chair at the far corner of the room. The towel, rubber pants, and Alma Lee's night gown were knotted in a ball on the floor. Naked, except for a blanket wrapped around her shoulders, Alma Lee rocked in silence, tears streaming down her beautiful face. Cassia quickly made her way to the other woman, knelt in front of her, and took each of her hands. "What's wrong, Alma Lee? Please tell me so I can help you."

Alma Lee pointed to the soiled towel. "I don't like wearin' that…that there…towel." She cast her eyes down in shame. "It's embarrassin' to have to be cleaned and changed like I've been." She met Cassia's gaze. "I'm not a baby. I'm a grown woman."

"You're right, Alma Lee, and no one thinks of you as anything but a grown woman. You are a very brave woman who has been strongly grieved," she soothed. "All of us have taken into great consideration the reason for your condition and know you need time to get past the tragedy you've been through."

"The medicine Mama gives me before bed makes me too sleepy. When I feel the need to use the pot, I try to get up, but I am too weak to do anythin' but fall back to sleep. And then when ya come in the mornin', I'm wet," Alma Lee explained. "But this mornin' was different, 'cause I didn't drink all the tea Mama gave me before bed. When she left the kitchen for a spell to help Ruth Ann with her hair, I dumped the tea in the sink. Then early this mornin' when the need struck me, I tried to make it to the pot…honest and truly I did. I knew what I should do, but by the time I got that awful towel off me, it was too late," Alma Lee went on. "And I ended up wettin' in the towel." She frowned. "I was so mad at myself for bein' so stupid."

"You are anything but stupid, and I don't want to hear you say such a thing about yourself again." She took a handkerchief from her pocket and dried the other woman's tears. "You're doing remarkably well, and I'm so very proud of you. Do you hear me?"

Alma Lee nodded.

"Perhaps it's time to stop giving you the sleeping powder."

Alma Lee's face brightened. "Do ya think so, Cassia?"

She smiled and hugged Alma Lee. "Yes, I truly do. We'll still cover the bed with a rubber sheet for a time, though. Just until we're sure you won't have any more accidents."

Alma Lee sighed. "I reckon that would be a wise thing to do."

Pulling back, she searched the other woman's face. "But I want you to promise me you will stop feeling embarrassed or stupid, even if an accident should occur. If you stop pressuring yourself and instead take each day as it comes and each new accomplishment as a sign you're healing, you'll get through all of this quicker and with a positive spirit."

"I promise," Alma Lee agreed.

After leaving the Boyd homestead, Cassia would go on to put in a full day's work either seeing patients at the office, going on house calls, or clinic duty. Not to mention, since her engagement, the wedding preparations. She hired Olivia Beachum to make her bridal gown, so there were the nightly fittings to attend. And family obligations also lined up…dinner at Brodie's parents' home, dinner with her parents, invites at Brodie's sister, Shailyn's home, Nora Dodd's home, and this evening, dinner in Willow Creek at Brodie's other sister Betsy's home.

She sat quietly in the wagon, letting the beautiful spring night air clear her senses and play havoc with a few wisps of curls framing her face. It was the first real moment of this entire day, so far, she was required to do absolutely nothing but relax.

"You've been rather silent tonight. Are you feeling ill?" Brodie inquired concerned.

She stifled a smile. Her husband-to-be would always be a doctor first, worried for her health. "No…just relaxing, I suppose."

"We should have done this Willow Creek dinner on the weekend."

She stretched her back. "All is fine, Brodie, really. I'm actually enjoying the ride and being able to absorb the peaceful silence of the night." Then, with a sigh she added, "Sometimes it's nice to just sit quietly and not have to be doing anything in particular."

"Lately, my love, I've become worried about you. And if you ask me, you work too hard."

She glanced his way, catching his frown. "You should talk, Brodie O'Clarity."

His frown deepened. "It's different for me."

She arched a brow. "Oh, really. How is that?"

"I'm a man," he stated flatly.

She giggled at his determined conviction of the statement. "Well, I am truly grateful for that wonderful fact," she teased. "But men can get sick and tired from overworking just as well as women. Look at what happened to your father."

"Yes, but my father is an elderly man, and you're just a wisp of a thing."

She folded her arms across her chest, a bit determined herself. "I'm just as hardy as you."

"You go from sunup to sundown, and rarely do I see you stop to have a proper meal," he scolded softly. "And if this keeps up, I'm going to be making a house call to your sickbed."

Brodie was right; she was wearing herself thin. If she didn't slow down and take some time to relax, she might not make it to her wedding. She stifled a yawn. "I hear you, Brodie. Really I do. But so much depends on me at this point in my life. How can I turn my back on Alma Lee when she's coming along so well? Or not keep my word to Ruth Ann?"

"I think I might have an answer to that, honey," he said. "My father's been itching to get back to work."

She gasped. "Oh, Brodie, do you think that's wise?"

He nodded. "He's well enough now and bored as hell. Not to mention driving my mother mad."

She giggled again. "My mother thinks your mother is a saint."

"Well, her halo is fading rapidly."

"So, what's the plan then, if Sean comes back to work?"

"I was thinking, for now, he could take on the office patients. It would give him set hours, more of a controlled entry back into the job. And it would free you up to work only house calls and two days at the clinic."

She smiled. "I think such a schedule just might work out to everyone's benefit."

"I thought so myself." Then he added with a mischievous grin, "And then come the evening, you'll be all mine."

They all sat down to a delicious dinner. Betsy served venison stew and homemade rye bread. A peach cobbler for dessert finished the meal, accompanied by a steaming cup of herbal tea. After Betsy's three boys were tucked into bed, the two youngest wanting Uncle Brodie to give them a piggy-back ride to their rooms, the adults sat down to talk.

"Have you chosen a maid of honor yet, Cassia?" Betsy inquired.

"The other night we had dinner with Nora and Cameron Dodd, and I asked her to stand up for me…to be my matron of honor."

Betsy nodded. "I figured she'd be the one you'd ask, as the two of you were inseparable growing up."

She took a sip of her tea, placing the delicate china cup carefully back upon its saucer. "And I can't tell you how sad I was to be away when she and Cameron were wed."

"I'm sure, had you been here, Nora would have chosen you to stand up for her as well," Betsy concluded.

She sighed. "I'm sure of it too. We always talked of such things as girls. I'm just sorry I let Nora down."

"You did nothing of the sort," Betsy countered. "Besides, you were there to deliver her baby, and the way I hear it from Maggie Granger," she added, "you saved Nora and her son."

She shrugged. "I was just doing my job."

"Nonsense," Brodie chimed in. "You went above and beyond, as you always do."

Betsy giggled. "I'd say your husband-to-be doesn't admire you much," she teased. Then she leveled her gaze on Brodie. "And dare I ask who you've chosen to be your best man?"

Brodie arched a brow. "It certainly can't be Tucker, not with his pending circumstances. By October he'll be settled in San Francisco, helping his father-in-law run a ranch and taking care of a wife and baby."

Betsy frowned. "He did make a mess of things, didn't he?"

Brodie nodded. "I'd say it wouldn't be all that horrible if he loved Jessica, but I don't believe that was ever the case." He sighed. "And I have a feeling it never will be."

"Poor Jessica," Betsy muttered.

Brodie downed the rest of his tea before answering. "Well, let's at least hope Tucker will be a good father."

"So, then... Who will stand up for you?" Betsy probed further.

"I've contemplated asking Paul Rhinehart, a young lawyer from Atlanta I met in Boston. He boarded at Widow Danfield's boarding house with me. We shared a bathroom and had many late night talks."

"Hopefully not while in the bathroom," his brother-in-law, Michael teased.

They all laughed.

"No, not in the bathroom, although come to think of it, that was the only place Widow Danfield wouldn't have been able to hear us." He arched a brow. "That woman was a champion at being nosy, as well as the town gossip. She could have put Maggie Granger to shame."

Michael shook his head. "That bad, huh?"

"Sadly enough, yes," Brodie said.

"And has Paul agreed?" Betsy inquired further.

"I haven't asked him yet," Brodie said. "I believe once we've set a concrete date, I'll write him."

Shifting to the edge of her seat, Betsy glanced at Cassia. "Have you a time in mind?"

"October when most of my family living overseas can attend," she said. Turning Brodie's way, she smiled. "And the earlier the better, so I've been told." She reached for his hand. "How does the first Saturday in October sound?"

He smiled. "Sounds swell to me.

She returned his smile. "Good, then it's a date."

"And I shall write Paul this evening," Brodie said.

"Now that a date's settled, I want to know all about your gown," Betsy began.

"Brodie, how about we let the women talk of the wedding preparations over tea, and we move to the parlor to enjoy a whiskey," Michael interrupted.

"Sounds like a plan," Brodie agreed. "Besides, I'm not supposed to know anything about the gown, isn't that right, honey?" He glanced at Cassia with a mischievous gleam in his emerald eyes.

It was Betsy who answered. "Oh my, bad luck for sure if any details are spilled."

She frowned. "I thought it was only bad luck if a groom saw the gown before the wedding."

"No. He's not to know a thing," Betsy corrected. "That first glance of the bride coming down the aisle must be the groom's first look. The impact is far greater, more romantic that way."

"Then come away, Brodie." Michael stood to make his way to the cupboard where he kept the whiskey and reached for a couple of shot glasses. "We wouldn't want you spoiling the impact."

"Heaven forbid." Brodie chuckled and followed Michael.

Betsy moved to sit beside her, occupying Brodie's seat. "I've learned from my mother that Olivia Beachum is sewing your gown. Is she using a pattern?"

Cassia took another sip of tea. "No, I wanted something unique, mine and mine alone. And Mrs. Beachum is doing a splendid job. She's incorporated all my ideas and wishes into a gown that will be so amazing. Well, the whole process is so exciting."

Betsy smiled, her green eyes twinkling. "Oh, Cassia, I can't wait now until October. What about Nora? Is Mrs. Beachum making her gown too?"

"No, Maggie's making Nora's gown in a very pale blue."

"And is your gown pure white?"

"No, more of an off white. The shade is called "candlelight," and the fabric is satin, lace bordering the neckline, sleeves, and the hem."

Betsy's eyes widened. "Have you made the headpiece yet?"

"No, I haven't thought that far ahead." She downed the rest of the tea.

"I only ask because the veil I wore to wed Michael was my paternal grandmother's. I'm sure you've heard the stories of it being one of only a few items Mama could bring to America?"

Cassia nodded. "Along with the tea cups, saucers,

and the engagement ring."

"Yes, and the veil is an off shade of white. It's of the finest Irish lace, so delicate and beautiful. It could be your something old and something borrowed if you chose to wear it," Betsy offered.

She reached out to affectionately squeeze the other woman's hand. "Oh, that would be so wonderful. Thank you."

"If I show it to you now, would you be able to tell if the shade matches the gown?" Betsy said.

"Yes, I'd be able to tell."

Betsy stood, motioning for Cassia to follow her up the stairs. "I keep the veil safely tucked away in the hope chest at the foot of our bed, wrapped in blue tissue paper. I'm the only one so far to wear it since its travels. Shailyn preferred to wear a picture hat on her wedding day."

They had to pass Michael and Brodie sitting in the parlor on their way to the staircase. One quick glance at Brodie—brows furrowed and lips pinched together—brought a sinking feeling to the pit of her stomach. She tried to catch his eye, but he was too intent on what Michael was saying to notice she passed by. What could the two men be discussing that would put such a strained, worried expression upon Brodie's face? With Betsy urging her toward the top of the stairs, she wasn't able to hear what Michael was saying, but his words seemed to frighten Brodie right out of his skin. It didn't take but a second to realize whatever Brodie was hearing, greatly upset him. And in turn, upset her and made it hard to concentrate on the task at hand. She tried her best to focus on what Betsy was conveying, the story she was telling about her own special day, and the history of the veil as she lifted it from the cedar chest and removed the blue paper wrapping. But Cassia's thoughts were on Brodie. Obviously, the men were speaking about something very serious and troublesome, but what could it possibly be? And why did the bad news affect Brodie so horribly?

"Do you think the veil will match?" Betsy broke through her thoughts.

She gasped when Betsy placed into her hands the most exquisite lace veil. With Brodie and Michael's conversation forgotten, she examined the remarkable headpiece. "Oh, Betsy, this is so elegant. I've never seen such intricate tatting, such fine lace, in all of my days."

Betsy smiled. "I know. The handiwork is perfectly exceptional. Now, can you tell if it will match the gown's material?"

"Yes. It will match," she said, her heart racing with excitement. Running her finger over the design, she added, "I don't think there are enough wonderful words to describe how magnificent this veil is, and you honestly don't mind me borrowing it?"

Betsy shrugged. "What good is it just sitting in my hope chest when it can be worn on the head of a beautiful bride?"

"Oh, Betsy." She reached over to hug her sister-in-law to be. "I could not be luckier or as happy. Again, thank you so much."

When they finally made it downstairs, the veil again wrapped in the blue tissue paper and carefully placed in a small carry bag, the men were discussing a lighter subject. Brodie, now looking more at ease, stood when she entered the room, sliding over on the sofa to make room for her.

"And from the look upon your faces, you must have told Cassia our good news," Michael surmised.

"Hush now, Mike. This is Brodie and Cassia's evening. Our news can wait a bit longer to be told," Betsy scolded.

"Nonsense," Brodie chimed in. "Good news is welcomed at any time…especially now."

"Yes, please tell us," Cassia added, wondering if Brodie needed good news *especially now* because of his emotional discussion earlier with Michael.

Betsy smiled, moving to sit on the arm of Michael's chair. He placed a loving hand upon her thigh. "We're expecting a baby."

She felt her heart leap with joy for these two marvelous people. "Oh, Betsy." She made her way to the other woman and once again embraced her.

Brodie stood, nearing Michael to shake his hand. "Congratulations!" As he hugged his sister, he bombarded her with a series of medical questions. "Have you been examined yet? How far along are you? Are you having morning sickness, paying attention to eating well, and getting enough rest?"

Betsy blushed and held up a halting hand. "Hold on, Brodie. You know, I still can't get used to discussing such things with my brother."

Brodie arched a brow. "I'm a doctor, Betsy, and I want to make sure my sister is taken care of during her pregnancy."

"I can answer all those questions," Michael said. "We have one of Willow Creek's finest doctors on the case. The baby is due a few weeks before Thanksgiving, so she is four months along, definitely she has morning sickness, eats fairly healthy when she isn't feeling sick, and most nights she is in bed by nine in the evening."

"Oh, hush, Mike," Betsy scolded again. Leveling her gaze at Brodie, she added, "After birthing three babes already, I'm sure, by this time, I know how to take care of myself."

"Yes, but you see for the very reason you have three other children to contend with, you're spread thin, and that causes me to worry." Brodie hugged his sister. "And let's face it; you're not getting any younger."

Betsy pulled back from the embrace and playfully slapped Brodie on the arm. "I can run circles around you any day, even while expecting."

After Cassia helped Betsy clean up, ignoring her adamant protests, the time arrived for them to leave. She hugged Betsy goodbye at the door. "Thank you so much for the delicious dinner and the loan of a beautiful veil. I will take extremely cautious care of it. Who knows, that little bundle of joy you're nurturing just might be a girl who will one day wear the veil herself."

Betsy smiled. "I love my boys, and I gladly welcome another, but a girl would be so grand, for sure."

On the ride back to Eagle's Landing, Brodie seemed preoccupied. Not wanting to appear meddlesome, she chose her words carefully. "Did you enjoy the evening as much as I did?"

"I did, thank you, my love." He kept his eyes alert to the dark surroundings.

She tried again. "You and Michael always seem to get along so well."

Brodie shrugged. "Not hard to do, since we've

basically grown up together. After all, the McCrea's and the O'Clarity's came to America together, remember?"

She nodded. "But he's also such an interesting conversationalist. His line of duty, as Willow Creek's sheriff, certainly gives him fuel for talk."

"And given me fuel for worry," Brodie mumbled.

Now, the opening was made for her to dig deeper without seeming nosy. "What exactly are you worried about?"

"Something Mike told me sets hard with me," he finally admitted. "And I want to talk further on it with you, but…"

"I'm listening," she said, her curiosity growing.

He sighed heavily. "Because you had such a good time tonight, I didn't want to ruin your evening by having it end on an upsetting note." He turned to look at her. "So, I thought I'd wait until tomorrow to warn you."

Her heart immediately raced. "Warn me about what?"

"Mike's working a case," he began. "A very disturbing case…more so than usual."

She swallowed hard. "And what does this case have to do with me?"

"A man by the name of Becket Attwater has escaped from a Nevada asylum for the criminally insane," he continued to explain. "This maniac has already covered a tremendous amount of ground. He's made his way to Phoenix and murdered two women there. The authorities found their naked bodies, compromised, strangled, and floating in the river."

She gasped, glancing cautiously to the darkened

land they passed. Suddenly the serenity of the night turned ominous and frightening. "And does Michael think Attwater is headed this way?"

"Yes, Cassia, he does." Brodie reached out to hold her hand.

She held tightly to the warm, safety of his grasp. "God, Brodie, what if…if…"

"I know, I know," he interrupted. "I could think of nothing else but you riding that bike all over Eagle's Landing, sometimes late at night, while Mike was telling me all this."

Now she realized why Brodie looked so strained, so upset during his conversation with Michael.

"And I believe Mike was worried for you too, that's why he confided it all to me."

She inhaled sharply. "What can be done? I must go on house calls. It's my job to be there when I'm needed."

"I don't want you out at night, for that I'm certain," he stressed clearly, his voice slightly shaken with his adamant request. "As far as the day, Ruth Ann's with you when you go to the clinic. There's strength in numbers. Mike said all the victims were women who were alone, taken at night. Perhaps we can work something out where Ruth Ann can also go on house calls with you, advance her medical training. She'd probably like that."

"No doubt, as she begs me for more time in the field," she admitted.

"I know you go to help Alma Lee every morning, and I don't expect you to give that up." He squeezed her hand affectionately. "I admire your dedication, and I wouldn't want you to leave the situation before Alma

Lee's ready to go it on her own."

"Especially now, to abandon her when she's making such progress… Well, it's not something I would want to happen."

"So, I will take you and put your bicycle in the wagon. From there you and Ruth Ann can go about your day." He frowned. "Does Ruth Ann have a bicycle?"

"Yes, John Tyler restored an old one for her to use."

"Good, then you two can get around swiftly," he deliberated. "And when I'm finished my day, I'll swing by the Boyds' residence to pick you up."

"What about my gown fittings with Olivia Beachum?"

He frowned. "There's plenty of time from now until October for you to continue your fittings, isn't there?"

She nodded. "Olivia's a fast worker. In only a short time, she's made good progress, so I suppose further fittings can wait a bit."

He glanced at the road ahead. "Mike's really on this, Cassia, so I have no doubt Attwater will be apprehended soon. But until he is, I'd like us to stick to a plan and ride on the side of caution."

She eyed the trees at the side of the road. "What sort of action will Michael and his men take to warn the public?"

"He's already placed a *wanted* poster in the post office and is holding a town meeting in Willow Creek tomorrow night. He's also going to call your father and will ask him to make an announcement in church on Sunday for everyone to gather later that evening at the parish center," he explained. "As I understand it, Mike will deputize a few of our town's men. Of course his brother, Patrick and his father, Mickey, will want to be part of this, as they both have excellent investigator skills and law enforcement credentials. And along with the other men, there will ultimately be a force available to comb the area for this fiend and be legally authorized to take action upon apprehension."

She moved nearer to him on the wagon's seat. "I'm scared, Brodie...for all of us."

He wrapped an arm around her shoulders and pulled her even closer. "I am too, honey. I am too."

Chapter Twenty-Six

At church the following Sunday, Reverend Holmes announced a mandatory town meeting to be held that evening at seven in the parish center. A few in the congregation questioned the gathering.

"I can only say it is a very important request by the Willow Creek Police Department, and extremely essential everyone attends," Reverend Holmes replied.

Sitting beside her mother in the pew, Cassia felt Amanda's hand close around her wrist. "God help us through all of this," she whispered.

All she managed was a nod, her own fears playing havoc with her thoughts. When she returned from dinner at Betsy and Michael's home on Thursday evening, she sat with her parents, and after explaining about Becket Attwater, her mother immediately went around and secured the window locks, shutting those already opened, and checking the front and back doors. True to his word, Michael phoned their house on Friday, explaining the horrendous situation further and incorporating her father's help.

Sunday dinner was hard to swallow. Brodie joined them, and even though everyone kept the conversation light and centered on commonplace topics, the atmosphere was thick with worry and uncertainty. Before leaving for the parish center, she and Brodie walked hand in hand around the garden. Memories of him proposing gave her heart a smile, despite the insanity looming other places in the world.

"It's hard to believe, looking at my mother's beautiful blooms, the world can hold such depravity and fear," she pondered aloud. "The women Attwater murdered were probably daughters or mothers or someone's love. They woke in the morning, facing the day like every other, not realizing it would be their last. All this simply because a sick, fiendish soul, whose life may have been tormented, felt the urge to end theirs." Tears rose to choke her. "And that same horror could happen here to anyone of us...to me."

In one fluid motion, he pulled her to him. She could feel the rapid beating of his heart against hers and smell the clean citrus and musk scent of his flesh.

"You have nothing to fear, my love," he whispered against her temple, his strong yet gentle arms a momentary safety net surrounding her. "I will make sure no harm comes to you. And after Mike and his men inform the townspeople of this dangerous culprit, he will not stand a chance in hell at hurting anyone in Eagle's Landing or any place else."

She wanted to believe his words, wanted to feel safe again, but deep inside she feared the worst. And it loomed heavy upon her shoulders like a weighted tool, sinking deep, consuming her until it took root in her very soul. "This has made me wonder if we're ever really safe. Attwater isn't the only derelict loose in this world."

"Well, right now he's the one we need to catch."

She sighed heavily. "One derelict at a time, I suppose."

At the town's meeting, Sheriff Michael McCrea

and two of his men informed the folks of Becket Attwater, explaining in detail how dangerous a man he was. The women gasped, the men talked over one another. And then the questions began. The law officers made a more than accurate attempt to be informative and honest about the situation. And for those questions that couldn't be answered at this time, strong support and speculation were added.

"Now, I need to call upon several men to keep watch here in Eagle's Landing. Only those certain they can deal with the situation, prevail with justice, and move forward to primarily keep the peace, will be deputized," Michael announced.

It was no surprise to her when the other two McCrea men, Mickey and Patrick, and several of the town's Apaches stepped up. All of them knew how to read the land, were excellent trackers, and the Apaches were formidable fighters. Her brother Gabriel and his son Ethan were the first of the tribe to make their way to the front of the meeting room. Even though Rising Sun and Falling Star weren't her biological aunt and uncle, related to her mother's first husband, Proud Eagle, she had grown up calling them as such. They lived next door, and Rising Sun was kind, loving, and taught her many ways to appreciate and respect the earth and nature, as well as cook traditional meals. Their son, Rising Star and his son, Kuruk—or Bear, as he was called, came forward as well. And though Little Elk and his wife, Owl Woman was long deceased, their memories lived on. Their son, Night Wolf and his son, Micah, also rose to the call. Two other townsmen made their way to be deputized, but the person who responded next shocked her the most...John Tyler

Boyd. When he walked up to join the rest of the men, her heart sank.

Leaning toward Brodie, she whispered, "Hasn't his family met with enough tragedy already, but for Trudy to possibly lose her boy as well."

"He's no longer a boy, but a young man doing his duty to keep his town safe, and no doubt thinking for his sister's sakes," Brodie whispered in return.

"What if it were Patrick Junior or one of Betsy's boys?" she said. "You wouldn't want any of them going on this manhunt."

Brodie sighed. "That's very true, but my nephews still have a father, so they don't need to be the man of the house. That's not the case for John Tyler. In a way, I'm kind of proud of him."

On second thought, so was she. "I just pray no harm comes to him."

Gabriel addressed the gathering now, standing tall and handsome in his buckskin pants and white shirt. She could almost guess how relieved he must be to have his wife, Riley and daughter, Anita away in England until the fall. "Any man," he began, "who would like to learn the Apache tracking method and hand-to-hand combat skills is welcome to meet with me or any of the other tribesmen for lessons. We will be at the wickiups located at the edge of the creek after this meeting ends. We'll be happy to go over some things then, as well as set up a schedule for further lessons." He motioned to Mickey McCrea and Patrick. "And you all know the investigator abilities of these two men, so they will also be on hand to share their skills."

After Gabriel spoke, many more townsmen agreed to join the manhunt and decided to also come forth to be deputized.

"I'm pleased at the turnout and the man power we've legalized tonight," Michael said. "Now, I have one more speaker wishing to be heard." He smiled at Amanda, sitting in the front row. The two of them, to this day, held a special bond. "The floor's all yours, Mrs. Holmes."

Cassia smiled to herself, knowing very well why her mother asked to speak…not to the crowd, but to the women.

With squared shoulders and strong determination, Amanda Holmes made it to the front of the room. "Ladies of Eagle's Landing, I am calling upon you to be a part of protecting yourselves, as well as the other women in this town." Pausing, she looked around the room. "You all know my past, the years I spent as an Apache wife. To cope with such a time, I learned the Apache ways of survival just as well as the men in the tribe." When she smiled, a twinkle of humor shone bright within her sapphire blue eyes. "Given, I am now a woman in my seventies, but that number is only the amount of years I've lived thus far upon this earth. It is, in no way, a number that has hampered me in carrying out my daily duties or keeping up with the grand scheme of things. I still have many good years ahead, and I tend to live them to the fullest. I also don't intend for Becket Attwater to end those years prematurely. And I am certain neither do you. So, I propose hand-to-hand combat lessons for the women." Amanda quickly glanced in Cassia's direction and arched a questioning brow. Knowing what her mother was up to, Cassia nodded. "My daughter, whom I've taught the Apache fight throughout the years, will help me to instruct any of you interested in acquiring the same skill. We will gather back here at the parish hall tomorrow evening for the first lesson. But remember, don't travel here alone. There is strength and safety in numbers." Then finally she added, "Please take a moment to think about my proposal, as training will not be easy. And should you decide in favor of my instructions, please take another moment to sign your names on the register sheet I've supplied, located on the foyer table."

Brodie chuckled lightly. "Now I know why you were such a scrappy little girl."

She smiled. "I did beat Tucker a few times when he got out of hand, didn't I?"

"And so, where were you when he punched me in the jaw?"

She sighed heavily. "All kidding aside, Brodie, I still fear this man—Attwater."

He grew serious. "And you should, my love; we all should. But Attwater's not walking into a town where the folks are unprotected or caught off guard. And I think that makes a huge difference in our favor."

She hoped he was right.

Chapter Twenty-Seven

Tension in Eagle's Landing grew three weeks into the authorities' search for Becket Attwater. Brodie felt it like a crawling insect, creeping about and settling deep inside his own thoughts. A few times he attended the men's combat class, amazed at how stealthy and quick the Apache way of fighting actually was. Keeping up was morally difficult, as to accomplish the effect properly, hurting an opponent was necessary. The oath he swore to do no harm rang loud and clear within his moral fiber. Would he...could he maim or kill another human being if he had to? His answer came swift enough when he pictured Cassia at the mercy of this monster.

Yes, I could kill him, without blinking.

And so he listened and learned and carried his hunting rifle. It would only be the second time he would use it, if need be. The first time was when he was fourteen. He thought he'd be this great hunter, able to feed his family on the game he caught. He had excellent aim, at practice he always struck his target, lined-up cans on a fallen log. But his heart broke after bagging a rabbit. Seeing the tiny rodent's lifeless body, due to the fatal shot he fired, left him with much grief. After burying the rabbit in a makeshift grave and asking the good Lord's forgiveness for its demise, he put the rifle away. It remained in the corner of the barn until last week, when he dug it out of storage, cleaned and loaded it. Now it had a permanent place beside him in the wagon. Cassia eyed it reluctantly a few times in the beginning, but now, after several weeks into the manhunt for Attwater, he almost believed she took the rifle's presence as a welcomed security.

He was also impressed by the women's combat progress. While watching Cassia bend, kick, and dance her battle strategy, he became immensely absorbed...and physically excited. Picturing her free of any clothing while in action led him to take a few nightly walks to cool off before driving her and Amanda home. He was amazed at the turnout. There had to be at least thirty women in the class. Of those in attendance he knew about half, Nora Dodd, Maggie Granger, as well as Muriel Dodd—his childhood school teacher. Watching her strike a fighting pose was indeed strange. This was the woman who helped him master his sums, know the difference between a verb and a noun. Now, she was learning how to battle a criminal and fight for her life. God forbid that time should arise.

Ruth Ann Boyd and her mother, Trudy were present, but not Alma Lee. He hadn't seen her since the day he was called in on her false pregnancy case. Trudy had asked him to stay away. It saddened him to know he failed a patient. If it weren't for Cassia gaining their trust and making progress with Alma Lee's condition, she could have been lost to reality forever.

As he glanced around the room, he recognized Rowena Cooper and her daughter, Clara Morris, the herbal growers. The two women supplied him with many homemade tinctures and balms, which aided the patients he called upon. There was Olivia Beachum and

Flora Washburn, two unlikely candidates, yet they were bouncing around, learning to defend themselves. Katie McCrea, his sister, Shailyn's mother-in-law, and Katie's daughter, Trina, were also present. The McCrea family came over from Ireland with his family—Mickey, Katie, and their four children, Michael, Patrick, Trina, and Mary.

Michael became his best friend, and he was a good and honest man. Now, he was an honest and caring lawman, doing his best to keep folks safe from harm. No one will ever forget the role Mike played in alerting the townsmen to the kidnapping of Amanda Holmes by Denton Hall, a former Reservation Agent. Mike's quick wit aided in Amanda's rescue, and forever they share a special bond. No wonder, as his future mother-in-law had an exciting past. Her time living with the Apache was the stuff great folklore is made from. In truth, the town's existence was basically due to her strength and foresight to bridge the gap between races.

He smiled to himself when he spotted his mother, Sadie O'Clarity, his sister, Shailyn and her nine-year-old twin daughters, Megan and Marta. All of them were taken fully out of their elements, as they jumped around, shouted out, and twisted their bodies to unusual positions. Their differences didn't matter here tonight, whether slim or fat, young or old. All of them were determined to keep Attwater from claiming his next victim. He prayed quietly their efforts paid off.

After making sure Patrick McCrea had Sadie, Shailyn, Katie McCrea, and his nieces packed comfortably in his wagon, Brodie gathered up his riders. He remained silent on the ride to the Holmes's residence, as he listened to Amanda and Cassia planning their next lesson. Wisely Amanda scrutinized her class, picking out which of the women needed to work on shifting from side to side, while some others needed to become flexible with their kicks and more forceful with their punches. As he learned more of the strategy, he admired the cleverness and dedication to getting it right. And to think, his own beautiful wife-to-be, was a little power house, taught to stick up for herself in the face of danger. She was feminine, yet hearty—dainty, yet strong. And the combination excited his male senses beyond what he expected.

"You're awfully quiet tonight." Cassia placed a hand upon his arm. She sat between him and her mother on the wagon's seat, closer than usual, and their thighs touched.

Her proximity and show of affection sent shock waves of desire through his body.

"He's probably thinking, what sort of family are we, that he's chosen to marry into," Amanda teased.

He was thankful for the elder woman's humorous remark, as it helped him to take the focus off Cassia's very near presence.

Cassia giggled—the lilting, golden sound of her mirth was like the halo of sunlight pigmenting her hair—and at this point a most needed and joyful noise. "I can't blame him."

He chuckled now, some of the tension lifting from his shoulders. "After tonight, I've decided, it would be extremely unwise for me to ever get you really mad."

Chapter Twenty-Eight

Patrick Junior was now gainfully employed as Cassia's traveling assistant. With Becket Attwater still at large, Brodie insisted on her having another traveling companion, for those times he was not available. Today, the two of them rode their bicycles to Nora's house.

"When would you like me to return for you?" P.J. inquired. Although he was only eleven, he was tall for his age and solidly built. Thus the reason Brodie thought he'd be the perfect bodyguard, or at least intimidate danger to keep it at bay.

She stifled a smile at his professional manner. "How about in three hours?"

"Will do." He left her safely at Nora's front porch.

Once inside, Cassia marveled at the beautiful table Nora spread for their afternoon gathering. How she missed being with her dear friend. As children they were inseparable.

"It's nice having you over for tea." Nora filled another cup for each of them. "With your work schedule and now the fighting lessons, I don't know how you manage to have time to spend with Brodie."

"I think if we didn't work together, there wouldn't be a whole lot." She accepted the piece of lemon cake Nora handed her.

"Well, that's why I haven't invited you over

sooner," Nora went on. "I didn't want to put any further pressure on an already packed agenda."

She sighed, sitting back in her chair. "But this is exactly what I need. Just some time to be me with a dear friend over tea and lemon cake and just relaxing."

Nora arched a brow. "Would talking about wedding plans be an intrusion on this relaxed time you're having?"

She giggled. "No, I'd welcome the chance."

Nora smiled. "Good, because Mama and I have finished my matron of honor's gown, and I'm anxious to show it to you while the baby's still napping."

When Nora brought out the gown, Cassia gasped. Maggie and Nora's creation was amazing, as every stitch was perfect. And the light blue satin and lace combination truly complemented her gown, which would make the two of them a beautiful sight to behold when they walked down the aisle.

"I couldn't be more pleased," she said, adding praises and compliments to their handiwork.

"Oh, I am so relieved the gown meets with your approval," Nora confessed. "And now that I've lost my pregnancy weight, I am actually anxious to put it on and strut about in it."

"Truthfully, I'm getting excited myself, and I can't wait until this manhunt for Becket Attwater ends so I can once again travel to the Beachum house when I want and without a companion for my fittings."

Nora shivered at hearing Attwater's name. "Now, no further talk on that matter. Only happy talk today, and I've a curious thought to ask."

She giggled. "Why am I not surprised? You've always had curious thoughts."

Nora giggled too. "And they always landed me over Mama's knee for a paddling."

She laughed harder now, the pure joy of having fun with her dearest friend a luxury she missed. "Well, don't worry. I won't repeat history."

Nora wiped tears of joy from her eyes with a napkin. "And I thank you greatly for that. Sometimes I think that old wooden spoon was used more to redden my backside than it ever was in Mama's kitchen."

"So, what is your curious thought, as I'm curious as well," she said, drying her own eyes.

"I was just wondering," Nora said, taking a deep breath to calm her giddiness, "where do you and Brodie plan to live after you're married?"

She arched a brow, suddenly serious. How could she have overlooked such an important factor? "That's a good question, and one I've no answer for."

Nora's face lit up, reminding her of all the times her bright ideas started out wonderful, but ended up with them in trouble. "I might have a solution."

"Nora Granger Dodd, keep me in suspense any longer, and I might find a wooden spoon."

Her friend laughed. "Remember, I can run faster than you."

She leaned forward in her seat. "Yes, but I pull hair harder."

Nora held up a surrendering hand, "All right, all right, you win. I was thinking how Mama's little apartment, the one she occupied before she married Papa, might work out nicely for you and Brodie."

She frowned. "Are you referring to the quarters behind the General Store?"

Nora nodded. "I've come to think of it as Eagle's

Landing's rite of passage home for newlyweds."

"And why is that?" she prodded.

"Right after Mary McCrea wed Jake Mulligan, they moved into the space, before permanently moving to Brooklyn, New York, that is," Nora explained.

"One of my classmates in England, by the name of Celeste Foster, was from New York City. She was the person who introduced me to nail polish," she reflected. "I wonder how far away Brooklyn is from where Celeste lives in the city?"

Nora shrugged. "I haven't a clue, but New York sounds fascinating. Mary writes me about an underground railway system that takes folks all over the city, as well as an amusement park called Coney Island, which has all sorts of grand attractions to enjoy."

She sighed. "I miss Mary. The three of us always had so much fun together."

"I miss her too," Nora agreed.

She frowned. "How did Mary meet Jake Mulligan?"

"Jake is my mother's nephew by marriage," Nora explained. "As you probably heard, my mother was a widow when she came to America."

"Yes, I've known that since I was a little girl," she admitted.

"Well, Mama's first husband's name was Colton Mulligan. After he died, Mama came to this country to be with the only family she had left, your sister-in-law Riley, who is one of her long, lost cousins," Nora went on.

"So, Jake Mulligan is related to Maggie's first husband?"

"Yes, Jake Mulligan is one of Colton's brother's

sons," Nora confirmed. "And a cop who came to America for a new and better opportunity. He looked Mama up, since she was kin and came for a visit about four years ago. That's when he met and fell in love with Mary, and then six months later, wed her. It was Michael McCrea who found him a policeman's job in Brooklyn." Nora shrugged. "Anyway, back to the apartment."

"Sorry for getting you off track," she apologized. "Go on, I'm listening."

"Mary and Jake lived there until their daughter was born, so they had room enough for a baby."

Cassia giggled. "Well, there will be some time before we need to address that situation. With both of us working, starting a family isn't something that will happen right away."

"But it's good to know there's room for a baby, right?" Nora countered.

She nodded. "There's no harm in always being prepared."

"Cameron and I lived in the apartment for a time after we were wed." Nora paused a moment.

"Since there was enough room there for a baby, why did you and Cameron move out?"

Nora sighed. "Cameron's father thought it would be wise for us to invest in a home, with being in the law field and all. More prestige, I suppose. My father-in-law helped with the down payment. Now Cameron has the room for a home office, to see client's now and then on off hours, and that sort of thing. Also, this house affords us the room to hold work-related dinners."

"I would say, for the sake of Cameron's career, the move was a wise decision," she said.

"Then living at the apartment could be a wise career move for you and Brodie too, since you'd be living right next door to Doctor Sean's medical office."

"Yes, it could," she agreed.

"It really is quite nice and very cozy. You could fix it up, like I did, to be a little love nest, as it has lots of potential."

Her frown deepened. "It's been eight years since I've been back there, so I can no longer picture the floor plan."

"There is a nice sized parlor area, a decent kitchen with a small dining space, two adequate sized bedrooms, and a bathroom which was added when Mary and Jake moved in," Nora explained. "Right now, the space is being used for storage. But a lot of what's there can be thrown out, as it's just broken items. And the rest of what isn't trash can be moved to the new storage area, which was added on two years ago to expand the store as well as to furnish a bathroom for customers." Nora frowned. "Haven't you been in the store since you returned from England?"

"No, truth be told, I haven't. I've been so busy with work, and since my mother does the shopping, I really had no need to stop," she explained. "Even though it is so close to the medical office, as you pointed out."

"You should take a look, perhaps after you get done with a shift at the office," Nora urged. "All in all, I think the place just might fit your housing needs."

"What about privacy?"

Maggie Granger still managed the store daily. Though she was a nice enough person—helpful and caring—she was also the town snoop and gossip. The last thing Cassia needed was for Maggie to hear and repeat all of her and Brodie's private business.

Nora cocked her head sideways. "It would be very hard to hear anything beyond the long breezeway connecting the apartment to the store."

She frowned. "Breezeway…what breezeway?"

Nora's brows rose. "Cassia, you seriously should take a gander at the place and refresh your memory." Then Nora did a bit of refreshing for her. "Don't you remember the breezeway where you, Mary, and I hid the bucket of frogs?"

Sudden recollection filled her thoughts. "Yes. Yes, I do now."

"Well, that keeps store sounds away from the living quarters, and vice versa," Nora said. "And when Mary and Jake lived there, they had a private door built off the side of the breezeway so they wouldn't have to enter the living quarters through the store, as Mama always had to do when she occupied the place."

"Then the apartment really sets off from the store, like a little home all in itself?"

"It does at that," Nora confirmed.

"If we decided upon this place, we'd want to change the locks, though."

"I can't blame you there. Mary and Jake installed a new set, as did Cameron and I when we moved in." Nora smiled. "So, what do you think of my idea?"

She pondered the notion further. "Well, I'll have to talk it over with Brodie first, of course. But otherwise, if he agrees, it sounds like this could be an answer to our housing problem."

Nora beamed. "And to think, this time my bright idea didn't end with me getting a thrashing."

She giggled. "I'd say there's hope for you yet, my

friend."

When P.J. arrived to escort her home, they took a detour to the O'Clarity homestead. P.J. hoped to sample some of Sadie's molasses cookies he'd heard she baked fresh that morning, and Cassia hoped she'd be able to talk to Brodie about the apartment.

As the two of them rode up to the house, P.J.'s professionalism flew right out the window, along with him, dropping his bicycle and flying up the stairs for those molasses cookies. She shook her head and smiled. He was after all just a typical eleven-year-old boy. She secured her wheels and then properly did the same for P.J.'s bike, before making it into the house herself.

The O'Clarity home, in all the time she ever entered it, was usually in a state of calamity and more times than not filled with happiness and good old Irish cheer. So, it was a complete and utter shock to enter the abode today and find the place subdued and the occupants morose. Even Irish wakes were livelier than the atmosphere she stepped into. Scanning the faces of those seated in the parlor, her heart sank. Sadie was wiping tears from red-rimmed eyes. Sean, seated beside her on the sofa, had one arm around her shoulders while patting her arm with his other hand. Brodie stood by the fireplace, holding a letter—his face ridged and pale. Everyone was very quiet, the house still except for the sounds of P.J. helping himself to the molasses cookies in the kitchen.

Immediately the excitement and euphoria of what she talked over with Nora left her heart, as it sank to her toes. "What is it? What's happened?"

"We've lost a grandchild today…a little boy, and his mother," Sean explained in a shaky voice. His words started Sadie's tears once again.

Her first thought was of Betsy and her unborn babe. Had she miscarried and then lost her own life as well? Was the letter Brodie held news from Willow Creek? Panic and nausea assailed her in one blow. Quickly she sought out a seat and took it, calming herself to keep from fainting or getting sick. Her thoughts flew. *Why would the news come by post when it could be relayed by phone? And at this point in Betsy's pregnancy, it would be too soon to decipher the sex of the child.* Finally, finding her own voice she broke the silence. "I don't understand, who…?"

"The letter is from Tucker." Brodie folded it neatly and placed it upon the mantel. After clearing his throat of emotion, he continued, "Jessica miscarried two weeks ago. The baby was…was a boy." He paused, swallowing hard. "She hemorrhaged to death."

Cassia gasped, tears filling her eyes and spilling over. "Oh, no—no."

Aggravation, anger, and disappointment were etched upon Brodie's face. "And my beloved brother, good enough to at least get a letter off to us, has left Phoenix for San Antonio, Texas." He chuckled sarcastically. "I'd say he couldn't even wait until the poor girl's body was cold to leave her."

"Enough, Brodie," Sean scolded. "Yer attitude's not helpin' matters in the least."

"I'm sorry Pa…sorry Ma." He combed his fingers through his russet curls.

P.J. entered the room. "Can I please have a glass of milk with my cookies, Grandmamma?" With his mouth caked in cookie crumbs, he glanced around the room. "Why's everyone so sad?"

Cassia stood. "Come, P.J., I'll pour you a glass of milk."

"Nay, let me." Sadie rose from the sofa. "I think 'tis best I stay busy." She placed an arm around P.J. "Come, Lad."

"But why is everyone so sad?" P.J. asked again.

"Let's get ye that milk, and I'll try to explain." Sadie escorted P.J. into the kitchen.

Sean sighed and stood. "I'd better be callin' Betsy and Shailyn. 'Tis only fittin' they hear this news as well." He took his leave to use the wall phone in the hallway.

She made her way to Brodie, wrapping her arms around his waist. He buried his face into her neck and pulled her close. "I'm so sorry for your loss, honey," she whispered. "Sorry for all of you, Jessica, the baby, and her family."

"I wonder if my brother is all that sorry," he muttered.

"I'm sure he must be hurting as well." She pulled back to search his face. "Why, don't you think he is?"

He arched a brow. "If anything, he's probably more relieved, since he didn't want to marry the poor girl to begin with."

She frowned. "Surely you must give your brother more credit than that, my love. His not wanting to marry Jessica and not feeling sorrow over her death are two very different things. And what of his son? He has to be grieving the loss of his baby."

He shrugged. "Perhaps he grieves for the baby, but I doubt he's all that heartbroken over Jessica's death."

"We mustn't think the worst, Brodie," she tenderly cautioned. "He's still your brother, and family has to stick together. If Tucker comes back to Eagle's Landing, needing to be surrounded by the support of his family during this difficult time, you must be in the frame of mind to comfort him."

"He won't be back, Cassia," he said flatly. "He's on his way to Texas, and I doubt we'll hear a thing from him for a very long time."

Sadie poked her head into the room from the kitchen doorframe. "Ye'll be stayin' for dinner, right Cassia?"

"Oh, no, please don't go to any trouble…"

"Nay a bit o' trouble, and I won't be takin' no for an answer," Sadie returned. "Like I said before, keepin' busy is best for me." She forced a smile. "Now, give a call to yer mother, so she won't be frettin' ye've been snatched by the derelict roamin' about, and then come help me peel potatoes. I've got a recipe or two I've been meanin' to share with ye, anyway."

Cassia admired Sadie O'Clarity. Even in the face of sorrow, she pulled the family together with her skill to be organized, clear-headed, and supply sustenance. She was a strong yet tender woman. Fierce love for her family and friends made her a trusted being, always able to be counted on and responsible to carry through in all situations. She hoped she'd be the sort of wife and mother Sadie was. As well as her own mother, who lived through all sorts of adversities, yet remained centered and strong for those she loved and cared about.

P.J. also stayed for the delicious Irish stew dinner. His presence helped the atmosphere, as he rattled on about his expertise in frog catching and his assessment of the critters before he mercifully granted them release.

"Nora, Mary, and I liked to catch frogs," she said, wiping her mouth with a napkin. "We hid a bucket of them once in the breezeway behind the General Store." She frowned. "I'd forgotten all about the ordeal until today. Nora reminded me while we were having tea."

Sean chuckled. "Seems like a strange thing for ye women to be discussin' over tea."

She replaced the napkin on her lap and sat back in her seat. "Well, actually we were discussing the apartment behind the store. In fact, that's why I had P.J. escort me here instead of my house this afternoon, so I could talk to Brodie about the place."

Brodie frowned. "Why is that?"

"Nora thought it would work out well as our first living quarters, after we're married."

Brodie's frown deepened. "Is it even livable?"

"According to Nora, all it needs is a cleaning, as there are some items stored there, and then a bit of decorating."

"Aye, I remember Mary McCrea movin' in there when she married Jake Mulligan," Sadie chimed in. "Went to visit them a few times, after their baby was born, and thought the place was quite nice."

"And 'twould be a real convenience to ye both, being 'tis next door to the medical office," Sean added.

Brodie sighed. "And also convenient for Maggie Granger to know all of our business."

"I thought the same thing," she agreed. "But Nora said the distance between the store and the apartment is separated by a long breezeway which keeps the store activity and the apartment dealings private from each other. Nora also said when Mary and Jake moved in they had a private door built on the side of the breezeway so the apartment dwellers don't have to go through the store to enter their quarters. And we could always change the locks, should we decide to take the place."

"It sounds promising," he pondered.

"That's what I thought. Perhaps we can go over there in a few days, and look around the place, before we make a decision," she offered.

"And if ye like what ye see, perhaps we can all get together, clean it out, give it a paint job, and furnish it," Sean countered.

"Aye, I've got lots o' furniture ye can have," Sadie offered. "As I'm sure Shailyn and Amanda do as well. So, ye'll be up and housed in no time."

"Might be a grand idea if Brodie moves in as soon as the place is ready," Sean added.

"Aye, 'twould probably be best that he does," Sadie agreed.

Brodie chuckled. "Are you two trying to get rid of me?"

Sadie and Sean smiled devilishly at each other.

She giggled. "Oh, Brodie, it looks like your parents could use some privacy too."

"Why do they need to be private?" P.J. questioned.

Sadie strategically changed the subject. "Have ye room for dessert, laddie?"

"I sure do," P.J. strongly confirmed.

Sadie took her grandson by the hand. "On yer feet, Lad," she coaxed. "Come into the kitchen with me, then. Ye can help me slice the peach pie I made, and brew us all a wee bit o' tea."

Chapter Twenty-Nine

A weekday service was held at the church. Though no one really knew Jessica Matthews O'Clarity, or the son Tucker named Daniel Sean O'Clarity, many of the town's folk attended. Cassia teared up several times, as Reverend Joshua Holmes's comforting and moving words came forth from the pulpit, easing grief and ensuring courage for those left to carry on. Often she wondered how he did it...saw the positive and cherished sides of unhappy and negative situations. Truly he was a man of strong faith and conviction for the Lord, and all serving Him meant. His link to the Almighty was amazing and inspiring. Whenever she questioned her own faith and strayed far from hope, her father was there to help her back on the right path.

He taught her many times by quoting scripture. "As Psalm 16:8 reads, 'I have set the Lord always before me,' " he'd begin. "Do you understand what that means, Cassia?" And before she could answer he'd tell her. "It means to set the Lord between you and your fears. Visualize Him protecting you, keeping you safe, and linking you to His abundant grace and glory."

Another inspiring virtue he had was complete trust in God. Whenever Joshua Holmes was asked to meet at a place, he'd say, "I'll be there, God willing."

Once she asked, "Papa, why do you say, God willing?"

"Because, Cassia, none of us really have the foggiest notion of what tomorrow might bring, even with all our careful planning," he'd explain. "No one expects to die today, but somewhere, someplace, someone has taken their last breath."

"Then, in truth, we can lay claim only to this very moment," she'd respond.

"Aye, so use your time wisely, baby girl, as the hours belong to God, not us. And be grateful for each new day you live to see."

After the service, folks gathered in the parish hall. Amanda Holmes whipped up an amazing feast in only the few short days she had, spreading a meal of fried chicken, baked beans, homemade biscuits in gravy, and a spinach salad upon the table.

The next day dawned quiet. It was a beautiful Friday morning, and Cassia had no house calls other than to visit Alma Lee. Today was a milestone in her patient's recovery, as she, Trudy, Ruth Ann, and Alma Lee planned to do a bit of shopping at the General Store for material. Ruth Ann offered to make them all sundresses to wear at the upcoming annual Strawberry Festival held in town. Summer had arrived with a blazing sun and sweltering days, perfect for new sundresses and straw hats. Besides, a shopping spree always lifted her spirits, and so she planned one for Alma Lee.

While she waited for P.J. to escort her to the Boyd's home, she wondered if she was indeed using her time wisely, as her father so many times preached. With the threat of Attwater lurking about, it seemed she wasted a lot of precious time waiting to be accompanied to and from a place, instead of just going about the day as she should. Lately, she'd become disgusted with the whole inconvenience, especially since P.J. tended to be late to his duties. She had the strong feeling he no longer took pride in his job, as the lure of swimming in the creek or hunting down frogs with his friends was so much stronger.

By the time she made it to the Boyds' residence it was close to noon.

"So sorry," P.J. apologized. "But I couldn't find my swimming trunks."

"Never mind." She tried to stay calm. "Let's just get on our way now."

Alma Lee, now able to wash and dress herself, paced frantically in the parlor when Cassia entered the home.

"She didn't think ya was comin'," Trudy said.

Nearing Alma Lee, she took her trembling hands in hers. "I'm sorry to be late, but I'm here now and ready to have a fun day, if you're still up to it."

Alma Lee sucked in a breath. "I'm ready."

On the way to the General Store, Cassia kept the conversation light, telling her three companions about the apartment.

"I reckon it'll serve a good purpose, bein' it's so close to the doc's office and all," Trudy figured. "I'd say ya can't beat a better place than that for ya two to live in, that's for sure."

"No, the location is perfect; let's just hope the rest of the place suits our needs as well," she admitted.

Maggie graciously welcomed them, showing them the new sundress material she had in stock, making suggestions on different patterns that worked best with each fabric, and then serving fresh-baked biscuits and lemonade to replenish their energy. All in all, it was a grand time, and Cassia was so pleased Alma Lee was enjoying her time out, laughing and feeling at ease with so many people milling about.

But just as they were ready to leave, Murial Dodd and Nora stopped into the store, utilizing the buddy system while Attwater was at large, with Nora wheeling little Cameron Jr. in a baby buggy. Alma Lee's happy face suddenly became crestfallen when her glance settled on the baby. Slowly she made her way to the side of the baby buggy and gently reached down to caress the child's small hand.

"He's beautiful," Alma Lee said softly.

"I thank you kindly, Alma Lee," Nora answered.

Then raising her gaze to Nora, Alma Lee added, "Yer truly blessed."

Nora swallowed hard, casting a quick glance in Cassia's direction. As far as anyone in town knew, Alma Lee had lost her baby, and Nora struggled for the appropriate response at a time such as this?

It was Maggie who came to the rescue. "Saints be praised, 'tis a busy day here, for sure. So, me darlin' daughter," she went on, politely escorting Nora and the baby buggy to the back room, "as long as ya thought to stop by, I'll be thankin' ya kindly for a helpin' hand with the paperwork." Turning to Murial Maggie added, "And I've got new material to show you."

Trudy picked up on Maggie's motive and took Alma Lee by the arm, ushering her to the door. "I reckon we've takin' enough of yer time as it is, Maggie, so we'll be off now as well."

On the ride home, Alma Lee remained eerily still, taking to staring ahead with vacant eyes once again.

Cassia feared all the hard work everyone, including Alma Lee herself, put in these last few weeks to get her back on track was now for naught. Seeing Nora with her baby immediately crushed Alma Lee's spirit, brought her loss back to her in volumes. It all had to be so painful to endure.

Once back at the Boyd homestead, she helped Trudy with dinner. Alma Lee refused to eat, adding to everyone's concern.

"She can't go through this. None of us can go through this again," Trudy whispered.

"It was the first time she's been out and seen a baby since her illness. It all had to be quite a shock and immensely exhausting," Cassia reasoned. "Let's not jump to the worst conclusions."

"I pray yer right, Nurse." Trudy gathered the dirty dishes to wash from the table.

Cassia took Alma Lee up to her room, helped her to undress and bathe, all the while talking as cheerfully as she could muster about the pretty patterns and material purchased earlier. But Alma Lee stayed silent.

Ruth Ann brought up a cup of tea. "Mama added a pinch of the sleepin' powder," she whispered. "Should I get the towel wrappin'?"

"No, let's give her a chance to come back to herself," she said. "But we should at least cover the mattress with the rubber sheet."

After only a few sips, Alma Lee refused the tea. Placing the cup aside, she assisted Alma Lee into bed. Then Cassia made her way downstairs to join Trudy and Ruth Ann. The three of them sat on the front porch, waiting for P.J. to arrive and escort her home.

"That bad man runnin' around these parts is makin'

275

everyone's life all mixed up," Ruth Ann commented.

"My mother, who lived thirty years in a tent with no more than a canvas flap for security, is afraid to open a window," she offered.

Trudy grunted. "I can't blame her."

"It's sure gonna be a mighty hot summer for sleepin', with no air," Ruth Ann added.

P.J.'s arrival time came and went, and it appeared to everyone Cassia had been forgotten.

"I can't be leavin' Alma Lee alone, not in the state she's presently in. And I wouldn't allow Ruth Ann to be riding ya home, 'cause then she'd be returnin' by herself. But if ya can wait for John Tyler, whose out on a watch and should be home in an hour or two, he can take ya home. Yer welcome to rest here 'til then," Trudy offered.

She sighed, gazing up at the dusky sky. "I think I'm going to head out on my own, before it gets too dark."

"No, ya can't be doin' that, Nurse," Trudy protested. "Not with danger lurkin' about as it is."

She sighed again. "On such a nice night as this, there's probably many people out and about, going to the store for a cool bottle of pop or a stroll. I think if I ride my bicycle out in the open, away from any trees and keep along the busy streets, all will be fine."

It was with great reluctance Trudy and Ruth Ann allowed her to leave, the two strongly reminding her of the *traveling with a companion* rule. But she was fed up with wasting any more time. Attwater hadn't been seen or heard from in weeks. Perhaps he moved on from the area or was attacked by a wild animal and lay dead somewhere. Either way she was going to take herself home.

To her relief she did see a few wagons driving by, as well as a couple or two taking an evening stroll. One couple she followed a small distance behind until she neared Amelia Lane and Ethan Drive. Once she spotted her home on the corner, her confidence grew, and she rode faster, away from the others to cross the street, toward her destination. But before she made it to the other side, a wagon cut her off. The bicycle swerved to the left, and she lost control. She landed hard, injuring her left ankle. A large man, wearing a red bandana and one gold, hoop earring, pulled the bicycle off her and tossed it aside like it was made of paper. Carefully he helped her to stand. Her ankle throbbed with pain, and she faltered.

The man caught her and scooped her up into his arms. Then he carried her over to a small, shabby rig. He placed her on the seat, beside a child—a girl about six or seven—with long, fiery red hair. Cassia knew who they were—gypsies. She had been warned as a child to stay away from their camps, whenever a band of them settled for a time at the edge of town. Whether it was a myth or the truth, she obeyed, least she be kidnapped and taken far away from home.

"Please, ma'am, tell me you are not harmed," the man said.

"Just my ankle's a bit sore, but I am otherwise fine. And I just live across the way." She gestured to the house on the corner. She started to climb down from the seat, wanting to put as much distance between him as possible. "So, I am sure I can make it home."

"Please, I cannot let you go. My wife needs your help," the man pled. "I know you to be the one who always travels with the doctor and works at the clinic."

She felt even more uneasy now, hearing he'd been watching her. "I can show you where to find the doctor, sir?"

"There's no time. My wife…she's havin' trouble birthin' our baby."

She gestured again to the house a few doors down the street. "As I said, I live there. Let me go inside a moment to fetch my medical bag," she stalled. If she could get into the house, she would phone Brodie and have him take this call.

But the gypsy man was too desperate. "You will stay put and come with me now." He pulled a knife from a leather sheath that hung from his belt.

"I cannot help your wife without my bag," she tried again.

In one fluid motion, he pressed the tip of the knife's blade against her side. "I said you will come with me now."

"Please, ma'am, my mamma needs help. She needs you," the little girl cried. "Or she will die. I know she will."

She glanced at the little girl sitting beside her. Large tears ran down her face. And in her eyes was a mixture of fear and sorrow. Immediately Cassia's heart went out to the child. How would she feel if her mother needed help, and there was no one she could trust or turn to?

"Very well," she agreed. "But your father must put away his knife, now."

"Please, Papa, do as she asks," the little girl begged. "For Mama's sake."

"You will give me no trouble, then?" the man said.

She turned to look deep into his large, chocolate eyes. They mirrored his young daughter's fear and worry. "No. No trouble. I will come willingly to help your wife, as it is my duty to help others."

He hesitated, arching a bushy brow.

"You have my word." She reached down to grip his arm. She felt him trembling. Her gaze locked defiantly with his as she slowly pushed his hand and the blade away from her side. "Now, put away the knife."

Chapter Thirty

It had been one of the longest days yet for Brodie. He helped his father with office calls all morning and then ran the clinic all afternoon. Just as he was about to go home, he was called to go on two emergency house calls. Now, as it neared ten o'clock, he was finally able to sit down and eat the fried chicken and applesauce his mother left for him in the ice box.

With his parents already tucked in bed, the house was quiet, except for the ticking of the mantel clock. He closed his eyes, relishing the silence. After a long, hard day like this one had been, all a man needed was food, a little piece and quiet, and his lady love warming his bed. Soon, he'd have the latter to enjoy as well. Visions of Cassia naked beneath the quilt, waiting for him, brought a satisfying thrill to his loins. Lately, it was getting harder and harder to keep such scenes from his thoughts. How he would ever make it to October, he didn't know.

It was the knock on the back door that brought him from his delicious musings. "Saints preserve us. Don't tell me my day still isn't through," he grumbled to himself. He opened the door to find Gabriel Eagle, Ethan Eagle, and Patrick McCrea standing on the porch. The look in their eyes made his heart race. "What is it?"

The three men entered the kitchen without invitation. Patrick pulled out a kitchen chair for Brodie to sit upon.

He shook his head in refusal, terror coursing through every vein in his body. "Tell me what's happened?"

"It is my sister," Gabriel choked out hoarsely. "Cassia is missing."

Missing! How could one word strike such horror in a man?

He did sit...had to sit...the room spun. He swallowed hard, the thundering of his heart echoing in his ears, throughout his body. "What do you mean Cassia's missing?" he finally managed to say.

Patrick ran his fingers through his hair. "P.J. was supposed to fetch her from the Boyd's home, and he forgot." He fisted his hands by his side, his eyes welling. "He forgot...he forgot," Patrick repeated, his voice raising. "I just switched that boy's bottom so hard he won't be able to sit for a week."

"Did anyone go to the Boyd's residence to see if Cassia was still there?" he probed. "She knows enough not to travel alone, so she could still be..."

"She's not there, Brodie," Gabriel interrupted. "It seems she tired of waiting for P.J., realized he'd forgotten her, and decided to make it home herself. Trudy was concerned for her safety, so when John Tyler got off patrol duty, he was sent to my parents' house. It was then Cassia was discovered missing." He took a deep breath before continuing, "That's when my mother became hysterical, and John Tyler came looking for me. After I sent John Tyler home, since he'd put in a full day on watch duty, I quieted down my mother somewhat. Ethan and I followed the trail we believed Cassia might have taken and came upon her bicycle. It was tossed on the side of the road, just down the street from my parents' house." Gabriel paused, clearing his throat from emotion. "So it looks like she almost made it home…almost."

"But she didn't…she didn't. So why are we sitting around talking about it and not out there looking for her?" Brodie shouted.

"I've got every man I could locate combing the town, and Michael's been called. He's bringing the hounds," Patrick informed him.

By now Sean and Sadie were awake and entered the kitchen with confused, groggy expressions.

When Patrick explained the situation, Sadie gasped, her hand going to her throat. "Mother of God," she whispered, tears pooling in her eyes. "I'll get meself dressed immediately and go to Amanda. The two o' them shouldn't be alone at a time like this."

"I'm right behind ye, my love," Sean chimed in.

"I thank you both," Gabriel said.

He made his way to the door. "Let's go, then. We've got to find her. I've got to find her before…"

Patrick interrupted sharply. "Brodie, it would be best if you stayed here."

The blood rushed to his head with a roar. "Like hell I will, Patrick!" His eyes blurred with tears, and he quickly wiped them away with the back of a hand. "I know these woods, this area, better than any of you." His voice broke. "I'll find her if I have to tear the town apart."

"Then you will come with me and Ethan," Gabriel said, his own face filled with torment. "And the three of us will tear this town apart together."

Chapter Thirty-One

The ride to the gypsy's camp seemed like an eternity to Cassia. Her ankle throbbed, as it had begun to swell, and the night air chilled her flesh to the bone. She shivered, wishing she at least had a sweater. But this morning, when she dressed for only a shopping spree, a sweater wasn't necessary. All she donned was a three-quartered sleeved blue blouse, a blue and white checked skirt, and sandals. She didn't even carry a satchel, sticking her change purse and the keys to her house and the clinic, tied together on a leather cord, in a pocket of her skirt. She had no idea she'd be out after dark, having to deal with the wilderness. Besides being fearful for whatever came next, she was in pain and extremely uncomfortable.

The man drove the wagon in silence out of Eagle's Landing, over the covered bridge, and into South Eagle's Landing. They passed the clinic, closed for the weekend, the small hotel, and many resident homes before coming upon a patch of backwoods and turning down a secluded road. The darkness enveloped her heart as did her fear, and she shifted uneasily in her seat.

About a mile down the dank piece of wasteland, the little girl placed her small hand on Cassia's arm. "We are almost there," she whispered. "I am Roxanne, and my father is Niko."

The child's small gesture to comfort her meant a great deal and she forced a smile. "My name is Cassia," she responded softly.

"Thank you for coming to help my mama," the little girl whispered again.

If Niko heard them talking, he made no sign of it or attempted to stop the conversation, and this encouraged her to a small degree. There might be a good chance he wasn't a bad man or out to hurt anyone. He was just desperate to get help for his wife.

It was then she silently prayed. *Lord, guide my hands tonight. Let all be well for this woman I go to help, the baby, and for me.*

It wasn't much longer that Niko halted the wagon in front of three covered wagons parked in a semicircle. A campfire was burning at the center of the arc and a few people, two elderly men and women, a middle-aged man, and two small boys appearing to be about six and four in age sat around the flames.

When Niko helped her out of the wagon, the pressure she put upon her ankle to stand sent shocking pain shooting through her leg. Her balance faltered, and once again Niko gently and courteously helped her to remain upright.

He pointed to a wagon situated to her far right. "That is my wagon, where my Ramona is in labor."

She nodded, inhaling sharply as she walked in the direction where she was needed. Climbing into the home on wheels was even more difficult than walking. But bracing herself slightly, carefully using the fragile frame of the archway, seemed to suffice. Once inside, she scanned the dimly lit abode. Nothing but a few chairs, pillows, a small table with a lit lantern upon it, and a feather mattress furnished the area.

Immediately, what came into her mind, were the stories her mother told of living for several decades in a wickiup. Hearing about the primitive housing and daily survival had her both stunned and awed. Yet she couldn't fathom such an existence as reality. How anyone could truly survive, throughout all seasons, living in such a fashion was beyond real comprehension...until now, seeing it all unfold before her eyes.

On the mattress set upon a thin, wooden plank, a woman with long, fiery red hair lay writhing with pain. Beneath the sheet, barely covering her breasts and the juncture of her thighs, she was naked. Another woman, older than the expectant mother with hair the same shade of the blackest night, knelt beside the mattress, swabbing the patient's neck and face with a moistened cloth.

"Ramona, love, I've brought the midwife." Niko made his way to his wife.

Ramona held out her hand to him. "I knew you would find her."

Niko knelt on the other side of the mattress, pulling Ramona into his embrace. "All will be fine now." He rubbed his wife's naked back in slow, circular motions.

She hobbled over to the mattress, looking down at the laboring woman.

Ramona's large, green-gray eyes locked with hers. "Please, help me."

"My name is Cassia Rose Holmes, I am a midwife and a nurse, and I will do everything I can," she assured the woman, kneeling beside the mattress.

"If my wife and baby die, you also will die," Niko

threatened with wide eyes.

Ramona turned her gaze briefly to her husband. "Niko, hush with such talk," she scolded.

Niko bowed his head, like an admonished child. "I could not bear it if anythin' happened to…"

"Nothin' will happen to me," Ramona interrupted. "Now, go. Leave this work to the women."

Reluctantly Niko stood, looking back at his wife for a long moment before he left the wagon. Niko looked as though he feared he'd be seeing his wife alive for what might be the last time.

"Forgive my husband." Ramona turned onto her side. "He will not harm you, so no need to fear. He is just very worried over this birth. I have been too long in too much pain."

"How long have you been in labor?" She hoped to get a timeline on Ramona's situation.

"For near to two days," Ramona confessed. After inhaling sharply, she went on. "My other three children slipped easily from my body. But this one is stubborn…like my husband," she added, forcing a smile.

Cassia's heart went out to the woman. In all her pain, she tried to make her feel at ease as did the little girl. Like mother, like daughter, she supposed, returning the smile. "I am not afraid of your husband. I see he is just worried for you and the baby." Gently she pushed aside a lock of red hair from Ramona's sweaty brow. "Now that I am here, all will be fine."

Ramona relaxed a bit, taking a cleansing breath. "This is my mother, Maria." She indicated the other woman.

Maria inclined her head politely. "Tell me how I

can help."

"I had no time to grab my medical bag," she began. "In it I keep gloves and a gown to put over my clothes, which I wear to insure sanitation." She looked down at her bare hands, quite dirty now from falling off her bicycle. "I will need hot water, soap, and whiskey, if you have it, to cleanse my hands properly. Also towels and a sharp knife, that also needs to be clean."

Maria nodded, leaving to fetch the items requested.

"Does my baby not come because somethin' is wrong?" Ramona's eyes filled with tears.

"I won't know anything until I examine you," she said. "But whatever the circumstance, we will work together—you and me—to do the very best we can."

Again Ramona forced a smile. "Yes, we will do our very best."

When Maria returned, Cassia sterilized her hands the best way she could and removed the sheet covering Ramona. Carefully she examined her breasts and felt around her very swollen abdomen. Then, cleansing her hands once again, she made way to examine Ramona internally.

It was then Ramona cried out with the urge to push.

"Ramona, you must not push." Cassia positioned herself between Ramona's thighs. "Instead, take deep breaths, try to relax, until I'm finished examining you."

"I will try, but it is hard not to want to push." Ramona moaned.

"I know, Ramona," she sympathized. "But remember, we need to work together."

"I will remember," Ramona choked out hoarsely.

Cassia instructed Maria to help Ramona scoot farther down on the mattress, hanging her buttocks off the slightly raised edge. Then she showed the older woman how she wanted her to hold onto Ramona's legs.

As the perineum, the section between the vaginal area and the anus, expanded, Cassia didn't see the baby's head, but the purplish color of the prolapsed cord. And instantly she knew why Ramona was having such a hard time delivering…the baby was breech.

Chapter Thirty-Two

Before Brodie joined Gabriel and Ethan on the search for Cassia, they drove Sadie and Sean over to the Holmes's residence. Gabriel wanted to check on his mother, and Brodie wanted to make sure his parents made it safely to their destination. With Cassia missing, he didn't need or want any more of his loved ones in jeopardy. Knowing his sisters were safely settled in their homes and his parents stayed with Reverend Holmes and Amanda freed his thoughts to focus on finding Cassia.

Amanda ran into Sadie's embrace, the two weeping and consoling each other. His heart broke for his future mother-in-law, as she clung to her friend for moral support. Cassia's parents had always been good to him and his family. In the early days of their arrival to a new land, it was Joshua and Amanda who helped them to settle in by showing them the new ways of a country that offered them much more than from whence they came. His proposal to Cassia now insured he would be a part of this heartwarming and honest family, as she would be a part of his. It was no wonder all the people gathered in the Holmes's house felt the pain and fear of Cassia's disappearance and prayed the mission would be a rescue and not a recovery.

Brodie spotted Reverend Holmes standing alone in the parlor, gazing out the front window. No doubt hoping he'd see Cassia making her way up the front walk, all this just a horrible mistake. He neared the elderly man and stood silently beside him, a small sign of support and solidarity on his part toward his future father-in-law.

"You are to go, then, with Gabriel and Ethan to find my daughter," he said, his tone calm, soft, as though he were having an ordinary conversation.

"Yes, and although I am not deputized, I will hold nothing back in actively rescuing her from whatever circumstance she is in," he vowed.

Joshua Holmes remained looking out the window. "My daughter is resilient, like her mother. The two of them only need the smallest measure of hope to be courageous enough to carry on—survive—and strive to return to those they love."

"I know Cassia will be clever and brave, wherever she is and in whatever circumstance she finds herself in," he countered. "I am the one ready to fall apart."

"It is always harder for the loved ones left behind to cope, but together we must expect a good outcome tonight, and in doing so, we will all find good wins out, more than not," he advised. Turning to glance at Brodie, his eyes brimming with unshed tears, the reverend added, "I am too old to go on this rescue mission. My mind is willing, my heart yearns to be the one to find her and bring her safely back to her mother, but my body is too weak…too old and tired to withstand such rigors. So, I ask you, my son-to-be, to bring my precious baby girl back to us."

Brodie's eyes grew moist, his heart breaking for this father who loved his child. He would feel the same if it were his daughter in peril. "You know, sir, I love

Cassia with every fiber of my being."

"Aye, I know this to be true," Joshua agreed.

"Then you must also know I will not stop searching until I find her, and bring her home. On this you have my word."

"Then go with God. Do at all costs, what you must," Joshua whispered, turning back to gaze out the window.

He left his parents' wagon at the Holmes's residence and followed Gabriel and Ethan on foot into the woods. In one hand he gripped his shot gun and in the other a flashlight. His heart beat like a drum, echoing throughout his body, into his ears, to the top of his head. The pulse at his neck throbbed. Every part of his body was on high alert…aware of his surroundings and every move Gabriel and Ethan made. He watched them, admiring their excellent tracking skills. The ease and familiar way they went about the search, comfortable with the wilderness they trudged through despite the inner turmoil they had to be experiencing, gave him a higher regard toward them. His two companions crawled on the ground, sniffed the area like dogs, left nothing unturned as no sign was considered too small or insignificant. They were patient, steady, stealthy, and wise with their every move.

"We have come as far as we can from this end of town," Gabriel announced about an hour into the search. "It would be wise for us to double back. McCrea's men are meeting in a clearing about a mile south of here, near the creek, and have brought in the hounds. We would do well to check in with them to see what news they might have."

As they drew nearer to the clearing, he heard the

barking hounds, their howls high-pitched with excitement. A mixture of dread and hope washed through him, as the dogs could have come upon either a living or a dead body. Men, their flashlights beaming in the distance, followed the dog's trails. At the juncture of a path not far from the creek, several men stood. The dogs halted beside them, sniffing a body lying on the ground, draped with a blanket. He, Gabriel, and Ethan shared horrified glances before proceeding farther.

Michael McCrea spotted them and made his way to where they emerged. "About twenty minutes ago we found a woman's body beside the creek." Michael paused, biting his bottom lip. "She has short blonde hair and blue eyes."

He went numb, as the blood drained from his head. The bond he had with Cassia, the love and devotion etched deep within his heart was so strong, so much a part of his life that if the woman found was her, he no longer would have a reason to live.

Gabriel's voice shook. "Is it my sister?"

"We can't tell." Michael ran a hand through his hair. "She's been badly beaten so her facial features aren't recognizable."

"My mother said when Cassia left the house this morning she was wearing a blue blouse and a blue and white checked skirt," Gabriel supplied.

"Not a help to us at this point, Gabriel." Michael cast his eyes to the ground. "The woman has been stripped of her clothing." He inhaled sharply before raising his gaze. "The only way we might get some answers is if we take the body to the Willow Creek examiner for an autopsy. And even then we could still be in the dark as to who the woman is, as well as it taking weeks for any other results."

"Let me examine the body," Brodie choked out, his stomach turning inside of him.

"Brodie, you don't have to put yourself in this position," Michael said.

"Yes. Yes, I do." He swallowed back the nausea rising in his throat. "We need to know instantly if it's Cassia. And if not, then we need to continue our search before the trail grows cold."

"He speaks the truth," Gabriel agreed. "Let him examine the body."

"But how will you tell if it's her?" Michael questioned.

"I can tell if it's *not* her," he said. "As a doctor I've examined and delivered the babies of many women. I can tell if this woman has ever been with a man or had a pregnancy."

"Whether she's ever been virtuous or not wouldn't be something you could determine now with an examination." Michael cleared his throat nervously. "From the blood it's evident she's been severely and brutally compromised."

Brodie closed his eyes for a moment, willing himself not to black out. "Saints preserve us," he whispered. Of all the horror and death he's witnessed throughout his medical career, nothing could compare to the gore of the scene he was about to set his eyes upon. Then a thought struck him. "Let me see her feet."

Michael frowned. "What can the woman's feet tell you?"

"In this case, everything." He made his way to the body on shaky limbs. Slowly he knelt, placed the shotgun aside, and lowered the flashlight. With trembling hands, he pulled back the blanket from the woman's feet and examined her toes…carefully.

Bringing the light close to each digit, he searched for the pink nail polish. There was not a trace of the pale paint, but something else caught his eye. There, on the left ankle bone, he spotted a birthmark in the shape of the number eight. Frowning, he forced himself to remember where and when he'd seen this birthmark before. And then it came to him, in a sickening and disturbing rush. Dropping the flashlight, he stood, running over to a tree. Bracing himself against the trunk he began to vomit, losing all the contents of his stomach. An intense pang of sorrow gripped his heart, a heart he could feel bleeding, if that were possible, for the woman lying brutally murdered a few feet away. And then he thought of Cassia. Where was she? Was she scared, suffering, and desperately fighting for her life? Would she be Becket Attwater's next victim? It all became too much to bear, and he lost all resolve. Falling to his knees, he wept loudly, not caring who heard him or what any of the other men might think. It was then he felt a hand upon his shoulder. He turned to look up at Gabriel. Even in the dark he could make out the other man's anguished-filled eyes. They mirrored Brodie's own heart.

Gabriel's words trembled with his emotion. "Is the woman Cassia?"

He swallowed hard, forcing his voice to come. "No," he finally managed to choke out.

In an instant, relief washed over Gabriel's face. "Do you have an idea, then, as to who the woman might be?"

He nodded and slowly stood. "Tell Mike he needs

to send someone over to the Boyd residence." After taking a deep breath he whispered, "Because that's Alma Lee Sloane."

Chapter Thirty-Three

Besides the situation of delivering a breech birth, the covered wagon's draped walls seemed to close in on Cassia. No air circulated within the wheeled dwelling, causing the perspiration to form on her forehead and drip into her eyes. Not wanting to contaminate her clean hands, she raised her arm to wipe her brow upon her sleeve. Sweat trickled down her cleavage, as well as her back, causing her shirt to become wet, the flimsy material sticking to her flesh. Not long ago she was shivering from the night chill, but now her adrenalin was in full force, and she was as hot as an oven. It was the case for Ramona as well. Her entire body glistened with sweat, as she lay writhing with pain. And the dark, loose tendrils framing Maria's face spiraled into damp curls.

She closed her eyes a moment to calm the inner turmoil rioting deep within the pit of her stomach. Here she was, in the middle of nowhere, with none of her medical equipment or supplies, and facing a difficult birth. She'd never delivered a breech baby and only saw it done once. Taking a few deep breaths, she called sternly and desperately on her medical training to recall the procedures she must take to save Ramona and her baby.

"What is it? What is wrong?" Ramona choked out hoarsely.

Slowly Cassia opened her eyes, her gaze meeting Ramona's. "Your baby is breech—coming out buttocks first."

"And how will you help her?" Maria sternly responded.

Cassia inhaled sharply. "The only way is to turn the baby."

"Have you ever done this?" Maria probed.

"No, but I've seen it done—once," she admitted.

"Then once will have to do," Maria said flatly.

She licked her dry lips, removing herself from the fear coursing through every vein in her body, the throbbing pain of her swollen ankle, and the extreme heat of her surroundings, and put every effort into concentrating on the next move she needed to make.

Instantly she realized the breech position is an incomplete sphere and the cord could very easily slip down around the baby's legs. But as far as she could tell, the cord was still pulsating normally. And that was a good sign. As the perineum continued to extend, Cassia could see more clearly the baby's buttocks. It appeared the baby's right buttock cheek would emerge first from under the pubic bone.

"The baby needs to come as slowly as possible, Ramona. The slower, the better," she strongly emphasized. "So try not to push."

Ramona, her face contorted with pain, nodded her response.

The baby, with legs curled up, needed to be rotated to safeguard the best position for delivery. Carefully she inserted a hand into Ramona's birth canal, latching her fingers over the baby's legs. It was fortunate Ramona had already given birth to three other children, as her body was stretched enough for Cassia to navigate her hands successfully within the woman's womb. If this was Ramona's first birth, the situation would have been very grave. A Cesarean section would have been the only plan of action, something Cassia could not have performed. Gravity helped at this point, pulling the baby's body to hang from the vulva, which helped to sustain flexing the head.

"The baby's legs are sliding out," she announced, as a gush of blood followed, soaking the front of her blouse. "Please, keep from pushing just yet, Ramona." A long piece of the cord also came out, and she could see it throbbing…the baby's life blood as the child was still attached to the placenta. Even though the baby was half born, until the nose and mouth were clear, the placenta was what sustained life.

With Ramona's next contraction, more blood flowed, staining her skirt. Then the baby slid out as far as the shoulders.

"The baby must not catch even the slightest chill, so I will need something to wrap her in," she said.

"Her?" Ramona gasped.

Cassia smiled. "Yes, you have a daughter, Ramona."

Maria left her post at holding Ramona's legs to fetch the clean towels she'd brought in earlier and sat on the small wooden table. She also grabbed a knife, cleaned it with the whiskey, and set it within Cassia's grasp.

Quickly Cassia wrapped the baby, also using the towel to ensure a good grip on the child's body, and turned her one fourth of a circle under the pubic bone. As she was doing this, the right shoulder was delivered.

Another contraction helped Cassia to grip the baby under an arm and rotate her clockwise, delivering the left shoulder. Now, just the head remained.

"Push now, Ramona, with everything you've got," she said.

But even with the next contraction, the baby's head remained inside her mother. Silently Cassia prayed gravity would again help the situation. Up until this point, she had been bracing the baby with her hands, but now she let the child go, dangling a bit from the mother. Surely, with the next contraction, the head would be born. But again that wasn't the case. Leaning forward, she placed her hands on Ramona's abdomen. When Ramona had another contraction, she pushed on her stomach just above the pubic bone. The baby's mouth and nose were finally exposed. Quickly she wiped the baby's face clean with one of the towels, freeing the mouth and nose the best she could of mucus. With the last contraction, and more pressure on Ramona's abdomen, the entire head was born. No longer did the baby need the life line of the placenta to breath. After she cut the cord with a knife, the baby gasped and cried...music to everyone's ears.

She placed the infant in her mother's arms, then sat back to take a long, cleansing sigh of relief.

Thank you, Lord for linking us strongly to Your grace and getting us all safely through this.

"If you were not here my daughter and her baby would have died." Maria clasped Cassia's hand and squeezed it affectionately.

After Ramona was washed and dressed, and the baby cleaned and diapered, Niko and the other children came into the wagon.

"What will we name her, Ramona." Niko marveled over his new daughter.

Ramona turned to Cassia. "I like your middle name. Rose, wasn't it?"

"Yes." She moved to sit nearer to the wagon's door flap for air.

"I shall call her Rose, then," Ramona decided.

Later, as she sat by the fire eating a bowl of vegetable stew and enjoying the delicious spicy flavor of the gravy, Maria knelt in front of Cassia.

"Let me take care of you, now," the gypsy woman said. With gentle and nimble fingers, she spread a minty smelling salve on Cassia's ankle and bound it with a clean, cotton strip of cloth. "We will break camp in the mornin', as we are to move on. But before we leave, Niko will take you home."

She nodded a response, too tired to argue the fact she needed to leave. She feared her family would believe something fiendish happened to her, most likely assuming she'd been snatched by Becket Attwater. No doubt the deputized men would be gathered and searching the town for her. Gabriel and her parents would be devastated. Brodie would be beside himself. To put them all through such worry made her heart ache. Plus, her clothes were stained with dried blood. But to rip Niko away from Ramona and the baby, just to please her, seemed cruel and selfish.

Maria draped a blue and white, crocheted shawl over her shoulders "My mother makes these shawls." She knotted the cape in front to cover the blood stains. After Maria set a blanket and pillow for her by the fire, she promptly joined her. "I will sleep with you beneath the stars."

An elderly woman, thin and rather frail, her pure white braid reaching to her waist, slowly made her way to where Cassia and Maria lay. She also held a blanket and pillow in her hands. "May I join you?"

"Aha, is Papa's snorin' botherin' you again, Mama?" Maria stood to help her mother arrange the blanket and pillow beside her own.

"And the fact he drank too much wine celebratin' another grandchild's birth makes him snore even louder," the old woman confessed.

"This is Cassia, the midwife who saved Ramona and the baby," Maria said. Then turning to her, Maria continued the introduction. "This is my mother..."

But before Maria could tell the elder woman's name, the old gypsy interrupted. "Move closer to the fire, Child, so I might see your face clearly."

She complied, moving closer to the old woman and searching her freckled face.

Maria's mother gasped, placing a wrinkled hand gently upon Cassia's cheek. "My eyes deceive me. How can this be?"

"What is it, Mama?"

"This woman...she is Amelia Gregory. But how can this be?" the elder woman said with astonishment. "This woman is young, and Miss Amelia would be..."

Cassia frowned, this time it was her turn to interrupt. "How do you know my grandmother?"

Chapter Thirty-Four

"Your grandmother?" the elderly gypsy woman gasped.

"Yes, Amelia Gregory was my grandmother," Cassia confirmed.

"Aha, that explains the resemblance." The other woman's brows rose. "Then you must be Amanda's daughter?"

Her frown deepened. "Yes, Amanda is my mother, but how do you know my family?"

"Before I married Marcus Zappone, I was Thea Johnson, your mama's best friend," the elder woman claimed.

She reached for Thea's hand, encasing it within her own. "I have heard many stories about the fun you and my mama had as young girls. She said you would stay often with her family while your father was away trapping and fishing."

Thea smiled. "Ahh, those were good times. Times I will never forget. Your grandmother treated me with love, respect, and kindness, tried to help me many times by givin' me clothes and other things a young girl growin' up needed to have." She sighed heavily. "But my father was a proud man, didn't take well to charity, and I was not allowed to reap the benefits of Amelia's generosity."

Men and their misplaced pride—like Ned

Beachum. "Mama still speaks to this day about your father just up and leaving, and how she never saw you again," Cassia relayed.

Thea sighed again. "It was the worst day of my life as I loved your grandparents and your mother like family."

She frowned. "Why did your father leave?"

"I was only seven at the time, and Papa had just returned from one of his trips. Miss Amelia invited him to stay for dinner. If I recollect right, I had taken a fancy to some ribbons Amanda owned." She shrugged. "I reckon I stole the ribbons, and somehow Papa found out. He was shamed by my behavior, as he was also a God fearin' man. Amanda knew I'd get a paddlin' for my deed, as I confided in her many times the way Papa punished me. So she lied and said she'd given me the ribbons. Papa didn't believe her. Right there and then he turned me over his knee, raised my skirt, and paddled my naked behind in full view of Miss Amelia, her husband, and Amanda."

"I'm so sorry," she sympathized.

Tears formed in Thea's eyes. "The heat of shame washed through my whole body, so much so that whenever I think of it, I can still feel the humiliation. I tried to place my hands over my backside to cover my nakedness, but Papa kept pushin' them aside, thrashin' me harder and harder. All I could think of was how I disappointed Miss Amelia. I remember glancin' over at her and hopin' she wouldn't hate me. But her kind, lovin' face mirrored my disgrace and agony, not scorn. I grew weaker and weaker from Papa's blows. That's when Miss Amelia stood and pulled me from Papa's wrath, held me tight, and rocked me like a mother

303

would a small babe. She scolded him, told him he was never to degrade me in such a way again."

"Her reaction stemmed from the fact she was abused the same way by her own father," Cassia explained. "And she never would allow such punishment to befall upon Amanda, nor did my mother ever reprimand her children in such a fashion."

"Aha, now I see why Miss Amelia came so strongly to my defense," Thea mused aloud. "That night Papa packed up what little we had, and we left for California," she continued. "We settled in a small town called Grover's Ridge. When Papa went on his fishin' and trappin' trips, I stayed alone in the crude, one-room cabin we lived in. I learned quite well how to take care of myself, but I was very lonely. It was the summer I was fourteen that I made friends with a band of gypsies camped near our cabin. I kept their presence from Papa, so I wouldn't be forbidden to visit them. While Papa was away, they were my saviors, feedin' me good food, makin' me laugh. I enjoyed the music, the colorful clothes, and the friendship. When Papa returned he was sick with pneumonia. I didn't know what to do or how to help him, so I went for Katerina, the gypsy healer. She did all that she could to make him well again, but he was too sick. After Papa died, the gypsy men buried him by the cabin, and the women took me in. I married Katerina's son, Marcus, when I was eighteen, and so here I be. Now, tell me how my good friend, Amanda has done," Thea concluded.

Cassia told Thea about Proud Eagle, and her mother's time living with the Apaches before marrying Joshua Holmes."

"Strange to think," Thea reflected, "how we both

bridged a gap, her with the Apaches and me with the gypsies."

"Won't you come along when Niko brings me home, to see my mother once again?" she hopefully inquired. "I know it would please her greatly."

"It would please me as well, but it is best I remain here with Marcus. He is too old to be worryin' over my whereabouts. Besides, as soon as Niko returns, we must leave the area. Stayin' too long in one place is not wise." Thea gave Cassia's hand an affectionate squeeze. "It must be a divine, heavenly plan for your family to bless mine. First with Miss Amelia, being so kind and carin' to me and all...and now with you, savin' the life of my granddaughter and her baby. When you finally get home, tell Amanda my heart, my sincere appreciation, and my prayers will always be with her and her family."

At dawn Cassia woke to the smell of coffee. Maria handed her a cup along with a piece of cornbread. While she ate, Niko readied the wagon. After checking on Ramona to make sure there was no hemorrhaging and little Rose to make sure her lungs were clear, Cassia was satisfied both were doing very well. She gave Maria and Thea a farewell hug and slipped off the shawl.

"No, that belongs to you now, Child," Thea said. "The colors bring out your eyes."

After thanking the elder woman and hugging her again, she joined Niko in the wagon, and they were on their way back to Eagle's Landing.

"I don't know how to thank you for helpin' my wife as you've done." Niko kept his eyes on the road ahead. It was a foggy morning, and visibility was extremely poor.

She wrapped the shawl tightly around her shoulders, the morning mist chilling her flesh. "There's no need for thanks. I just did my job."

"I haven't anythin' to pay you," Niko continued.

"That's hardly true, Niko. Your people gave me dinner, tended to my ankle which feels much better, gave me a night's lodging, a beautiful shawl, and fed me breakfast. There's no need for further payment."

As Niko drove the wagon out onto the main road of South Eagle's Landing, the howling of hounds could be heard in the far distance. He halted the horse, turning to her with a worrisome frown. "The hounds must be searching for you."

Instantly she knew why he looked so troubled. In truth, he held her at knife point to get her to come with him. In the eyes of the law, he committed a crime. He'd be apprehended, thrown into jail, and convicted of kidnapping. Never would he be able to return to Ramona and the children.

"Go, leave me here." She turned to climb down from the wagon.

He placed a restraining hand on her arm. "You will not make it far with that injured foot."

"And you will never make it home if the men guiding those dogs see you." She pushed aside his grasp.

Niko ran a hand through his hair. "But you are defenseless against danger."

Niko spoke the truth. She had nothing, no weapon to use in case she came upon a problem. Suddenly the thought of Becket Attwater lurking within the fog sent a rush of fear down her spine. Yet knowing what could happen to Niko if the search party found him, frightened her even more.

"I will be fine as the clinic is not far from here." She patted her skirt pocket. "And I have a key to get in." Instantly she breathed a silent prayer of thanks for that key, because today was Saturday and no workers were expected. "I will be able to use the phone, call for help, and stay safely inside until someone arrives. Now, you must go."

He nodded and came around to the other side of the wagon to help her down, securing her as before until she could stand firmly on her feet. As soon as she was stable, he climbed back into the wagon and drove away. She stood for a moment, watching him disappear into the fog. Outside of the howling hounds, all was still.

Slowly, not to aggravate her sore ankle further, she took careful steps. As she made her way down the block in the fog, the cold morning vapor again chilled her. Adjusting the shawl once again to stay warmly around her shoulders, she continued until she came upon the back path to the clinic. She was about fifty feet from the door when she reached for the leather cord of keys in her pocket. As she fumbled to find the one to fit the lock, she was rushed from behind and knocked to the ground. Stunned, she dropped the keys. In the next quick second, a fist slammed against her jaw. Immediately she tasted blood, her senses reeling from the blow and the sound of the hounds fading.

Her worst nightmare was taking place, and she struggled now to stay conscious and keep her wits about her. Her gaze traveled slowly to the massive presence looming above her. He was tall, broad, a monster in the flesh.

"I won't be able to give ya all the attention I usually take with them their hounds not far from my trail," a deep voice rasped. "But just a taste, before I go into hidin' again, will have to do."

She fought to clear her vision and focus on the man's face before her, a round, plump façade with a jutting chin and large, droopy lips. "Becket Attwater!"

He cackled like the crazed human being he was. "At your service, ma'am."

His black, pig-like eyes leered down at her, sizing her up and no doubt picturing how he'd make her another one of his victims. But she wasn't having any of it. Frantically, her eyes searched for the keys. They'd fallen a few inches away from her left knee. She'd never make it to retrieve them, hustle with an injured foot to the door, unlock it, and safely barricade herself inside the clinic before Attwater could attack her again. He was too big, strong, and quick. But she wasn't about to let this depraved man have his way with her either. Not without a fight, anyway.

But what do I have to fight him with?

Then her brother, Gabriel's words instantly came to mind. *Anything can be made into a weapon if you use it right and hold it effectively.*

She lunged for the keys, pain radiating down her face to her neck from the blow she sustained, and gripped them between her fingers. When Attwater came down to grab a fist full of her hair, she blindly swung out at him, not caring where she stabbed his flesh.

He shrieked like a wounded animal and jumped back, holding his arm. Blood seeped through his fingers, red droplets raining to the ground. "You little bitch," he roared. "I'll make sure you pay double for that."

She scrambled to her feet, praying her injured ankle held her weight. Pain jotted through her leg as she broke into a run, but she kept on...one foot after another...trying to put as much distance between her and the fiend pursuing her. She screamed as loud as her lungs allowed. "Help, someone help!"

Then he was upon her—reaching for the shawl around her shoulders and tossing it aside. In one fluid motion, he thrust her hard against the trunk of a large tree. His mammoth hands covered her entire throat, as he lifted her off the ground and squeezed the life from her body. She dropped the keys and struggled for air, her fingers trying desperately to pry his grasp from her throat. Her feet dangled and kicked, sandals flinging from her feet while Attwater banged her head, shoulders, and spine repeatedly against the tree's trunk. Her vision blurred, and her ears rang as she fought for breath. And then, just as her hands fell to her sides and her body grew numb, the sound of a gunshot broke the silence. Attwater's hands suddenly released her throat, and he stumbled back. She dropped to the ground in a heap, gasping for air.

"Cassia!" Brodie raced to her side and gathered her into his arms.

She clung to him, coughing and gasping as the air entered her lungs. Tears wet loose tendrils, sticking them to her face.

He pushed the curls from her eyes. "Breathe, just breathe. You're all right now, honey. I've got you. I've got you, and I'm never letting you go."

She could make out his face now, his tears welling in fearful eyes as they frantically surveyed the front of her bloodied blouse. "It's not my blood," she choked out. "It belongs…it belongs to…to Ramona," she managed to say, before everything went black.

Chapter Thirty-Five

When she regained consciousness, she found herself lying on one of the clinic's examining tables. The curtain was closed around her, and she could hear many men's voices talking nearby. Every part of her body ached, as did her mind's eye—playing repeatedly the horror she'd gone through. The ankle Maria so carefully bound was bared, and a cool damp cloth replaced the wrappings. Another moistened cloth gently swabbed her face and neck, pulling her fully to her senses. Slowly she opened her eyes to find Brodie standing over her. It was his tender touch she felt.

"It's over, honey. Attwater's dead," he whispered, washing her neck. His eyes filled with moisture as he gazed upon the bruises Attwater's hold left upon her flesh. "He had you by the throat, choking you. And I just lost my mind. So I…so I shot him in the back of the head."

She held out her arms to him, and together—while embraced—they sobbed. It was a clear fact both had taken the oath to do no harm. So, for Brodie to shoot someone and end his life, he had to have been brought to the edge of fear and moved by the sheer love he held for her. But he vowed he'd never let any harm come to her, and today he kept that promise. Still and all, it was no wonder he sobbed as they held each other close.

"I was so scared I'd lost you." He buried his face

against her neck. "And I knew I couldn't go on if that happened, because you are so much a part of me—of my life. We are bound in every way."

She stroked his deep russet curls, swallowing her tears and inhaling his comforting and familiar scent. "I feared I'd never see you again, Brodie. As my lungs were being robbed of air, my thoughts raced to everything I was standing to lose…to all the days, months, years I was going to miss being with you. Laughing with you, working by your side, loving you at night, making a home and having children. And those thoughts hurt worse than anything physical Attwater was doing to me. It was though my heart was bleeding."

He pulled back, gently caressing her bruised jaw and frowning down at her blood-stained blouse. "I felt the exact same way, Cassia. I could feel my heart bleeding as it only beats for you. But now we're going to have all those things together that you mentioned, honey. And the mad man is dead, so he will never be able to hurt another human being again." His face hardened. "I hope his soul rots in hell."

She flinched in agony when she tried to move her left leg, her sore ankle shooting pain to her shin and knee.

Immediately his handsome features softened with concern. "Enough talk now. It's time for me to tend to your wounds, my love."

"Outside of my jaw, ankle, and the ring of fire around my neck, I have no open wounds," she quickly conveyed. Glancing down at the front of her blouse, she added, "The blood is not mine."

His frown deepened. "You said as much before you blacked out and mentioned a name…Ramona." He

312

cleared his throat. "Michael and his men are waiting to question you, when you think you're able to talk to them. Gabriel and Ethan are waiting to see you too."

She arched a brow. "Question me? Why would Michael need to question me about Ramona?"

Gently he took her hand. "Because of who she was...another of Attwater's victims murdered in this area. Obviously, for you to know her name, the two of you must have been held together. Mike needs to know where Attwater left her body."

"No. No, you don't understand," she interrupted, sitting up quickly. The room spun.

"Stay put, honey, until you regain more of your strength." He helped her to lie back upon the pillow.

Her voice trembled. "Ramona is a gypsy woman whom I helped through a breech birth. Last night, just as I pulled up to my house, a gypsy man and his young daughter came seeking my help. The call was an emergency, and there was no time to grab my bag. I've been at their camp all night trying to save both mother and baby."

"And did you save them?" He recaptured her hand and warmed it within his.

"Yes, both are fine." She sighed. "But I was so scared. I had no medical supplies or instruments with me, and I had to turn the baby. I've never done such a procedure before, and only saw it performed once. I put my hands inside of this woman's womb and navigated the baby to a better birthing position. Then the child's head was stuck, and I had to fiddle around to free it. But, thank God, all was fine. And then, this morning, the man started to drive me home again when we heard the hounds," she explained. "I feared he'd be detained because he is a gypsy. You know how that goes?"

He nodded. "Yes, there are a lot of small minds around. At times my own folks have been looked down upon, being immigrants from Ireland."

"Exactly, as my brother, Gabriel, who is often referred to as the half breed as well as the other Apaches in town, and the dark skinned folks who've migrated here from the southern states. Though it's been fifty-five years since slavery has been abolished, they still aren't considered equal." She paused a moment. "Please, don't get me wrong, Brodie. I don't fault or hold anything against Michael, for I think coming from Ireland himself he knows enough to be fair, but he still must answer to the protocol of the law, as he's sworn to do. And I couldn't take a chance this poor man—who only sought help for his wife— wouldn't be unnecessarily detained. So I told him to drop me off at the clinic. I thought, once inside, I'd be able to phone you, and while I waited for you to arrive, I could tend my sore ankle. But before I could get to the door, I was attacked by Attwater."

He frowned. "How did you hurt your ankle?"

"I was startled by the gypsy's wagon, as he came upon me in such urgency, and fell off the bicycle, landing on my ankle," she said. Then she frowned, suddenly realizing he indicated a second woman. "Why would Michael think Ramona was another of Attwater's victims?"

Brodie sighed heavily. "He murdered another woman before he grabbed you. The hounds found her body by the creek. I examined and identified her."

She swallowed hard. "Was she someone we know?"

He nodded slowly, his eyes moist.

Fear rioted within her chest. "Who was she, Brodie? Tell me."

He sighed again and kissed the top of her hand. "It was Alma Lee. And I am so sorry, honey. I know how much she meant to you and how hard you tried to help her."

The grief and horror of it all…Alma Lee dead, was just too much to bear. That poor young woman lost everything dear to her…her husband, the hope of a baby, and now her life. The thought of how horrible the end had to be for Alma Lee…alone, scared, with no one coming to her rescue…set a fire of pure sorrow burning within her she had no power to contain.

She screamed a sob at the top of her lungs, which echoed throughout the clinic, and covered her face with her hands. The curtain shielding her from the others in the room ripped open, and in an instant Gabriel had her in his arms, rocking and cradling her like she was still a small child. Often he soothed her, when she was little, in just such a manner. He, being so much older, was like a second father. And she felt no shame to curl into his embrace, like she'd done all those many years ago, allowing him to comfort her the way only family knew how to do.

"You are with those who love and care for you, especially your man, Brodie. He saved your life." Gabriel stroked her hair and kissed her forehead. "Everything will now be all right, baby girl."

The endearing name—*baby girl*—was what her father always called her. She hated hearing the loving words when she got older, but now she welcomed the sentiment. And somehow Gabriel knew what she needed…understood how much those words would comfort her and help relay the safety of a family member's strength. And so she felt free to release all of her sorrow. With her face buried beneath her older brother's neck—she wailed.

Ethan neared them and wrapped his arms around her, resting his head against her shoulder. "I am here as well, Cassia."

The three of them stayed entwined while she sobbed. No one spoke or interrupted, and she cried until she couldn't cry anymore. Then exhausted and spent, she let them take her home.

Chapter Thirty-Six

Cassia remained in her brother's arms until a wagon came for them and allowed him to hold her during the ride and carry her into the house. As they came through the door, her mother and Sadie gasped.

Sean broke instantly into professional mode. The elderly doctor, who took care of her so many times, began to bark out orders. "Get her to a bed, Gabriel, for me to check her wounds."

"The blood's not hers, Papa," Brodie instantly added.

"Nevertheless, get her onto a bed." Sean reached for his medical bag.

Gabriel carried her into her room. Sean, Sadie, and her mother followed closely behind. Gently her brother set her on the bed, placing another kiss upon her forehead. "You're in good hands now," he whispered, before leaving the room.

After the door was securely shut, her mother and Sadie set to work removing the blood-stained blouse and skirt. Then off came her slip, leaving her clad only in a brassiere and underpants. She was too exhausted to protest, too grieved to feel any shame while lying nearly naked before their eyes. Sean took her temperature and listened to her heart. Then he examined her head, shoulders, and back, which had scrapes and bruises from being slammed against the tree. He felt around her jaw, the front of her throat, and moved to her abdomen, checking for broken ribs.

As the doctor moved his hands to examine her pelvic region, he paused. "Cassia, were…were you…compromised?"

"No," she responded quickly. "Brodie arrived in time."

"Then there's no need to check ye further." He covered her with a sheet. From his medical bag, he pulled salve for her neck, jaw, and the scratches along her back. "I'll leave ye now, Lass, so the women can bathe ye and apply the salve. Then I'll return to wrap yer ankle." He gave her hand an affectionate pat.

Sadie and her mother left the room long enough to fetch wash clothes and towels, soap, and a basin of hot water. Together they stripped her of the rest of her clothes and bathed her. Like a child she was washed, arms raised, legs spread, and turned from side to side. Then they dried her, covered her bruises with salve, and dressed her in a nightgown and robe. All the while she stayed silent, accepting the personal care. It was easy to fall into such sadness you didn't mind others tending to private matters—those parts of your body otherwise held modestly. This must be how Alma Lee felt during her great despair. It was just easier not to have to cope with anything other than breathing, and let others do all the worrying for you. But then, she still had Brodie— the man who was the love of her life. If nothing else, coming to grips with tragedy and carrying on was worth it just to be with him. The thought of sharing her life with him brought her a measure of strength. But when her mother coaxed her to sit at the dressing table to have her hair brushed, she spotted the discarded clothes in a pile on the floor. In a rush the day's events gripped her again, the impact so fierce, she had to fight back becoming physically ill.

Swallowing the bile threatening to choke her, she cried out, "Burn those clothes, Mama. Burn them…burn them all, because I never will want to wear them again."

"As you wish, my darling." Her mother moved to retrieve the garments.

Sadie quickly stepped in. "Let me be doin' that for ye, me friend. Ye stay with yer daughter and help her to set things right."

Amanda reached out to affectionately pat Sadie's arm. "I thank you for being here for me…for all you do."

While Sadie went through the skirt's pockets, removing the change purse she found in one and setting it aside, she added, "I'll see what I can feed the men, as they must be hungry and thirsty. Then I'll bring somethin' in for Cassia."

"Again, thank you, Sadie." Amanda turned to help Cassia to the dressing table. "Now, sit, let me brush your hair. And when we're done here, Sean will wrap your ankle, and you can have a bite to eat."

"I'm not hungry," she mumbled. "Besides, I've got to go to the Boyds' house."

Amanda arched a brow. "You're not in condition to go anywhere."

Her eyes filled with tears. "You don't understand, Mama. Alma Lee is dead—murdered."

"I know. Michael called from the clinic when they found you and gave us the devastating news about Alma Lee." Amanda sighed. "I wouldn't doubt it if the whole town knows by now, as gossip travels fast in Eagle's Landing."

"I wanted so much for Alma Lee to recover and be happy again," she said.

"I know you did, dear. And we are all so sorry— for her passing and her family's loss," Amanda said. "But we're also very grateful you're all right."

"I've got to pay my respects, comfort her family during…during…"

"What sort of comfort will you be," her mother interrupted, "as bruised and exhausted as you are at this very moment?" Amanda pulled a handkerchief from her pocket and wiped the tears streaming down Cassia's cheeks. "Besides, it's your father's place to visit the family, as he will know the right words to say. And no doubt Sean will accompany him, so he can medically soothe whatever distress ails Trudy and her children. In a few days, when you're able to walk properly on your foot, you and I will go over to see them."

"Yes, you're right, Mama," she agreed. The last thing any of the Boyds needed was to see her battered, swollen jaw, and the choker of bruises around her neck. Brodie hadn't disclosed Alma Lee's condition, and she was thankful for his discretion as she wouldn't have been able to handle how she succumbed to her death. But in view of what Attwater did to two other women and what he tried to do to her, the actual cause of Alama Lee's demise had to be horrendous. She closed her eyes, sorrow coursing through every part of her body. "I pray the Lord was with Alma Lee at the end, Mama."

"I know He was." Her mother hugged her and kissed the top of her head. "Of that I am sure."

She sat on the bed while Sean wrapped her ankle. Her father, coming into the room, plopped down beside her. Gently he reached for her hand. Without saying a word, he comforted her. His peaceful presence wove a cocoon of security and love around her. She knew, when he closed his eyes and bowed his head for a moment, he was praying.

Then he stood, his eyes searching her face. "God's grace is greater than our woes, baby girl. Don't let the light He's given you to share, go dim with your sorrow." After kissing her forehead, he whispered, "I will give those grieving Alma Lee's loss your love." Sean left as well, to accompany her father to the Boyds' home, just as her mother had said.

Ethan looked in on her before taking himself back to his house next door. Gabriel followed soon after. Both men looked exhausted, after being up all night searching for her. Come to think of it, everyone had yet to sleep in their beds. Truth be told, lying on the ground beside the campfire hadn't really afforded her much sleep either.

Her brother had the shawl, her sandals, and keys in his hands. "I found these things on the ground when Brodie carried you into the clinic." He placed the shawl over a nearby chair, the sandals beside her bed, and laid the keys on the nightstand.

She glanced at the leather cord holding the keys and sighed. "Those keys helped in saving my life."

Gabriel frowned. "How so?"

"I remembered what you said...how anything, if used right and held correctly, can be applied as a weapon. I set the keys between my fingers, and when Attwater reached for me, I stabbed him in the arm. I believe that action bought me some time until help arrived."

Brodie was the last one to check on her. "I wanted to wait until your family had time with you," he explained while caressing her face.

"But you are family," she countered.

He hesitated a moment before he made a reply, and the pause concerned her. "Not yet, I'm not."

She frowned. "Brodie, what…"

"No more talk, honey." He pulled her close for a hug. "You get some rest, and I'll be back later, after I've done the same." He lowered his lips to hers for a kiss and whispered against her mouth, "I love you with all that I am." Then he was gone, departing with his mother to his home.

That left just her and her mother. After a quick trip to use the bathroom, Cassia tried to rest. But within an hour, delicious aromas sprung from the kitchen. Her mother was making bacon and eggs. Since she barely touched the tea and toast Sadie made for her earlier, her stomach groaned with hunger. She climbed out of bed, slipped on her robe, and reached for the shawl before joining her mother in the kitchen. Able now to put more weight on her foot, due to Sean's expert bandaging, she examined the shawl in her hands. It had sustained a bit of abuse…pulled slightly apart and soiled…during her scuffle with Attwater. But her mother was skilled in repairing yarn made garments, as well as knowing how to hand wash to clean and block while drying. Together she and Amanda sat and ate the small meal, while Cassia explained about the gypsies and Ramona's breech birth.

"Then that would explain why your bicycle almost

made it home, but you didn't," Amanda mused aloud.

"And I met someone else while at the gypsies' camp...someone you know. Her name is Thea Johnson," she began. She handed the shawl over to her mother. "She made this," she added, going into more detail. Amanda held the shawl against her heart and hung on her every word Cassia spoke, listening spellbound.

"I always wondered what happened to Thea—one day there, the next gone," Amanda admitted. She glanced at the shawl, fingering the few frayed pieces of yarn. "I'll fix and wash this for you."

"No, I want you to have it. I know Thea would want that too," she said.

Her mother sighed. "She was my best and dearest friend, and I missed her terribly after she left town."

"She said she missed you too, and grandmamma," Cassia relayed.

Amanda shook her head amazed. "Imagine, after all these years I finally get an answer as to what happened to her. And to think my daughter saved the life of my best friend's granddaughter and her baby." She smiled. "Thea bridged the gap with the gypsies, as I did with the Apaches. What a pair we are," she marveled.

Cassia cocked her head sideways. "Funny thing is, Thea said the exact same thing when I told her about Proud Eagle and your time as a warrior's wife."

Amanda's smile broadened. "Well then, I'd say it just goes to prove, great minds think alike."

At that point the mantel clock chimed the noon hour. She yawned, hardly able to keep her eyes open.

Amanda stood, making her way over to where

Cassia sat. "Come, time for sleep."

She took the hand her mother held out to her. "I can barely hold my eyes open," she confessed while her mother walked with her toward her room.

"No doubt the effect of the sleeping powder Sean gave me. I put a bit of it in your tea," Amanda admitted.

"Mama..." she began to protest. Then she clipped her words, laying her head on her mother's shoulder. She was just too tired to argue.

"Do you need to use the bathroom first?" Amanda inquired, as she'd done many times before putting Cassia to bed when she was a little girl.

"No, I'm good," she said, yawning again.

"Then to bed with you." Amanda helped Cassia off with the robe and adjusted the quilt for her to snuggle beneath. After tucking her in, Amanda climbed onto the bed, beside her. "You'd never take an afternoon nap unless I lay down with you, but right now I'd say we could both use a bit of shut-eye." Stifling a yawn, she added, "I hope your father comes home soon as well, so he can get some sleep."

Cassia rubbed her sleepy eyes. "He never thinks of himself."

"That's what he has me for," her mother commented. "Why do you think a spouse is referred to as *the better half?* I'm his, and he's mine. It will be that way for you and Brodie too. Now, roll over onto your side."

Cassia obeyed, and her mother gently rubbed the lower region of her spine. Her tender touch made Cassia sigh as the tension left her body. For now, grief could take a break. She was safe, home in her bed, with her mother here to tend her. Whatever else transpired in the hours, days, or months to come, could wait. This was the time she needed to heal. Hope sprang, as she remembered her father's words. *God's grace is greater than our woes.* She will be counting on that grace, clinging to such a thought to get herself through this tragedy. And she would also care for her inner lamp, making sure it didn't go dim so she could share the light of love, hope, and compassion with others.

Slowly Amanda brought her hand to rest upon Cassia's backside. Back and forth she rocked her. "I used to soothe you like this when you were little, after you had a nightmare or felt ill."

"I'm too old now for you to be rocking my bottom, Mama," she mumbled, feeling her body grow limp with fatigue.

"Nonsense, you will never be too old for me to comfort, because you'll always be my baby. And one day, when you're a mother, you'll know exactly what I mean," her mother warned.

She smiled to herself, thinking of the time when she'd be holding her own baby close to her heart, and then sleep overtook her.

Chapter Thirty-Seven

The aroma of her mother's cooking stirred Cassia's hunger once again, this time waking her from her slumber. She sniffed the air—chicken stew and homemade bread, she deciphered, her stomach longing for a taste.

She glanced at the nightstand clock. It read five p.m. "Goodness, I've slept the day away," she mumbled, stretching her bones before leaving the bed. She dressed in a casual, off white, pull-over top, and a yellow cotton skirt before slipping on a pair of moccasins Rising Sun made for her when she first returned from England. She arranged her hair with care, wanting to look presentable for Brodie, when he visited later. Truth be told, she was a little concerned he hadn't already tried to call. His hesitation and remark about not yet being family left her unsettled. But then again everyone was in dire need of rest. He might still be sleeping himself, or simply decided not to disturb her.

When she entered the kitchen, her mother was busy at the stove, and her father sat reading the paper at the table. His specs hung down his nose as he scanned the page before him. "How long have you been home, Papa?"

His eyes rose to meet hers. "I returned about two hours ago."

She frowned, taking a seat opposite him. "Then

you haven't gotten much sleep."

"He hasn't gotten any," her mother chimed in, turning from a simmering pot on the stove, to glance annoyed at her father. "So, it will be an early bed call for you tonight."

"Now, Amanda, don't be coddling me so," her father objected. "I've gone all night and day without sleep before, and it didn't kill me."

She knew why her mother worried. Joshua Holmes was well into his eighty-fifth year, though quite healthy and vibrant in many ways. Yet he was still a very elderly man, and going twenty-four hours without sleep could be detrimental.

"But I will do as you wish, and take myself to bed after dinner," he reneged, always accommodating Amanda. "And how much longer will it be until the meal's ready to be served?"

"Another thirty minutes should do it." Amanda sliced the homemade bread on the cutting board.

"Good, just enough time, then." Joshua set his glasses and the newspaper aside. Standing, he put out a hand to her. "Come with me, baby girl, as we need to talk."

Once in the parlor, Joshua sat in his favorite stuffed chair, so old it fit the mold of his body. Cassia took a seat on the sofa. "First, I want you to know I spent a great deal of time with Trudy and her children. We talked, she reminisced about Alma Lee, and then we prayed." He shook his head. "It won't be easy for them, as swallowing the bitter taste of grief never is, but they are God-loving folks and their faith will help them through." He sighed, sitting back in his chair. "I believe losing a child is the worst loss a person could endure.

So many facets of that child's life cross your mind…the times you cared for them as a baby, changing their diaper, feeding them a bottle and the bathing, rocking, reading bedtime stories. And then how you molded them as they grew, teaching them right from wrong, showing them how to be self-sufficient, and preparing them for adulthood." His eyes filled with tears. "The eight years you were in England were very difficult ones for your mother and me. We missed you terribly. Many nights I'd catch your mother in your room, touching your pillow or hugging that old teddy bear you've had since you were five. I would have my moments as well. And yet, we knew you'd return to us, and we'd have more chances to love and enjoy you. I can't imagine how Trudy must feel."

She swallowed the tears stinging her throat. "How can you ever get over something like this, Papa?"

"You don't, Cassia, but in time a person does learn to live with tragedy," he said, leaning forward in his seat. "Take into consideration your mother's tragedies. She lost her mother at a very young age and saw her father slain by the Chiricahua. With all that heartache, she still managed to carry on after losing her home and having to conform to a way of life foreign to her upbringing. After being captured by the Chiricahua, stripped and humiliated, she rose up to fight them for her escape, shooting and killing one with an arrow. She lived in fear for her children when the Apache village was taken over by white agents…enduring their suppression, starvation, and secretly coping with one of her daughter's rape. Then she was forced to send all her children away for their safety. Not to mention the eventual loss of Proud Eagle, and her being kidnapped by a Reservation Agent."

She gasped. "Though I've always known these things have happened to Mama, I am still amazed upon hearing them. Her strength is more than admirable."

"And those who don't know her would never suspect anything so traumatic has ever happened to her. And the reason is she embraces life, doesn't give up or give in because she grieves, and draws courage from the love she gives and takes from her family," he added.

"And yet all the grief and horror is still there, lurking in the back of your mind or etched deep within your heart," she countered. "I've seen it with the military men I tended during the war while in England. They suffer from shell shock—an aftermath of fighting, killing, and seeing their friends die in front of them. I've had nightmares myself just from caring for them and watching many succumb to their wounds. And now…and now…"

Her father reached out to take her hand. "Breathe. Take your time."

"Now Alma Lee is dead, and I keep seeing Attwater's face. How he leered down at me, what I knew he wanted to do to me, and then seeing him shot in the head." Tears spilled from her eyes. "Papa, how do I… How will I get past it all?"

"By dwelling on the good things," he said softly. "Your mother told me about the gypsies, how you saved two lives. In the scheme of things, Attwater's escape and you leaving the Boyds' house alone despite the pending danger led up to you being in that gypsy camp at the right time to help a woman and her baby."

"Just as you've always taught me to believe, there are no coincidences," she mused aloud.

"Aye, baby girl," he agreed. "And though we don't always like or understand why things turn out the way they do, the Lord has good reason…a master plan far greater than anything we could imagine."

"You always know what to say and when to say it, Papa. Constantly you offer others a plate full of nutritional food…only for the soul," she reflected.

"I just trust in the Lord to guide my tongue," he humbly admitted. He squeezed her hand affectionately. "And with that in mind, I need you to trust and have faith for those results destined to come. Shine a beacon of hope on those who need it, like the Boyds and Brodie."

She frowned. "Brodie?"

"Aye," her father said. "He's having a hard time coming to grips with the fact he killed a man—monster or not—a life was taken by his hand. The fear he endured throughout last night's search, and then coming upon Attwater attacking you, has left him with his own case of shell shock."

She gasped. "How do you know all this, Papa?"

"After I left the Boyd's homestead, I dropped Sean off at his house and decided to go in to talk with Brodie. Sean thought he'd be asleep, but I knew differently."

"Why did you know differently?"

He arched a brow. "Because of what I said to Brodie before he left to search for you." Joshua paused before continuing. "I told him to do whatever it took to save you…at all costs. And that's just what he did."

"And so, now you somehow feel you gave him your blessing to take the action he did?"

"Aye, though I'm sure he would have done the

same with or without my permission, I still can't help but feel responsible. And now the poor chap's dealing with blood on his hands."

She stood. "I must go to him."

Joshua reached for her arm. "Nay, Cassia." He pulled her down to sit back upon the sofa. "Brodie needs to think the matter through by himself tonight. So, if you're expecting him to visit... Well, I don't believe you'll see him this evening."

She sighed and nodded. "Were you able to comfort him any?"

"Aye, as we talked I could see some of the tension departing from his shoulders, and the creases along his brow relaxed," he conveyed. "As I was leaving, Sean insisted he take something to sleep, so I'm hoping he listens to his father. Rest is what he needs...and time...and that goes for you as well."

She stood, making her way closer to her father and wrapping her arms around his shoulders. "Thank you, Papa, for always being there for me and everyone else. Truthfully, I don't even want to think what I'd do without you."

"God willing, you won't have to worry about that for a while." He returned her hug with one of his own.

"Yes, God willing," she repeated.

It was just then her mother peeked around the door frame. "Dinner's ready, my loves. So, come and get it while it's hot."

Chapter Thirty-Eight

Cassia was given a reprieve from going to church the next morning, her father understanding her need to avoid the questions and gossip for which a small town is famous. It was only the second time in her life she missed services—as her father was quite strict about her and Amanda attending Sunday worship. A stomach ailment kept her home all those many years ago when she was just seven. Not being able to keep anything down or venture too far from the toilet granted her permission to remain home. Rising Sun had stayed with her then, while her mother accompanied Joshua to church. Today Cassia stayed home alone.

After the midafternoon meal, her father went into the bedroom to take a nap while she and Amanda sat in the parlor, working on an embroidery piece. At that point Brodie still hadn't called her or come over, and her concern level rose.

"Give him time," Amanda advised.

"I'm trying," she said, forcing her focus on her sewing.

By late afternoon there was a knock on the back door. She took the call, her ankle much better and only giving her a slight limp. When she opened the door, she found Brodie standing on the stoop. His emerald green eyes still looked tired, and his russet curls were in disarray. She rushed to him, wrapping her arms around his neck.

"I love you, Brodie," she whispered against his mouth before capturing his lips with a kiss.

His immediate response eased her heart, as he pulled her close and deepened the kiss. "Cassia, honey…marry me."

She giggled. "I am, in October."

"No, I mean sooner…much sooner." He pulled back to search her face.

"Come into the garden where we can talk," she advised. Once they were seated upon a bench, she probed further. "Why don't you want to wait until October as planned?"

He took a deep breath. "Because I need to be beside you each night, not three streets away, wondering if you're all right. I need…no, I want to touch you, make love to you, and be your family…the one called upon to take care of you…the only one you turn to when you need comfort."

"But Brodie, I do turn to you," she protested.

"No, no you don't, Cassia… You didn't… You turned to Gabriel. And I understand, because we're not wed." He ran a hand through his unruly hair and took another deep breath. "But you see, as your husband, I would rightly have been the one you would have turned to. I would have rocked you in my arms, carried you home, placed you in our bed, examined you, and bathed your wounds."

Suddenly everything became perfectly clear. This incredible, loving man had killed for her, saved her life in the process, and yet she turned to her brother. "Brodie, my Brodie," she whispered, taking his face between her hands. "If you only knew how much you mean to me, how many times I think of you when we're not together. How I trust you and admire you, depend on you, need you, want you, and love you, you'd be so overwhelmed."

"Then overwhelm me. I'll welcome it. I want it. I want you." He placed his hands over hers. "I want you in my arms, all night—every night, and then waking with you in the morning."

"All right," she decided. "When, then do you want to make me your wife?"

"Within six weeks…just enough time for me to fix up the apartment behind the General Store, and for you to have Olivia Beachum finish your gown."

"What of the family members far away, especially my sister-in-law, Riley and niece, Anita and your best man, Paul? None of them will be able to attend on such short notice," she pointed out.

"I talked to Gabriel this morning, and he's leaving for England in two days to escort his wife and daughter back home. He said he needs her with him—feels empty without her around, and I can't blame him. And as far as Paul goes… Well, the truth is, with all that's been going on, I've yet to contact him. But I've decided I want family standing witness to my marriage instead. Someone who shares how much I love and care for you. So, I asked Gabriel to be my best man, and he agreed. Besides, in October, when your sister in England and the one in Ireland, and their families can travel here, we can have another big party."

She smiled. "You've put a lot of thought into all of this."

"I've thought of nothing else."

Her smile broadened. "I can help with the

apartment renovations, and I'm sure we can count on friends and family to chip in as well."

His eyes twinkled, mirroring her excitement. "I've already decided on asking P.J. He's devastated about forgetting his obligation to see you home, blames himself for it all. So, helping with the apartment can be part of his amends...outside of not being able to sit so well since his father gave him one hell of a thrashing."

Moving her hands to fold in her lap, she lowered her gaze. "Poor P.J. In truth, he isn't at fault for any of what happened. I am."

He lifted her chin with a finger. "That's not true, honey."

"Yes, Brodie, it is. I am completely responsible for leaving the Boyd home on my own. Trudy offered for me to stay, said John Tyler could drive me home when he got off duty, but I didn't listen."

"And because of that you were in the right place at the right time to save a woman and her baby," he defended.

"Though that part may be true, I'm still responsible for Alma Lee's death," she said, tears welling in her eyes.

He frowned. "How can you believe that?"

"Because it's the truth, Brodie. That Friday afternoon, I encouraged Alma Lee to come along to buy material at the General Store. She was doing so well, had returned to her old self. And Ruth Ann wanted to make us all sundresses for the Strawberry Festival in two weeks. So, I thought it would please Alma Lee to pick her own material pattern. And all went well for the better half of the outing until Nora came into the store pushing her baby in the carriage. Alma Lee's happy face dropped to her knees. So crestfallen and sad were her features, I wanted to cry. She neared Nora's little son with a longing in her eyes, then admired the child with heartbreaking admiration."

"Saints preserve us," he whispered. "That poor, poor woman."

"On the way home she didn't talk, went back to staring as she'd done before. All the weeks of working with her, the challenges she tried to overcome, were all for naught," she went on.

"You had no idea Nora would stop by the store with the baby," he defended again.

"True, but I did know Alma Lee was very vulnerable. I should have given it more time before suggesting an outing." Then, with the realization again of Alma Lee's fragile state of mind, something horrible struck her thoughts. "Brodie, didn't you say her body was found by the creek?"

"Yes," he said.

She gasped. "Oh dear Lord, I think Alma Lee meant to drown herself, her depression and sorrow just too much for her to bear any further."

"But Attwater got to her first," he supplied with a frown.

"Yes...oh God," she moaned.

"Then, Alma Lee's demise rests on my shoulders," he admitted flatly.

Now she frowned. "How can you even say such a thing?"

"Alma Lee needed professional help. As wonderful as you were to her and as hard as you tried, you weren't qualified to read the signs or decipher them properly. As you just admitted, she was vulnerable, but you tried to push her forward anyway. That's why Alma Lee needed psychiatric care. If I hadn't presented that fact so bluntly, so frighteningly to Trudy Boyd, Alma Lee might be somewhere now, getting the help she deserved." His face saddened. "I failed her. I failed a patient."

It was her turn to defend his actions now. "No matter how you presented the facts, Trudy wouldn't have agreed. Her lack of understanding and trust filled her with fear, and that would've prevented her from ever allowing the professional help you offered. No one can make someone do something they don't want to. I'd say no one's to blame." She took his hand and brought it to her lips for a kiss. "Come," she coaxed. "It's time for us to go on with our own lives. And a good start would be to tell my parents our nuptial date has changed."

He nodded, a slow smile spreading his full lips. "Let's go, then… We've got a wedding to plan."

Gabriel stopped by the next day. Cassia would remain home until midweek, giving her ankle time to heal strong and her bruises to fade a little more. So, she was available to receive her brother's visit.

Gabriel handed her a small, black case. "I wanted to give you this before I left for England."

She smiled, loving when someone gave her a gift. Quickly she unlocked the lid. But her smile turned to astonishment when she got a look at the case's contents. "A gun?"

Gabriel nodded. "And you're to keep it somewhere on you at all times, especially when you're out and about on your own."

She frowned. "You want me to carry a gun?"

He nodded again. "It is much better protection than keys."

Carefully she pulled the petite-sized pistol from the case, holding it out by its black pearled handle as though it had teeth.

He chuckled lightly. "You'll get used to it, once you learn how to shoot it properly. I've asked Ethan to give you lessons."

Upon closer examination, she read aloud the words etched on the barrel. "H and R Fire Arms, Worchester, Massachusetts...twenty-two."

"Twenty-two is the caliber. H and R stands for Harrington and Richardson, the company that produces the gun. The establishment is located on Park Avenue in Worchester, Massachusetts. The make is a Young American...double action, small frame centerfire revolver," her brother explained. "This weapon is a vest pocket model, self-cocker and uses modern, smokeless powder cartridges. Ethan will be over in a few days with the ammunition and to give you your first lesson."

She inhaled sharply. "Gabriel, I don't understand anything you just said."

He took the gun from her grasp and placed it back in the case. "You will; just wait for Ethan."

"But I don't wear a vest," she protested.

"Then always wear something with pockets," he countered.

"It will weigh me down," she objected again.

"It is a small gun; you will cope," he said. Then folding his arms across his chest he added. "You are like this, you know, because my mother and Josh never spanked you."

She playfully slapped him on the arm. "You're one

to talk; you were never spanked either."

"I should have had the good sense to interfere. Wait, perhaps it is not too late." He reached for her and pretended to put her across his knee.

"Stop, stop, Gabriel." She wiggled free from his grasp and protected her bottom with both of her hands. "I am a grown woman now, engaged to be married."

"Yes, I know. Brodie asked me to be his best man," he announced proudly.

She smiled. "Thank you for agreeing."

He nodded once more. Then pointing a finger at her, he playfully provoked her again. "You better be a good wife, or else Brodie will spank you."

She arched a brow. "He damn well better *not* try."

****

The next day Cassia and Amanda paid a visit to the Boyd homestead. Amanda made a peach cobbler and brought along a few jars of homemade jam. John Tyler wasn't around, as he still worked with Patrick to keep the town at a safer level. Though Attwater was dead, danger of any sort could arise. That was precisely why Patrick remained a law enforcement figure for Eagle's Landing, hiring Ethan and John Tyler to assist him. Trudy was subdued, appearing like the floor had been pulled out from beneath her, and rightly so. Ruth Ann seemed to handle it the best. Cassia believed, in Ruth Ann's case, she put so much love, consideration, and hope in what she did and in how she lived, that a strong cocoon of faith kept her shielded from complete despair. As Cassia and her mother were ready to depart, Ruth Ann handed her a folded piece of material. Upon closer scrutiny, she recognized the fabric as the one she had chosen for her own sundress, the light green background peppered with bouquets of white, yellow, and pink flowers.

"I finished it for ya last night," Ruth Ann said. "I made mine as well, and Alma Lee one too. I've been workin' ever since word came about her death. Keepin' busy's helped me through, as I've got to stay strong for Mama." The younger woman's eyes filled with tears. "Alma Lee will be buried in her dress, though no one will see…can't have the coffin open 'cause of what that monster did to her." She reached out to gently finger the bruise on Cassia's jaw. "Reckon he'd have done the same to ya if help hadn't come."

Ruth Ann's words brought strongly to mind the force of Attwater's blow, and she swallowed back the tears rising to choke her. "Oh, Ruth Ann, I am so terribly sorry for your loss."

"For yours too, as my sister was someone you loved and cared about as well," Ruth Ann reflected.

"Yes. Yes, she was at that," she admitted.

"Well, like Reverend Holmes said when he paid a visit, God's got a plan. Besides, we will all see each other again one day. Right now, Alma Lee's gone on ahead…went to be with her husband." Ruth Ann shook her head sadly. "Lord knows how much she missed him. Now they're together again."

"Amen to that," she whispered.

****

The following weeks leading up to the wedding day were busy ones. Alma Lee's funeral was extremely emotional, Cassia herself coping hard. Brodie remained faithfully by her side throughout the ordeal. His presence was the only thing keeping her from falling apart. A week later, to her surprise, Ruth Ann showed up with her family to the Strawberry Festival wearing her sundress. Cassia wore hers as well. The two of them raised a glass of lemonade in honor of Alma Lee's memory.

After work most nights, she helped Brodie paint the apartment walls, sand down the floors, and clean the appliances, counters, toilet, tub, and sinks. P.J. helped, with an overly accommodating attitude, laying down a rug in the parlor and hanging curtains. Ethan lent a hand, as did Shailyn, Nora, Maggie, and Rising Sun. Furniture was given to them by both her and Brodie's parents, Betsy, Shailyn, and Muriel Dodd. Vernon Washburn was even nice enough to make them a table and chairs set for the kitchen. The quality of his expert craftsmanship would last many years to come, as the table top consisted of one very strong piece of oak wood and the legs held on by wooden pegs instead of nails. In three weeks' time, the place was ready to live in and Brodie moved in.

Cassia's gown was finished. Betsy's veil completed the look beautifully, and several women in town agreed to bring a hot dish, a meat dish, and a vegetable dish. Amanda supplied the flowers, Sadie made the cake, and Patrick handled the beverages.

The second Saturday in August dawned sunny with a slight breeze. Amanda, Riley, and Anita helped Cassia dress in her gown and veil. Having them back home for her special day meant everything to her. Even Silas made it back to Eagle's Landing, deciding to stay in town until after the holidays. She glanced one more time around the room she'd slept in throughout her life. Now, it was empty of her belongings, as everything had been taken to the apartment the night before.

As her father walked her down the aisle, he teared up. "I never thought I'd make it to see this day." Slowly he handed her over to Brodie, and whispered, "I know you'll take care of her now."

Willow Creek's Reverend Benjamin Newcomb officiated. The church, decorated with white and pink roses, was magnificent, as was the music. But it was Brodie's expression when she met him at the altar she'd remember for the rest of her life. The love he held in his large, emerald eyes which filled with tears of joy, made her heart soar with happiness.

A reception was held in the church's hall. About seventy-five people attended. Thankfully there was more than enough food and drink to go around. They forfeited a honeymoon away, opting instead to save their money for an automobile. Brodie was sick of getting rained on while driving the wagon, and she was tired of getting around on a bicycle. So, the first night she would sleep in her new apartment would also be the first night she'd be with Brodie.

Butterflies fluttered in her belly when he carried her over the threshold. As he set her gently down upon her feet, she looked around the parlor, admiring all the little extra touches they added to insure their little love nest would be cozy and comfortable. As well as all those friends and family members who helped them. The whole place was a labor of love. With that in mind, it was easy to feel at home.

He poured them a glass of wine, and after removing her veil and placing it aside, they toasted their new dwelling and the life they'd now share. The heady taste of the burgundy warmed her throat and rose to her head. She felt light, happy, and ready to be with her husband.

He took the goblet from her and placed the two glasses on a nearby end table. "Welcome home, Mrs. O'Clarity," he said before his long, hot, passionate kiss sent her senses whirling. Then he took her by the hand and led her to the bedroom.

Chapter Thirty-Nine

"Let me help you off with your gown," Brodie offered, excitement rising through every part of his body. He had waited a long time for this night—to be with Cassia in the *Biblical Way*, as his parents referred to it. His fingers fumbled as he unfastened the tiny pearl buttons down her back.

She kicked off her heels before pulling the gown off each of her shoulders. He watched as she freed her arms from the sleeves, one by one, slow and easy as not to tear the delicate lace. Then she slipped the gown to her waist, wiggled her shapely bottom to get the material past her hips, and dropped it to her ankles. It was like watching a choreographed dance, and it mesmerized him. She laid the gown over a nearby chair and did the same routine with the slip, tossing it on top of the gown. Then she sat on the edge of the bed to release the garters holding her stockings. One by one she rolled the silk coverings down her shapely legs, off her heels, past her pink toenails, and placed them on the chair with the slip and gown. This left her clad in only a brassiere and panties.

His mouth went dry. As a doctor, he'd seen many naked bodies, belonging to both men and women. But this body…this beautiful, shapely body standing half naked before him—full, perky breasts erupting from the low-cut neckline of the brassiere, and a trim waist bared to his eyes...belonged to his wife—the woman he would soon have the privilege of making love to.

"I'm going to draw a bath." She walked past him to the bathroom across the hall and disappeared behind the closed door.

He swallowed hard, anticipation swelling his loins. As he undressed, he heard the tub fill with water and then the swish of her descent. Would she come to him naked? Or would she be shy, afraid, timid and cry when he touched her? She had never known a man in this capacity, and it worried him he'd say or do the wrong thing to scare her.

I must remain patient and understanding.

He was down to his underwear when she called out to him. "Brodie, would you please bathe me?"

For a moment his legs froze, yet his blood rushed hot to his phallus. Immediately he swelled, his manhood hard and moist in his shorts. Inhaling sharply, he reached down to reposition himself, not wanting to intimidate the stars out of her, and made his way to the bathroom. Slowly he opened the door.

She held out a bar of soap to him. "Do you mind?"

His voice cracked as he neared her and took the soap. "No, not at all."

Calmly, she lay back in the white, claw-footed tub and closed her eyes. Her ample breasts peeked out just above the water's line. The nipples were a soft shade of pink, hard, and perfectly round. He fought the strong urge to lean over...suck one, and roll his tongue around the tender peak. Instead he knelt beside the large-framed tub on the plush bath mat that had been placed there. He was grateful for his height, as it afforded him the length to reach her over the large tub's ridge, and dip his hands into the warm water. He lathered the soap and gently cupped her right breast, washing her with the fragrant lavender suds.

She groaned with pleasure and arched her back a bit, thrusting her rounded flesh against the palm of his hand.

Her bold response took him by surprise, and he hesitated to continue.

She opened her eyes, soft blue orbs searching his face. "Is something wrong, Brodie?"

He licked his dry lips. "I…I…just don't want to…to frighten you by moving too quickly."

Gently she took his soapy hands within hers. "Let me tell you something, honey. Married to an Apache, my mother learned what happens in the marriage bed can be fulfilling and pleasurable to both a man and a woman. The tribe's women were not as prudish as the white women of my mother's generation. They were free from such protocol and loved their husbands as their bodies craved. Between my mother's schooling on such matters and my medical education, it was easy to become aware of my own body and confident enough to embrace its needs without feeling ashamed." She smiled, moving her wet hand to stroke the side of his face. "Though I've remained chaste, wanting only to give myself to the man I married, I am far from ignorant or naïve as to what takes place between a couple after they wed, nor do I fear it. Understanding and enjoying intimacy is just as essential for the woman as it is for the man. With both of us admitting and satisfying our wants and needs, telling each other what does or does not please us, we'll have a better marriage. I want our bodies to connect as well as our minds and hearts. So, I trust you to take care of me and to bring me to the point you'd want me to bring you. And none of that is going to happen for us if we're not open and honest with each other about sex, or willing to be free with our bodies in the process."

He swallowed hard. "Saints preserve us. I feel like a kid in a candy store...a very big, delicious candy store, and I don't know where to start first."

She giggled. "Where your hand started out works for me."

He smiled. "Me too."

She closed her eyes again as he washed her breasts, caressing and pinching the hardened peaks. Then he moved past her abdomen and to the juncture of her thighs where he played with the patch of golden hair framing her womanhood. She spread her legs wider, affording him the ability to circle with the tip of a finger her bud of passion. He teased her with slow, easy strokes. She groaned with pleasure.

Her passion caused his phallus to throb and ooze, wetting his shorts. "Honey, I'm openly and honestly telling you I need to take you into bed now."

She opened her eyes. "I'm ready for that as well."

In an instant she stood, emerging from the water like a love goddess, naked and ripe. He got to his feet, and for a moment he just feasted his eyes upon her. Slowly he visually roamed the length of her, memorizing each facet of her glorious being.

"My body tingles when you look at me like that," she said, a spark of blush coloring her cheeks.

He smiled to himself. As free and as willing as his young bride was, her innocence and decency still prevailed. "Do you like me gazing so long on your naked body?"

"Yes," she said breathlessly. "Very much so."

His hands trembled when he reached for a towel and gently dried her arms, breasts, torso, backside, and legs…right down to her pink toenails. She stood quiet and still while he wiped the moisture from her body. Then he tossed the wet towel aside and reached for her robe, dressing her in the light pink, silk garment before embracing her. The front of the robe opened when she wrapped her arms around his neck. Her full, soft breasts met with his bare chest. The feel of her nakedness against his drove hot surges of yearning through him. He hoisted her into his arms, and she wrapped her legs around his hips. Without hesitation he stroked her backside, cupping and squeezing each of her buttock cheeks.

"Every time you touch me, you cause new and wonderful sensations to ripple through my body," she softly admitted, burying her face beneath his chin.

"I love you, Cassia," he whispered, kissing her forehead and carrying her to the bedroom.

Once he placed her onto her feet, she slipped off the robe and climbed into bed. He stood looking down at the beautiful woman he was fortunate enough to spend the rest of his life with, before removing his own shorts. His male member sprung forth so hard and erect, it could fly a flag.

Her eyes went to the thick shaft, and she smiled. "Looking at you also makes me tingle."

He returned her smile. "Me too."

"And do you like it when I gaze so long at your nakedness?"

"Yes." He climbed into the bed beside her. "Very

much so."

He rolled toward her now, capturing her lips with a kiss, his tongue exploring the tender flesh of her mouth. Then he moved to her left breast. She entwined her fingers in his hair and gently scratched his head. Her touch felt good, and it relaxed him as he sucked, teasing the hardened nipple with his tongue. When he moved his hand to rest between her thighs, she spread her legs. Again he found the button of desire hiding between her woman's fold. Back and forth he flicked the tip, feeling her grow moist with his touch. She groaned with pleasure when he increased the rhythm. As her ardor mounted, she arched her back…trembling with passionate spasms beneath his touch…crying out his name as her climax exploded.

His sex throbbed and oozed for a release. "Are you ready for me now, honey?"

"Yes," she whispered, her breathing rapid.

He mounted her and entered her womanhood, pushing through the virgin barrier. For a moment her body jerked, and he halted.

"No, don't stop." She brought her hands to rest on his backside. Gently, she stroked his buttocks, her fingers making circles around his flesh.

He entered her fully now, the hot, tight canal enveloping him with unimaginable ecstasy. "Oh, God, Cassia," he choked breathlessly as he drove himself in and out, bringing on his own eruption. And when he did, he filled her—his hot juices sprouting like a geyser. It flowed from him along with his energy. He fell beside her, exhausted. She moved to cocoon her body to his, one arm across his chest, a leg strewn over his hips.

He wrapped an arm around her and pulled her close. "I love you, Mrs. O'Clarity," he whispered.

"I love you more, Mr. O'Clarity," he heard her say before he fell asleep with a smile.

****

Settling into married life was a joy for Cassia. She and Brodie had a routine during the week, working a few days side by side and then a few days apart. Unless a dire emergency took place, they generally made it home together at a decent hour to have dinner or sup at a family member's home. She was grateful her mother taught her at a very early age how to cook. Nightly she'd make a good meal for them both, proud to be able to fill her hardworking husband's belly after a long day.

Two weeks before Thanksgiving, Betsy not only gave birth to a girl, but twin girls. She named one after her mother, Sadie, and the other after her father by using the female version of Sean, which turned out to be Shauna. They were the second set of twin daughters born to an O'Clarity sibling with Shailyn's girls, Megan and Marta being the first.

Holding the sweet little bundles of joy gave Cassia moments of wishing for a child of her own. Brodie too was totally enamored with the smallest members of the family. She knew, when the time came, he'd be an amazing father. So far, despite their nightly passions, nothing on such a spectrum had come to pass. So for now, the two of them enjoyed the twins.

Time passed quickly until it was only a week before Christmas. She had no calls that day, and Brodie was only scheduled to work until four p.m. His time to arrive home for dinner came and went. A phone had been installed for them in the apartment, so after waiting a proper span of time, she rang him at the office to see what delayed him. If he had some sort of emergency, he just might need her assistance.

But the operator couldn't get through. "Sorry, ma'am, that line has been disconnected."

Immediately an uneasy feeling swept through her. There was no reason the phone should be unusable, as there was no storm brewing outside. Truth be told, it was a calm, warm day for late December. And Brodie would never purposely disconnect the phone.

"Operator, could you place a call over to the police station?" Since the Attwater murders, a makeshift police station had been set up on the upper level of Mickey McCreas stables where Eli Granger lived before he married Maggie. "Please reach either, Patrick McCrea, John Tyler Boyd, or Ethan Eagle. Tell them to hurry to Eagle's Landing Medical Office immediately."

The medical office was a stone's throw from the apartment, so she slipped on a jacket and headed for the door. As she came upon the side window of the office's back room where Brodie did paperwork, she glimpsed him sitting at the desk. Something about the way he looked, tense and on edge, brought her concern to an even higher level. As she moved closer to the window, she gazed around the room to see if Brodie was alone. To her horror, Clayton Matthews stood about two feet away, aiming a gun at Brodie's head.

She gasped and fell back from the window. Why would Mr. Matthews be in Eagle's Landing, and why was he threatening Brodie?

Her mind whirled with what she should do. Waiting for Patrick, John Tyler, or Ethan could be a while, especially if they couldn't be located right away.

And Brodie was in danger now. Then her brother's words of warning echoed in her head. *Never leave the house without the gun, especially if you are alone.* Well, she hadn't. Slipping her hand into the right pocket of her jacket, she reached for the gun and quietly made her way to a side door.

Only she, Brodie, and Sean had a key for this entrance. In her left pocket, she kept all her keys. Reaching for the leather cord, she found the correct one, slowly unlocked the door, and dropped the keys back into her pocket. With great care she opened the door ajar, as when it was opened fully it tended to squeak. She was thin enough to slip through the small opening, not bothering to close it for fear of making too much noise.

On tiptoe she crept down the long back hall and noticed the phone had been ripped from the wall. She raised the gun and held it between both her hands. Ethan had given her lessons all last summer, and although she wasn't a "crackerjack" shot, she could manage to hit a target. Her heart raced, and her hands trembled. Hitting targets and shooting people—if need be—are two very different things altogether. Could she make such a decision if she had to?

Brodie made the decision for me. He killed a man to save my life. Now, I must be there for him.

As she neared the door she could hear Mr. Matthews' voice. "I will only ask you once more for the whereabouts of your brother."

Brodie's voice shook, yet he answered calmly. "And I will tell you again, as I told you several times before, I don't know where he is. Last I knew he was headed to San Antonio, Texas."

"I've been there, combed the city, and even hired a private detective," Matthews spat. "The bastard's nowhere to be found."

Brodie tried being diplomatic. "Mr. Matthews, I understand how upset you are over your daughter and grandson's death. When we received the news, we were all very grieved as well. We even held a service for them both in church." He sighed. "But what you're doing now, trying to find Tucker—get revenge—isn't going to bring them back."

"Maybe not," Matthews argued. "But it will even the score, avenge their death. And since I can't find Tucker, I will do the same to him as he's done to me, take away his family. After I blow your head off, I'm going to do the same to that pretty little wife of yours."

That's when Brodie's face reddened. "You leave my wife out of this."

"She's the reason Tucker treated my daughter so shabbily…always throwing to her face how she came between them…how much Cassia meant to him. He made my Jessica cry herself sick. I reckon that's the reason she lost the baby, hemorrhaged, and died. Then that poor little boy—my little, Daniel, died too." Matthews raised his gun and cocked the trigger. "Now, you're both going to pay."

That's when she pulled the trigger of the pistol she was holding. The shot rang out in the room, and the bullet hit Matthews in the left buttock.

He dropped his gun, let out a yelp of pain, and fell to the floor. Blood soaked the man's trousers as he writhed in agony.

Brodie reached for a pair of scissors on the desk and went to the injured man, cutting away his trousers to expose the wound.

"The bullet just grazed him," he explained as he examined Matthew's bared bottom. He looked up at Cassia who stood in a state of shock. "All will be fine, honey," he reassured her, taking a moment to stand and pry her hands from the gun. "He's only got a flesh wound." Then he smiled, planting a kiss on the tip of her nose. "Good shot."

"Not really." She wiped the tears streaming down her cheeks with the backs of her hands. "I was aiming for his knee."

Chapter Forty

June 1920

Brodie hated leaving Cassia alone at night, now that she was six months along with child. As a doctor he knew anything could happen at this point in a woman's pregnancy, and being far from her unnerved him to no end. How she put up with his constant coddling was a wonder, though she did protest when he adamantly advised her last month to stop working. He examined her often for signs of bleeding, took her temperature, listened to her heart, and watched what she ate, drank, and if she got enough rest. He made a point of having her tell him the color of her urine and the consistency of her bowels…as well as when she did and didn't have a movement. At this point he knew his wife's body better than his own.

"I'm knowledgeable in the medical field as well, Brodie," she'd say exasperated. "Don't you think I'd know if something was wrong?"

"Second opinions are always wise."

Their calculations estimated the time of conception to be the night she shot Clayton Matthews. So upset was she, and traumatized over shooting a man, that calming her brought an entire night of physical closeness. Thus, she conceived—a happy result to what could have been a disastrous outcome. Clayton

Matthews was sent to jail for his attempt on Brodie's life and died four months later from complications due to diabetes. And Tucker sent a Christmas card that didn't arrive until February with the postmark of Melbourne, Australia.

Now he was on his way home from a late, emergency call for Mr. Sweeny, who broke his leg in two places and dislocated a shoulder while trying to cut down a tree. He was tired and gassy, as the hurried pastrami sandwich he downed earlier bloated his insides. He should know better by now. Eating pastrami in a rush never did work out well for his intestines.

As he navigated the horse in the pouring rain, the cold, nighttime drops pelted his face, dripped down his collar, and drenched him thoroughly. "Soon, we'll have that automobile," he muttered to himself. "And I won't have to get soaking wet like this anymore." His in-laws had offered them the money, as Cassia had a bit of an inheritance coming, but he wanted to purchase his first automobile on his own merit, or was it simply a case of pride. "Saints preserve us," he muttered again. "Cassia's right. I'm becoming like Ned Beachum."

By the time he settled the horse in his parents' barn next door, he was so wet, his boots squeaked when he walked. When he came into the house, all was silent. He quietly, not to wake his sleeping wife, stripped off his wet clothes and boots at the front door. Making a mess of the parlor rug wasn't a way to keep a pregnant wife from getting upset. Naked, he tiptoed to the kitchen and pulled a towel from the laundry basket of clean clothes. After drying his hair and shoulders, he bent to wipe his feet. That's when he heard her soft voice behind him.

"You've gotten me all hot and moist down here, watching you do that," she said.

He turned to find her standing in the kitchen doorway, naked, and touching herself between the thighs. Her seductively just-awakened expression matched the sleep-tossed blonde curls, now long enough to fall to her shoulders, framing her face. Her breasts, even fuller and heavier with her pregnancy complemented her body, as did the perfectly rounded belly growing his seed. It was a beautiful and sensual scene that sent waves of excitement pulsating to his loins. Instantly he became engorged.

Her gaze went to his erect phallus and she smiled. "Come to bed."

"Oh, sweetheart, I won't make it that far, as I'm ready to spill myself right here and now." He reached her in one fluid motion, picking her up and setting her on the kitchen table. She lay back on her elbows and opened to him like a rose to the sun. He stepped between her thighs, which spread wide to accommodate him, her heels braced on the table's edge. With his hands on her raised bottom, he leaned forward to suck her nipples. She lay back fully on the table now, surrendering to his tongue, as it played with her erect peaks, moved to fondle her navel, and rested at the opening of her womanhood. Spreading her with his fingers, he exposed the pearl of ecstasy between her vaginal lips. With the tip of his tongue he flicked smooth, small strokes over the slippery nub.

"Oh, please, Brodie, go faster." She reached down to press his head against her. "Make my toes curl."

The musky, sweet scent of her flesh, and her explosion as he complied, brought him close to his peak. As soon as she was fulfilled, he entered her hot, wet sheath. The table shook with his thrusts but held strong, allowing him to erupt like a volcano. Spent, he dropped his head upon her rounded belly.

"I was going to put a flowered centerpiece on the table today," she began. "Now I'm glad I didn't."

He raised his gaze to find her again up on her elbows and looking at the vase of flowers resting on a counter across the room. He arched a brow. "I will never, as I sit here for my meals, look at this table the same way again."

She giggled. "We could have held off, made it to the bedroom."

He arched a brow. "Hell no, honey. That wasn't happening. But I think I can get you there now, before my legs totally collapse."

****

Gently he placed her on the bed. "Did I make your toes curl?"

"Not just curl, but tremble too," she admitted with a smile, rolling onto her side. He climbed in bed beside her. Cassia felt the warmth of him at her back. Just as he laid a hand over her belly, the baby kicked. She smiled and pushed her bottom against him.

Instantly he hardened. "I'd say no one is ready to sleep just yet."

"It appears so." She got up on her knees and jutted out her bottom for more of his sensual touch. He mounted her from behind, fondling her breasts with one hand and the area between her legs with the other as he entered her. She tightened around his thick, hot member. As his finger motion increased, his thrusts quickened. Everything inside of her heightened to such arousal, her body freely reacting to the sensual stimulation she'd grown to crave. She arched her back, pushing her raised derrière up against his genitals, feeling his manly sacs, now almost a part of her.

"Saints preserve us," he breathlessly managed. "You get me so hot."

Yes—hot…they were both hot. And when her body could hold out no longer, she released the most satisfying and intense spasm she could muster. Like fireworks on the Fourth of July, she burst, shattering a thousand different pieces of desire throughout her being. He erupted along with her, his body trembling with his release. Then they both collapsed; her on her side and him on his back. Their rapid breathing was the only sound in the room until Brodie let go of gas. The sound, rumbling for a span, then fizzling out to a long whistle, made her giggle.

He reached over and playfully pinched her bare bottom. "What's so funny, Mrs. O'Clarity?"

She squealed at his unexpected action. "You could power a steamboat with that force of gas, Mr. O'Clarity."

He chuckled lightly. "As a doctor, my rule of thumb is to release what ails you, for the sake of a healthier body, especially if you've eaten a pastrami sandwich on the run."

"You know what my Aunt Marrietta's rule of thumb is on this matter," she baited.

"I can only imagine," he countered.

"A chap who breaks wind in the presence of a lady, is no English gent," she said, mimicking her aunt's British accent.

He chuckled again and pulled her close. "Well, you

see, that can hardly be a rule pertaining to me."

She snuggled as close to him as her belly would allow. "And why not?"

"Because I am an Irish doctor who happens to be your husband," he said proudly.

"And I wouldn't change that for anything in this world," she vowed, raising her lips to his, whereby he captured them with a kiss.

Epilogue

Eagle's Landing, Arizona, January 1996

As the limo pulled up to the arena, Cassia Rose O'Clarity and her great granddaughter unbuckled their seatbelts. Amanda ran around to open the door. "Are you nervous, Granny?"

Cassia made a little shrug. "Yes, a bit. I never spoke to a large crowd before."

"Well, this is your special day, so enjoy it," her great granddaughter advised.

As she walked into the arena, she recognized so many faces, memories flooding her thoughts. In the front row sat her three sons, and three daughters, now all in their seventies. Brodie Junior, or B.J., as he was called, was her oldest. He was a doctor, like his father and grandfather. Then twin boys, Joshua and Sean, named for the other two men in her life she loved and respected, were born two years later. Twins were something far from unusual in the O'Clarity family. Cassia's father, Reverend Joshua Holmes, lived to see her sons born. After his passing Cassia's nephew Ethan and his wife, Raina, one of Rising Sun's granddaughters, moved in with Amanda. She left the house to them after she died. Cassia's father-in-law, Doctor Sean O'Clarity, succumbed to a second heart attack just after Mandy...her name a derivative of

Amanda…the first of her three daughters was born. Sadie O'Clarity then moved to Willow Creek to live with Betsy and gave the O'Clarity home to Cassia and Brodie. Shortly after, Joslyn…called so in honor of Sadie's middle name…and Marrietta, named for her aunt, was added to the family. And once again the O'Clarity home was bustling with children. It was convenient having a doctor for a husband, as Brodie delivered all their babies. With her throughout all things, good and bad, he loved her passionately until his own passing ten years ago. She missed him more and more each day, as he was her rock, her best friend, her lover, and her heart for sixty-seven years. They supported and completed each other, always doing their very best. In the end that's all you can do, as the next breath is never promised. After Brodie's death Cassia had a new-found empathy for her mother. Losing one man you loved was tragedy enough, but Amanda lost two. Her courage to carry on in both instances fueled Cassia's determination to do the same when rendered with the same circumstance. Though her mother had been long gone from this world, she still guided Cassia through the grief.

As she took her seat and waited for the program to begin, she reached for the chain she wore around her neck, once her mother's, and fingered her husband's wedding band hanging there. Both pieces of jewelry were treasures of time, as was the engagement ring and wedding band she still wore. One day she would leave these heirlooms to one of her great grandchildren, so the beautiful memories they held would never die.

Now, the first speaker, an elderly woman a few years younger than Cassia, walked to the podium.

When she spotted Cassia sitting in the front row, she smiled warmly.

"My name is Doctor Ruth Ann Boyd-Turner and my brother, John Tyler and I owe who we are and what we've accomplished to Cassia O'Clarity. She cared for my sister before her death and then for me and my brother. She encouraged John Tyler to stay in school and to further his education. He went into law enforcement and later entered politics, becoming an Arizona congressman. As for me, Cassia paid for my tuition to medical school which is where I met my husband, Doctor Eastman Turner. Together we founded The Alma Lee Sloane Woman's Hospital in South Eagle's Landing, a facility that addresses all women's issues, from pregnancy to mental health." Her smile deepened. "Your father was right, Cassia. God had a plan. And I'm so blessed you were a part of it all. Happy Birthday and thank you for all you've done."

Another elderly woman took the stage. "My name is Anna Beachum Grant, and I owe my success to Cassia O'Clarity as well. She encouraged my mother, Olivia, to do alterations and sewing, bringing her customers. I helped and after graduation Cassia strategically, not to wound my father's pride, set up a scholarship for me to attend fashion school. Today I am a designer. The Beachum-Grant label is noted throughout the United States and Canada. In honor of the one who gave to me, my company gives back to many charities. Thank you, from the bottom of my heart, Cassia…and Happy Birthday."

Then it was time for her to take the stage. When she stood at the podium she received a standing ovation. "Goodness," she giggled. "And I haven't even said a word yet." The audience chuckled and sat down.

She looked around the room. "I can't help thinking how wonderful it would be for my mother, Amanda Gregory Eagle Holmes to be here right now to witness how the town she initially funded has grown. She used to tell me of a fantasy she had as a child, whereby she could fly wherever she wanted, or send a message through the air. With the convenience of planes and computers, we can do all those things my mother only dreamed about. She was a true pioneer woman, who could shoot with a bow and arrow and a spear. Yet, she could play the violin, cook, and crochet, keeping the home fires burning. Even before she married my father and fostered this town with the foresight of my brother, Gabriel Golden Eagle, she braved enemy attacks, kidnappings, and survived living in an Apache village as a warrior chief's wife during the infiltration by the white agents. And still she managed to bridge the gap between the races. Today all the faces I see in the audience are the product of my mother's melting pot. She passed away at the age of ninety, mindfully sharp until her last breath. And it was her request to be laid to rest between the two men she loved and married Reverend Joshua Holmes and Chief Peter Proud Eagle. He called her, Golden Lady."

A word about the author...

Roberta C.M. DeCaprio is a freelance writer of all genres in romance and woman's mainstream fiction. A prior "sexuality" columnist for *A.B.L.E.D. Women* magazine, and former Assistant Editor for *Independence Today* newspaper, (both publications dedicated to the needs and rights of the disabled), Roberta has insight into the problems other physically challenged people face due to living herself with a walking impairment.

She is a self-published author of a book of poems, *Once Upon a Sonnet*, has won awards for her poetry, and been published in several anthologies.

Ms. DeCaprio is a graduate of the Writer's Digest School and Cornell Cooperative Extension. She held office from 2002 to 2004 as newsletter editor for Capital Region, her local chapter of the Romance Writers of America, interviewing such published authors as Elaine Raco-Chase, Valerie Hansen, Barbara Daly, Sue-Ellen Welfonder, Mary J. Forbes, Sharron McClellan, Mariah LeGrand and the late Kathleen E. Woodiwiss for the former monthly publication, *Capital Romance*.

A mother of two, and grandmother of four, Roberta shares her upstate NY home with two dearly loved cats, Mikko and Misha, and her artist/screenplay writer husband with whom she's collaborated on a script for a *24 Hour Film Race* in 2015 and a sitcom that has won the attention of a producer.

To view Roberta's back list, read excerpts from her books, and check out her blog, log on to:

www.robertacmdecaprio.com
www.thewordmerchantssociety.blogspot.com